Rogue Destiny: Beginings

A Rogue Destiny Novel

Paul Tallman

OLIVERHEBERBOOKS

To Tina, the love of my life,
Whose unwavering support, love, and belief
in my writing, made this silly little book possible.

Chapter 1
The Angels of Avalon

Ren B'gatti raced down the halls of a mountain citadel as the fabric of reality tore apart around him. Outside the picturesque windows, a violent maelstrom raged in an ever widening chain of destruction. Violent bursts of lightning flashed inside the roiling thunderclouds that shook the foundation of the earth. An icy shiver rushed up his spine because he knew a storm of this magnitude meant only one thing.

He rounded a corner, his bare feet sliding on the marble floor as he stopped in front of a heavy wooden door. He grabbed the doorknob. It was locked.

"Claymore!?" Ren shouted. He pounded on the wooden door with his fist. "Open up! It's me!"

No response.

Ren pounded harder. Nothing. Stepping back, he ripped open his shirt. Buttons flew as he focused his thoughts on a mythical creature renowned for its raw power.

His body changed. Hair sprouted over his naked torso. Twisted horns grew from his forehead as the shape-shifter expanded in size to a massive, broad-shouldered minotaur. His loose pants stretched against the thick, sturdy legs.

Ren lowered his head and lumbered forward, his hooved

feet clicking off the stone floor. He slammed into the door with the full strength of the minotaur. The wood cracked under the impact but did not give way. He backed up and crashed into it again. This time, the doorframe buckled inward in a shower of splinters. He stomped through the broken debris into an expansive study. The smell of gunpowder assailed his senses.

The first thing he saw was his partner, Claymore, lying on the floor in a pool of his own blood. Next to him lay his smoking revolver. Panic gripped Ren. He never gave into abject fear, but a tight ball of dread formed in his stomach. Beyond Claymore, Minstrel Cotty, the reigning governor of the local region, slumped in his chair at a spacious desk with two bullet holes in his chest. His lifeless eyes stared off into space.

A soft gust of wind blew through the study. Ren saw a swirling wind move like a dust-devil in the desert across the back of the room. It swept past Cotty's desk, blowing papers onto the floor. The whirlwind dissipated to reveal a cloaked figure.

The dark form pulled a sconce on the wall. A bookshelf slid open to reveal a hidden passageway. Ren lumbered forward with a roar, still in the shape of a minotaur. A shrouded face turned toward him before disappearing into the darkness of the tunnel.

A groan behind him brought Ren to a stop. He looked back to see Claymore push himself up from the floor. He released the minotaur's form, shrinking back to his five-and-a-half foot natural shape, and dropped to his knees next to his partner. The twisting guilt in his stomach eased now that he saw Claymore was alive.

Ren had felt something was amiss when he left to bring their ship around, but he told himself it was only paranoia. Claymore always had everything under control. He was the hero, not Ren, and the shape-shifter was fine with that.

"Are you okay?" Ren asked. He helped Claymore sit up.

"I'm fine." Claymore gave a painful smile at Ren's concern. He touched the blood on the back of his scalp with his fingertips. "I was arguing with Cotty when someone struck me from behind."

"Whoever it was disappeared down a passageway behind

that bookcase," Ren replied. He pointed to the lifeless body at the desk. "But we have a bigger problem. Cotty's dead!"

"Dead?!" Claymore repeated. "That means—" He tried to climb to his feet, but his legs gave out as he rose.

Ren caught his arm and helped him to a plush chair near the fireplace. There was an iron poker on the floor at his feet. Ren picked it up. The end dripped red with blood.

"How far has the world deteriorated?" Claymore leaned back in his chair and closed his eyes. "Can you see any words yet?"

Ren peered out the windows into the heart of the raging storm. Black inky water dripped down the panes of glass. Lightning flashed across the sky. He saw nothing but the fiery storm clouds.

"Not yet," he responded. "But it won't be too long now."

The sound of steel-toed boots echoed down the marble hallway. Claymore glanced at a crate on a table behind Ren. "There's a scepter with a blue gem in there. Hand it to me."

Ren rummaged through the straw-filled crate. The footsteps grew louder. He pulled out a two-foot long silver scepter with a translucent sapphire embedded at the end and tossed it to his partner's outstretched hand. A moment later, the hardened faces of several citadel guards crowded the doorway, curved swords in their hands. Claymore forced himself to his feet and pointed the scepter at the open doorway.

"I'd step back if I were you!" Claymore yelled at the men. "*Imperius-elaito!*" The sapphire on the end of the scepter glowed, illuminating the room in a blue, hazy light.

The armored guards scattered as a ray of brilliant light shot from the end of the rod. Ice crystals filled the air and the temperature in the room dropped. The shaft of light hit the wall across the hallway. A torrent of frozen white created a thick sheet of ice that filled the hall and the doorway. Tendrils of icy mist rose from the now impassible entrance.

Claymore tossed the magical relic back into the crate and

holstered his revolver. He staggered to where Minstrel Cotty lay, checking his neck for a pulse.

"He's gone," Claymore rumbled, shaking his head in disbelief. "There's a rabbit-hole less than a mile from here. That has to be where the assassin headed." He disappeared into the passageway with Ren on his heels.

"Are we going after them?" Ren asked as they descended into the pitch blackness. He ran his hand along the wall, following the sound of Claymore's boots on the stone steps ahead of him.

"There's no time," Claymore said. "We have to get off this world. Where's the ship?"

"It's on the roof," Ren replied. "Who would want to kill Cotty?" His voice was a whisper, but it echoed in the narrow stairwell.

"I have no idea," Claymore replied. "But they're trying to frame us for his murder."

Claymore reached the bottom and pushed open a wood panel to a large food pantry at the back of a kitchen. The thunder outside rattled the pots and pans hanging against the walls.

"We can take the stairs through the east room!" Claymore yelled over the increasing intensity of the storm.

They bolted through the dining area to a long, wide hall that opened into a central gathering area. The windows shattered above them. Ren covered his head from the raining shards of glass. Burning winds blew through the room. The hall was empty except for a handful of household staff running to a nearby corridor. Claymore grabbed the arm of a young woman as she rushed past with a terrified look in her eyes.

"Please, you must come with us!" Claymore pleaded. "We have a ship that can take you to safety!"

"You're going to fly in this storm?!" she shouted. "No airship would survive! The lower cellars are the best place to hide!"

"You will die if you stay here!" Claymore insisted. "This maelstrom is of supernatural origin and it's going to bring the entire mountainside down! Please, you have to trust me!"

She pulled her arm away and ran after her companions.

"We don't have time to help people!" Ren yelled over the turmoil.

Claymore turned to him, a thin trail of blood oozing down the side of his head. "After all our time together, you still haven't learned the value of every life. That is what the Raconteurs do. It's who we are."

"We can't take all of them with us!" Ren argued.

"No, unfortunately, we can't," Claymore replied. "But we'll give anyone who listens the opportunity to save themselves."

Ren nodded in agreement to avoid any further argument. He hated getting tangled in the affairs of other people, but for some reason, it mattered to Claymore. Ren was content playing sidekick, letting his partner's moral compass guide them both.

The depths of the citadel shook under their feet as the storm continued to gather strength. Cracks appeared on the tiled floor and along the walls. Ren headed up the stairs when a thunderous crash came from the hallway where the servants had sought shelter. Smoke and dust billowed out from the collapsed corridor. A moment later, the young woman emerged from the cloud of rubble, coughing and covered in soot. An older man stumbled out next to her. They both rushed back to the staircase.

"We decided we'll take our chances with you!" she said as they reached Ren and Claymore.

"What's your name?" Claymore asked.

"Tamryn!" she shouted through the surrounding chaos. "And this is Caillou."

Claymore nodded to them. "Good to meet you both! Let's go!"

Ren ascended the steps ahead of the others, dodging people running down past them. Claymore held tight to the banister with one hand and climbed each step with an effort. Although he could barely stand, he pleaded with anyone they met to come with them. By the time they reached the highest floor, he had convinced three more of the household staff to join them. Unfortunately, too many others had refused the offer of salvation, not believing their end was at hand.

Ren retraced his steps to the roof where he had parked their ship, *Righteous Indignation*. He paused to take a deep breath before opening the utility door to the environmental nightmare that awaited them outside. A blast of scorching heat hit him as he pushed the hatch open. The air felt thick with the fires of a smelting furnace. Ren and Claymore exchanged a glance. Each knew what the other was thinking. The end of this world was at hand.

Across the flat roof, their sleek ship waited for them. The sixty-foot long, world-hopping slipstream had a smooth and elegant design, built of a technology beyond anything found on this world. Its polished, dark blue exterior shimmered under the bursts of lightning.

"What is that?" Tamryn yelled. "It's not like any airship I've ever seen!"

"That is how we escape the storm!" Ren replied.

"Get them out of here, Ren!" Claymore shouted. He propped himself against the doorframe, letting the others by him.

"Follow me!" Ren shouted to those around him. Shading his eyes from the burning inferno. Amid the tumultuous gusts and dark rain that poured from the skies, he sprinted forward, outpacing everyone. The brutely hot winds tore through him. Scalding drops of black rain splashed his face, arms, and naked torso as he reached the ship. He opened a small hatch and pulled down a lever. The clamshell doors at the center of the vessel split apart. A set of stairs descended as the others caught up to him.

"Go! Go!" Ren ordered, waving them up the steps into *Righteous Indignation*. Lightning flashed overhead, revealing massive words written across the sky. Tamryn stopped to gawk at them.

"What is happening?" she yelled, her hair flaying in the wind.

"Get in!" Ren shouted at her. "Everything will be explained once we're safe!"

The enormous words faded from view as quickly as they appeared. Tamryn nodded and climbed the stairs. Ren realized Claymore wasn't with them. Across the rooftop, he saw his partner down on one knee. Ren sprinted to him.

"Don't worry about me," Claymore said, waving him away with a hand. "Get the others out of here before it's too late."

"We're all leaving here together," Ren replied. He pushed his shoulder under Claymore's arm and half-carried, half-dragged his friend the rest of the distance to the ship. Once inside, Ren pulled the lever to close the doors, dampening the relentless pounding of the winds outside.

Claymore stumbled to the row of passenger seats and dropped into the closest one. His face and arms were raw and blistered from the brief exposure to the fires of the Crucible. He laid his head back, teetering on the edge of consciousness.

Ren looked at the others. They were alive, but all suffered the same burns on their exposed skin. His own face and torso flared in pain at the slightest movement.

"Ren, I'm in no condition to fly," Claymore mumbled. "It's up to you to get us out of here."

"I can do that," Ren replied. He glanced across the terrified faces staring up at him. He was now the one in charge, whether or not he wanted to be.

Rn opened a storage compartment. "Tamryn, there are bandages and a first aid kit in this locker," he said. "See if you can get Claymore's head to stop bleeding. Everyone else, buckle in tight and hang on!"

Ren went up the steps to the cockpit. He slid into the pilot's chair and started up the engines. He'd flown slipstream Runabouts many times before, but never inside a collapsing world.

A moment later, *Righteous Indignation* lifted from the rooftop. Turbulent winds battered the ship from all sides. Ren pulled the throttle back and gunned the Coldfire engines. He tightened his grip on the steering wheel as the ship ascended into the violent skies.

Outside the windshield, crimson lightning flashed again. Words reappeared on the sky ahead of him. Sentences and paragraphs stamped into the DNA of the world around them. This time, the letters did not disappear. The *Crucible Event* was hitting its crescendo. They were out of time.

The aerodynamic design of the slipstream sliced through the air with reckless speed. Ren fought the controls to maintain their upward trajectory as the ship bucked and jerked under him. The letters and words in the windshield grew larger. He hit a button on the console. A loud ping echoed through the cabin. A pulse of light shot out from an arcane gem embedded at the front of the ship.

The radiant point struck the word canopy, exploding in a cacophony of brilliant, earthy colors. A ripple spread across the surface of the edge of the world as a keyhole appeared.

An alarm flashed on the dash, indicating the temperatures outside the ship were increasing to the point of damaging the hull. Ren glanced over to see a wall of flames engulfing the side windows. The skies crinkled and burned around him, like paper thrown into a fire.

Ren seldom doubted his own abilities, but now he felt the icy grip of uncertainty seize him. The art of jumping in and out of a written world was a delicate skill. He had performed it many times before, but never under this kind of life and death gambit.

The ripples moving across the surface of the word canopy slowed, and the keyhole began to contract. If he could get through the opening before it closed, they'd reach the safety of the Void Between Worlds. If not, the fires of the Crucible would consume them.

Ren opened the engines as wide as they would go and hoped for the best. Winds buffeted the slipstream, but she steadily gained altitude and the keyhole drew closer. His grip on the wheel tightened until his knuckles ached.

The keyhole was only a narrow slit in the sky when *Righteous Indignation* reached it. With one final desperate effort, Ren threaded what remained of the opening. There was the momentary shifting of realities as the slipstream emerged into the blackness of the void.

Outside his window, hundreds of soft glowing globes appeared, floating weightless in a vast sea of blackness. These were the other worlds of the Mythic Cosmos. Behind him, a world-shattering implosion rocked the ship. Ashes and debris flew past his window, but they were clear of any danger. Ren leaned back in his seat and sighed.

Once his heart stopped pounding, he relaxed his death grip on the steering wheel. He set the destination of the auto-navigation system to Rogue Destiny and climbed out of his chair to check on Claymore.

His partner lay back unconscious in his seat, his head wrapped in white bandages. Tamryn sat next to him, her singed hair framing a sad expression of relief. The other survivors looked the same as she did, tired and scared.

"How is he?" Ren asked.

"As good as can be expected," Tamryn replied. She held up a syringe. "The bleeding stopped, and I gave him a shot for his pain. Now, do you want to tell us what's going on?"

Ren shook his head. "We need to wait for Claymore. He can explain these things better than I can."

"No, I demand answers!" Caillou shouted, standing up. "You will tell us what happened! What was that firestorm? I've never seen anything like it! Take us back at once. We have families. We have to make sure they are safe!"

Ren could tell from his clothing he was a civil servant of some sort, and by his demeanor, he wasn't used to being told no. He took a deep breath, because for once he was not in the mood to argue. How could he tell the five individuals seated in front of him that everything they had ever known was now nothing more than dust and debris floating in the void? He usually cared little for the feelings of others, but the impact of what he was about to tell them was not lost on him.

"You have no place to return to," Ren stated matter-of-factly. "Your world has burned to ash."

"What do you mean *burned to ash*?!" Caillou yelled. "You're saying it's gone?!"

"That's all I can tell you for now." Ren replied. He turned back to the cockpit.

"Don't just walk away from us!" Tamryn yelled after him. "Not after spouting cryptic words of worlds being destroyed by fire and there being no place to return to."

The young woman's eyes were full of unspoken pain and grief. Ren knew she wouldn't like the truth once she heard it. None of them would. No one ever did.

"Okay, don't say I didn't warn you," Ren said. He paused before continuing. "What I'm about to tell you will be difficult to comprehend. Your world has been consumed in a fiery cataclysmic called a *Crucible Event*. You five are the sole survivors from the pages of a book called *The Angels of Avalon*."

"You expect us to believe that?" Caillou said. "That we are just characters in a book?" His eyes filled with despair as he spoke the words out loud. A moment later, the reality of those words hit him. He sat down in his seat and said no more.

"I told you it would be difficult to comprehend," Ren replied. "The comforting familiarity of the life you knew is over. Nothing will ever be the same again. Take a moment to think about that, and you'll realize I'm telling you the truth."

Silence filled the cabin for several heartbeats. The woman at the end of the row broke into tears. The man next to her dropped face into his hands and began sobbing. Caillou stared at the floor. The fifth survivor closed her eyes and sat unmoving in her chair, showing no outward display of grief. Ren could tell Tamryn was trying to process it all.

"So what happens to us now?" she whispered.

Ren smiled for the first time since the chaos began. "That's the only bright spot in all of this. You'll be resettled in Rogue Destiny until you decide what you want to do next."

"Rogue Destiny?" Tamryn asked. Her voice trembled. "Is that where we're going?"

"Yeah, it's a city," Ren replied. "A place of refuge for the lost and wandering. It'll give all of you a chance to start your lives over. Now you should try to get some rest. I need to send a message to let my employer know what has happened."

Ren returned to the cockpit. His body ached from the exhaustion of what he had just gone through. He ran his fingers through his wild hair, brushing ash and debris to the floor. The blistering burns that covered his arms and torso were already beginning to heal. In the day or two, any sign of the injuries will have completely disappeared. It was one of the many perks of being a shape-shifter.

He looked at the dashboard, dreading the message he should have already sent. The Raconteurs needed to know what had happened. He picked up the receiver, cleared his throat, and spoke.

This is Ren B'gatti, acting pilot of *Righteous Indignation*.
Raconteur badge number 2947.
It is my duty to report that the novel, *The Angels of Avalon,*
has been destroyed after the death of its *Logos Personae,* Minstrel
Cotty.
Claymore Ives and I escaped with five survivors.
We are in route to Rogue Destiny.
Estimated arrival eight hours, twenty-three minutes.
Righteous Indignation out.

Ren made sure the message was on a secured line and hit send. He sat back in his chair. Despite the fact they had escaped a horrendous catalyst, he could not shake the feeling that this was only the beginning of their troubles.

Chapter 2
Aftermath

Ren landed *Righteous Indignation* on a circular landing bay inside the secure walls of the Raconteurs' headquarters. He switched off the engines and stretched his tired muscles before taking a deep breath. Pushing himself up from the pilot's chair, he went back to check on his partner.

Claymore sat in his seat, staring off into space. His head wrap was stained with dried blood. Ren could tell he was still in a lot of pain. His partner came out of his daze and looked up as Ren approached.

"I need to talk to Gideon," Claymore said. Ren followed him along with the survivors of *The Angels of Avalon* down the steps of the ship onto the stone tarmac.

Sebastian Poe, the Raconteurs' chief mechanic, met them at the doorway to his subterranean garage. He was an imposing figure from a cybernetic world, that hobbled about on a metal leg.

A portable, artificial lung encased his upper torso. A long, black tube sprouted from his back, snaking behind him across the floor to an apparatus in the workshop's ceiling. The cord pumped life-giving oxygen into what remained of his internal organs.

"He's waiting for you down in the WayFinder room," Sebastian said as they reached him.

"Thank you," Claymore replied.

"How bad is it?" the cyborg asked.

"As bad as it gets," Claymore answered. "If you could have someone move *Righteous Indignation* somewhere the authorities won't find her, I'd appreciate it."

"Of course," Sebastian replied, clapping Claymore on the shoulder with a metal hand. "We'll get through this. We always do." The cyborg led the way down the ramp into the expansive underground facility where the Raconteurs' fleet of slipstreams was built and maintained.

Behind them, Ren could hear the survivors whispering. They seemed intrigued by the cyborg's mechanical limbs and metal skullcap sprouting with antennae. Sebastian bid them farewell, returning to a workbench where he was dissecting an engine core. Claymore took the group down a stairwell under the garage to a large door. He glanced at Ren before opening it.

A short, stout man in a dark tailored suit and black gloves turned as they entered. Around the room, a score of operatives sat at work stations. Each monitored the various screens of the massive WayFinder that stretched across the entire back wall of the room.

"I am so glad you're safe," he said. "And these are the citizens you saved from *The Angels of Avalon*?"

Claymore nodded. "Yeah, the only ones we could convince to come with us."

"Welcome to Rogue Destiny, my friends," Gideon said with a pleasant smile. "I wish we were meeting under better circumstances. My name is Gideon Dumas. I am the co-founder of the Raconteurs. We will do our best to make you feel welcome here in your new home. You must be famished. We've had food and drink brought down from the kitchen. Make yourselves comfortable."

He motioned to a long table at the far end of the room, where silver platters heaped with meat, breads, desserts and vegetables waited for them. Ren's stomach growled, reminding him he hadn't eaten in quite some time. He met Tamryn's eyes. She gave him a sad smile before turning away.

"Eat and rest here for now," Gideon said. "Your sleeping arrangements are being finalized next door. You'll be provided with a bath and clean clothes, along with a warm bed as you get adjusted to your new life here in Rogue Destiny."

Claymore glanced back at the survivors. "If you'll excuse us, I need to speak to Gideon privately," he rumbled. "If you need anything else, anyone here can help you. We'll be back shortly."

Ren opened the door to the office he and Claymore shared. The cramped room sat at the end of a lonely hallway in the back of the public house, the Obtuse Turtle. Claymore took the chair behind his cluttered desk. Gideon paced the floor in thought. Ren leaned against the wall.

"There will be long-term ramifications for the Raconteurs," Gideon said. "What are your thoughts, Claymore?"

"Somebody knew we were going to be there," Claymore replied. "Minstrel Cotty told me a competitor had made a move on his smuggling operation, but he wouldn't tell me by who."

"Any theories on who that might be?" Gideon asked.

"That's a long list," Claymore replied. He put his bandaged head in his hands. "Natascha's mother, Idalia Devi, is the first to come to mind. Or it could be any number of people on the Common Council. Bonfar Nil or Palacios Vosch come to mind."

Gideon nodded in agreement. "And let's not forget Mordecai Davos and *The Society of the Black Rose*. They have their fingers in every illegal activity in the City."

Claymore rubbed his face vigorously. "I couldn't shake the feeling that Cotty and I weren't alone," he said. "Every so often, a slight draft would pick up around us as if something unseen moved about the room. Then I was hit from behind."

"Someone else was there!" Ren said. "I saw a cloaked figure escape down a passageway behind the bookshelf as I broke through the door. So, what do we to do now?"

"Would you know the assassin if you saw them again?" Gideon asked.

"Probably not," Ren replied. "It happened so quickly. All I saw was a black robe hood. That narrows it down to half of the people in Rogue Destiny."

"You and I should probably hole up somewhere," Claymore replied. "Until we track down whoever is behind this."

The intercom on his desk buzzed. "Sir, this is the front desk. Inspector Morris Rance is here asking to speak to you."

"Is the Inspector alone?" Claymore asked.

"No, sir. There is a... rather large contingent of police constables with him."

"Please send them down to my office, Katrine. Thank you." Claymore clicked the intercom off.

"That was a little quick!" Ren quipped. "We need to go. We can fly *Righteous Indignation* somewhere safe until we figure this out!"

Claymore stood up from his desk. "No, I'm going to turn myself over to the Inspector." He winced and touched the bandage wrapped around his head. "I am in no shape to run. Besides, they know I'm here. If I disappear now, it will only give the Common Council a reason to come down hard on the Raconteurs. Ren, you should make yourself scarce. See if you can hunt down any leads about who is behind this."

"No!" Ren argued. "I'm not leaving you to face this alone!"

"I'm the one the Council wants," Claymore said. "Once they have me, it'll take the pressure off the Raconteurs. I've done nothing wrong, so I'm confident we'll win this in court. Gideon, I hope you'll be willing to represent me at trial?"

"Without hesitation," Gideon replied.

"You don't have to do this," Ren said. "There has to be some other way." Claymore's moral principles aggravated him. His partner was too trusting of a legal system that would never treat him fairly.

"Every decision I make is for the good of the Raconteurs," Claymore said. "That's the only thing that matters in the end."

A knock on the office door interrupted them.

Claymore glanced at Ren. "Go!" he whispered.

Ren morphed into a brindled-colored house cat. He stepped out of his discarded pants and padded to the bottom shelf of a bookcase, where he curled up.

"Come in," Gideon replied, kicking Ren's discarded pants under the desk as the door opened.

Inspector Rance entered. Three burly uniformed officers dressed in the traditional black and scarlet colors of Rogue Destiny's law enforcement bureau stood outside the doorway. The Inspector was a tall lanky man in an overcoat and fedora. He sported a thick mustache and bushy eyebrows. A cluster of more officers stood outside in the hallway.

"How can I help you this evening, Inspector?" Gideon asked politely.

"Thank you for not making this more difficult than it already is, Gideon," Inspector Rance said. He dug into the pocket of his coat and produced a folded piece of paper with the wax stamp of Rogue Destiny's highest governmental office on it.

"Claymore Ives, I believe you know why I am here," he said, his voice level and professional. "This is an order signed by the General Protectorate to take you and Ren B'gatti into custody for the destruction of the novel, *The Angels of Avalon*. You both are to be held in Lazaranth Prison until a full investigation has been conducted."

"I understand," Claymore said without emotion. "You'll get no resistance from me." He held out his hands while a constable stepped in and shackled his wrists.

"Is that really necessary, Inspector?" Gideon asked coldly. His large dower eyes revealed his disgust at the use of the restraints.

"I'm sorry, but its protocol, Mr. Dumas," the Inspector replied. "Now where can we find Mr. B'gatti?"

"He's around here somewhere," Claymore replied. "He might still be down in the garage talking to Sebastian. If you hurry, you may catch him. Also, you'll find five survivors from *The Angels of Avalon* in our communications room."

Inspector Rance nodded toward the door. "Spread out and find B'gatti," he said to his officers. "And round up the survivors for questioning."

The cluster of uniformed officers rushed off down the hallway. Once they were gone, the Inspector closed the office door. When he turned back to them, the stern gaze of his profession was gone, replaced with a sadness for what duty had forced him to do. His eyes swept the room like he was looking for something. He stopped when he saw the cat sleeping on the shelf of the bookcase.

"I'm sorry about this whole mess," Inspector Rance stated, shaking hands with Claymore. "I'm sure all this will be cleared up once our investigation is complete."

"Like I said, Morris, I understand," Claymore said with emotion. "No hard feelings. You're only doing your job."

"Then you're a better man than me, Mr. Ives," the Inspector replied with a somber smile.

"So tell me, Inspector," Gideon asked. "How did news of this tragedy reach the authorities so quickly? Claymore and Ren had just returned not a half hour ago."

"All I know is the Common Council received an anonymous message telling them that *The Angels of Avalon* had been destroyed in the fires of a *Crucible Event*. That was five hours ago. We received a signed arrest order shortly thereafter and were told to wait for Claymore Ives and Ren B'gatti to land so we could take them into custody. The whole thing looked very orchestrated if you ask me."

"Of course it was," Claymore growled. "I knew we were set up. Whoever killed Minstrel Cotty planned to leave me and Ren holding the bag. With no physical evidence of the crime, it'll be easy to blame us for the murder of millions of people."

"Could any of the survivors have witnessed something that could exonerate you?" the Inspector asked.

"Doubtful," Claymore said. "We had been there less than a day and stayed holed up in Cotty's study the whole time."

"Why were you there?"

"Minstrel was involved in an expansive smuggling operation of magical artifacts and relics stolen from various magical worlds. He knew me as a high-end dealer he could buy and sell through."

"Was he acting strange or anything?"

"He was on edge, like he knew something was about to happen. Kept arguing about things we had already agreed to..."

There was a knock on the door. Inspector Rance turned to Gideon.

"I will get further information to you when I can," he whispered.

"Thank you, Inspector," Gideon replied quietly with a slight bow. "We'd appreciate anything you can find."

The door opened, and one of the uniformed officers stuck his head inside. "Sir, we couldn't find any trace of B'gatti."

"Doesn't surprise me, Officer Hines," the Inspector replied. "B'gatti is a trickster, a skin-changeling who could be hiding as anyone. You may have even questioned him without knowing it. But he cannot escape us forever."

"The ship *Righteous Indignation* was not in the landing bay," the constable added. "But we did locate the five survivors and have taken them down to the station for questioning."

"Mr. Ives?" Inspector Rance said somberly. "It's time we go." Two officers took hold of Claymore by each arm and escorted him out of the room. Inspector Rance tipped his hat.

"Please contact our office if Ren B'gatti shows up again," he said. "I'm sure you are aware of the harsh penalties for harboring fugitives of the city. Good day, Mr. Dumas."

"Good day to you, Inspector." Gideon shut the door after them. Ren leapt off the bookcase shelf to the floor, where he morphed back into his true form.

"So we're just going to let them get away with this?" Ren asked.

"We have no choice, Mr. Bugatti," Gideon replied. "We cannot stop them from arresting Claymore any more than we can break him out of police custody. The ramifications of either would destroy everything the Raconteurs have built. And if we cannot continue protecting the written worlds, then millions of more lives will meet the same fate as those from *The Angels of Avalon.*"

Ren felt his temper flare. "Then what are we going to do?" he asked.

"We will have to prove Claymore's innocence at the trial," Gideon said thoughtfully. "No one but Claymore was there when Minstrel Cotty was killed. Not even you, correct?"

"That's right. I left to get the ship," Ren replied. "By the time I got back, Minstrel was dead, and the Crucible fires were already burning in the skies. Claymore was unconscious on the floor. We barely made it out alive."

"Defending him will be difficult," Gideon admitted. "Every bit of evidence was destroyed when *The Angels of Avalon* burned. My guess is the prosecution will rely on the testimony of the survivors and what they saw that day."

Ren ran a hand through his wild hair. "So, what are our chances of proving his innocence?"

The look in Gideon's eyes said it all. "As it stands now, it will be difficult, if not impossible."

Chapter 3
Tribunal Court

Natascha Devi sat alone at the end of a long bench, where one of her closest friends waited for the verdict to come down from Rogue Destiny's highest court. Her fellow Raconteurs filled the first several rows at the front of the dimly lit tribunal chambers. Final arguments had been made, and the Tribunal Judges had excused themselves to their inner chambers to decide the fate of Claymore Ives.

His trial had not gone well. The five survivors from *The Angels of Avalon* were kept sequestered until the opening day of the trial, making it next to impossible for Gideon to prepare an adequate defense without the prosecution looking over his shoulder.

All five testified before the court during the hearing. The first three had nothing of value to say, except to confirm they saw no one outside of the household staff present in the citadel that day. The fourth gave testimony that she had seen Minstrel Cotty with Claymore Ives and Ren B'gatti throughout the afternoon of the murder.

The last one to take the stand gave an account that was the most damning. He told the court he had witnessed an argument between Minstrel Cotty and Claymore Ives, while bringing a tray of afternoon tea to Minstrel's study. The door was locked, but he heard shouting coming from inside. He knocked and was told to go away by Cotty. A short time later, the skies above the citadel turned into fire and storm. He broke down in tears while describing how he watched his world burn from a window of the slipstream, *Righteous Indignation*. What little hope Natascha had left began to falter.

The criminal system of Rogue Destiny was simple. If there was adequate evidence to make an arrest, it was left to the accused to prove their own innocence. The defendant had to convince the court the evidence against them was not strong enough to warrant a conviction. Or prove their innocence with a credible alibi or witnesses of good moral character to speak on their behalf. In the end, the final decision of guilt or innocence lay in the hands of the seven judges overseeing the proceedings.

Gideon mounted as strong a defense as he could, arguing the evidence against Claymore was circumstantial at best. He stressed the fact that no one had actually witnessed Minstrel Cotty's murder and argued the presence of a secret passageway behind the bookcase in Cotty's study could have easily been accessed by the actual assassin. Unfortunately, the passageway's existence could not be corroborated by any of the other witnesses.

Claymore craned his neck to look at the Raconteurs behind him. His gaze drifted down the row of friends and comrades, many he had personally recruited into their ranks. He nodded to each in turn, then stopped when his eyes met Natascha's. They stared at each other for several heartbeats before he gave her a final pensive smile.

She forced herself to return the gesture, although doing so brought a tear to the corner of her eye. The last thing she needed was to get emotional now. She wiped it away and forced herself to remain stoic in front of the mass of spectators behind her.

Natascha's stomach tightened as the High Judge Magistrate appeared from behind a curtained doorway. Her face was hidden by the traditional red and black mask of Rogue Destiny's judicial system. The entire courtroom rose to their feet. Six similarly dressed judges followed her out, their dark robes trailing behind them.

The High Judge ascended the steps to the tall podium that loomed over the accused. The other judges took the ivory chairs set in a half-circle around the man that brought them there today. Slanted beams of sunlight from the domed ceiling created an ominous contrast of shadow and light. It shined down on where Claymore stood chained to the floor.

"Before we hand down our verdict, there is an outstanding issue we must address," the judge's voice echoed across the crowded courtroom. "Claymore Ives' accomplice, Ren B'gatti, has continued to elude capture. So it is the decision of this court to double the bounty on his head to fifty thousand gold sovereigns. This amount is to be paid to anyone with information leading to his capture and arrest." She paused a moment before looking down at Claymore.

"Claymore Jonathan Ives," she said. "You stand before us today charged with the most heinous of crimes, the genocide of a written world. This court seeks justice for the countless lives lost in the pages of *The Angels of Avalon*. After an exhaustive examination of the evidence presented to this Tribunal, you have been found guilty in the murder of Minstrel Cotty. And upon the death of the Novel's central character, that sacred, mystical connection between the Story and its *Logos Personae* was severed, causing events to be set in motion that ended with *The Angels of Avalon* being consumed by fire."

The High Judge continued. "It grieves this court to see how far the once great Raconteurs have fallen in recent years, but that is a matter for another day. By the power given to this court by the Commonwealth of Rogue Destiny and her surrounding territories, Claymore Ives, you are to be sentenced to death by hanging one week from today. So has it been ordered, so will it be done. Do you have any last words?"

Murmurs erupted from the crowd of spectators in the

packed Tribunal Chambers. Many of the Raconteurs around Natascha protested loudly amongst themselves. The High Judge raised her hand and motioned the crowd to silence.

Claymore shifted in his chains. His strong shoulders pulled against the shackles that bound his ankles and wrists to the circled marbled platform. He lifted his head as high as the iron collar allowed. Natascha's jaw tensed, watching him try to maintain what little dignity he had left.

"I am not responsible for the death of millions of people," Claymore said, his voice steady and confident. "I swore an oath long ago that I would protect the innocent with my life. There are sins I will someday answer for, but the crime of genocide is not one of them."

The High Judge nodded. "In accordance with our laws and traditions," she said. "I will now open the floor to any calls for Final Mercy. Does anyone want to submit evidence or testimony on behalf of Claymore Ives that would cause this court to reconsider its sentence of death?"

The ancient tradition dated back to the days of the City's founder, Baltazar Gheddi. Because this was a capital crime, tradition demanded that anyone in the courtroom could make a plea for leniency in the court's judgement. It held the condemned had a right to a last-minute reprieve that might sway the judgement of the court. If no one stepped forward to challenge the death sentence, it became irrevocable. That was Final Mercy.

Any reprieve to the death sentence was left to the sole discretion of the High Judge. That was how justice was done. It was a brutal system and rigged so those in power held onto that power. Corruption ran deep in Rogue Destiny.

As if on cue, the wide doors at the rear of the great hall opened, and Medesto appeared. He ambled up the main aisle toward the front of the courtroom, his hard soled dragon-skin boots echoing in the silence. When he reached the defense attorney's table, he pulled an envelope from inside his coat and handed it to Gideon Dumas.

Gideon took the envelope and stood up from his seat. He lifted his dower eyes toward the High Judge. "We have just received additional evidence I think is very relevant to my client's case. May I approach, your honor?"

The judge motioned him forward, and he walked toward the steps leading up to the dais. A voice behind Natascha spoke. "It is a sad thing to witness the greatest protector of the Mythic Cosmos convicted of a crime he clearly did not commit."

She turned to see a short, portly man in an expensive suit and black bowler hat with an umbrella hanging from his arm. The strange man sat down beside her, removed his hat, and gave her a pleasant smile behind a graying goatee and mustache. A sparkling blue eye winked at her as he held out his gloved hand. He did not fool her for a second.

"Nigel Bishoff," he said, introducing himself. "And you are Natascha Devi, whose alter ego is the infamous Doctor Enigma. You work for the Raconteurs, do you not?"

Natascha did not shake the offered hand. "What are you doing here?" she said in a low voice. She looked around. No one sat close enough to overhear their conversation.

"Where else would I be?" Nigel said with a look of surprise. The man shifted his feet, like he was uncomfortable in the shiny hard-soled shoes he was wearing.

Natascha leaned into the man's ear and whispered, "This is not a joke, B'gatti. The entire city is searching for you. They'll be watching the crowds, expecting you to show up. If you try anything to free Claymore, innocent people will get hurt."

"This whole thing is a setup by the Common Council," Nigel whispered. "To settle old scores with Claymore and the Raconteurs. I'm not going to let that happen."

"I agree," Natascha whispered. "This is not fair."

The portly man's demeanor changed. His blue eyes grew dark. "Then what are we going to do to correct this travesty of justice?" His voice brimmed with anger.

"The Raconteurs are agents of the law," Natascha said.

"There is nothing we can do, even if those responsible were standing in this room at this moment."

"Even if that law condemns an innocent man to death?" Nigel asked, fitting the hat atop his head. "Then what good are your laws? And if the Raconteurs can't protect their own, what good are they?"

Natascha knew trying to reason with Ren B'gatti further was pointless. It was never good when he got like this. She laid a hand on his coat sleeve. His arm rippled under her fingers as he prepared to shift into something that would throw the crowded court proceedings into chaos.

"Please wait, I beg you," Natascha whispered. "Gideon is about to play his last card." Nigel's body relaxed, and he remained in the borrowed face of Nigel Bishoff.

"Okay," he huffed. "For now."

Natascha looked up as Gideon reached the podium. He handed the letter to the High Judge, turned on a heel and walked back down the steps.

The High Judge stared at the letter in her hand. She broke the wax seal on the envelope and unfolded the paper inside. Her expression remained hidden behind the red judicial mask as she read it. Natascha could not gauge the impact the letter's words had on her, but she watched an amused look appeared Gideon's face as he returned to his seat.

After what seemed an eternity, the High Judge Magistrate folded the letter and slipped it into the pocket of her cloak. She gathered the six other judges to her. They spoke in inaudible whispers for several minutes. The crowd noise in the courthouse rose as people discussed the sudden change in the direction the hearing had taken.

The High Judge walked back up to her dais. She looked momentarily at Gideon and the Raconteurs, then cleared her voice and spoke. "This court has received additional evidence which has caused us to reconsider our original ruling. After deliberating, we have decided to dismiss the sentence of death. Instead, Claymore

Ives will serve life imprisonment inside the walls of Lazaranth Prison. So has it been ordered, so will it be done." The Judge's gavel came down on her podium with the resounding echo of finality.

The courtroom erupted into hundreds of converging conversations. Gideon glanced at Natascha and smiled. A small squad of court security came in and surrounded Claymore. The chains holding him to the floor were unlocked, and they led him away. The noise in the Tribunal Chambers became deafening. Natascha gave a sigh of relief.

"Happy now?" she said, turning to Nigel. His seat was empty. She saw him moving through the crowd toward two burly security guards who stood at the exit. Nigel pulled a wallet out of his jacket and dutifully showed his identification to them. They motioned him through. Nigel Bishoff disappeared with the crush of people into the outer foyer of the building.

A steady crowd pressed in close as the audience emptied from the main gallery. Natascha pushed through the line. She flashed her Raconteur badge at security, then hurried through the open doors of the courthouse to the plaza outside the front of the building. She searched the expansive area for Nigel but didn't see him anywhere. Someone grabbed her arm, and she spun to see Tempest Vondersteen glaring down at her.

"What was that all about?" the Raconteurs' Senior Operations Officer asked. "Who were you talking to?"

Tempest was a tall woman with dirty blonde hair pulled back in a tight bun and towered over Natascha. She may have been a recent hire, but her voice was that of someone who was used to being in charge, who took their job seriously. Medesto ambled up behind her. He scanned the crowd with a brooding gaze.

"Ren was here, wasn't he?" the chief field agent of the Raconteurs rumbled. The stout, four-foot tall gnome scratched his scruffy beard. It wasn't a question. Natascha looked out over Ampersand Boulevard, the major thoroughfare in the City's downtown district.

"Yeah," she said. "No one's seen him since Claymore's arrest, but he asked me to help bust Claymore out of Lazaranth. I told him I couldn't do that. He didn't like that answer."

"Of course not," Tempest spat. "He's a trickster with allegiance to no one but himself. Makes sense he'd show up today to cause trouble. The Raconteurs have put up with his nonsense for far too long already."

Natascha gave Tempest a sour look. "If I could just talk to him," she said. "I know I could make him see reason."

"Claymore was the only thing holding him to the Raconteurs," Tempest replied. "Why stay around when your one ally will be locked away in prison for the rest of his life?"

Natascha ignored the comment. On an empty bench next to the fountain, she spotted a bowler hat and umbrella. She walked over and picked up the hat, searching the crowd for any signs of Ren.

"What do you think, Gideon?" Tempest asked loud enough for Natascha to hear. "I may be new to the organization, but it's always been obvious to me that B'gatti was never cut out to a Raconteur. He's always been more trouble than he's worth." Natascha turned to see Gideon walking up to them.

"I have to disagree with your assessment, Tempest," Gideon said. "Mr. B'gatti has the potential to become a great Raconteur, perhaps one of the greatest we have ever employed. I believe there is more to him than just what we see on the surface."

"Either way," Tempest replied. "I'm guessing this will be the last time we'll ever see him."

Natascha scanned the crowded courtyard again, hoping in vain to spot the elusive trickster. He wouldn't just leave, would he? Not without saying goodbye.

"So, tell me, Gideon," Tempest asked. "What was in that letter you gave to the High Judge Magistrate? It certainly sent a shock wave through the most powerful court in the City."

Gideon nodded in agreement. "When I realized my defense would not keep Claymore from the gallows, I quickly gathered incriminating evidence on as many of the Judicial Judges as I could. Every one of them has had compromising dealings with Rogue Destiny's most powerful crime lord, Mordecai Davos."

"Brilliant," Natascha said.

"I agree," Gideon quipped, quite pleased that his gambit had paid off. "The letter given to the Judge contained detailed dates, account numbers and banks where the money connecting them to Mordecai's illegal operations were hidden. It simply stated that if Claymore's sentence of execution was not reduced, the incriminating evidence would be released to the public by the end of the day. Such corruption never looks good on the highest court in the land. Even the Common Council could not ignore that, and they were forced to reconsider their sentence. The resulting scandal would ruin every judge on the Tribunal."

"Well, we're going to have to brace ourselves for the retaliation that'll be coming from all sides," Medesto said. "The Common Council already has it in for us. Now the Tribunal Court has reason to join them."

"Of course," Gideon said. "We will have to watch our backs, as we always have. But I am not above poking the dragon when the life of one of our own hangs in the balance. Given the short time, I could only gather evidence on four of the judges, and I was forced to play with the cards I had. The accusations in the letter were broad enough that I knew the others would fall in line out of fear of what I may have on them. It was a gamble, but it paid off in the end."

Medesto agreed. "The impact of what happened in that courtroom today will resonate throughout the City," he replied grimly. "Once again, the Raconteurs will be the topic of conversation in every corner of Rogue Destiny. We deserve some decent publicity after everything we've been through these past few weeks."

"Couldn't you have them declare Claymore innocent of the crimes against *The Angels of Avalon*?" Tempest asked.

"I was ready to force them to release Claymore," Gideon

replied. "He and I discussed the issue at length, but he insisted someone had to pay for a crime of this magnitude. If not, the Common Council would come down hard on the Raconteurs. He decided to take full responsibility for what had happened upon himself. Other things came up in our conversation that I cannot speak of at this time. Let's just say he is dealing with dark issues that go far deeper than the trial."

Natascha could not listen any further to their conversation. One of her closest friends had just been condemned to life in imprisonment and another had taken off, maybe forever. She walked to the edge of the courtyard steps, looking out over the crowded boulevard for any sign of Ren.

Across the wide street, on the slanted roof of a clock-tower, a black raven perched. The bird was a favorite of Ren's. It stared at Natascha for the longest time before its spread it wings and disappeared over the rooftops.

"You're never going to find him." Tempest said, standing behind her, arms crossed with a sanctimonious smile on her face. "If he has taken off, good riddance to him. He was never one of us."

Despite her anger at Tempest's words, Natascha knew she was right. No one would find Ren B'gatti if he didn't want to be found.

Chapter 4
Lazaranth Prison

A black raven perched in a tree under the shadows of the massive walls of Lazaranth Prison. Ren B'gatti stared out through the eyes of the bird down the mountain road at the cityscape below him, deciding on the best course of action. If the Raconteurs would not help him free Claymore, he would do it himself.

Ren remembered nothing of where he came from before finding himself in the great City of Rogue Destiny, but he never worried about such things. He preferred to live in the moment, reveling in doing what those around him were incapable or unwilling to do. Claymore was being sent to an impregnable prison stronghold, and Ren would be waiting for him when he got there.

His argument with Natascha left him empty and angry. Without her help, attacking the prison transport would be futile and only get Claymore killed. So he waited, deep in thought about how he would free his partner.

Getting inside Lazaranth Prison would be easy enough. He'd done it before. But getting Claymore out alive posed a problem. He decided his first step was to reach his partner. Together, they could figure how to get back out again.

Since the night of Claymore's arrest, Ren had spent his days staying out of sight. He prided himself on maintaining a number of false identities throughout the City. Each was created to give him a place to hide if the time ever came for him to part ways with the Raconteurs. But the stress of being on the run and watching over his shoulder had taken a toll on him. He'd become paranoid, constantly moving from one place to another, never knowing who might be closing in on him.

He heard the rumbling of the armored prison trucks before he saw them. A convoy of three massive prisoner transports came up the curving road that led to a stronghold built into the side of Mount Perdition.

Ren took to the air, flying over the vehicles to the entrance. He landed gently with outspread wings on a lamppost near the front gates. After the armed guards followed the proper protocols, the tall gates slowly swung open, and the trucks rolled through, one by one.

The parking area in front of the entrance was congested with vehicles, prison transports, trolleys, and foot traffic. The adrenaline of getting inside a place deemed impenetrable welled up in him. Near the lamppost was a tall, broad-leaved tree, perfect for concealment. He flew into the thick foliage. Once out of sight, he increased his focus and shifted into the smallest shape his willpower would allow him to take. A moment later, a large housefly flew out of the leaves.

Ren could turn into a raven with a mere thought and able to hold the form for hours. The shape was natural and instinctive. It was a part of him, like putting on a comfortable pair of shoes. He could sustain the shape of any creature roughly his own size almost indefinitely, even while he slept. But condensing his five-foot-seven-inch frame and 135 pounds of mass into a tiny insect was another matter. It took his full concentration to hold the shape for any length of time. The pressure in his head was immediate.

Ren buzzed past the gun turrets and guard towers unnoticed, flying in the lazy zig-zag pattern of a fly. He dropped over the highstone walls into the courtyard where the prisoners were being unloaded.

Below him, throngs of civilians went about whatever business brought them to the prison. Armed guards were everywhere. Important-looking people from every walk of life passed through the security checkpoints.

He saw Claymore step down from the last prison truck, his hands and feet shackled. He was one of a dozen prisoners shuffled through a set of secure doors, separate from the main lobby. His partner stood in line between two heavyset prisoners, both sporting proud beards, bald heads, and thick, heavily tattooed arms. The guards led them through a hall full of armed security to a larger group of convicts waiting to be processed. Overhead, a tiny housefly followed.

An authoritative man with a clipboard separated the prisoners into smaller groups. Three guards took four prisoners, including Claymore, to an elevator next to another security checkpoint. Ren flew down through the doors as they closed and landed on the wall near the ceiling.

Thirty seconds later, the doors opened to a dimly lit, dank hallway. Etched into the wall in front of them were the words *Sublevel 13*. The judicial system of Rogue Destiny did not discriminate between gender or genre, human or non-human. All crimes were equal in the eyes of the law, and punishment doled out without prejudice.

The prisoners shuffled to a stop at the next checkpoint. Two were separated from Claymore's group and taken out of sight by two other guards waiting for them. Ren stayed with Claymore, knowing they would throw him into the deepest hole they could find. One where only the worst criminals in Lazaranth were housed.

The guards took Claymore and the other prisoner down a long, dank hallway farther and farther into the bowels of Lazaranth. Finally, they stopped at an enormous iron door with words engraved across it. *Sublevel 13 - Cellblock 27: Restricted Area.* The sentry on guard duty looked over the prisoners' papers before opening the door. A rush of cold air hit Ren as the heavy doors swung in without a sound.

Cellblock 27 was laid out in an oval pattern. Ren estimated there were at least fifty cells throughout the level. The first in the row had a scar-faced man lying on a threadbare cot, reading a newspaper. He sat up as the first guard unlocked the cell door next to him and motioned the prisoner beside Claymore inside. "Your clothes, Addison," the guard said as he tossed a black-and-white striped prison uniform into the cell. The man called Addison changed and handed his street clothes back. The guard locked the cell door, and they ushered Claymore up the corridor.

Ren clung to the wall. The strain of holding the tiny form was increasing. The pounding in his ears grew louder. He had only a short time before he needed to shift back. Across from him, a large broad-shouldered man with a bull neck leaned against the bars of his cell. His mallet-sized hands rested on the crossbar of his cell. His black hair was slicked back, and his soulless eyes were that of a killer. He paid no mind to the new prisoner as they passed, his gaze never leaving the stone floor. A strange darkness emanated around the man. The shadows he cast across the floor seemed to stretch far past what was natural.

The guards passed a concrete cell that was set back from the others. Thick walls kept whoever was inside isolated from everyone else. The front of it had two narrow windows and a small opening at the bottom of the door to pass food to the occupant. Ren's curiosity became too great, and he flew to the window for a look.

Inside the cell, a long serpentine figure with a human torso lay curled up and sleeping in the corner. The serpent's wedged-shaped head was encased in a shiny black containment mask that covered its eyes. The torso of its long body rose and fell in a rhythmic pattern as the creature slept.

The clank of a cell door brought Ren back to the problem at hand. He and Claymore had been in impossible situations before, but he began to harbor doubts about how he would get his partner out of here alive. They were currently thirteen stories below a high-security fortress, inside the tallest mountain in the Sojourn Archipelago. Hundreds of highly trained personnel stood between them and freedom. He pushed those doubts away, confident they could fight their way out of here if it came down to it. He flew back to the three guards surrounding his partner.

The front guard motioned Claymore into the small cell with the butt of his short rifle. The other two stood back with their guns ready to react if the need arose. Claymore offered no resistance as he stepped into the barren cell. Once inside, he put his cuffed hands through a slit in the bars. The guard removed shackles on his hands and feet. He changed out of his street clothes into the striped prison uniform without a word.

The prisoners around them look out from their cells for a moment before returning to the activities of their busy day. The guard checked Claymore's door to make sure it was locked and spoke into a handheld device, indicating every prisoner was secured.

Ren waited on the wall outside Claymore's cell for the guards to leave. A strange aroma filled the air from the cell next to him. He crawled down over to peek inside.

A man in filthy robes with a gaunt face, unkempt beard and long ratty hair hanging in his face sat crossed legged on the floor. A small tin of incense burned in front of him. He murmured softly to himself, his eyes closed, oblivious to anything that might disrupt his meditation. The man was wasting his time if he was trying to conjure any sort of magic. The islands of Rogue Destiny existed within a dead zone, so there was no magic to draw from within her borders.

In the cell across from him, a woman dressed all in black sat at a desk, writing with a feather quill pen. She stood out among the other inhabitants of the cellblock in both dress and manner, but Ren understood the most dangerous individuals often appear nonthreatening on the surface. The lady was in here for a reason.

The pressure in his head was becoming too much to bear. Ren would need to abandon his tiny disguise before he lost his hold on it completely. After several more agonizing moments, the guards departed, and the prison block fell silent. Ren dropped from the wall and flew between the bars into Claymore's cell.

His partner lay stretched out on a narrow cot, staring at the ceiling. Ren buzzed to the back of the cell. With a thought, he released his hold on the insect's form, morphing back to his actual size. He crouched in the darkness, waiting until the throbbing in his head subsided.

"Claymore?" Ren whispered.

"Ren?" Claymore rose from the cot as the trickster stepped out from the shadows. The prison garb Claymore wore could not conceal the muscular frame underneath. He stared at Ren for a long time without speaking, his expression confused, as if he had lost his train of thought. After a moment, the turmoil in his face vanished, and he gave Ren a tired smile.

"What are you doing here?" Claymore asked. He snatched the blanket off his bed and threw it to Ren. The naked trickster wrapped it around his waist.

"I've come to discuss the terms of your escape," Ren replied. The welcoming look on Claymore's face faded. Layers of anguish and distress replaced it.

"I'm not leaving," he said at last.

"Has everyone gone mad?" Ren hissed. "First Natascha, and now you!"

"You don't understand," Claymore whispered. He winced and pressed a hand to his temple. "Something is wrong with me. I don't feel like myself anymore."

"Why haven't you said anything before now?" Ren found himself more confused than ever.

"Because I had it under control," Claymore muttered. "Or I thought I did. But the head injury I suffered from the assassin's attack has only made it worse. Something inside me has broken. It's not physical. It goes deeper than that. My injuries have healed, but the events of that night have left a scar on my soul."

"You look exhausted. When was the last time you slept?"

"I don't know. When I do, I have dreams, words really, coursing inside my head that repeat over and over. It's been driving me mad, so I don't sleep."

The glare of a flashlight appeared outside the bars. Claymore stepped in front of Ren, shielding him from the light. Ren backed into the darkness, blending his skin tone in with the shadows.

"Talking to yourself, Prisoner 7987?" The prison guard checked the confines of Claymore's world with the flashlight. The beam fell on a rat in the corner, standing on a blanket. Satisfied nothing was amiss, he shined his light back at Claymore. "Lights out in five. You and your friend have a pleasant night."

Claymore watched the guard as he left to complete his rounds, then sat down on his cot, running his hands through his hair. Ren stood up on his hind feet and morphed back into his proper form. He picked up the blanket and wrapped it around his waist.

"None of it matters anymore," Claymore said, descending again into melancholy. He scratched the back of his head vigorously and stared through the bars of his cell. "I'm out of the game. After *The Angels of Avalon,* there are no more worlds left for me to save."

Ren laid a hand on his shoulder. "You're not responsible for what happened."

"I know," Claymore choked out. Water crept to the edges of his eyes. He licked his lips. "But a world burned, and millions died, because I was not who I needed to be."

Ren had never seen his partner in such despair. It was not how he expected their reunion to go. There was supposed to be fighting and heroics, with violence and bloodshed mixed in for good measure.

Claymore Ives had always been the exemplary hero. The one who remained strong when those around him faltered. He was the personification of everything the Raconteurs stood for, always in control, easygoing with a quick laugh. Nothing ever got to him. Everyone wanted to emulate him, most of all Ren. He found it hard to breathe. His stomach tightened, and he swallowed.

Ren tried one last desperate plea. "There's supposed to be another way out of Lazaranth," he said. "An errant doorway that leads to a series of tunnels somewhere in the depths of Mount Perdition. It was here before they built the prison. If we find it, we can get out. Then Natascha would have no choice but to help us."

"That's just a myth," Claymore growled. His tone bordered on anger. "A rumor no one has ever been able to verify. It's supposedly the original doorway that brought Baltazar Gheddi to these islands. There are no rabbit-holes inside Mount Perdition. The authorities would never allow secret tunnels into of their impenetrable stronghold."

"Maybe it's a rabbit-hole that can only be entered from the other side. There are thousands of rabbit-holes throughout these islands."

"Ren, you need to get out of the city," Claymore said. His tone suddenly calmed. "The Common Council won't stop until you're in custody or dead. By now, they've brought in bounty hunters and assassins to hunt for you. Find somewhere to hide where no one will look for you until you can figure out your next move. They have their scapegoat, and that'll take the pressure off Gideon and the Raconteurs for now. But whatever you decide to do next, it doesn't involve me."

Ren was taken aback by the statement. "You want me to leave you down here to rot?" he said. "You're not thinking straight, you just said so yourself. Let me get you out of here and we'll figure this out just like we always have."

"No, Ren, this is different," Claymore whispered. "Something's wrong with me. I don't know what it is, but my cognitive abilities are waning. My thoughts are cloudy and more confused with every passing day. And the nights are even worse. I haven't slept in weeks. Words I don't recognize flow through my mind, and they get louder every day. I can't make them stop."

"Then let me help you." Ren took a step closer.

Claymore raised a hand to keep him back. "You're not listening to me. Nothing makes sense anymore. I'm losing the ability to discern between right and wrong. Out there, I'd only be a danger to everyone around me. In here, I can push back against the madness growing inside me."

"Right and wrong is whatever you decide," Ren replied. "Every world has its own laws and moral absolutes. They're never the same from Book to Book. Killing is bad in some places, but acceptable in others. I've tried it your way, but after seeing how justice works in Rogue Destiny, I've decided to making my own rules from now on."

"Stop saying that," Claymore rumbled. He held the side of his head like the words hurt to speak. "Good and evil are not arbitrary. There are absolutes, and we must never let evil win. I have dedicated my life to that. If we lose that fight, then there is no hope left for anyone. I fought to get you into the Raconteurs because I could see good in you. I knew you would stand on the side of the angels if given the chance. There were those who thought you didn't belong among us, but I brought you on, anyway."

"I'm not here to argue moral philosophy with you," Ren said. "I came to get you out."

Claymore's demeanor changed. He hesitated, like he was now uncertain of his own convictions.

"I said I'm not leaving," he said, his expression dark. There was an irritation in his voice that only came out when he was tired of arguing. "I think you should leave."

Ren didn't understand what was happening. Physically, Claymore looked unchanged. He stood as tall and strong as ever. But he was missing that uncompromising confidence that had kept the Raconteurs together through the worst of times. Gone was his swagger and devil-may-care attitude that overcame every impossible situation he had ever faced.

Ren had never gotten emotional in front of his partner, and he was not about to start now. Claymore was the soul of the Raconteurs, quick-witted, decisive, and never without a plan. The person standing before Ren now was no longer that man. He swallowed his confusion and pain, replacing it with anger and anguish. His world was crashing in around him, and he was out of places to run.

He felt empty and abandoned by everything he knew. He had tried to trust the Raconteurs, but they had failed him. They were supposed to be fighting to bring Claymore back into their fold. Now, even his partner was telling him to leave, to run from everything he had ever known.

"I'll go," Ren replied. "But know one thing. If I'm ever forced to choose between you or the Raconteurs, I will always side with you."

"I know," Claymore whispered. He grabbed the trickster's head and pressed their foreheads together. "We are brothers and always will be. No matter what happens, that will never change. But everything ends. We had a good run, but that time is over. I'm fighting a battle I cannot win. Go. Save yourself. Get out of Rogue Destiny before it's too late."

Ren turned away, peering out into the cellblock. It was dark and empty. He felt alone in a way he had never known before. He had no memory of where he came from before falling from the sky and finding himself in the City of Rogue Destiny. That made his short time with the Raconteurs the culmination of his entire life. And now, he was being told to walk away from that.

"Ren?" Claymore said. The distance and loss of focus gone from his eyes. "I've always believed in what you are capable of becoming. Never forget you are a Raconteur. That means accepting life as it comes, the good as well as the bad. We are the ones who protect those who can't protect themselves. We guard them from dangers they are not even aware of. If the Raconteurs fail, there's no hope for anyone. Remember that."

Ren dropped his eyes to the floor but said nothing. His partner was going mad right in front of him and refused any help. He left without another word between them, transforming into a housefly and flying between the bars of the cell.

He flew past the rows of prison cells, realizing he had no place to go. Everything he cared about involved Claymore and the Raconteurs. Now he wandered through a dark cellblock with no idea what to do next. A fury rose within him. It was a cold anger. One he would hold on to for a long time.

Ren decided at that moment he would leave the city. Travel to the farthest reaches of the Mythic Cosmos, where he could lose himself, never to be seen again. The Raconteurs had betrayed him, and now so had his partner. He was done with trying to be the hero.

At the northernmost point of the Rogue Destiny, stood a small shop on a quiet lane. It dealt in many things, legal and not so legal. The owner was a spry old woman who Ren considered more than an acquaintance, but not quite a friend. For the right price, she would allow passage through one of the many doorways hidden in her cellar. Any one of those rabbit-holes would take him away from this accursed city forever.

Chapter 5
Somewhere in the pages
of The Crimson Masque

It was a dark and stormy night. Lightning flashed across the sky while black clouds thundered their fury. A frigid rain blew in from the north. A rickety wagon trundled down the muddy road in a heavily wooded area twenty miles south of Paris. Its two occupants were cold, tired, and at the end of their patience. In the distance, a lone wolf gave a long, mournful howl.

Natascha sighed into her gas mask. "We've been at this for days," she said. "I'm beginning to wonder if he's out here?" Her long coat and cowl thermally insulated her against the relentless downpour, and she knew she was warmer than her stout companion.

The driver of the wagon pulled down his hood against the torrential rain and cold winds. Rivulets of water rolled off his bulbous nose. "Our intelligence indicates he should be," Medesto grumbled. "The field house said there's an individual who is *not* a character in this Story running around the countryside outside Paris. A highwayman who goes by the name Talbot Mundi. He's had several run-ins with the *Logos Personae* of this world, Arsene Vidocq, but Mundi isn't mentioned in any of the stories. It could be our boy."

"Yeah," Natascha responded. "This is as likely a place as any we've been to. Ren hates boredom, so he's not going to be hiding as a fishmonger or candlemaker. He'll be running around out in the open, causing mischief of some kind or another."

Under different circumstances, Natascha would have been on top of her game, excited to explore the pages of a new Story and hunt down their missing trickster. She wore the accouterment of her alter-ego, Doctor Enigma, and was ready for a fight. But now she was tired. The weeks of sleepless nights searching for a shape-shifter who did not want to be found were catching up to her.

The Echo Transponder in her gloved hand lit up. "Hold on,' she said. "I'm getting some bio-scan readings. Around the next bend, there are two humans on horseback. One on each side of the road, hiding in the trees. It might be him. You continue down the road while I circle in behind them."

"Be careful," the gnome warned. "He'll most likely be under the influence of the Muse, and that will make him dangerous and unpredictable."

Natascha agreed and tucked the scanning device into a pocket inside her coat. She grabbed the wooden pole supporting the lantern and jumped down from the wagon. Her boots sank in the rain-soaked muck and splattered her long coat. She adjusted the Peacemaker Lightning gun holstered at her side and worked her way through the trees to where her transponder had shown the heat signals originated. She spotted the highwayman among the trees and moved in silently behind him.

"Easy, boy," Talbot Mundi said, as his horse shifted restlessly under him. He patted the beast's neck. "This will be over soon."

A stifled cough came from the darkness across the road. "Quiet, Catalonia," hissed Talbot. His partner grumbled inaudibly, but probably knew better than to start an argument in the middle of a robbery. Natascha watched the muddy road from behind a tree for Medesto.

Right on cue, the creak of wagon wheels caught the outlaw's attention. He pulled a flintlock pistol from under his black cloak, then gave a sharp whistle to his confederate. The dim glow of a lantern appeared as the wagon rounded the bend. Talbot pulled his handkerchief over his face and urged his horse out of the trees. Natascha crept toward the edge of the road after him.

His partner, Catalonia, appeared from the dark trees across the road, her mask pulled up and a pistol in hand. Medesto jerked on the reins, pulling the horses to a stop.

"Stand and deliver your goods!" Talbot bellowed, pointing his flintlock pistol at the wagon's lone occupant. He tossed a set of empty saddlebags to Medesto. "Put anything of value in that and be quick!"

Medesto caught them with one hand. His face was hidden in the shadows of a rain-soaked hood. He laid the saddlebags on the seat next to him and pulled the hood back to reveal his bearded face with a prominent nose and salt-and-pepper hair. Dark eyes stared at the two outlaws from under his bushy eyebrows.

"Hello, *Talbot*," Medesto said. "It took us forever to find you."

"Just give us your gold and we'll be gone," Talbot said, motioning with the pistol towards the saddlebags. "Try anything and I won't hesitate to shoot you."

"That's good to know." Medesto climbed off the wagon to the muddy road and approached the outlaw with a brazen swagger. Talbot dismounted his horse and met him halfway.

Medesto was much shorter than Talbot's towering six-foot plus frame but stood defiant in front of the highwayman. The stout gnome stood four-feet tall with broad shoulders and a short, scruffy beard. His deep-set black eyes looked at Talbot with a sly grin as he stood toe to toe with him, his bravado unfazed by their difference in size. Natascha moved down the side of the road next to the highwayman's stallion and laid a calming hand on its flank. Both Medesto and Talbot remained transfixed on each other.

"Do I know you?" Talbot growled. His pistol remained on Medesto.

"You should," he replied. "My name is Medesto. We worked together for years. Then you disappeared on us. Does the name Ren B'gatti mean anything to you?"

"No," he answered.

"We've traveled across a dozen worlds looking for you, Talbot," Natascha called from behind them.

The highwayman spun around at the sound of her voice and leveled his pistol. Natascha raised her hands. She caught a quick flash of recognition in the highwayman's dark eyes, but it vanished an instant later.

"We're here to help," she said calmly.

Medesto scratched his short beard. "So you're a highwayman now?" he asked. "Running around in a Story you have no business being in?"

"Who sent you? The Crown?" Talbot spat, a confused look in his eyes. He stepped back so he could keep his pistol on both of them. "No, you're too short to be a proper soldier."

Medesto seemed amused by his response. "You really don't remember us, do you?" he asked.

"No!" Talbot replied. He seemed to hesitate for a moment before raising his flintlock again.

"Then you are further gone than we feared," Natascha said. "I assure you I was not sent by any authority of the state, nor am I in league with the Crimson Masque. We came here to talk."

The howl of a wolf echoed over the wind and rain, closer than before. This time it was answered by a second howl.

Catalonia shifted in her saddle, searching the surrounding darkness. "Kill them, Talbot, and let's be gone," she said. "The monsters are close. Let them keep their gold. There will always be other travelers."

Medesto looked around the rainy darkness. "Was that a were-wolf?" he asked.

"They are called *Loup-Garou*," Talbot said. He pulled a large silver cross out from under his cloak. "They run thick as thieves in these forests, but this will keep them at bay."

"You're thinking of Draculas," Medesto chuckled.

"Draculas?" Talbot said.

"Yeah, vampires, vampyres, Nosferatu, the blood-sucking

undead," Medesto said. "You know... Draculas? A cross doesn't work on a werewolf. Silver is what you need. It poisons the blood."

"The Loup-Garou fear the Holy Cross as much as any vampire," Talbot protested. The outlaw never took his eyes off either Raconteur.

"You're mixing up your mythology, but that doesn't matter right now," Medesto said. "Does the name Rogue Destiny mean anything to you?"

"Who's that?" Talbot hissed.

"It's a place," Natascha said. "A great city at the center of the Mythic Cosmos. You called it home before you ran off. This will make more sense once we get you off-world."

"I'm not going anywhere!" Talbot barked his anger rising. The highwayman pointed the flintlock at her.

The thud of heavy horse hooves shook the ground. Natascha turned to see half-a-dozen riders galloping up the road toward them. The leader of the brigands wore a mask under a black hood. Arsene Vidocq, the *Logos Personae* of *The Crimson Masque*, had arrived.

"It's an ambush!" Talbot yelled. "Catalonia, run for it!"

Catalonia fired at the approaching riders, and a cloaked figure fell from his horse. Chaos exploded as several pistols answered in return. Talbot's partner flew from her saddle.

"No!," Talbot cried as his partner-in-crime landed in the muddy road. He glanced back to Natascha and Medesto, his face hot with anger. "I'll deal with you when I'm done with them!" The outlaw grabbed the saddle horn and pulled himself onto his stallion. He jerked the reins around to face the approaching riders. Although outnumbered, Talbot charged at breakneck speed toward Arsene Vidocq and his infamous band of Black Cloaks.

"Ren, get back here!" Medesto yelled.

"If I am to die this night," Talbot bellowed, spurring his horse forward, "I'm going to make damn sure I take the Crimson Masque to hell with me!"

The flintlock in his hand thundered, and a second rider fell to the mud. When he reached the masked leader, Talbot launched himself from his saddle. His arm caught his rival around the neck, and he pulled Vidocq from his horse. They crashed to the ground in a tangle of limbs. Talbot landed a blow, knocking the red porcelain masquerade mask from his face. Vidocq returned a punch to Talbot's chin, and the two men rolled out of sight down a roadside ravine.

"Medesto, get back!" Natascha shouted. She pulled a small canister from under her coat and threw it in front of the three remaining riders. The metal cylinder exploded in a cloud of white smoke. The effect of the somnambulic gas was immediate. The horsemen emerged from the cloud, gasping for air and swaying drunkenly in their saddles. The horses stumbled forward before collapsing to the ground. Moments later, the Black Cloaks and their steeds lay unmoving in the mud.

Medesto pointed to where the highwayman had disappeared from sight. "We can't let Ren kill the *Logos Personae!*"

"I'm on it!" Natascha yelled. She hit a button in her glove and a green mist rose around her as she ran to the ditch. The hulking figure of Talbot Mundi emerged from the ravine, dragging the limp form of Arsene Vidocq behind him. He dropped the unconscious man onto the muddy road and pulled a second flintlock pistol from his belt.

"This is where our rivalry ends, Vidocq!" Talbot shouted. He pointed the pistol at the unconscious man at his feet and cocked the hammer back. "I may even take the title of *Crimson Masque* for myself."

"I cannot allow you to kill him, Talbot!" Natascha said. "You think you are part of this Story, but you are not. If Vidocq dies, the world around us will become nothing but a fiery memory of smoke and ash. You need to lay down your weapons and come with us."

Talbot turned the flintlock on her. "And if I don't?" he snarled. His eyes flared and the grip on the pistol tightened.

Natascha gave a sigh, unintimidated by the flintlock pointed at her face. She saw no glint of recognition in his eyes. Was he really so far lost to the pages of this world that he would shoot her?

"Then I will have to make you," she answered. "This is not a fight you can win, Talbot."

"It won't matter if you're dead," Talbot said with a sneer. The pistol went off with a crack of thunder and smoke.

The lead ball passed harmlessly through Natascha's ghostly form, striking a tree across the road. Natascha stood speechless for a heartbeat before recovering her senses. She had just been shot by one of her closest friends and confidants.

Talbot stared at her for a moment, then shrugged nonchalantly. "Be gone, phantom!" he spat, shoving the smoking flintlock back into his belt. The outlaw stomped through the rain to where his tricorn hat lay. "I have no time for your nonsense. I have already lost too much this night."

He pushed his hat onto his matted hair and walked to where Catalonia lay. The young woman was dead, hit twice in the chest by the barrage of bullets. Talbot brushed the hair from her face, and he kissed her forehead. "I'm sorry, my love," he muttered.

Medesto walked toward Talbot, with his hands out, letting the distraught outlaw see him approach. "We're sorry for the loss of your friend," he said. "But please hear us out. You are not who you think you are."

Talbot looked back at the prone form of Arsene Vidocq, rage burning in his eyes. He rose to his feet and drew his saber as he moved toward his rival, but Natascha stepped between them. The highwayman continued forward, expecting to pass through the apparition as easily as his bullet had. Natascha's gloved hand pressed against his chest to stop him.

"I said you are not going to hurt Vidocq," she said.

Chapter 6
On the Edge of the Abyss

Talbot stared down at the hand pressed against his chest. "So you *are* flesh and bone, phantom."

"When I have to be," Natascha replied.

"Lead balls may have no effect on you," Talbot roared. "Let's see if cold steel does." He brought his saber down with enough force to split open her gas mask. His pain and anger at the loss of Catalonia flashed across his face.

Natascha dodged to the side, knocking his sword arm away with the palm of her left hand. She pulled two fighting sticks from under her coat and readied herself for the next attack. Talbot came at her again, swinging the blade. She stepped beyond the saber's reach, and a blur of clashing sword and sticks ensued. Natascha met every assault with a counter block. Talbot's frustration grew each time he failed to strike his foe. Both were sweating and breathing hard before long.

The two-foot long fighting sticks were lightweight and made from wood strengthened by alchemy to the point of tempered steel. She knew Ren's skilled with a blade. He often carried a sword with him whenever he grew bored with shape-shifting.

A wolf howled, this time much closer.

"Hurry!" Medesto yelled.

"I'm trying," Natascha shot back. She caught Talbot's next attack with crossed sticks in front of her. The blade stopped inches from her gas mask. She pushed the sword to the side and knocked the highwayman's feet out from under him with a strong leg sweep. Talbot crashed to the ground.

Natascha saw the opening she had been waiting for. She struck Talbot's sword arm at a cluster of nerves endings. The blow would cause a brief paralysis in his arm. At the same moment, she dropped the other stick and reached into her coat.

Talbot climbed out of the mud to his feet. The saber slipped from his useless fingers. Natascha smiled from behind her goggled mask. She swept in and slapped a small adhesive patch onto the exposed flesh on the side of his neck.

"Now, if you're finished, we need to talk," Natascha said, picking up the saber and tossing it aside. Medesto ambled up next to them.

The outlaw held his incapacitated arm, spewing profanities. His steely eyes boiled with fury and took a step toward Natascha. He swayed, then stumbled, and dropped to the mud.

"W-what have you done to me?" Talbot rumbled, his voice filled with disbelief. He touched the small square patch stuck to his neck with his good hand and tried to pull it off, but the fingers were clumsy and uncoordinated.

"It's only a minor nerve inhibitor," Natascha said, standing over him. "The effects are temporary. Just enough to lower your defenses and bring you out of this delusion."

Natascha threw back her hood. There was an escape of trapped air as she pulled the gas mask from her face. Raindrops speckled her forehead and cheeks. The cool droplets were a nice reprieve from the stifling confines of her alter-ego's costume. She slipped the mask inside her long coat and spoke into a transmitter concealed in the collar of her coat.

"Gustav, we're ready for pickup," she said.

"I am still searching for a place to land," a mechanized voice responded. "The trees are too thick to set down near you."

"Let me know when you find a place to set down," Natascha said. "And hurry." She pulled off her gloves and approached Talbot with her hands up in a gesture of peace.

"We didn't come here to fight you," she said, her voice soothing. "But you were too far lost to listen to reason, so drastic measures had to be taken. Your interference with this Story will have very dangerous consequences. You must remember who you are, and that this world has no control over you." She held her hands on both sides of Talbot's face. She didn't touch him, but he still flinched.

"May I?" she said. The curiosity in his eyes indicated she may be getting through to him. She could tell he wanted to know who she was, even if he still wanted to kill her.

"Look at me." She stared into his volcanic gray eyes. "Do you remember who I am?"

"We were together once, weren't we?" he said, softly. "In that tavern in Barcelona."

Natascha laughed. "You wish. We were close, but never that close. Now focus!" She could tell somewhere in the deep recesses of Talbot's mind he recognized her.

A second wolf howled in the opposite direction from the first.

"There's movement in the trees!" Medesto shouted, pointing into the darkness. "I'll do what I can to hold them back while you get Ren to the ship! Just hurry!"

"I'm working as fast as I can here!" Natascha yelled back. "These are not the ideal conditions to be doing this!" She looked down at Talbot. "I'm sorry about this part."

"For what?"

"That I don't have time to do this nicely." She drew the Peacemaker from its holster under her coat. It was a round, metallic pistol with a small node at the end of the barrel. She adjusted the setting on the side of the weapon, and it hummed with the charge of electricity. Talbot clumsily lifted his hands in front of him, but his limbs were heavy and hard to control.

"Wait," he mumbled.

Enigma held the weapon up. "Don't worry, it's on its lowest setting." She pushed Talbot back to the ground with her boot and pinned him there. He tried to push up, but there was no strength in him.

"No, you'll—" Talbot protested.

"I'll be fine. My boots are insulated," she said. "You might feel a little something, though."

Talbot started to argue further, but she fired the Peacemaker. An arc of blue, green and red electricity hit him in the chest. He twisted in pain as the potent current coursed over his body.

Doctor Enigma stepped back from him. "Talbot Mundi is not a character in *The Crimson Masque*," she said. "You are Ren B'gatti, a trickster and shape-shifter of dubious character, and a general pain in the ass. And you do not belong in this Story."

As she spoke, a ripple went through Talbot's muscled physique, over his thick arms, and down to his hands. His body twitched, convulsed, then Talbot Mundi changed. His shape melted, unrecognizable for a moment, then changed into a different, much smaller individual. His muscles spasmed a few more times as he coughed violently.

"Did you just shoot him?!" Medesto yelled.

"It was on the lowest setting!" Natascha retorted. "We don't have time to be gentle! He'll be fine!"

Ren B'gatti sat up in the icy rain. The highwayman's clothes hung loosely on him now. His oversized pants spilled over the cuffs of his boots. He unbuttoned his heavy cloak, letting it drop to the mud before he pulled off his gloves.

Ren had a strong, slender face with almond-shaped eyes that were always two different colors. At the moment, one eye was green, and the other a reddish orange. Their hue might change again as the trickster settled into his natural state.

His body was half the physical mass it had been moments before. Nowhere close to the herculean proportions, Talbot Mundi boasted. The highwayman's dusky skin changed to a swirl of earthy colors and then dissolved away, leaving Ren with the complexion of sun-bleached bones.

His pale skin was as white as the blank page, devoid of color. Dark swirling tendrils of pigment crept across his exposed chest and arms in slow, fluid motions. His incisor teeth extended slightly longer than they should. It gave him a feral appearance whenever he smiled.

To a casual observer, the markings appeared as ornate tattoos decorating his body in careful, deliberate patterns, But unlike tattoos, they crept over his skin in a continuous motion. Natascha knew this came from the pooling of the trickster's skin pigment whenever he assumed his true form.

He stared up at her. She could tell from his eyes that he recognized her now. Natascha grabbed him by the hand and pulled him to his feet. Ren was shorter than her by a couple of inches, but his muscles were lean and tight without an ounce of fat. She hated him for that. The fog lifted from his eyes. He looked into her face for a moment before recognition struck him.

"Natascha," he croaked and collapsed into her arms. "What are you doing here?"

"Rogue Destiny needs you." She gave him a smile. "We have a bit of a situation. Can you stand on your own?"

"I don't think so," Ren mumbled. His legs gave out under him, and he plopped back into the mud.

"Do we have him back?" Medesto yelled, running up to them.

"We do!" Natascha answered. She turned back to Ren. "But the effects of the Peacemaker and the nerve inhibitor will take a bit to wear off."

"What happened?" Ren muttered. He ran a hand through the large tuft of black hair.

"I pulled you back from the edge of the abyss," Natascha said. "We almost lost you to this world." She pulled on her leather gloves and spoke into the collar. "Gustav, what's your location?"

The rumble of engines echoed somewhere above the trees. A moment later, a sleek, wingless craft appeared over them, silhouetted against the stormy skies except for the blue glow of its engines. There was the crackle of static from Natascha's collar. "There's a clearing five hundred yards north of your position," a robotic voice said. "I'll meet you there."

"Our ride's here," Natascha said to Ren. "Let's get you home." She pulled her gas mask back over her head and grabbed Ren's hand to pull him up. His legs wobbled under him before he fell into her arms. Natascha held him until he got his feet under him. The smell of wet animal hung heavy in the air.

"The Loup-Garou are close," Ren said. He held onto Natascha, struggling to keep his balance. "And I'm in no shape to fight."

"You won't have to," Natascha said. "We just need to get to the ship." Medesto followed, watching the dark trees alongside the road.

Ren glanced back at the Crimson Masque and his men lying in the road. "Aren't we leaving them to the mercy of the Loup-Garou?"

"Not to worry," Medesto said. "The monsters won't bother Vidocq and his co-horts. It's not part of his Story. We're the intruders here. Good to have you back, B'gatti."

"Great to be back," Ren muttered. He swayed and clung tight to Natascha's arm.

The three trudged up the road in the mud and rain as fast as Ren was able. Natascha held him up on one side and the gnome on the other. As they rounded a bend, the sleek, sixty-foot-long Slipstream Runabout, *Nevermore,* sat in a clearing shrouded in the glow of her landing lights.

"Gustav, we have you in sight," Natascha said. "We'll be there in another minute, but we're not alone out here." She pulled her Peacemaker from its leather holster.

"Copy that," Gustave responded. "I'm picking up two large shapes heading toward you. The closest is about fifty yards out to your left and moving fast."

Medesto stopped in the middle of the roadway, his wet hair

matted down in the rain. "Get Ren to the ship!" he yelled. "I'll hold them off!"

A giant shape leapt from the shadows and hit Medesto in the side. The gnome rolled across the road in a tangle of fur and fangs, coming to a stop with the beast on top of him. He caught the snarling snout by the throat with both hands as it snapped at him.

Medesto twisted the slavering mouth away from his face and pulled his legs up under him. He pushed out with his boots, throwing the werewolf off him. The monster crashed into the bushes alongside the road. An instant later, it came charging out and leapt into the air at Medesto.

The gnome grabbed a storm fallen tree limb. He jammed the butt of the thick branch into the mud. The broken end caught the beast mid-jump. The force and weight of the werewolf's body drove the makeshift weapon deep into its chest.

The raging werewolf struggled to free itself, but the jagged limb was lodged too deeply in its chest cavity. Medesto lifted the branch from the ground and, with an inhuman amount of strength, tossed the monster away from them into the trees.

Natascha continued forward with Ren in tow. The trickster walked on his own now, if only barely, but he was gaining more strength with each step. They had covered half the distance to the ship when a deep, guttural growl broke through the darkness to their right.

A second werewolf emerged from the trees. Its flaming eyes glowed in the falling rain. Lightning flashed overhead, revealing hunched shoulders behind a thick, misshapen snout. Long, sharp teeth glinted in the flashes of light.

Natascha dropped Ren to the mud and fired her Peacemaker. The monster charged forward as the full charge of the lightning gun hit it. The night lit up around them. Ren threw an arm up to protect his eyes from the blinding flash. Natascha's tinted goggles prevented the light from inhibiting her vision. The werewolf stumbled and collapsed to the ground in a pile of fur and claws. She helped Ren up and half carried him toward the waiting ship.

"Gustav! Open up, we're here!" she yelled into her comm. The side hatch opened as they reached the slipstream.

Natascha helped the stumbling trickster climb the steps. Ren rolled to the carpeted floor of the dimly lit interior. Medesto ambled up a moment later and Natascha hit the button to close the hatch.

"We're in, Gustav, go!" Natascha yelled. The engines of *Nevermore* fired as the ship lifted from the forest floor. Natascha slipped into the co-pilot seat next to Gustav 7. She pulled the gas mask off and tossed it on the dashboard.

"I'm guessing you found him," he asked in his flat, mechanical manner. Gustav 7 was a seventh generation Sojourn Automatronic Utility Bot, of Natascha's own design. He was the size of an upright vacuum cleaner. A small gyroscope spun rhythmically inside his clear elliptical-shaped head. Three of his six utility arms pulled levers and turned knobs to get *Nevermore* in the air.

"We did," Natascha replied. "Now get us out of here!"

Chapter 7
Lost and Found

The interior cabin of *Nevermore* had two rows of seats facing each other. Ren took the seat closest to the cockpit. He was still breathing hard from their escape. The familiar hum of the slipstream's engines soothed his tired mind. Random aches and pains radiated throughout his body. A moment later, he looked up to see Medesto watching him.

"You okay?" Medesto asked with genuine concern in his deep voice.

"You're bleeding," Ren replied, changing the subject. He hated to show any weakness, even to those he considered his friends.

The gnome touched the left shoulder of his corduroy jacket. His fingers came away red. "Must have caught a claw back there," he muttered, poking at the injury with a thick finger. "Blast it! I liked this coat too. Not as nimble as I used to be, but it barely broke the skin. It takes more than razor-sharp claws to cut into my thick hide."

"Medesto, we'll drop you at the courier ship," Natascha said from the co-pilot's chair. "Then we can head back to Rogue Destiny together."

"You brought two ships?" Ren asked.

"So we could cover more ground looking for you," Medesto

said. "It wasn't easy finding a shape-shifter hiding amongst the population of a world."

Ren's skin itched and tingled as the nerve inhibitor began to wear off. He stretched his arms to find his muscle control returning. He propped himself up into a sitting position.

Natascha turned around in the co-pilot seat, her eyes filled with concern. "How are you feeling?" she asked.

"Bruised and dizzy, but I'm doing okay," Ren replied, scratched his arm vigorously. "The whispering in my head has stopped." He watched out the window across from him as *Nevermore* cleared the top of the trees. The rain outside had subsided to a drizzle. In the distance, sixteenth-century Paris blazed in the early morning dawn.

Natascha climbed from the co-pilot's chair to sit next to him. "We almost lost you down there." She put a hand on his arm. "A few chapters deeper into the Narrative and you would have been beyond our reach."

"I had forgotten where I was," Ren said. "Everything seemed so real." He blinked and rubbed his eyes, then ran a hand into his hair.

"That's because you let her inside your head," Natascha said. "The Muse may be an intangible, impersonal force, but she's always there, just beyond the mind's eye, seducing you into believing you belong here. She wants you to think you're a part of her world. Her incessant whisperings invade your thoughts until you forget who you are or why you would ever want to leave. If we hadn't found you when we did, you would have become just another character in Her Story."

"Yeah, I'm starting to remember." Ren lay back in his seat and closed his eyes. "I remember leaving Rogue Destiny after I went to see Claymore in Lazaranth Prison. He told me to get out of the city before the authorities found me, so I did. I wandered about for a while, through one rabbit-hole after another, until I found myself here. I found the Story interesting, so I stayed."

"So, you just fell under the influence of the Muse?" Medesto asked. "That's interesting. Natascha and I have been here searching for you for days and have had no problem closing our thoughts off from Her."

"You calling me a liar?" Ren snapped.

"No, of course not," the gnome replied.

"It sounded like you were."

"I'm just saying you may be misremembering what happened," Medesto said. "It wouldn't be the first time someone tried to disappear into a Story. I get it. I've been there myself."

"As have I," Natascha added. "All that matters is we found you before any permanent damage was done."

"That you came here to lose yourself in the Story. Doesn't that about cover it?"

Ren struggled for an answer. "You heard Natascha. It wasn't on purpose! I fell under the seductive whisperings of the Muse. Couldn't help myself and all that." It was a pathetic response, one even Ren didn't believe. He had walked dozens of worlds and knew it took no effort to push back against Her.

"Don't give me that!" Medesto huffed. "What you did was dangerous and stupid! If you leave yourself open to her influence, She will take you every time, but it *never* happens against your will! Not without you letting your guard down. You were trying to disappear into this Story, weren't you?"

"So you were just hiding out?" Medesto rumbled. "Then how did you end up inside the middle of the Narrative, playing kabuki theater with the *Logos Personae?* When Gideon finds out you tried to kill the Story's main character, there'll be hell to pay."

Natascha squeezed Ren's arm. "If we hadn't stopped you," she said. "Everybody within the pages of *The Crimson Mask* would have perished."

Ren stared out his window but said nothing. He was embarrassed his comrades had found him acting so recklessly. He didn't do it on purpose. Or did he? Even now, as they were about to leave the world, he could feel the Muse murmuring in the back of his mind, coaxing him to stay.

Medesto continued. "The ramifications of messing with the Narrative are catastrophic. The Raconteurs exist to hunt down anyone that attempts to interfere with the Story or its *Logos Personae*. It's the unpardonable sin to disturb the rhythm of a world's continuity. *The Crimson Masque* is not some playground here for your amusement. The lives we're dealing with are as real as you or me. Didn't you learn anything after *The Angels of Avalon?*"

Ren had no answer. Maybe it was because he had given up on being a hero. With Claymore incarcerated, and his lingering anger at the Raconteurs, he had suddenly found his life was suddenly without direction. He didn't remember letting the Muse take him, but there was a lot he could not recall from his time in *The Crimson Masque.*

"I haven't been gone that long, have I?" Ren muttered after a time. "It feels like I just got here."

"That's more of the Muse's trickery," Natascha replied. "You've been gone for over a year."

"So, what are we going to do here?" Medesto asked. "This is a major violation of the Seven Laws."

Ren looked over to see Natascha staring at him. She gave him a smile that didn't quite reach her eyes.

"So, what happened?" Medesto asked with a sigh. "What led up to you trying to kill Vidocq?"

Ren knew better then to answer the question directly. He was clever, and even more than devious when backed into a corner. How was he going to talk his way out of this? He took a deep breath to clear his addled thoughts.

"I met Catalonia on a street in Paris," he said. "We hit it off, and she introduced me to Arsene Vidocq. He and I became rivals for Catalonia's affections, as well as the territory around Paris. It felt like walking in a dream that you didn't mind where it took you. I didn't mean for things to get out of hand like this." That was as close as he was going to come to an apology, and Natascha seemed satisfied with it. Medesto did not.

"Catalonia was an integral part of the Story," Medesto replied. "You tore at the fabric of the Story with your interference, and she and Vidocq Masque will never be together now."

"How was I to know she was such an important player?" Ren argued. His body tensed and he sat up, his anger flaring. "She's the one who suggested we move in on Vidocq's territory!"

Medesto gave a harsh laugh. "She wouldn't have if you hadn't been messing around where you weren't supposed to be!" He grabbed the armrests of his seat, ready to push himself to his feet.

"This is not the time, boys!" Natascha said. "We're still on the clock. Ren is back to his old self and leaving voluntarily. *The Crimson Masque* will realign itself. The Narrative will make adjustments for the absence of a secondary character like Catalonia. It happens, otherwise none of us would have been able to leave our homeworlds without disastrous results. There was no permanent damage done, and no one has to be any the wiser."

"I'm just saying," Medesto grumbled. "Gideon isn't going like it when he hears about this."

"Then don't tell him," Ren replied. The gnome gave him a quizzical look. "Natascha said you needed my help with some situation. Say nothing to anybody about what happened, and I'm in. No questions asked."

"Just like that?" Natascha said. "You don't even know what the job is."

"You said I could trust you, right?" Ren grinned for the first time since coming out of his Muse induced hallucination.

"Of course," Medesto said. He sounded almost indignant. "We've always been on your side."

"So here I am, trusting you," Ren said. He sat up in his chair. "Don't tell Gideon how I almost killed Vidocq. It was a terrible mistake—one I won't make again. You keep your word and I'll keep mine, an eye for an eye and all that."

Natascha let go a laugh. "That's not quite what that means, but I get what you're saying."

Ren's voice changed to a serious tone. "The alternative is I go to war with the Raconteurs because no one's putting me in Lazaranth Prison."

"No one's here to do that," Natascha replied. "I can keep quiet. Medesto?"

The gnome scratched his beard, appearing to weigh every possible outcome. Ren was using their own words to see if he could trust them. It wouldn't be the first time the three covered for each other. He was sure it wasn't the last time, either.

Ren knew there were things from Medesto's own past that he was not proud of. Nobody knew the actual details, but the gnome's guilt would come to the surface from time to time. Despite their seemingly constant arguing, he made Medesto laugh. Ren knew the gnome had a certain soft spot for his antics. Besides, they had little choice but to agree with his demands. The Raconteurs needed Ren more than he needed them.

"One day you'll realize that the Raconteurs look out for their own," Medesto said at last. "But you can never pull this kind of stunt again. Next time, Gideon may send others who will not be as forgiving as we are."

"Understood," Ren said.

"So, you'll help us?" Natascha added.

Ren grinned. "Yes, I will."

The gnome's gruff disposition seemed to lift, and his bearded face broke into a crooked smile. "Talbot Mundi, the highwayman, huh? An interesting choice of faces to choose, don't you think, Natascha?" he asked. "Looked an awful lot like the founder of a certain group of that we all know and admire."

"Talbot wasn't *anything* like Claymore," Ren quickly replied. "He was an original personae I created from nothing." He looked at Natascha for support, but she only laughed.

"Oh, sure," she teased. "It was all there, the square jaw, the physical build, even the attitude. Your hero worship is as strong as ever, B'gatti. But now it's all agreed, you're a Raconteur again, and the three of us are back together."

"What did Claymore call us?" Ren wondered aloud.

"His *Mighty Triumvirate*," Medesto said. "And if he was here, he'd be laughing at all of us."

Ren sat back in his seat. That had gone easier than he'd thought it would. Despite his bravado, he did not want a war with the Raconteurs. He knew that was a battle he could never win.

Nevermore flew over the forest for several more minutes before slowing above a wide clearing beside a winding river. The cabin vibrated as the landing gear lowered. The slipstream descended and set down next to a smaller ship.

"Why the courier ship?" Ren asked. "Where's your rig?"

"*Subtle Chaos* is in the shop," Medesto said. "I crashed her again and Sebastian's been taking his sweet time getting her back up and running. This one's a loaner."

"Does Sebastian know it's been loaned?" Ren wondered out loud.

Medesto grinned. "He does by now."

There was a hum and the side hatch of the ship opened. Medesto picked up a black leather traveling bag he took with him everywhere and stomped down the steps to the pine-needle floor of the forest. Ren stretched out in his seat and closed his eyes.

"You coming?" Medesto asked.

Ren looked out the hatch to see the gnome waiting for him. "I was going to ride back with Natascha and Gustav."

"No. You're riding back with me. We need to talk."

"I'm exhausted, and just want to sleep."

"You can sleep just as easily in the courier ship," Medesto said.

Ren turned to Natascha, his eyes pleading for a reprieve from the lecture that was sure to accompany him all the way back to Rogue Destiny. She only winked at him.

"Father wishes to speak to you alone," she said, looking sad and shaking her head. "You have a lot to answer for."

Ren could only grin back. "I thought that we just settled all that."

Natascha put a hand on the Ren's shoulder. "Thank you for

doing this. Many lives will be saved now that you are back with us."

Ren shrugged. "That's what a hero does, isn't it?"

"*In Medias Res*, B'gatti!" Natascha said as she closed the hatch. *Into the middle of things.* The Raconteurs' motto actually made Ren smile.

The storm clouds had broken up and an orange dawn cracked the eastern sky. Ren's mind was awash with all the events of that night. Medesto waited as the trickster came down the steps with reluctance.

The slipstream they would take home was a courier transport, small and practical, the color a dull gunmetal gray. The ship delivered goods and dignitaries from their respective literary worlds back and forth to Rogue Destiny.

Medesto pulled a small rectangular box from his coat pocket and pressed a button. The gull-wing doors on both sides of the ship rose.

He tossed his traveling bag behind the pilot's seat and climbed in at the controls. He inserted the black box into a slot on the dashboard. The console lit up, and he started the engines. The steel hull vibrated gently as the Coldfire engines warmed up for the journey ahead.

Ren crawled in on the passenger side. The passenger side floor on his side was littered with paperback books. He picked up one that caught his eye and kicked the rest aside to make room for his feet.

"What's this?" he asked. The paperback in his hands was a romantic pirate novel titled *Plundered Hearts*.

"Those are all the places we searched for you," Medesto replied, turning on the overhead light. "Gideon deduced where you might have gone. He said it would be a place with minimal magic, cause you hate magic. High adventure with no technology, so you'd be harder to find. Natascha and I compiled a list, and we've been knocking them off one by one. The field house in Paris had reports of someone wreaking havoc throughout the countryside. *Someone* who was not a character in *The Crimson Masque.* We hoped it might be you and flew out to investigate."

Both doors of the ship closed in unison. Ren settled in as Medesto fiddled with the controls and revved the ship's engine. He reclined his seat and absently flipped through the paperback in his hands.

Medesto adjusted the navigation screen on his right, then hit the comm button on the dash. "*Nevermore*, we're ready for liftoff."

"Roger that, *Wayward One*," Gustav's robotic voice answered. "We'll follow you out."

Medesto eased the control throttle forward and the route thrusters kicked in. The smaller ship lifted off the ground, climbing slowly into the predawn sky.

Once clear of the trees, Medesto turned the ship skyward and opened the engines up. A flock of birds altered their course to avoid collision, squawking in protest as the flying speedster shot past. Ren stared out the small port window, watching the continent of Europe disappear beneath them.

"I'm still a wanted outlaw in Rogue Destiny," he said.

"No one will know you're back in town," Medesto replied.

The two occupants fell silent in the confines of the cabin. The only noise was the gentle hum of the engines and the clinking of glass behind their seats.

"What's in the wooden crates?" Ren asked.

"I like to bring Gideon samples of the wines from the different worlds we visit," Medesto answered. "I always make an effort to indulge his obsession by bringing him back a taste of the local vine-yards we visit. He insists the best vintage came from the most unexpected sources. So what better place to find an excellent wine than Paris in a paranormal world full of supernatural terrors?"

The slipstream gained altitude, flying higher and higher toward the star-speckled sky. The world disappeared below them. Ahead lay a few cloud banks, but beyond that was nothing but a vast sea of stars.

Medesto shook his head and chuckled to himself. "Ha! You

have all of Literature to disappear into, and you let yourself get swept away in a grim, dark fantasy where you get to play outlaw. That says a lot about you, B'gatti."

"Paris is nice this time of year." Ren replied, not looking up from the paperback. He yawned and fidgeted in his seat, trying to find a comfortable position.

The gnome straightened up in his seat. The stars faded from view, consumed by a strange glow that emanated from the sky itself. It was not sunshine. There was no source for the light, it was just there. The slipstream had reached the apex of the world, where the clockwork function of *The Crimson Masque* ended, and the larger realities of the universe took over.

"Hang on," Medesto muttered. "We're approaching the Veil."

Chapter 8
Into the Void

In the distance, small, hazy letters appear on the sky. There was no pattern or order to the random consonants and vowels. It was as if they had been typed haphazardly upon the heavens.

As the ship drew closer, the writing became clearer and more discernible. Individual letters slowly became words, and those words became sentences. Soon, the sky was blanketed by overlapping words, sentences, and paragraphs. They had reached the outer edge of *The Crimson Masque*.

This was the last barrier between the Story and the infinite blackness that lay beyond. Every world was protected by a word canopy. Although unseen by its inhabitance, the words knit the world together. It bound its denizens to the Narrative, where they lived their lives unaware of what lay beyond the confines of their world.

The veil of words formed the foundation of the Story. The cornerstone upon which everything else was built. The words formed its mountains and waters and cities. It caused the Narrative to pulse and flow, rousing its players to move and interact within the Story. It dictated the random comings and goings of its people, the conflicts, the heroics, and the tragedies.

The canopy kept the novel's inhabitants safe from anything

that was not part of the Story. But the Raconteurs knew ways around its protective shielding. The slipstream's engines protested against the strain, but Medesto held its course. He pressed a couple of buttons.

"Punch drive engaged," the gnome announced calmly. "Opening a keyhole."

Medesto knew Ren had traveled to *The Crimson Masque* on foot, through the network of rabbit-holes that connected every written world. Although slower than piloting a slipstream it was easier for Ren to move around undetected.

The gnome punched a button on the dashboard. An audible ping reverberated inside the cabin. An almost invisible pulse of light shot out from the ship's nose into the massive wall of words in front of them. The word canopy rippled as if a pebble had been dropped into a quiet pond. A small oblong opening appeared. The shimmering effect expanded over the surface and the Keyhole grew larger. A violent turbulence of air escaped through the opening. The ship slowed a bit as the outside air pressure increased.

The suction caught hold of the slipstream and their speed picked up as they drew nearer. Medesto pushed the engines to their limits, and the cabin shook as the ship regained the lost momentum needed to pull itself from the world's gravity. The steering wheel bucked and fought him for control.

"Hang on, we're threading the needle!" Medesto announced. He tilted the ship slightly and hit the keyhole with practiced precision. They passed through the opening into the darkness of the outer cosmos.

The temporary doorway flashed with arcs of static electricity that dissipated as the keyhole closed behind them. The outer surface of the pale globe returned to its natural state of shifting greens and blues. Ren glanced out his window to see *Nevermore* emerging from a second keyhole not far from them.

Blackness went of forever, broken only by hundreds of more drifting globes floating weightless around them. The glowing orbs spilled out across the dark backdrop like dice randomly thrown onto a table. The courier ship sped through the darkness toward home.

"*Nevermore*, you make it through?" Medesto said into the comm.

"Roger that, *Wayward One*," Gustav 7 replied.

A blue light on the dashboard flashed, indicating a message was waiting for them. Medesto clicked on it. A static-filled voice Ren recognized came over the speaker.

"Hello, anyone in the area? This is *Fool's Errand*. Can anyone hear me? This is an urgent request for assistance..." Static interrupted the next few words. "... under fire and requesting backup. Sending coordinates. Again, we request immediate assistance. This is *Fool's Errand*. Situation critical."

The transmission ended.

Medesto flipped on the ship's Wayfinder screen at the center of the dashboard. Three overlapping directional circles appeared on the screen, overlaid by a navigational compass. A line moved clockwise over all three screens as it zeroed in on the source of the distress signal. He turned a knob to widen the search parameters.

"Was that Cedric Keating?" Ren asked.

"It was," Medesto said, his voice hard. "Last thing I heard, he and Artimus Montagu were investigating a disturbance out beyond the ninth ring. This message is over seven hours old. *Nevermore*, do you have a lock on the distress signal?"

"Roger that, *Wayward One*," Gustav answered. His mechanized voice had an unusually serious tone to it.

"Can you tell if anyone has responded?" Medesto asked.

Natascha's voice came over the line. "Not that I see. Gustav and I will take this. Deliver your passenger. Tell Gideon we'll check in as soon as we know what's going on."

The comm went silent. Medesto clicked it off as they watched the sleek form of *Nevermore* alter her course. The slipstream stood silhouetted against the glow of an enormous world until she disappeared into the distance.

Medesto navigated the courier ship through the blackness. The light of the soft-glowing worlds hung weightless as far as the eye could see. Each orb was an autonomous literary world whose inhabitants lived unaware of what lay just beyond the confines of their doorstep. He watched dozens of worlds pass by his window. The Raconteurs could not protect them all, but they did what they could, and that would have to be enough.

"The Void's quiet tonight," Medesto commented, trying to ease the tension in the cabin. "We hit a violent electrical storm coming across. Worst I've ever seen in a while."

Ren didn't respond. He lay back in his seat with his eyes closed, obviously not in the mood for small talk.

"Sorry Natascha used her Peacemaker on you," Medesto said. "You were pretty far lost to the world's influence. I suggested giving you a sleeping drug. She was afraid that wouldn't bring you out of your Muse-induced haze and restore you to the happy, carefree trickster we all missed."

A smirk appeared at the corner of Ren's mouth. He opened his eyes. "I would have done the same thing under those circumstances," he replied. "I know she even enjoyed it a little."

Medesto chuckled. "Well, you did try to kill her—*twice*."

Ren gave a halfhearted shrug. "So, what do you need my help with?"

"Several weeks ago, there was a breakout from Lazaranth Prison. Everyone inside Block 27 simply disappeared from their cells. No one knows how. They were just gone."

Ren pushed himself up in his seat. "Claymore?" he asked, showing more enthusiasm than Medesto had seen so far. The gnome knew he'd piqued Ren's interest and had his full attention.

"Claymore's in the wind," Medesto said. "We're still investigating the details of how this could have happened, but for now, it's a mystery. Claymore is not the concern right now."

"So what am I here for?"

"I'm getting to that," Medesto replied. "The prison escapees somehow ended up on an island in the middle of the Dreaming Sea called Bones Martyr Isle. Once we learned what had happened, we moved in to stop them. But when the first Raconteurs arrived, they walked into an ambush by a contingent of soldiers sporting high-tech weaponry. We lost several agents in the firefight that followed. Despereaux and Lazlo Quinto were among them. You didn't know the others."

"Despereaux's dead?" Ren said.

"Yeah," Medesto said. "The fugitives escaped through the labyrinth of rabbit-holes speckling the island. How fifty-seven high-security prisoners could get from their secured cells to a tiny pile of rocks in the middle of the ocean remains a mystery."

The cabin fell silent. Medesto stared out his window and said nothing. His chest tightened with a sharp pain, reliving the deaths of his fellow Raconteurs. His grip on the controls of the slipstream tightened until he feared he might tear it from its steering column.

"This doesn't sound like something I can help you with," Ren finally asked.

"I haven't gotten to the strangest part yet," Medesto said. "A few days after the breakout, we received word that a forgotten record's archive, hidden inside the dystopian, gothic horror novel, *No More Tomorrows*, had been ransacked. Several agents flew out to investigate. We lost three more. There have been six more archives torn apart by these marauders since then. It's like they're searching for something."

"What?" Ren asked.

"That's what we're hoping you'll find out for us."

"And you're worried Montagu and Keating ran into them."

"Exactly," Medesto sighed. After the death of our agents, Gideon decided we needed to change strategies. That's where you come in. He wants you to infiltrate the band of outlaws. Get inside their ranks and find out what they're up to."

"And no one has seen Claymore since the breakout?" Ren asked.

"No," Medesto said. "Everyone in the city is looking for him, but so far we've had no luck. Gideon assumed he'd contact us when he was ready, but he never has. For now, we need you to focus on the task at hand. You help us untangle this mess, and I will personally help you hunt for Claymore."

"I'm just saying we could use his help," Ren argued.

Medesto sighed. Ren would not let it go. But the gnome had to be careful with the tone in his voice. The Raconteurs needed Ren's cooperation, and he did not want the conversation to turn into an argument, as it so often did with the trickster.

"Let's get one thing clear," Medesto said. "This is not about finding Claymore. You promised to help and I'm holding you to that. The escaped fugitives have been easy enough to track by the destruction they've left behind. It's stopping them. That's been the problem. If this distress signal turns out to be a lead to them, we'll need to be ready to act. So, it was decided you getting inside the band of outlaws undetected was the best for all of us."

"Easy for you to say," Ren quipped. "I'll be the one inside the belly of the beast."

"Don't act all indignant," Medesto said. "You love hiding amongst the enemy undetected. That's why we need you. You're the only one who can do this."

Ren tried to suppress a smug smile, but failed.

"Just tell me what happened?" he asked.

"I'll do my best," Medesto said. "But it's still raw."

Chapter 9
Bones Martyr Isle

Medesto felt his eyes mist as he recalled the events of that night. His jaw tightened. He scratched his salt and pepper beard, staring out the front window, unable to look at Ren. His voice broke slightly as he spoke.

"The first prisoners started disappearing from their cells around midnight, although we knew nothing about it at the time. Sebastian was in his shop when the Wayfinder started picking up erratic power surges off the northeast coast of the island. Then electrical grids started going down and before we knew it the north half of the city had blacked out. Sebastian pinpointed the source of the disruptions to an unimpressive island in the middle of nowhere called Bones Martyr Isle. Its only distinguishing trait is it's a cross-roads for hundreds of ley lines. Kinchlow Jepson and his rookie partner, Lumen Addicott, were the first to investigate in their rig, *Fool's Paradise.*

"Our first thought was something big and nasty was trying to get through the rabbit holes again. The energy surges were distorting communications. So, it was a couple of hours before Sebastian received a faint distress signal from *Fool's Paradise.* We weren't sure what we were up against, so Gideon sent every available agent out there."

"Where were you?" Ren asked with more than a bit of accusation in his tone.

"I'd just returned from a rather brutal confrontation with a flock of harpies that took up residence in a fairy tale story," Medesto said quietly. He knew what happened that night was not his fault, but if he had gotten there sooner, maybe things would have played out differently. "I was tired and needed to decompress. With communications down, it took time to find me. I was playing cards at a little pub on the west side. I flew *Subtle Chaos* out as soon as I received word."

The gnome paused to gather his thoughts before he continued. "On any map, the island is nothing more than a speck. But as you get closer it turns out its size is all an illusion. Once you over it, the tiny island is actually hundreds of square miles in size. It's just another of Rogue Destiny's many quirks. They say the concentration of so many ley lines distorts its true appearance.

"Bones Martyr is covered in a thick mist, so visibility is nearly impossible. As I reached the island, the intense concentration of ley lines wreaked havoc on navigation, but I had a good idea where they might be. I flew in low through the canyons to the remains of an abandoned waystation at the mouth of a mystical labyrinth that lead to the countless rabbit-holes under the island.

"I descended through the fog until I saw Lazlo's slipstream, *Blood and Fortune,* parked along the wall of the canyon. There was no movement around it, so I continued further up the gorge, until I came upon the wreckage of two other slipstreams. One was *Mischief Maker*. It looked like she had crashed. Not far beyond her lay *Fool's Paradise*. She was shot full of large caliber holes. Her engines were still smoking. Then I heard the gunfire.

"Amid the chaos of smoke and fire, I saw Despereaux and Shuli Vox, pinned down in a rock cleft. They were exchanging fire with a squad of heavily armed soldiers near the entrance to the labyrinth. I brought *Subtle Chaos* in low hoping to draw the soldiers' fire and give them a chance to get out of there.

"The plan worked very well. My ship was hit by a barrage of

high-caliber gunfire that ripped through the fuselage and disabled my engines. As I went down, I managed to crash into the soldiers. The few survivors disappeared into the gaping mouth of the labyrinth.

The impact jammed my hatch, so I was pounding my way out when Shuli and Despereaux appeared at the window. Once I got the door open, I grabbed the Tommy gun from my bag, along with a couple of extra drums of ammo. Together, the three of us followed the soldiers to the labyrinth's entrance.

Despereaux said they hadn't seen any sign of Kinchlow or Lumen, but she had talked to Them on the comm. Lazlo and his partner, Haddock Todah, were last seen heading into the labyrinth to find the missing Raconteurs when they ran into a handful of soldiers and the shooting started. We had no idea what was going on, but knew we had to go in after them.

Moving along the canyon wall, we concealed ourselves among the rocks until we reached the gaping entrance of the labyrinth. Despereaux signaled us from the doorway of one of the outbuildings. She and Haddock were almost to the entrance before they ran into gunfire. Haddock had been hit by some kind of plasma weapon. We ran to where Haddock lay, but it was too late. He had been hit by some sort of burning substance. His skin was scorched and melted. His face had been half burned away.

We had to leave Haddock where he was and push on into the labyrinth, trying to get a reading on what was going on inside. We hadn't gone far when we heard voices. I peered over the edge of the passageway into a vast cavern. Below us was an abandoned waystation and its adjoining buildings.

A man in a trench coat stood on the porch of the waystation, addressing an assemblage of fifty or more dressed in prison garb listening to his every word. He was very animated, gesturing with his arms like a politician trying to get votes. Two individuals stood behind him. One was a large individual dressed in black with a wide flat-brimmed hat. The other appeared to be a cyborg that reminded me of Sebastian Poe. Our two missing Raconteurs knelt in front of the crowd at the foot of the speaker.

"We were too far away to hear what he was saying," Medesto said. "I didn't recognize him, but he was in charge. A squadron of soldiers kept their guns on the escaped fugitives, but also watched the dozens of tunnels that fed into the cavern."

Lumen and Kinchlow were rookies who had joined a few months prior. Like most Raconteurs, both had previously been bounty hunters, so they should have known better than to run off without backup. One sentry spotted us and opened fire. High-caliber weapons tore up the rocks and melted the ground around us. That's when all hell broke loose.

The crowd of prisoners scattered when the shooting started. Soldiers pulled Lumen and Kinchlow to their feet, and they disappeared into the catacombs at the far end of the cavern. Most of the prisoners followed them, while a few sought refuge in the surrounding tunnels. The speaker who had rallied the fugitives was escorted away by the cyborg.

"We exchanged fire with them before the remaining soldiers pulled back into the darkness of the catacombs. They outgunned us, both in numbers and firepower, yet they pulled back. That should have been our first warning. We rushed forward, trying to keep the soldiers that held Lumen and Kinchlow in sight.

The retreat of the soldiers emboldened us. We took off after them, concealing ourselves between the rocks and an abandoned building. By the time we reached the entrance of the labyrinth, there was no one in sight.

Twenty years back, two brothers started a business venture on the island. They built departure stations and a marina where boats would transport patrons traveling to and from Rogue Destiny. They advertised how the catacombs beneath the island led to a thousand different worlds. The signage welcoming travelers to Rogue Destiny was still up on the cavern walls.

"But rabbit holes run both ways. Not all of those doorways leading to the island came from hospitable worlds. The constant traffic started to attract hideous things drawn there by the concentrated hum of so many ley lines. Rumors began to crop up about the nasty things that roamed the deep corridors of Bones Martyr Isle. Indescribable monstrosities from the darkest corners of Literature that wandered those tunnels at will.

The brothers eventually abandoned their investment. What kept coming through the rabbit holes was more dangerous than anything they could handle. Both died in poverty years later.

"Shuli and I led the way through the opening of the labyrinth with our weapons ready. The main tunnel was as silent as a tomb. Lazlo and Despereaux trailed behind us, watching for any ambush. We followed the twisting passageway down into the black depths of the island.

"The air grew thick and closed in around us the further we descended. Every so often, we heard movement down one of the side passages. We stopped at a track of dark slime and blood that marked the passage of some beast. You'd never catch me roaming those catacombs alone. Too many dark and dangerous things prowling about.

Rusty lights were strung up along the corridors, but the electricity was out. We passed dozens of tunnels branching out in every direction, listening, but there was no sign of where they went. I have to say there was a creepy stillness to it all. We just wanted to find our missing comrades and get out of there, but we had no idea where they were. We followed them deeper into the catacombs.

That's when the screams began.

They didn't come from any single direction, but seemed to echo down every corridor. They were answered by distant gunfire. It was obvious the fugitives' intrusion roused things from the shadowy corners of the labyrinth. Ahead of us we heard the rending of bodies and crunching of bone followed by gunshots and blood-curdling screams.

The only light beyond our flashlights was a greenish glow from the veins of the ley lines pulsating through the walls. We passed more tunnels, listening for any indication of where our companions might be.

Then we stumbled across the first body. It had once been a large male, but now was a gooey mess of muscles and bones splattered across the walls of the tunnel. Bits of prison garb were visible among the gore. Whatever creature did the deed was large and efficient. We were facing worse things down there now than armed soldiers and desperate prison escapees.

I told the others to kill their flashlights so we wouldn't attract attention. We followed the dim glow of pulsating veins in the ley lines, hoping somehow to reach Lumen and Kinchlow. Sporadic bursts of gunfire erupted ahead of us. We headed toward it. The shooting ended as quickly as it began, and the tunnels grew deathly silent. We came across several more bodies. Some were soldiers, others were more prisoners.

We stopped when we saw the passageway blocked by what looked like a fallen log. It gleamed shiny black in the low light and was as thick as I was tall. The tentacle recoiled when I stepped toward it, and retreated into a side tunnel dragging the body of a prisoner away with it.

I stood at the mouth of the tunnel as Despereaux and Shuli rushed past. I've gone toe to toe with some nasty things during my service in the Raconteurs. But I think I was never more scared than at that moment, not knowing what waited ahead. Not for myself, but for the others down there with me.

We saw flashes of gunfire up the passageway and headed into the thick of the fighting. Sections of the walls and floor burned red and orange from a sulfuric smelling chemical fire around the two Raconteurs. In the glow, I saw a handful of soldiers battling a reptilian creature with long barbed quills running down its back. It resembled dragons I'd seen before, but it was quicker and didn't exhale fire. Its spiny tail slashed the soldiers, cutting down several of them before their gunfire caused it to retreat down a connecting passageway.

We rounded a corner to see Kinchlow and Lumen kneeling in

the center of the tunnel, their hands tied in front of them. Behind them, a soldier stood with a pistol pressed to Lumen's head.

"That's far enough!" he shouted. We stopped in our tracks. Shuli stood at my side. Lazlo and Despereaux watched the tunnel behind us.

A gaunt individual appeared out of the smoke behind the soldier. He wore a full-length coat and had his shoulder-length hair combed back with a neatly trimmed goatee. Soldiers flanked him on each side.

The tunnel turned icy cold, and the stench of death blew down the corridor. A massive shape separated from the shadows and floated up behind the man. The hunched figure wore a tattered black cloak. The hood was pulled down to hide the monster's face. Only its jawbone protruded from under the cowl.

The soldiers became visibly uncomfortable in the presence of the ghoul and separated to let it by them. It drifted through the air to take a place at the leader's shoulder.

"I don't recognize you." I told the man. "But your sidekick there is the Grimm Jester. So that must make you Mordecai Davos."

The gaunt face broke into a smile. "And you are?"

"Medesto Bodenhammer."

"And you're an agent of the Raconteurs, I presume."

"He didn't know who you were?" Ren asked. "Everyone in Rogue Destiny knows who you are."

"I thought that was strange too," Medesto replied.

"Are you sure it was Mordecai?"

"That's what he claimed," Medesto said with a shrug of his shoulders. "No one has ever laid eyes on him and lived to talk about it. But the Grimm Jester was there with him and only Mordecai controls that monster. The situation was baffling."

"What happened?"

"We just want our people!" I yelled at him. "No one else needs to die here. Let them go and we'll leave."

The standoff lasted for several more seconds as the leader

weighed his options. Finally Mordecai shouted, "Go!" He waved Kinchlow and Lumen over. The two prisoners stumbled to their feet and headed toward us.

Kinchlow was in bad shape. He bled badly from a gunshot wound to his abdomen. Lumen limped toward us, but she had no visible injuries. We had our people. Now we needed to get out of there alive. The tunnel fell silent as neither side moved. Slowly, we inched our way back down the tunnel as two of the soldiers escorted Mordecai away from us.

Mordecai turned back, his face empty of any emotion. "Kill them," he ordered and was gone. The remaining soldiers opened fire. Kinchlow and Lumen were both hit in the back before they reached us. Lumen fell into my arms. Lazlo caught Kinchlow and helped him stay on his feet.

Bullets struck the surrounding walls, followed by a sizzling ball of red plasma that hit the rocks next to Lazlo. He threw Kinchlow to the side as it exploded in a molten splash that splattered across his face. It melted the stone, Lazlo's skin and everything it touched, then ignited into a low burning, intensely hot fire that spread across the surface of the wall. Lazlo fell to the floor of the tunnel, writhing in pain.

I grabbed his arm and pulled him around the bend where there was some protection. The chemical weapon ate away at his skin and clothes. He rolled on the ground, screaming in anguish. There was nothing I could do. His eyes met mine, his face contorted in agony. Then he was gone.

Despereaux pulled a grenade from her shoulder bag and threw it down the passageway to buy us time to get away. The explosion tore up the tunnel and the soldiers with it.

The Grimm Jester burst from the smoke. I emptied my Tommy gun into the approaching wraith, but my bullets had no effect on it.

The monster went after Despereaux. Even though he was wounded, Kinchlow stepped in to stop the monster. He was a big man, but the wraith knocked him aside like he was a rag-doll. His body slammed into the wall with bone crunching force. I knew he was dead before he hit the floor.

The Grimm Jester grabbed her by the throat and lifted her off the floor. Something dropped to the floor under Despereaux and rolled it beneath her and the floating ghoul. I shielded Lumen with my body as the incendiary device went off.

"The blast engulfed both Despereaux and the Grimm Jester in flames. The force of the explosion rattled the cavern, knocking debris from the ceiling. We didn't wait for the smoke to clear. We knew Despereaux was dead, but her sacrifice made it possible for us to escape.

"I could feel the heat and fire behind us as I followed Shuli down the first rabbit-hole we came to. I was afraid of what we might run into in there, but we took it."

"We came out on a hillside of an urban fantasy world. By the time we reached the nearest city, Lumen was gone. Bottom line is we lost five Raconteurs that night. Only Shuli and I survived. I apologize for rambling, but that was a lot to sort out in my head. I can see that black cowl and jutting jawbone with the cruel smile."

Medesto watched out of the corner of his eye. Ren shifted restlessly in his seat. The guilt on his face was evident. The trickster was impulsive, headstrong and selfish, but his loyalty to his friends was unquestioned. If anything good could come from that horrific night, Medesto hoped it would push him to fully commit to their wild plan.

"And you never saw Claymore?"

"No, it was too dark and chaotic," Medesto replied. "Once the shooting started, the prison escapees scrambled for cover in all directions. My only thought was rescuing our missing comrades and getting out alive."

Ren suppressed a yawn and stretched his arms out in front of him like a cat. The massacre at Bones Martyr Isle was enough to make him seethe, but he was too tired to commit to a proper rage. Reliving the events had not been easy for the gnome.

"But after that, I go look for Claymore alone. It seems he wants nothing to do with the Raconteurs after everyone abandoned him. Or else he would have contacted you."

Medesto yawned loudly in response. "Mordecai and his marauders will surface again soon enough, and we'll be ready when he does. Then we'll look for Claymore. The cosmos is a big place. It's easy to lose yourself out there, but we found you, didn't we?"

Ren tossed the paperback onto the dashboard and slouched down in his seat. "It's been a long day, and I'm suddenly very tired."

The gnome nodded, not taking his eyes off the control panel. "That's the aftereffects of the Muse's influence. You'll be back to your normal irritating self soon enough."

Ren yawned again. "How far to Rogue Destiny?"

Medesto synced the navigation system with the WayFinder. The auto controls took over and the courier ship adjusted course. Medesto checked the clock on the dashboard. "We're about eleven hours out."

"Then wake me up when we get there." Ren rolled over and settled into his seat.

Medesto felt a grim satisfaction. Ren did care about more than just himself. The death of people he considered friends did affect him. That told the gnome, despite his doubts about using the trickster in this mad scheme, maybe it would work after all. Ren Bugatti was still a Raconteur at heart, whether or not he was aware of it.

During his time among them, Ren had made steady progress under Claymore's careful tutelage. But he had backslid since his old partner's fall from grace, and the founder of the Raconteurs wasn't here to help corral him anymore.

He shifted in his seat, trying to get comfortable for the long ride home. He dimmed the interior lights and stared out the windshield into the blackness. Wisps of mist and bits of debris floated by as the slipstream moved through the silent darkness of the Void. He flipped on music to pass the time. The soft improvised melodies of

1940s jazz filled the compartment. Good music made the long hours of flying more bearable, and it helped soothe his mind.

He and Natascha had traveled through dozens of Books along the outer rim looking for anything out of the ordinary that might lead them to a shape-shifting trickster who didn't want to be found. He was running on less than six hours of sleep in the last two weeks, but needed to focus a while longer until he got Ren back to Rogue Destiny. He turned the music up and rubbed his eyes.

The gnome understood Ren had been through a lot, and he felt bad for him — even if most of his problems were of his own making. The truth was, the Raconteurs were putting all their hope of stopping Rogue Destiny's most dangerous criminals in the hands of someone whose allegiance to anyone or anything was dubious at best.

But for the first time since the massacre at Bones Martyr Isle, Medesto allowed a sliver of hope to slip through. Gideon's plan to deal with the band of marauders would work. It had to. As long as Ren did not find out the truth about Claymore Ives until after he helped them.

Chapter 10
The City of a Thousand Moons

Ren woke with a start as the courier ship jerked. He stretched his limbs as best he could in the confined space and rubbed his droopy eyes. Next to him, Medesto seemed lost in thought, staring blankly out the window at the glowing worlds that filled the darkness of the Great Void.

"Any word from Natascha?" Ren asked.

"Nothing yet," Medesto said with droopy eyes and a half-stifled yawn.

"Do you think the distress signal is related to Mordecai and the escaped prisoners?"

"Hard to tell," the gnome replied. He switched the screen to its directional map. It showed they were nearing their destination. "Mordecai's made no effort to hide his movements, and there's been no discernable pattern to where he and his people will turn up next. They pop up here and there like a Whack-a-Mole game. We have dozens of Raconteurs in the field, dealing with the myriad of problems we always deal with."

"You get any sleep?" Ren asked, stifling a yawn.

"A little," the gnome said. "I let the WayFinder guide us home, but I've been monitoring a small leak in the left engine. It's giving us a bit of a lag. I didn't want us stalling out in the middle of nowhere."

Ren watched the radiant worlds streak by his window. After some sleep, his memory had returned in excruciating detail. The realization of what he had almost done hit him like a punch in the gut. If he had killed Arsene Vidocq in a fit of rage, millions of people would have suffered the same fate as those in *The Angels of Avalon*. The thought made him sick to his stomach.

In the distance, the soft glow of a flat, circular world came into view. It was a disk-shaped plane that rose at the edges like an enormous bowl filled to the brim with water. The slipstream passed above the outer edge and came out over a vast ocean. Ren could make out latitude and longitude lines that crisscrossed the bottom of the clear, deep sea as if the nameless world sat upon some great map.

The Dreaming Sea surrounded a chain of islands called the Sojourn Archipelago. The small courier ship slowly descended toward the largest of the islands, a crescent-shaped mass of land where a great city stretched out below them.

"There she is," Medesto said. His stoic voice cracked with uncharacteristic emotion. "Rogue Destiny, City of a Thousand Moons. The imperishable crown jewel of the Mythic Cosmos. She is the only thing that never changes. No matter how bad things are out in the field, She'll always be waiting for you to return. You don't realize how much you miss being here until you see Her shores again."

Ren nodded, but said nothing. Although he had abandoned Her, his heart still jumped at the sight of the ancient city. He would never admit that to anyone. But seeing his adopted city tore open old wounds, and he felt a familiar anger rise in him once more.

Rogue Destiny was different from the countless worlds that filled the skies overhead. There was no veil of words above her skies, no Narrative controlling the actions of her citizens. The island city was a place outside of time, where her inhabitants lived as creatures of free will. For better or worse, the city existed beyond the laws that bound the rest of the Mythic Cosmos.

The shining spires and minarets of the city's skyline met towers of brick and cut stone in a patchwork of architectural designs from a hundred different genres and cultures. Factories and commerce centers spotted the landscape beneath them. Futuristic glass skyscrapers stood next to ancient citadels. The river Ampersand wound through the heart of the metropolis. It flowed past the giant water clock that marked the governmental buildings of the bureaucracy class.

At the center of the City's largest bay, a massive spiral watchtower rose above anything around it. It had been built by the founder of Rogue Destiny a millennium before. The black stone monolith stood like some great sentinel watching over the City. Legend said the tower stood at the very center of the Mythic Cosmos, like the gnomon on some great sundial. The monolith was also rumored to contain the doorways to countless worlds and clues on how the city came to be. Some of the tales might even hold a bit of truth in them.

Ren watched the islands draw closer beneath them. He allowed himself the slightest of smiles. Medesto was right, there was no place anywhere like Rogue Destiny. Now he was back.

Shadowing the southern end of the island, surrounded by a series of low-lying bluffs, Mount Perdition stood. Halfway up its base sat the impregnable fortress, Lazaranth Prison. The courier ship slowed as they approached the western edge of the city.

Medesto kept a watchful eye out as he navigated through the airships and broadsides populating the skies over the island. He switched on the comm screen.

"Tin Man, this is *Wayward One*, requesting permission to land." No reply. Medesto rolled his eyes and sighed. "Hello? Sebastian, anyone down there?"

The console crackled in response. A distorted image of Sebastian's oil-smeared face appeared on the small screen. The metal skull cap on the right side of his head sprouted a handful of short antennae. The other half of the cyborg's head bore the crewcut from his days in the military. His face looked older and wearier than Ren remembered.

"This is Tin Man." Sebastian said, his basso voice short and gruff. "And don't use our real names, *Wayward One*. You never know who's listening."

"Ah, you are there," Medesto said. "I knew that umbilical cord of yours never let you wander off too far."

"You have permission to land, *Wayward One*," the static reply came back. "Put her down in the Byzantine. I'll meet you there."

"Please tell Gideon the package has been delivered," Medesto replied. He clicked the console to standby and slowed the ship to landing mode as they approached the landing bay.

Ren felt the thrusters kick in, and Medesto brought the small ship over to the public house known as the Obtuse Turtle. It was a large Victorian estate, remodeled into a spacious hotel that catered to the weary traveler. It came complete with restaurant and gaming rooms to pass the time. Behind the hotel, several walled off court-yards housed the Raconteur's fleet of slipstream Runabouts.

The courier ship descended to the Byzantine landing bay, the hull vibrating as the landing gear extended. Medesto set down on a designated space in front of a large cargo door.

Ren opened the hatch on his side and climbed out. Sebastian Poe walked toward them through the dust and smoke kicked up by the ship. A large wrench rested on one shoulder.

"Hello, Sebastian." Ren smiled at the mechanic with a wave of his hand.

The Raconteur's chief mechanic gave him a nod. "Hello, Ren. Welcome back." The cyborg continued to survey the courier ship for dents or scratches. He bent down to look at the undercarriage. "No visible damage," he muttered. "I wonder what shape my engines are in."

Medesto came around from the driver's side of the ship. He looked worn out, his legs heavy as he ambled up to the Raconteur's chief mechanic.

Sebastian's gaze locked in on the short, stout Raconteur. "You're running the engines too hot, gnome," he said. "How many times have I told you not to turn off the cooling regulators or mess with the dampers? You'll burn them out!"

"But she goes faster with the dampers off," Medesto said. He opened a compartment door on the side of the ship and started unloading gear. "Also, there's a slight leak in the left rear pressure line you'll need to check out. My guess is it's probably from running the engines too hot."

Sebastian loomed over Medesto, casting a massive shadow of muscle and metal that fell across the four-foot tall gnome. The cyborg extended his metal right hand. Medesto reached into his coat pocket and pulled out the small black box. The cyborg snatched it from his hand.

"Don't take my ships without permission again," he growled, not even trying to hide his agitation. "Or you and I are going to have words. And stop adjusting the engine settings. Everything's preset for a reason. I'm tired of having to replace most of the internal components every time you go for a joyride."

"I was on official Raconteur business and needed to get somewhere quickly," he said. "If you have a problem with that, take it up with Gideon."

Sebastian bristled at the words. He squared his shoulders and adjusted the grip on the giant wrench in his hand. Medesto ignored him and grabbed an empty pushcart that sat near the side of the building. He pulled it across the polished stone floor and began loading boxes from the courier ship's cargo bins onto it.

"If you'd only take the time to get *Subtle Chaos* up and running," Medesto commented. "Then we wouldn't have to keep having these awkward conversations, would we?"

Sebastian's eyes narrowed, and he gave the gnome a crooked smile. "I've already stripped *Subtle Chaos* down for parts. I'm in the middle of building a new slipstream on spec and didn't have time to recast all the engine components I needed." It was

Medesto's turn to glower. Both his hands curled into fists, his knuckles cracking.

"I was told to finish the new ship as quickly as I could," Sebastian said with a smirk. "If you have a problem with that, take it up with Gideon."

Sebastian hobbled to a circular cover on the floor of the bay. He pulled out a large nozzle and dragged the hose back to the courier ship. With a twist, he attached the nozzle to the undercarriage of the slipstream and opened the fuel line.

Ren helped Medesto finish unloading the cargo bins of the knick-knacks and trinkets the gnome gathered on his trip. Rogue Destiny did most of its trading with goods secured from outside its borders. Cultural differences became blurred. Commodities from countless literary worlds found their way to a city that itself was nothing but an eclectic fusion of cultures and societies.

"What was that black box?" Ren asked.

"It's the new key-box system Sebastian recently installed," Medesto told him. "For security purposes, all slipstreams have them now. A lot has changed in the last year, B'gatti. We've had to beef up security. The Common Council is breathing down our necks more than ever. I have a bad feeling they're up to something, and it ain't good."

He grabbed the handle of the pushcart and headed down the ramp into the subterranean garage. "As always, it's been a pleasure, Sebastian." The gnome quipped as he walked away.

Sebastian muttered some inaudible profanities regarding Medesto's parentage. He caught Ren looking at him.

"Welcome back, bud," the mechanic said, a sardonic grin on his grizzled face.

Chapter 11
A Differing of Opinions

Medesto directed the pushcart down a ramp into the depths of Sebastian's workshop and parked it to one side. He grabbed his black traveling bag and a bottle of wine from the wooden crate. Sebastian's iron leg impacted the ramp, sending a resounding echo throughout the garage as Ren and the mechanic joined him. Worn-out gears in the cyborg's knee whined in protest. Medesto knew he was putting off fixing it because it would take him away from the actual work that needed to get done.

The underground garage stretched under the dim lamps of a dozen workstations. Sebastian returned to dismantling an enormous engine suspended from the ceiling. The cyborg came from a dystopian novel of eternal war. He escaped with the help of Claymore, bringing his three surviving children to Rogue Destiny during the Raconteurs' formative years. A framed picture of him and his three children sat on the bench behind him.

Medesto led Ren through the maze of equipment. The trickster wandered off among the hanging power cords and diagnostic equipment. Several slipstream Runabouts sat in the garage, each in some state of repair or rebuild. All the ships ranged in length from fifty-feet to over a hundred. Sebastian and his crew maintained the

Raconteurs' fleet of slipstreams down here, away from the prying eyes of those who would steal their technology.

The walls around the workstations were covered in posters of the classic muscle cars from the late twentieth century on a world known as Terra or Earth. The cyborg's passion for that particular time period was evident in every ship he built. He took inspiration in the stacks of *Hot Rod* magazines he collected. The glossy pictures within the pages gave him a window into a world he would never know. His ship designs combined the sleek chassis of his favorite hot rods with the practical aesthetics of science fiction spacecrafts.

Sebastian had an admiration for the craftsmanship of those magnificent automobiles, but his dependency on the portable lung kept him from straying too far outside his garage. His dream of seeing them firsthand was not to be.

Medesto, on the other hand, had traveled to a multitude of Earths and had seen and ridden in many of the vehicles displayed in the posters.

Ren stopped and peaked through the cockpit window of a partially dissembled slipstream. The chassis had been stripped and painted a different color than he remembered, but its design was unmistakable.

"Is this *Righteous Indignation?*" Ren asked.

"Huh?" Sebastian grunted, looking up from his work. "Yeah, Claymore's old rig. The Common Council tried to claim it when he went to Lazaranth. We hid her offsite and told the authorities Claymore never boarded her here. The Council doesn't even try to hide their ambitions about seizing our technology, but that's never going to happen."

Ren climbed in through the open side hatch and slid into the pilot's seat. He gripped the steering wheel with both hands. The overhead console and dashboard dripped with unfinished wiring.

"She's beautiful," Ren said.

Sebastian stuck his head in the barren main cabin and admired his work in progress. "She will be when I'm done with her," he smirked, cleaning his hands with a greasy rag. "I'm upgrading the engines. Haven't decided what to name her yet, but when she's done, it'll be the fastest ship I've ever built. Like I said, a lot of its components are from the *Subtle Chaos* wreckage."

The cyborg glanced over at Medesto with a smug smile. Medesto ignored the comment. Ren didn't know what had caused the animosity between Sebastian and the gnome. It just always seemed to be that way between them.

"When I get back from this run," Ren shouted through the window cockpit. "I'll be happy to take her off your hands."

Sebastian let go a rare laugh. "Yeah, you'll have to take that up with Gideon."

"And that possibility is definitely open for discussion," a voice behind them said.

Ren looked over to see Gideon Dumas walking up to them. His large, dour eyes studied them with a reflective gleam. He stopped next to the open hatch as Ren climbed out.

"Welcome back, Mr. B'gatti," Gideon Dumas said. "Since I see no visible bruising, I assume your reunion with Medesto and Doctor Enigma was a peaceful one." He chuckled at his joke.

Medesto gave a smirk. "We came to a mutual agreement."

Gideon gave the gnome a knowing look, trying to deduce what kind of deal had been struck to get the trickster to return willingly. He was a student of the human condition and infinitely curious why individuals made the choices they did. His was a brilliant mind, and one underestimated the diminutive leader of the Raconteurs at their own peril. It was a mistake the gnome knew never to make.

Medesto didn't know if he liked the idea of Ren traveling the cosmos alone in his own slipstream, but it was obvious Gideon had entertained the idea. Now Ren only had to prove himself worthy of that honor.

"Thank you for agreeing to see us in our hour of need," Gideon said. "How was the trip back?" He put out a gloved hand in greeting.

"I slept most of the way," Ren said, shaking the extended hand.

"And Medesto, thank you for finding our wayward friend," Gideon added. "How did your search go?"

"Terrible food and little sleep," the gnome answered. "It wasn't easy, but Natascha and I found our boy and here we are. I brought you a case of wine from a vender's stall outside of 16th century Paris. It's supposed to be an exceptional vintage." He held up the bottle in his hand. Gideon's eyes lit up at the words.

"Thank you," Gideon replied with a slight nod of his head.

"Any word from *Nevermore* or *Fool's Errand?*" Medesto asked.

"Since the initial distress call, *Fool's Errand* has gone dark," Gideon replied. "*Nevermore* and *Midnight Run* are both headed there to investigate, but neither have reported in yet. I pray they reach Artimus and Cedric in time." He shook his head.

"Tempest and Charley are waiting downstairs. We can talk there in more detail." He motioned to a staircase leading to another level under the garage. "Shall we?"

"Who?" Ren asked.

"Tempest Vondersteen," Medesto said. "She came on shortly after the events of *The Angels of Avalon*, as our Chief Security Officer. You disappeared on us, so you never had the chance to meet her. She's hellbent on bringing the latest technology to the Raconteurs. Her assistant, Charley Lovejoy, has been working on ways to reconfigure the Wayfinder to give our agents in the field a more detailed mapping of a Book's interior."

Gideon led the way down a spiral stairwell. They passed a wide room full of operatives working at desks. They struggled to keep up with the information pouring in from the giant screen of the WayFinder that dominated the farthest.

Designed and built by the greatest minds Gideon could recruit, the WayFinder connected the Raconteurs' vast network of caretakers and safe-houses throughout the Mythic Cosmos. It was the lifeblood of the Raconteurs' work. The first indicator of trouble beyond Rogue Destiny's borders. It exhaustively scanned the heavens, tracking irregularities throughout the written worlds. The information was parsed, prioritized, and passed on for any needed follow up.

Two dozen smaller screens of varying sizes were hedged in around the WayFinder's mother screen and spread across the walls. The WayFinder kept watch over the movements of their agents in the field. Red lights at the bottom of the main screen indicated when there was a problem or if any Raconteur was in danger. Currently, nine lights were on.

On the far side of the room, there was a doorway to a small conference room. A large, round table sat at the center, with two occupants waiting. One was a young dark-haired woman, the other was a tall, commanding woman with a somber expression.

Gideon made the introductions. "Ren B'gatti, this is Tempest Vondersteen." The older woman nodded and gave them a tight smile. She eyed the torn and bloodied Ren shirt still wore, but said nothing.

"And this is her assistant, Constance Lovejoy. She maintains the Wayfinder and oversees the myriad of the technical resources the Raconteurs need to get their job done."

Without lifting her head, the girl's eyes came up. "You can call me Charley." Her attention returned to the small flat display screen she was fine-tuning.

Gideon scooted himself up onto a chair at the opposite end from the two women. A tall ice bucket filled with chilling beverages stood next to the table. "Please, help yourself to something to drink," Gideon said with a wave of his hand. "We have soda or any number of the Obtuse Turtle's personal house brews."

Ren took a bottle of soda from the ice, popped the cap with his fingers, and plopped down on the chair in the middle of the table, where he stretched out his legs. Medesto closed the door behind them and pulled the cork off the bottle of wine. He sat down next to the trickster, pouring himself and Gideon each a glass of the deep red liquid.

Gideon took a sip of his wine. "This is excellent, Medesto," he commented. The gnome lifted his glass in reply.

"I'm here," Ren said. He took a swallow from his soda. "So, what's the plan?"

Chapter 12
A Simple Enough Plan

"What has Medesto told you so far, Mr. Bugatti?" Gideon asked.

"Lazaranth Prison suffered a large-scale breakout," Ren said. "Several Raconteurs were killed trying to stop the prisoners from escaping these islands. More died tracking the fugitives while they're raiding old libraries. Now you need me to infiltrate the outlaws to prevent more loss of life and find out what they're looking for, so the Raconteurs can get to it before they do."

"Precisely," Gideon replied with a nod. "A handful of the escaped prisoners snuck back into Rogue Destiny and were recaptured. I've had the opportunity to question several regarding how they managed to disappear from their cells undetected. Each told me the same thing. In the dead of night, a strange glow appeared on their wall, then a circular doorway opened that led them to a desolate canyon on Bones Martyr Isle."

"How is that possible?" Ren asked.

"Since there is no magic in Rogue Destiny or anywhere in the Sojourn Islands," Gideon replied, "we can only assume it must be some mechanical apparatus we've never encountered before. Once free of their cells, the prisoners were ushered by armed soldiers to an area where they were greeted by a man we believe to be Mordecai Davos, who sought to recruit them for some great quest. He said everything in Rogue Destiny was about to change, and those who swore allegiance to him, and his quest would share in the spoils once he found what he sought."

"Why are the Raconteurs responsible for finding Mordecai?" Ren asked. "Isn't this a local issue that the General Protectorate and Common Council should be dealing with?"

"The moment they left Rogue Destiny, they became the problem of the Raconteurs," Medesto said. "We need you to find out why Mordecai's suddenly interested in dusty, forgotten archives."

"The question is why was cellblock 27 released, but no others?" Gideon said. "It makes me believe Mordecai was searching for one prisoner in particular. The others were released simply to create chaos. If we find out who that prisoner was, it could answer a lot of questions and lead us to whoever is behind this whole affair."

"I'll have no problem getting inside," Ren said. He took a long, slow drink from his soda bottle. "But if Mordecai is behind this, I'm surprised you'd involve me, considering how I almost ended up working for him?"

Tempest let out an audible gasp. Medesto shifted in his chair and took a drink of his wine. *Here we go.*

"That was a long time ago," Gideon said with a reserved smile. "Mordecai tried to recruit you shortly after you first showed up in Rogue Destiny, while you were still part of the street gang, *The Gentlemen of Fortune*, correct?"

"Yeah," Ren replied. "His people approached me at *The Pithy Fool*, where the Gentlemen liked to hang out and asked if I was willing to meet with Mordecai. I told them I would consider it, but only if I could talk to Mordecai face to face."

"And that meeting never took place?" Gideon asked. "You never saw the man himself, as I recall."

"No, all contact went through his lackeys. The night before I was to meet with Mordecai, Claymore showed up at *The Pithy Fool*. He convinced me to talk to you instead. You know the rest."

"Yes, we do," Gideon said. "Rumors of a shape-shifter running around the streets of Rogue Destiny had popped up all over the City. There are many different factions with an interest in you. Any one of them could have been responsible for the Lazaranth breakout. But Medesto said it was the Grimm Jester that he saw in the depths of Bones Martyr Island. So it had to be Mordecai holding his leash."

"What's next?" Ren asked.

"As we speak," Gideon replied, "There are dozens of Raconteurs scouring the Great Void trying to locate the fugitives. We must be ready to put our plan into action when the moment arrives. Once the man we believe to be Mordecai is located, a small team, led by Medesto, will escort you there so you can infiltrate their ranks as one of Mordecai's confederates."

Ren was insulted by the suggestion. "Thanks," he said, "but I don't need anyone watching over my shoulder. Just point me to where they are, and I'll do what I do best."

A sly grin appeared on Tempest's face. "What's the problem, B'gatti?" she asked, enjoying Ren's irritation. "Afraid everyone's trust in you isn't what you thought it was?"

Ren stared at her with indifference. "You're not coming with us, are you?"

"No, Tempest will not be accompanying you," Gideon interrupted. "However, she has agreed to loan you her assistant, Charley, to see if she can track this portal-creating machine. We believe Mordecai and his people are using to jump from world to world."

"Then this only concerns those who are going on this mission," Ren said to Tempest. "Not those who choose to stay behind and send lackeys in their place. No offense, Charley."

Tempest stiffened at the remark. Her eyes narrowed and her jawline tightened, but she said nothing.

Charley looked up. "No offense taken. If Tempest wants to go in my place, I'll be happy to stay here." She glanced at Tempest. Her smile disappeared under her supervisor's withering glare. Her attention quickly returned to the tangled wires in her hands.

Medesto swished his wine around, staring at the translucent liquid through the glass. "No one said you'd be doing this alone. How did you think you were going to get to Mordecai?"

"Gideon's going to give me a slipstream," Ren replied matter-of-factly.

Tempest gave a laugh. "Why would we give you a slipstream Runabout just because you asked?"

Ren stood up and leaned in toward the security officer. "You don't trust me, I get that? But Medesto trusts me, don't you?" He nodded his head at the gnome without breaking eye contact with Tempest.

"Absolutely," Medesto replied.

"Gideon, you trust me."

"Of course," Gideon responded. "That is why I asked you here today."

"Charley?"

"Don't know you," she said. "But you seem decent enough. And you have hutzpah, I'll give that."

Ren gave Tempest a wink. "You seem to be the only one with a problem and since you're not going with us this on this run, you need to sit down and keep quiet."

Medesto hid a chuckle behind his glass. Charley smirked, but did not look up. The gnome could tell she wanted to add something to the conversation. Tempest looked around at everyone at the table, then sank down in her seat. Medesto sat back in his chair, relieved she would not be going with them.

"Thank you, Mr. B'gatti," Gideon said. "Rest assured, the team will simply travel with you to assess the destruction these fugitives have left in their wake and see what work will be needed to repair the damage caused."

Ren gave Gideon a hard look, as if he weren't sure he believed that. Medesto could see the possibility of the conversation unraveling at any moment. The trickster hated nothing more than being kept on a leash.

"Once you're inside, Ren, you'll be completely on your own," the gnome assured him. "No one will be there looking over your shoulder."

"But proceed with caution," Gideon added. "These fugitives are among the most dangerous criminals the Raconteurs have come up against."

"Well, Mordecai is about to find out how dangerous I can be," Ren said.

"We are not sending you there to kill him," Gideon said, agitation building in his voice.

"That would certainly save lives," Ren countered. "Mordecai would kill any of us in this room if he had the chance. He didn't hesitate the night of the breakout. But if I kill him, his followers would scatter and whatever they're searching for will remain where it is. One death instead of many. Problem solved."

The room fell silent for a dozen heartbeats. Even Charley looked up at Ren's words. "I like this guy," she said. "He's straight to the point."

Medesto knew Ren was provoking Gideon, trying to give himself an excuse to back out on his promise. It might have been humorous if there wasn't so much at stake. But he knew Ren was pragmatic. In his mind, killing this mysterious leader outright was the easiest, quickest way to solve the issue at hand. He had to admit the solution had merit. It would save lives.

"This whole affair is bigger than just a prison breakout, Mr. B'gatti," Gideon said. "The city as a whole has become so corrupt these past years, and it continues to get worse with each new day. The breach in Lazaranth's security has given the criminal element of Rogue Destiny a new boldness. Once your job is complete, the Raconteurs will swoop in and bring Mordecai back in chains to stand trial in the public square. That will show the entire city that no one is out of reach of the Raconteurs."

"Then you can bring his dead body back, and drag that

through the streets just as easy," Ren replied. "Mount his head on a pike at the courthouse. That'll show the Raconteurs are still relevant."

"A public trial will show how good always must win out over evil," Medesto said. "That justice prevails in the end."

Ren took a moment to think about that. He pushed down the anger building up in him. "I know my way sounds harsh," he said as calmly as he could. "And I understand your argument. No one should play judge, jury, and executioner, but this is a unique situation. Mordecai is responsible for the death of other Raconteurs, some of whom were friends of mine. We need to respond in kind. Or does this go back to the whole good thing, bad thing?"

"It always goes back to right and wrong," Medesto replied. "The good is always worth fighting for."

"I understand you believe that," Ren said. "But my world isn't so black and white. I walk the wide swathe of gray in between law and chaos. We are at war here, make no mistake about that. In my experience, good does not always win out over evil. You have to watch out for yourself because no one else will. Just ask Claymore about that."

Medesto winced at that comment. He knew the bitter subject of Claymore would make its way into the conversation at some point. Maybe that was why Ren was goading Gideon with threats of killing Mordecai. So he could get out of helping the Raconteurs stop Mordecai.

"Bad things happen to good people sometimes," the gnome said. "There is no one more worthy of admiration than Claymore Ives. He is everything a hero should be. But he is free now, and I pray he finally finds some peace after everything that's happened."

"I won't argue with that," Ren nodded in agreement. "We're all fighting for something here, aren't we? Isn't that what Claymore always said?" Ren drained his soda bottle and set it on the table. "I'm hungry. I'm going to find something to eat."

"Good evening then, Mr. Bugatti," Gideon said. He set his

wine glass down. "My only request is that you stay out of sight and be ready to leave at a moment's notice."

"I'll be waiting," Ren answered.

Medesto watched the trickster leave. Ren was nothing if not unpredictable. His own sense of morality was unique. Only one person could ever reason with him, but Claymore wasn't there.

Chapter 13
The Devil You Know

The moment Ren closed the door, Tempest turned to Gideon. "You cannot seriously be considering this?" she said.

"Please do not antagonize our guest," Gideon replied. "His willingness to help is tenuous at best, but his cooperation is crucial if this plan is to succeed."

"Doesn't that tell us something about your plan?" Tempest asked, "We know nothing about this individual other than he worked with the Raconteurs for short time over a year ago. He was Claymore's problem then. He shouldn't be everyone else's now. It is a mistake to let him take point on this mission."

"I agree he's reckless," Gideon said. "But he fights for what he believes in."

"How does that help us trust him?" she asked.

"We give him something he can believe in," Gideon replied. "Something to fight for. He's lost his closest friend. After Claymore's arrest and imprisonment, he felt betrayed by everyone he knew. So much, in fact, that he left everything behind. He's hurting. It would be difficult to trust anyone under those circumstances."

Tempest sighed. "Gideon, you hired me as Chief Security Officer for a reason. My job is to oversee the daily operations and security of this facility. That authority includes deciding who is fit to be a Raconteur and who is not. I know a weak link in the chain when I see it. He admitted to our faces that he could have just as easily worked for Mordecai and the *Black Rose* as for us. What does that say about his character? B'gatti is too big a risk for a task of this magnitude."

"He says those things to get under my skin," Gideon replied with a sigh. "He enjoys resisting authority. In the end, he never worked for Mordecai. He's always been a trustworthy agent and is here under his own accord with no obligation to help us, yet he said he would."

Tempest's frustration rose, and her face flushed. "I've read through his file, and nothing in it gives me confidence." She pulled a small notepad from her jacket pocket and flipped through the pages. "We have no details on his background. No one knows his point of origin or how he ended up in Rogue Destiny. He has chaotic tendencies and consorts with thieves and criminals. In my eyes, he's as unpredictable and dangerous as any of those escaped fugitives."

She flipped through several more pages. "There's nothing here to indicate he can be trusted. He's a trickster, a changeling who lives his life as other people. Trust is not in his nature. This may not even be his true appearance. For all we know, he could be Mordecai himself. No one has ever seen the criminal's face, so it's not beyond the realm of possibility. Or he might be some shape-shifting demi-god or dark lord in hiding."

"I assure you, Ren is not Mordecai Davos," Gideon said with a tired smile.

Medesto chuckled. "And he's no dark lord or demi-god, either. Both take too much effort — he's too lazy for anything that requires effort."

"You cannot know that," Tempest replied, her voice rising.

Medesto straightened up in his chair. "I've worked with him long enough to know his loyalties lie with the Raconteurs in his own way."

"That still doesn't make him one of us," Tempest argued.

"I know what he appears to be and what his background is," Gideon said. "But I also know what he is capable of being. I believe he has the potential to be a great agent for good."

Tempest was undeterred in her argument. "His psych profile says he has no defined concept of right and wrong and doesn't particularly care one way or the other. He makes it up as he goes and consistently straddles both sides of the law, as is evident with his affiliation with this gang he's been connected to—" She glanced down at her notes. "*The Gentlemen of Fortune.*"

Medesto let go another laugh. "The Gentlemen of Fortune were not so much a gang as a group of misfits full of self-importance and big dreams. They were little more than hobos, and more of a threat to themselves than anyone else. Ren fell in with them when he first showed up in Rogue Destiny before we even knew he was around. But it's all a moot point. *The Gentlemen* are all dead now if I'm not mistaken."

Tempest scowled. "And what happens once he's inside Mordecai's inner circle? What's to say he won't be turned against us? We could be sending our enemy their greatest weapon."

"I said I'll vouch for Ren," Medesto said. "He's no criminal. Maybe a little cloudy on the whole good-bad thing, but he is a Raconteur at heart, even if he doesn't realize it sometimes. I've been out there with him in the field, and he's done nothing to make me doubt his loyalty. If he says he'll do this, he will."

"Then what about Claymore Ives?" Tempest flipped to the next page in her notebook. "Ren B'gatti abandoned the Raconteurs after his partner was convicted of the destruction of *an entire world.* B'gatti is still sought in connection with that crime. You said yourself, Gideon, Claymore is suffering from the *Paradigm Madness* and is no longer able to lead the Raconteurs because of what he was exposed to inside *The Angels of Avalon.* I know he's your founder and revered by the Raconteurs, but if what they say about that horrible madness is true, then he'll never be the man he once was. He could turn against us too."

"You're out of line, Tempest," Medesto growled. "That all happened before your time." He didn't raise his voice. Only the twitching of his mustache gave away the anger lurking under his calm demeanor. Claymore was a touchy subject for the gnome, as much as it was with Ren. He was not about to let his friend's reputation be dragged through the dirt by anyone. He knew Tempest was just doing her job and felt she was only protecting the Raconteurs, but she had overstepped her place.

Tempest leaned in over the table. "And now he's asking for a slipstream in exchange for his cooperation. What is stopping him from searching for Claymore instead? That alone should make you question his motivations in wanting to help us."

"So you need to keep it in perspective," Medesto replied flatly. "Claymore Ives founded the Raconteurs. He and I were close friends. His imprisonment was a blow none of us have completely recovered from. Neither Claymore nor Ren had anything to do with what happened in *The Angels of Avalon,* and when it comes to stopping this horde of criminals finding whatever it is they are after, then Ren is the best chance we have to stop more bloodshed."

"I have decided I am going to offer Mr. Bugatti his own slipstream once his mission is completed," Gideon said. "That should incentivize him to help us bring Mordecai in alive."

"I still think this is a terrible idea," Tempest said. Her eyes bore into the gnome. Medesto returned the favor.

Gideon took a sip of his wine. "Then what do you propose, Tempest?" he asked.

Tempest thought carefully before she answered. She looked to Charley, then to Medesto. "I trust your instincts, Gideon. I always have. It's the changeling I don't trust. So I think I should go with the team to monitor its progress. I'll be there to deal with the trickster if he steps out of line."

Charley glanced up from her scanner. "Does that mean I can stay home?" she asked, not trying to hide her excitement. "They won't need me if you're there. I'm so far behind on my reports and the maintenance on the WayFinder. It'd give me a chance to catch up on so much."

"I still want you to go," Tempest said without looking at her. "This kind of experience will do you good. It will show you the inner workings of rabbit-holes and their connection to the mystical ley lines that create them. You'll see firsthand how what the field agents do and how our work here helps them." Tempest poked Charley in the side. "And the fresh air and exercise will be good for you."

Charley sank down in her chair. "But you said..." she muttered under her breath.

"You will not be in danger, Charley," Gideon interrupted. "Nor will you be asked to carry a weapon if you do not wish. Your task will be to help with any technical support the team might need. I want you to record anything you can on this mysterious portal machine. If we could get our hands on that kind of technology, it would revolutionize the way we travel the Mythic Cosmos."

"So it'll just be the four of us?" Charley asked.

"No, there is one other I have asked to go with you," Gideon replied. "He will act as your guide once you're in-world. Tempest is correct when she says the knowledge you'll pick up will be invaluable to your work with the WayFinder. The team's purpose is simply to get Mr. B'gatti close enough so he can infiltrate the cadre of criminals. After that, you will return home. This is not a combat mission, so you should not encounter any fighting."

Gideon took another sip before he continued. "Mr. B'gatti is hot headed and argumentative, but he is exactly what this situation calls for. We have lost too many agents already, and I will not needlessly risk anymore lives."

"Except Ren's," Charley quipped.

"If Ren behaves himself," Medesto said, "and plays the role we are asking him to. He'll be in no danger. We'll have a dozen Raconteurs waiting to take over once we find out more about what Mordecai is up to."

"Mr. B'gatti knows the risks that lie ahead and has chosen to help us," Gideon added. He turned to Tempest. "Do you know why I want him for this assignment?"

"I have no idea," Tempest said.

"I chose Mr. B'gatti because I am less concerned with someone's current station in life and more interested in what they have the capacity to become. I look for individuals with great potential whose stories have yet to be written. Many of our best agents have had questionable pasts. If we held that against them, the Raconteurs would never have survived to this day."

"And I'm sure he will be nothing but trouble for us," Tempest replied.

"Ren has always shown great promise," Gideon said. "I agree his abilities may outweigh his maturity. And though we have not yet figured out who he is or where he's from, I have a suspicion when we do, we will find he is far more powerful than even he realizes."

Chapter 14
The Obtuse Turtle

Ren walked through the darkened garage to a corridor leading next door to the public house, the Obtuse Turtle. He went up a flight of wooden steps under the glow of an incandescent light to a door at the top. There was a ripple of shifting flesh as the trickster's features morphed. His height increased several inches, and his weight increased by forty pounds. The door opened onto a carpeted hallway and Ren emerged as one of the many faces he used for sneaking about undetected.

Alex Prospero had a nondescript appearance. Dark rakish hair, and a nonthreatening Van Dyke with nothing about him that would stand out in a crowd. Ren maintained several identities built around people that did not exist. The Raconteurs knew nothing of these other faces Ren used whenever he needed to be alone.

A couple of these make-believe personas even had their own living quarters and a loose circle of associates. But that was before he had left Rogue Destiny. He still had a hefty bounty on his head and could not walk around openly in public as himself.

Down the hall to his left was Gideon's private office, and to his right was the public area of the Obtuse Turtle. Ren was hungry and getting irritated because of his empty belly. But two obstacles still stood between him and a good meal.

First, he was still wearing Talbot Mundi's clothes. The ripped silk shirt hung loose on Prospero's lean frame and was dirt stained, torn open on one shoulder, and splattered with blood on the inside of his left sleeve. The black pants and boots were caked with mud, none of which would help him blend in.

Across the hallway from Gideon's private office, Ren found a closet full of articles of clothing left behind by forgetful travelers. The small room was thick with hanging coats, luggage, and other miscellaneous items. He switched the light on and closed the door behind him. A dozen abandoned suitcases were lined up against one wall. He pulled the largest one out, laid it down, and clicked it open.

He kicked off his boots, then removed the silk shirt and pants, throwing them all into a pile. Rummaging through the contents of the suitcase, he found an open-cuff white dress shirt. Though it looked wrinkled, it fit nice enough and had a comfortable feel on his skin. He pulled on a pair of dark pants with wide cuffs that would fit over his boots. The fabric was loose and breezy. He always felt claustrophobic in any tight-fitting clothing and never wanted to risk getting tangled up if he needed to shape-shift. Pulling on some abandoned boots, he threw Talbot Mundi's clothes in the suitcase, closed the lid, and slid it back into the closet.

Ren strode down the hallway to the front lobby of the Obtuse Turtle. It was another busy night at the public house as he wandered into the main lobby under the disguise of someone who did not exist. The public house's reputation and the word of mouth of its customers kept the place filled to capacity day and night. Gideon Dumas credited its continued success to the exceptional food and tight security maintained by JoBucco, the head of hotel security and lead chef for the nightly dinner menu. JoBucco also happened to be a minotaur, which alone demanded people's respect. He and his security team were ever present, making sure the eclectic mix of guests was having a good time and everyone was behaving themselves. No one on the security team was squeamish about cracking heads or expelling unruly customers out into the street.

This brought up the second obstacle to filling Ren's empty belly. He had no money, but that could be remedied with minimal effort on his part. Ren pushed his way through the crowded lobby towards the dining room. The crush of people jarred and bumped him.

He dodged a young couple in contemporary dress. The man struggled with several suitcases while the woman held a tiny bundle in her arms. Ren moved around them and collided with a traveler who had his head buried in a map. The chart he was reading appeared to be a cosmological mapping of rabbit-holes commonly sold by street vendors throughout the City. They were notoriously inaccurate, as the confused man would eventually learn.

By the time Ren made his way to the dining room, his quick fingers had secured the traveler's wallet. Of course, Gideon and Medesto would not approve. Neither would Natascha nor Claymore. However, none of them were there to admonish him for taking it. Ren was hungry, and it was Gideon's fault there was no food at the meeting. He slipped the wallet into his back pocket.

Ren almost felt bad stealing from the unsuspecting, but he had to eat, and there wasn't much time before Medesto would come looking for him. He hadn't stolen from the young couple with the infant, so that showed personal growth, didn't it?

He stood at the edge of the elegant, dimly lit restaurant. The quiet ambiance was not what his head needed right now. He was restless and needed stimuli to take his mind off of what lay ahead.

Beyond the dining room, he saw the double doors that led to the gambling area and headed there. The sounds of rolling dice and the shuffling of cards filled the air as he entered. The ruckus of card players and the click of their poker chips hitting the gaming tables soothed his anxious thoughts.

He slid into an empty booth and pulled out his newly acquired wealth to see what he could afford for dinner. The wallet yielded enough paper money to keep him fed for a month. He laid it on the table and perused the menu. A man with graying hair, a red vest and ruffled shirt, appeared at this table.

"Ready to order, sir?" he asked politely.

"Yes, give me the thickest steak you have," Ren said. "Very rare, please. And what's your dessert special tonight?"

"A lovely, succulent chocolate soufflé with truffle shavings."

"Two of those, please, and a couple of soda pops."

"Are you expecting a guest? I can have someone watch for them."

"No," Ren replied with a wink. "It's all for me."

The server chuckled. "Very good, sir. I'll get that going right away."

"Thank you." Ren studied the crowd in the room. Several men and women played cards at the closest table. A burly man in a leather vest and black-collared shirt scowled and threw his cards on the green velvet tabletop. "Don't say a word, you mook, or I'll stuff your poker chips down your throat one by one," he growled.

Across the table, a quaint-looking gentleman in an old-fashioned suit and brown derby hat cupped his hands around the poker chips and pulled them to him. The round-faced man aggressively chewed on the end of an unlit cigar in his mouth, his eyes scanning the other players at his table.

The gaming tables near the poker game proved less interesting. The room was filled with people from dozens of genres trying to beat the house and each other in various games of chance. He returned his attention to the game next to him. After watching a couple more hands, Ren smiled to himself. The man in the derby hat would lose a hand, then quickly win the next two. He was cheating.

A server appeared with his meal. Ren's stomach rumbled as he cut into the steak and savored each juicy, bloody bite. He was halfway through the steak when he spotted Medesto on the far side of the restaurant near the lobby. The gnome squinted under the dim lights and craned his neck, searching the crowded tables. Ren grinned with amusement as the frustration grew on Medesto's face. What would it hurt to make the old gnome wait until he finished the best meal he would enjoy in some time? He dug his spoon into the chocolate desert.

Medesto ambled into the gaming room, carrying his traveling bag. He walked past Ren's table, then stopped and backed up, noticing the two bottles of soda. "Is it you?" he asked under a furrowed brow.

"Depends on who's asking," Ren replied. He took another spoonful of chocolate and washed it down with a gulp of soda. Medesto eyed the contents on the table, the bloody remains of the steak, and the two chocolate soufflés. He grumbled into his beard and sat down across from Ren.

"I'm not going to ask where you got the money," Medesto remarked. "Or the clothes. You ready to go?"

"I'm still eating," Ren said. He slid the second dessert across to Medesto. "Try some? It's delicious." Medesto stared at the chocolate decadence in front of him, sighed, and picked up a spoon.

The ruckus at the card table next to them grew louder. Accusations were being thrown around. Ren turned to see the burly man in the vest, his face red, pointing an angry finger in the face of the quaint little gentleman in the brown derby hat. The other patrons at the table glowered in his direction, too.

"You cheated!" the large man bellowed.

The accused man's eyes went wide. "I would never stoop to cheating at a game of cards. Certainly not with someone who plays as poorly as you do."

"Bullspit!" the man yelled. He stood up, his clenched fists quivering with rage. "Know how I know you're cheating? The full house you just laid down included the ace of diamonds. But I palmed that ace after the last hand so I could catch you in the act." The man pulled a card from his right sleeve and dropped a second ace of diamonds on top of the first one. "Why is there two of the same card?!"

"Perhaps it's you who is cheating," the gentleman in the derby hat said, unfazed by the accusations. "You're the one pulling cards from your sleeve."

"Save it! Nobody cheats me." The brute of a man came around the gaming table at the other card player. The smaller man waved his hands in front of him, like he was clearing away smoke around him. They were deliberate, practiced hand movements.

A second later, the man with the brown derby simply disappeared.

One moment, the man sat in his chair at the end of the poker table, and the next moment, he was gone. His tall chair teetered for a second before it toppled over.

The large man stopped in his tracks, not sure what had just happened. Medesto froze too, his spoonful of dessert held in mid-bite. "Did you see that?" the gnome asked.

Ren had seen it. At first, he thought his eyes were playing tricks and the small man had fallen out of sight behind the table. But everyone at the gaming table was also looking for the missing card player.

The bruiser stared down at the cards on the tables. He picked up what should have been a second ace of diamonds from the pile and laid it next to the other ace. From Ren's vantage point, one of the card from Rollo's hand was now a two of spades. The poker player pounded his fists on the tabletop. Cards and poker chips bounced off the table and rained down on the floor.

Underneath the poker table, Ren watched a mass of rippling air, like heat waves coming off a hot sidewalk. It was vaguely human shaped and appeared to be crawling out from under the poker table, away from the commotion.

Once clear, the human-shaped anomaly stood up and moved with purpose toward the main exit, the heavy glass doors that led to the restaurant. The barely visible shape pushed through the unsuspecting patrons, leaving people jostled and confused in his wake.

"Are you seeing this?" Ren asked. No one else seemed to notice this strange phenomenon playing out in front of them.

"See what?" Medesto said. He was still watching the confusion at the gaming table.

"Nothing." Ren wondered if he should get involved. This invisible card player was cheating his employer's establishment, but still. He took a bite of his dessert and thought about that. There was no money in it for him. He was tired, and his cushioned booth was extremely comfortable. He dug back into the soufflé with his spoon and stayed where he was.

There was no magic in Rogue Destiny, so it was obvious the card player was using some kind of high-tech cloaking device, no doubt stolen from some science fictional world to make himself unseen by the normal eye. Ren looked back at the man who had been cheated. He stared out over the crowd with a befuddled look on his face.

The invisible figure reached the exit, only to change direction as the twin doors burst open and two security guards entered. A tall woman followed them in. She spoke to a porter who had been present when the ruckus began.

The woman rolled her eyes and searched the room. Her gaze fell on the rippling of light and shadow running down the aisle between the gaming tables and gave chase, striding across the floor with a long, quick gait. Maybe Ren was not the only one who could see the strange anomaly after all. The fugitive card player rounded a corner to find the woman approaching fast. He reversed course and turned down the row of booths where Ren and Medesto sat.

The gnome returned to his dessert, but the trickster watched the invisible fugitive approach, and as he passed, Ren stuck a foot out. Something solid struck Ren's foot. There was a hard thump and a round little man in a black coat with tails and a top hat appeared out of nowhere.

Medesto's eyes went wide, not in surprise at a man appearing out of thin air, but in disgust. "Rollo Pennymaker," he sighed.

Rollo Pennymaker was an odd-looking man with a round, impish face and quick, darting eyes that took in everything around him. He wore a black tuxedo with gold buttons and white spats over polished black shoes. The little man could have been someone's chauffeur or a major-domo, or a barker from some traveling carnival sideshow. Whoever he was, he was not happy at the moment. He jumped to his feet and shot an indignant glare at Ren, then brushed himself off and picked up his black top hat. He turned to go, only to find the tall woman barring his way.

Rollo waved his hands again, and in a strange shifting of prism and light, disappeared from sight once more. The tall woman stepped forward and grabbed at the empty air in front of her. Her arm jerked violently as she pulled the unseen man from the floor with one hand.

"I'm mythic, Rollo," the woman said, agitation in her voice. "Your cheap street illusions don't work on me." Her arm stopped shaking and the small man in the black tuxedo became visible again.

"Hello, Bijou," Rollo said with a meek smile.

"How many times have I banned you from the Turtle?" the woman asked. "Yet you continue coming back. I see you in here again, I will break something. Got it?"

She handed Rollo Pennymaker to the two security guards as if he were as light as a pillow. "Gentlemen, please escort Mr. Pennymaker from the premises," she said. Rollo hung limp in their arms as the men carried him away.

Bijou turned to Ren's table. "Evening, Medesto, how have you been?" she asked with a touch of a Jamaican accent.

"Can't complain. Just got back in town," the gnome said. "That was impressive. You could see Pennymaker?"

"One benefit of being me," she replied with a wry grin. "I see things as they should be, and not how they appear. Who's your friend?"

Ren stood and offered his hand before Medesto could answer. "Axel Prospero. Nice to meet you."

Bijou shook the outstretched hand, a skeptical look in her eyes. "Really? I don't think that's quite right," she said. "So, the old elf was able to track you down, eh?"

"We did, but it wasn't easy." Medesto yawned, covering his mouth with the back of his hand. "Ren, you remember Bijou Antilles, don't you?"

"Only by reputation," Ren replied. "Bijou Antilles, a daughter of the Caribbean, and folk hero of the islands. Sought exile in Rogue Destiny for reasons she never talks about. Last time I was around, you had just started with the Raconteurs, but our paths never crossed."

Bijou shook his hand. "Well, it's good to finally meet you, B'gatti."

Chapter 15
Mementos from the Past

Bijou Antilles stood a drop over six feet, with lean muscles and an easy smile. She wore a clean, white, buttoned-down work shirt with suspenders and brown khaki pants over high riding boots. A wide red band of cloth held her mass of black hair back.

"My adventuring days are behind me now," she said. "Since I partnered with Gideon, I'm content running the Turtle and providing the occasional muscle work where it's needed. It's nice to finally meet the enigmatic Ren B'gatti everyone's always talking about. Gideon said you might be returning. I assume you've considered his offer, or you wouldn't be here. We could certainly use the help."

"I'm here to do what I can," Ren said.

"You could see Rollo too, couldn't you?" Bijou asked with a gleam in her eye.

The trickster shrugged. "He was a rippling blur in the air, but I could tell where he was."

"Interesting," Bijou remarked. "There aren't many who can see through his cloaking glamour."

"But there's no magic here," Ren said. "It's one of my favorite things about the city."

"Rogue Destiny has no magic of its own," Bijou said. "And

under the laws of *transmitigation,* the purveyors of magic cannot bring it with them from other worlds. Their magic is not a part of who they are, it belongs in their Story. Rollo's different."

"What I just saw looked an awful lot like magic," Ren said.

"Not everything is as it seems," Bijou said. "Illusions are only a portion of Rollo's capabilities. He's able to cloak himself because the glamour is an essence of who he is. He doesn't relinquish it at the doorway of a new world like others do. Although his abilities are greatly inhibited in Rogue Destiny, he's far more dangerous than he wants anyone to believe."

"How that?" Ren asked.

"As the story goes, he tricked a Faery Prince out of his fae magic," Bijou replied. "How he did that is anyone's guess. Now he's one of the biggest smugglers of contraband into the City. Deals mostly in stolen magical artifacts and items of substantial power, but he's not above moving anything that makes him money. I think he comes to the Turtle to meet with his buyers, but I've never been able to prove it. No one knows Rollo's full capabilities, but even I wouldn't go up against him in his own domain."

"So, how does Rollo get around *transmitigation?*" Ren wondered out loud.

"Every rule has an exception," Medesto said. "You can shape-shift on any world, right?"

"So far."

"Not everyone can use their abilities outside their own Story," Bijou said. "That puts you in a different category from others with extraordinary gifts. Medesto's legendary strength is also an exception to the rule. I've always wondered if he's this powerful away from his homeworld, how strong is he inside the pages of *The Forgotten Gods.* For whatever reason, the law of *transmitigation* differs from person to person. The primal laws of the cosmos are strange that way, and inconsistent, to say the least."

Medesto shrugged with a feigned disinterest. "That's just a family trait. Giant's blood in our veins and what not," he said. "And like you said, not everything is as it seems."

Ren looked at him with amusement. There was some great secret surrounding Medesto's unnatural strength and near invulnerability, but he'd never revealed the details to anyone.

"And what about you, Bijou?" Medesto asked, quickly changing the subject. "What did you leave behind to come to Rogue Destiny?"

"I am me wherever I go," she said with a grin. "A benefit of being mythic. Although I seem to have lost some of my abilities for doing miraculous feats."

Medesto chuckled as he pushed away the empty soufflé dish. "Like saving a fleet of fishing boats from a hurricane by tying their nets together and throwing it over the storm, and pulling it out to sea?"

"Could have happened," Bijou said. She shrugged. "People talk."

Ren studied the face of the woman standing at their table. There was an ageless quality to her he couldn't quite figure out. She could have been anywhere between her early twenties to early forties, yet her dark eyes held a depth of wisdom and an intriguing timelessness to them.

"You should come with us," Ren suggested. "We could use you in a fight." He could tell Bijou contemplated the offer, but after a moment she shook her head.

"Tempting," she said, raising an eyebrow. "I'd love to be there to bring those outlaws to justice, but I fear the Obtuse Turtle wouldn't survive long without a constant eye kept on her. Besides, I've seen enough excitement to last me a few lifetimes. You'll do fine out there without me. If the battle ever came to Rogue Destiny, I'll be the first one in line defending Her."

Medesto headed toward the main entrance of the Obtuse Turtle. Ren followed after him, before he detoured to the check-in desk in the front lobby. He pulled the stolen wallet out of his back pocket and laid it on the counter.

"I found this on the floor," he told the girl working the desk. "Please make sure it's returned to its owner."

The young lady gave him a pleasant smile. "That's very nice of you. Not everyone is that honest. Have a good evening, sir." Ren gave her a grin and started for the front doors. He could feel the gnome glaring at him.

"Found it on the floor?" Medesto remarked.

"I gave it back," Ren retorted. "That's what matters."

"After buying yourself dinner."

"Then tell Gideon he needs to have food at our next meeting."

The two left the public house through the wide front doors. The cool night air was refreshing on Ren's face. They walked along the sidewalk on Portmanteau Boulevard until Medesto stopped under the glow of a gas streetlight to hail a cab. A horse-drawn Hansom cab answered the gnome's whistle and weaved through the evening traffic to the curb in front of them. The floating carriage bobbed as they climbed in and settled themselves on the cushioned seats.

"I'm just over a few blocks, but I'm too tired to walk," Medesto said. He told the coachman the address and leaned back in his seat. The driver tipped his hat, shook the reins, and the weightless cab jerked forward as they merged onto the street. The cab bounced in rhythm with the click-clack of the horse's hooves on the cobblestones.

"Axel Prospero, huh?" Medesto asked. "That's a face I haven't seen before. You have any other clandestine personas we don't know about?"

"Too many to mention," Ren replied.

"Any other things you're hiding from us?"

"Probably."

Medesto lived in an apartment building, about a mile from the Obtuse Turtle. He paid the driver and grabbed his traveling bag. The two climbed up the stoop to the front doors of the ten-story structure. Medesto pulled his keys out and unlocked the decoratively carved front door.

Ren wandered the narrow lobby while Medesto stopped at a mailbox, opening the box with another key and pulled out a number of envelopes. He scanned each one and stuck them into his coat pocket. They crossed to the elevator. The gnome opened the elevator's collapsible metal gate and pushed the button to the top floor. Ren closed the gate behind them. The antiquated elevator rumbled up ten flights until, with a shaky jerk, it quivered to a stop. They exited.

"I came into some money recently," Medesto said. He unlocked the door to his apartment. "So I bought the entire top floor for the privacy." He dropped his traveling bag on a couch and clicked on a worn art deco lamp.

Ren shifted from his Axel Prospero persona and walked about the main room, taking in the expansive apartment's museum quality décor. In one corner, an enormous dragon's skull sat. Large turquoise eyes flashed as the lights came on. Its open mouth was fashioned into an easy chair, its lower jaw stuffed with cushions.

Every literary genre seemed to be represented in the room. Primitive bronze swords and high-tech armaments filled a dozen display in glass cases. Statuettes of mythical and famous literary figures stood on tables and shelves. A life preserver from a ship called the *Lusitania* hung on the bedroom door. The rest of the walls were adorned with bladed weapons of every type.

Ren thumbed through a shelf of vinyl records composed of blues and jazz composers. Next to the shelves an antique phonograph sat. He looked into the next room, where the oddities and curios continued. "You have accumulated a lot of junk over the years."

"I see them as mementos of a life well lived," Medesto replied. "When I moved in, I busted out the walls of all the adjoining apartments to accommodate my trinkets and baubles. It's nice to have reminders of where you've been and what you've seen. It makes the hard times a little less rough when you have good times to look back on."

Ren thought about that. He owned nothing himself. He wasn't sure if that was a good thing or not. Even the clothes on his back weren't his. He noticed a hookah pipe on the hearth of the fireplace, then a blacksmith's hammer mounted on the wall above it. The long handled flat-nosed mallet was massive.

"You still have the hammer, I see?" he asked.

"Yeah, if they want it back," Medesto replied. "They can come and get it. If you want to change out of what you're wearing, there are clean clothes in any of the spare bedrooms."

"You think they'll ever come looking for it?" Ren asked.

"They have to find me first," the gnome replied. "But who knows, anything's possible." He kicked off his dragon-skin boots at the front door. "Anyway, I'm going to bed. You'll find tea, coffee, and maybe soda in the icebox. Might even be something edible in the cupboards. There are several bedrooms visiting dignitaries used, so take whichever one you want. I've got the master suite because it has the most comfortable mattress. I'm a decent host, but a soft bed is where my hospitality ends. See you in the morning." He ambled off toward the bedroom, but he stopped at the doorway.

"What?" Ren asked.

"I almost forgot," Medesto said. He pointed to a wooden crate sitting on the dining room table. "That's a few of Claymore's personal effects we grabbed before the Council got to them. Just old knick-knacks and personal whatnots. Thought you might want to look through them. Might be some of your belongings in there, too."

"Thanks," Ren said. The handle of a holstered firearm was all he could see sticking out of the crate.

"And please be here when I wake up," Medesto added.

"Why wouldn't I be?"

"Because you have a tendency to disappear," the gnome replied, stifling a yawn. "And don't bother to go looking for Claymore. We've scoured the city for weeks and told every contact and informant we have to be on the lookout for him. Trust me, if he was in the City, we would have found him."

"I'll be here," Ren mumbled. He glanced around the main room, trying to decide where he wanted to sleep, but his eyes kept drifting back to the crate.

"Be sure you are." The bedroom door closed with resounding finality, leaving Ren alone among the trinkets and bric-à-brac of the gnome's world-trotting adventures. He stood there for a long time, staring at the wooden crate across the room, somehow hesitant to go near it. What could be in the box that he would care a whit about?

In his time with the Raconteurs, Ren had faced down horrors that would have kept most people from ever having a peaceful night's sleep again. But the unknown of what might be in the crate scared him more than anything he had ever experienced in the field.

Curiosity got the better of him, and Ren peered over the edge of the crate. He was more relieved than he should have been to see nothing but an assortment of rolled-up maps, postcards, and a pile of old snapshots.

He pulled the pistol from its leather holster. It was the original tracer gun Claymore had brought back from some mission. It was the prototype Natascha used to design the Raconteurs' own state-of-the-art Peacemaker. *Lightning in a gun*, she dubbed it. it was identical to the one she used on him inside *The Crimson Masque*. The non-lethal weapon was a favorite among the Raconteurs in bringing down the bad guys. It felt well balanced and familiar in his grip. He clicked it on and checked the light on the side. The charge was dead.

He rarely carried a firearm, preferring swords in combat when he wasn't shape-shifting. He holstered the pistol, wrapped the belt around it, and dropped it on top of the crate.

Ren pulled off his own boots, grabbed a fuzzy blanket from the back of the couch, and threw it over a shoulder. He took the box of memorabilia out onto the balcony overlooking the City. Sitting on a chair, he put it down in front of him and started picking through the contents.

He pulled out a stack of photos held together with string. They were snapshots of Claymore's career with the Raconteurs, from its founding to just before the incident in *The Angels of Avalon.*

Thumbing through them, Ren saw a lot of faces that were no longer around. In one photo, Claymore stood next to one of the first experimental Runabouts, the early predecessor to the slipstream. Its appearance was bulky and awkward compared to the ones that would follow.

The next picture showed Sebastian with his children gathered around him. The patriarch of the Poe family looked happier than Ren had ever seen him. His two daughters, Danique and B'Tori held him close on both sides while their cybernetic brother, Gossamer 99, towered over everyone.

The last of the photographs showed Ren when he first joined the Raconteurs. The picture showed him sitting around a table with Claymore, Sully, Medesto and Natascha, playing cards. An irritation flared up in him until it grew to a contained anger as he thought of how Claymore had been abandoned to the mercies of Lazaranth Prison. He tossed the pictures back into the crate. Too many memories were being dredged up, and he was exhausted by it all.

He curled up in the patio chair with the blanket wrapped tight around him and stared up at the multitude of worlds floating in the darkening sky. Nightfall never reached complete darkness over the city. It only settled into a deep twilight that cloaked everything in shadow.

Ren watched the flickering city lights through half-closed eyes as his thoughts drifted back to Claymore. He was convinced his partner was somewhere in the City. But how to find him?

Medesto and the others may not have found Claymore, but that didn't mean he wasn't out there. After a few minutes, Ren slipped into a dream of riding the Paris countryside as the outlaw, Talbot Mundi.

Chapter 16
Beggar's Row

Ren woke with a start, not knowing how long he had been asleep. It took him a moment before he realized where he was, back in Rogue Destiny on the balcony outside Medesto's flat. The sky above him had deepened to night.

Rogue Destiny was known as the City of a Thousand Moons, even though it had no real moons, stars, or sun. The lazy glow of celestial bodies overhead put him in a melancholy state of mind. The vast open sky was peppered with hundreds of shining orbs, some the size of moons, others nothing but tiny specks. These were the written worlds whose denizens lived out their existence, forever locked in the reoccurring cycle of their Stories. Never knowing the freedom that Rogue Destiny's citizens took for granted.

The crate of Claymore's personal belongings sat at his feet, partially covered by his discarded blanket. A breeze came in over the terrace as he rubbed his eyes and stretched, trying to clear the cobwebs. He stood up and looked over the sprawling cityscape in front of him.

The heartbeat of the city pounded in Ren's ears. He heard the sound of street music drifting up off the distant waterfront. It was familiar, comforting to him. The warm wind felt good on his face, and he realized he was free in a way he had not been in a while. His head was clear, no Muse controlled his thoughts, and no one told him what to do or what his responsibilities were.

He had questions that needed answering, and that always made him restless. He never waited around for things to fall into place on their own. With sleep no longer a concern, he needed something to occupy his mind and burn off the discontent building inside him. He smiled, wondering if the City's nightlife was as wild as it used to be and if Claymore was out there somewhere.

He gazed out over the ancient structures mixed in among the modern architectural designs. Glass spires, towers, and smokestacks spread out across the parishes, boroughs, and Victorian districts. Most of the City's denizens held tight to traditions and memories they carried with them from their homeworlds. Hundreds of diverging neighborhoods came together in a patchwork tapestry that made Rogue Destiny a place unlike any other.

He was still wanted by every legal authority in the City, but no one knew he was back in town. So wherever this night led him, Ren could move around undetected.

Ren glanced back at Medesto's bedroom door and remembered that he'd promised he wouldn't leave. With luck, he would be back before dawn and Medesto would be none the wiser. After all, it was the gnome's fault for leaving him alone to his own devices.

He unbuttoned the ill-fitting shirt he borrowed from the Obtuse Turtle, then stepped back from the edge of the railing and focused his will. Flesh and bones morphed at his command. His body shrank smaller and smaller, sprouting feathers as his arms spread into wings and he looked out at the world through the eyes of a raven. Ren hopped out of the pile of clothing, and with a flap of his wings, cleared the balcony railing. He flew over the rooftops toward his favorite part of the City.

His wings caught an updraft of wind, rising higher and higher toward the distant sounds of music. The night air was invigorating. It felt good to shift into something other than mundane bipedal forms he all too often had to take.

Beggar's Row lay in one of the oldest parts of Rogue Destiny. Beyond the festive lights stood the black spired tower of Baltazar Gheddi, the founder of the island city. One day, Ren would venture into the obsidian monolith and learn its secrets. But not tonight. He needed to stay on task and track down information on his wayward partner.

From the air, the narrow winding streets and alleyways of tilting stone and wood buildings created an intricate catacomb of passageways. The music grew as Ren glided between the buildings over the bustling crowds of night people. He landed on a slanted, shingled roof overlooking a crowded street. The entire area was lit with a multitude of colored lights pushing back the darkness. The music and bustle of the rowdy street crowds reverberated off the buildings. To the west lay the harbor that opened out to the Dreaming Sea.

It took Ren a minute to get his bearings. He flew down a side street, banked around a lofty bell tower and down among the chimneys to a flat rooftop. He landed under a water tank perched precariously on the edge of a six-story building of cut stone. In the shadows, he morphed back into his bipedal form.

The place was one of several hideouts he maintained during his time with the Raconteurs. After a yearlong absence, he knew the tiny apartment would have a new tenant, but he was there for something else. Even the greatest trickster in Rogue Destiny could not walk the streets naked. Fortunately, he had prepared for the situation. If the box was still there.

He looked behind a rusty generator and found the wooden box he had left there wedged in against the stone wall. Behind a loose brick in the wall was a small leather sheath containing a key to the padlock on the box.

None of his hideouts were elegant, and most weren't even practical. Nothing about the trickster was. The bounty money he received from his work with the Raconteurs had never been enough to make him wealthy, but it allowed him a place to maintain a stash of extra clothes.

As Ren dressed, a glint of something in the bottom of the box caught his attention. It was oval shaped, encased in a leather backing. A stylized compass design with a crescent moon was engraved in the dense metal. It was Claymore's Raconteur badge. The significance of what it meant was not lost on him.

He picked up the badge with a sad smile. He'd grabbed it in the confusion after his partner's arrest and kept it in hope of one day returning it to him. Claymore had always insisted a badge gave a Raconteur authority, but Ren refused to carry one. He slid his partner's badge onto his belt. Now he had some authority to throw around. And tonight he might need it.

Ren had chosen the apartment because of its quick access to the ground by way of a fire escape. After dressing, Ren chose the same face he had taken at the Obtuse Turtle. He climbed down the fire escape. A moment later, the goateed personae of Axel Prospero walked out of a dark alley, buttoning his shirt.

Ren was solitary by nature, preferring to do things alone. Beggar's Row was a place where he could lose himself in the crowded streets. He had missed the vibrations and rhythm of the place, the breath of the crowd and the height of the tall buildings hemming in the narrow streets. For the first time since returning to the island city, a sense of familiarity and a peace came over him. He was in his element here, more at home among these outcasts and misfits than with any royalty he had met in his travels.

He wandered the twisting, narrow streets, letting the music and the aromas of a hundred worlds wash over him. The crowded streets were a menagerie of cultures and genres. Rogue Destiny offered them something they could find nowhere else. A freedom from the predestined lives within their written worlds. The city's citizens were no longer bound to the Narratives of their Story. They were free to choose their own destiny, for better or worse.

Most citizens found their way to there by way of the mysterious doorways at the edges of their worlds. Others were told of Rogue Destiny by those that knew of its existence. Some remained, others moved on, lured by what else might be at the end of the next rabbit-hole. Either way, once someone learned the truth of their existence, that they were nothing more than a character in a Book, a whole new world of possibilities opened up for them. If they didn't go mad from the knowledge.

He turned a corner, edging past crowds of drunken revelers and street dancers. Glowing shop signs and paper lanterns hung from every storefront and restaurant entranceway, bathing the streets in an ethereal glow. Most of the buildings were many stories high, creating a canyon-like effect. Electrical wires stretched across the narrow streets, decorated with lanterns, banners and flags from hundreds of different worlds.

Many around him spoke in the common street tongue unique to Rogue Destiny. Ren's memory was sharp, and he quickly picked up on any new languages he came across at astounding speed. It was even faster in this case because he was familiar with it already. His mind was free of any memory loss from the Muse's influence, so he strode through the streets with purpose, listening to snatches of conversation from the people around him.

Buskers played at every corner, filling the air with music from steel drums to long-stringed lutes to hammer dulcimers. The sound vibrated the very air itself around him. Ren quickened his pace as his surroundings became more familiar. He knew where he needed to go.

He had no real plan in mind on how he would locate Claymore. His old partner would say start with what you know. He knew what he needed was to find the street gang he used to run with, *The Gentlemen of Fortune*. If anyone had heard rumors of Claymore roaming the City, it would be them. The thought that Claymore may not even be in the city came to mind, but he refused to entertain the idea.

Turning up a slanting narrow street, Ren found the place he was hunting for, *The Pithy Fool Teahouse and Lounge*. A hangout from a more untamed period in his life when he ran with a local street gang called *The Gentlemen of Fortune*, looking for trouble wherever they could find it. They were the only ones he's ever truly trusted. They wanted nothing from him but his friendship.

He walked through the front of the restaurant and looked around the boisterous environment. The establishment was a notorious haunt for the more unsavory inhabitants of Rogue Destiny. Grifters, killers, soldiers for hire all here to swap war stories, waited for their next chance at employment or working out the details of their next great con. Musicians played on the stage at the back of the room. Their eclectic music filled the air as couples milled about and danced in front of the stage. Law enforcement rarely wandered Beggar's Row unless there was a very good reason.

A fight broke out to his right, but half-dozen bouncers were on top of it in seconds, and the instigators were quietly escorted out the front doors.

The place was filled to capacity with a menagerie of patrons crowding the bar. Dozens of ethnicities, races and genus, human and otherwise, clamored to be heard over the noise. Ren saw a large booth in a back corner. He recalled the schemes of riches and glory that were devised at that table during his time with the *Gentlemen of Fortune*. In the end, all their talk never amounted to anything but unrealized pipe dreams. The thought made him sad. If he hadn't been recruited away by Claymore and the Raconteurs, no telling what they may have accomplished. They were good people, and he remembered his days with them fondly. He scanned the room but failed to see any of his ex-comrades.

The bouncer at the front door was a brute of a man, wide and well-muscled, a serpent tattoo curled around his sleeveless arm, disappearing under the leather vest and dreadlocks only to reappear wrapped around his neck and ending on the side of his face. The snake's head was opened mouth, with fangs ready to strike. He stared down at Ren with a snarl.

"I'm looking for a group of malcontents that used to hang out here," Ren said. "*The Gentlemen of Fortune?*"

The brute shifted his stance to a more threatening angle,

looming over Ren with small, cruel eyes. "Never heard of them." he growled.

"They're a vicious gang of miscreants wanted by every law enforcement agency in the city."

"Still haven't heard of them."

Unfazed, Ren continued. "Ok, maybe you know them by name. Tote Rossiter?"

"Nope."

"Oolong Bok, Sozo Vantage, Anon Ronin?"

"No".

"Mucluc Ludlow? Sojourn Kardia?"

The doorman's expression didn't change. "Mucluc works in the kitchen," he grumbled.

"Great, I need to ask him a few questions.

"I said he's working, so unless you're here to buy something, you need to leave."

Ren raised his eyebrows as the bruiser crossed his arms over his chest, trying to intimidate him further. Gideon had asked the trickster to keep a low profile, so he resisted the urge to show the doorman real intimidation. Instead, he pulled Claymore's Raconteur badge from his pocket and shoved it the bouncer's face. "This says I can."

"The Raconteurs don't have any authority here," the bouncer growled. Something in his tone sounded less convinced.

"That's where you're wrong," Ren replied. "Mucluc Ludlow is suspected in a serious of vicious murders and if I don't speak to him I'll have twenty agents down her in a matter of minutes. Then we'd have to shut you down for a couple of days until we check the credentials and background of every individual in here to make sure they're not wanted for some crime, either. I'm sure that will make your manager happy."

The bouncer thought about that. "You have five minutes."

"Thank you." Ren descended the steps and moved through the press of bodies at a causal pace, nodding to anyone who made eye contact with him. He made his way toward the bar. He felt the bouncer's eyes on him the whole time. He wasn't there to make trouble, but he needed to speak to Mucluc and find out where the rest of the *Gentlemen* were these days. One of them might have information on Claymore's whereabouts, or at least if anyone has seen him. He saw the doorway and disappeared into the kitchen area.

Mucluc Ludlow wasn't the brightest of individuals, but he was loyal to a fault — and certainly not the mass murderer, Ren told the bouncer he was. Never too good at taking care of himself, Mucluc relied on the *Gentlemen* to keep him safe. He'd wandered out from a children's book about monsters under the bed. He was one of a dozen creatures that showed up throughout the night trying to get the little boy to go to sleep. Mucluc had taken the moniker 'Ludlow,' insisting a last name would gain him respect among the denizens of the City. He argued everyone had a last name, so he should too. The group laughed about it, but the name stuck.

In Mucluc's mind, a last name would somehow make people overlook his 300 pounds of mottled green-yellow colored skin covered in warts and pustules, and his seven eyes that sat at various angles on his head. Little clusters of whiskers grew where they would in all directions. How Mucluc ended up in Rogue Destiny was a mystery, but everyone had their own story.

Mucluc Ludlow usually wore a white dress shirt and gentlemen's vest, both much too small for his doughy frame, and a tiny bolo hat perched on the top of his spiny head. He'd say it made him look respectable and would help him fit in with proper society. The monster from under the bed considered himself a dandy in his hat and fine clothes, warts and all.

Tonight, Mucluc wore a greasy apron and hairnet that did little to constrain his spiny tufts of hair. His squat, bowed legs were too short for his wide frame, and his thick, bulbous arms were too long. A tentacle that served as a prehensile tail was always twitching behind him. He waddled past Ren without a look, carrying a tub of dirty dishes into the backroom. The shape-shifter followed him to a steaming vat of soapy water. They were alone in the back corner of the kitchen, so Ren melted back into his natural persona.

"Hello, Mr. Ludlow," Ren said, mimicking Mucluc's deep-throated voice. "How are you this fine evening?" The monster's misshapen head turned toward him, and all seven eyes lit up. He almost dropped the tub of dishes he carried in his flippered hands.

"Reen Boogatti," he croaked. His toad-like mouth broke into a huge grin. "Where you been all dis time?" He set the tub down and pulled Ren in for a slimy, sticky hug.

"I've been away," Ren said, pulling away as soon as he could without appearing impolite. His shirt was wet and covered in a green mucus from the embrace.

"You still working for dat Geedeon who stealed you away from us?"

"For now," Ren said. "Where's Tote or the others? I need to talk to them."

"Oh, dey all dead," Mucluc replied, rinsing them off with a sprayer. "You and me da only ones left from dose days." He didn't look at Ren, but his mouth quivered slightly.

Ren watched the grotesque creature in front of him wash dishes in the filthy water and set them on a drainer at the end of the sink. By his physical appearance, Mucluc belonged inside a bad dream. But in truth, he was a gentle soul, lost and wandering. Like most of the City's inhabitants, he was just trying to find his way in life. His wide mouth overemphasized words as he spoke. Long streams of saliva stretched from his top lip to the bottom as if he were chewing a mouthful of taffy. His mouth always appeared to be smiling, even when he was angry or confused. He was a kind-natured but clueless beast. Ren always preferred the company of the bizarre and outcast.

"Is there someplace we can talk in private?" Ren asked.

"I like to," Mucluc replied, "but I have to get back to work before Mr. MacAvoy yell at me again."

"Mucluc!" a voice bellowed from the dining room.

All seven of Mucluc's eyes widened. "Oh, dere he is."

Ren morphed back into Axel Prospero as the owner of the voice emerged from the dining area. MacAvoy was a short, thick man with a neck beard, wearing a bright shirt spotted with pineapples. He stomped up to Mucluc and pointed a plump finger in the monster's face.

"Mucluc, so help me," he spat. "This is the last time I'm going to tell you to keep up with the dirty tables out there. They're backed up and people are waiting to be seated! The dishes are piling up in the sink and the garbage cans are overflowing again. Tell your friend to move along, or I'll fire you right now and you can leave with him!"

The doorman with the snake tattoo appeared in the doorway to the kitchen. "They're here," he announced. "You want me to take them downstairs?"

MacAvoy's face paled. He wrung his hands together and looked around at nothing before he took a deep breath. "No. I have to do it."

The bouncer nodded, and they left the kitchen together. Ren pulled the curtain back to watch MacAvoy push through the crowd out to the front doors of the restaurant. Three cloaked figures stood together at the top of the steps. The four of them huddled close for a moment before MacAvoy lead the three down the stairs and through the crowd.

"Who's that with MacAvoy?" Ren asked.

"I not know," Mucluc replied, staring over Ren's shoulder. "Not ever seen them before right now."

They stopped at a double door on the far side of the room. Several people sat at a booth next to it. They stopped laughing and drinking as MacAvoy's group reached them. One of the lackies stood up and opened the door for them with a slight bow.

"Where does that door go?" Ren asked, walking out into the main room.

Mucluc returned to washing the dishes. "Down under the Pithy Fool Teahouse and Lounge. There are secret rooms down there I'm not supposed to know about, but I do."

"I'm going to go have a look," Ren said.

"Dat not sound like smart idea."

"I won't be long," Ren replied. "I'll come find you after I'm done. I have questions I hope you can help me with." He walked back to the row of sinks full of dishes. There was a partition that separated it from the rest of the kitchen area.

"Dere will be lots of people round, so you better bring your best disguises."

"I will," Ren said. "Thank you, Mucluc."

"No problem." A grin spread across Mucluc's broad face. "Dat what friends for."

Ren unbuttoned his shirt and stripped down to nothing behind the partition. After hiding his clothes and shoes on a shelf in the back of the kitchen, he calmed his thoughts and focused on the image in his head. After a moment, his muscles quivered in response. Small and inconspicuous would get him in and out easily enough.

Mucluc chortled in glee as he watched Ren fly out of the back kitchen in the form of a conspicuously oversized housefly.

Chapter 17
The Spider and the Fly

R en buzzed along the ceiling, toward the five rough-looking individuals sitting at a table next to an arched doorway at the back of the room. He circled the area and landed on the top of the wooden door frame. The thought came to him that he was taking an enormous risk. One that threatened his mission with the Raconteurs and his efforts to find Claymore. That small part of his brain where he kept his common sense screamed at him to abandon this foolishness and go back to searching for his partner, before things spiraled out of control. He didn't listen.

The teahouse was an ancient structure full of history. The antiquated door frame in the rear of the room provided sizable gaps in the doorjamb, and with some effort Ren wedged his tiny insect body through the gap between the door and the frame. A darkened hallway was on the other side. Ren flew from the wooden frame, his buzzing wings echoed in the dark silence as they carried him down the hallway. There was another corridor to his right.

The sound of raucous revelry could be heard ahead. He followed the noise down a set of narrow stairs. At the end of the hall, the darkness was broken by the sliver of light escaping from beneath the gap of an ancient wooden door. Loud voices came from the room beyond. Ren landed on the floor for a peek inside.

The smoke-filled inner sanctum was dimly lit by several flat oil lamps on a long wooden table at the center of the room. Barrels sat along one side, and large kettles for the fermentation of beer stood on another. Shadows filled every corner. The flickering flames threw chaotic shapes on the walls. On the far side of the table sat an oversized man in an equally oversized chair. The gangsters' meeting seemed to be getting underway. The three council members sat together at one end of the long table. The Pithy Fool's manager, MacAvoy, stood away from the table, ignored by everyone.

Piqwic York was a fat, sweaty man whose gluttonous appetites were only overshadowed by his monetary acuity. Ren recognized him on sight. The man's pudgy face held small, deep-set eyes that disappeared behind rolls of fat whenever he laughed or smiled. Piqwic's love of money and his ability to hide it from the authorities was legendary throughout the City's underworld. It was this genius financial acumen that allowed the rotund man to walk among the criminal elite of Rogue Destiny. Ren knew that much.

The vulgar financier sat at the head of the enormous banquet table, entertaining a group of men and women. The chair he sat on was wide and sturdy, built to accommodate his girth. Four hardened enforcers stood watch over the proceedings. Each was armed and appeared ready to clamp down on any that might become disagreeable as the night progressed.

Around Piqwic sat the seven leaders from the City's dominant gangs, guilds, and criminal fraternities. All of them paid the *Society of the Black Rose* tribute in exchange for the right to conduct business within the city limits without fear of reprisal. Ren recognized most of the assembled gang leaders from his wilder days with the *Gentlemen of Fortune*. Directly behind Piqwic stood the largest human Ren had ever seen.

Odd Bod.

The man was well over seven feet tall, twice the width of any normal human, with large sloping shoulders, empty vacant eyes, and a protruding bottom lip. He had to weigh over 400 pounds.

Just the name of Mordecai Davos' Grand Enforcer instilled fear throughout Rogue Destiny. Odd Bod was the frequent subject of conversation during Ren's time with the *Gentlemen*. He had never met the man personally, but it was rumored the giant was responsible for hundreds of deaths and unsolved disappearances. The authorities of Rogue Destiny had been chasing him for years. The behemoth stood silent as a statue, hands behind his back. His half cast eyes stared forward with no emotion.

Ren's wings buzzed, and he lifted off the floor in a slow circle, buzzing past MacAvoy's ear before ascending above the table the gangsters gathered around. The stench of alcohol and tobacco filled the room.

The strain of holding his tiny form together was beginning to take its toll. Ren flew to the wall across from Piqwic, landing on a wooden ledge. Below him, Piqwic held the enraptured attention of his audience.

"This past year has been good for the criminal element of this fair city," Piqwic said, holding out his arms in a conciliatory manner. "And tonight, we are here to celebrate."

A great shout rose from the table. Glasses were clinked and congratulations passed around. Several servers stood ready with bottles of wine and other spirits.

Piqwic nodded to the head waiter, who clapped his hands twice, prompting the staff to move with precision around the crowded room. One server handed out the evening dinner menus, while others replenished empty glasses and replaced empty platters of appetizers with fresh ones. Piqwic sat back, reveling in the moment.

"Tonight, the ruling apparatus of Rogue Destiny," he said with a raised glass. "The Common Council of Public Sympathy and Eternal Vigilance sleeps in fear of us and what we have accomplished. They grow ever more corrupt and apathetic by the day. Those not already under Mordecai's iron grip are too frightened to stand against him. If they knew what was about to be unleashed upon the City, they would be even more terrified."

Another cheer went up. "To Mordecai Davos, the true emperor of Rogue Destiny!" someone shouted. Others followed with, "To Piqwic! To *The Black Rose!*"

A tall, fiery-haired woman, Cassandra of the Nine Sisters, furrowed her brow, then drained her glass and set it down loudly on the table. "I must ask why three members of the Common Council join us this evening. Just being seen in this part of the city will raise unwanted questions."

Piqwic emptied his own goblet and raised it to be refilled by a nearby waiter. "Each are vying for a position that has opened up within the *Black Rose*," he said. "A rare opportunity that does not come along very often."

"Then tell us about the rumors that Mordecai has left the city," Cassandra said. "Why would he be taking such a personal risk when he pays others to take those risks for him? Tell me, York, what is he looking for out there?"

Piqwic shook his head and chuckled. "Who can know the mind of Mordecai Davos? The Master does not divulge such things to his underlings." He shifted around in his chair, his great belly jiggling as he made himself more comfortable. "We have much to celebrate and much more to discuss about the coming new year. We bid goodbye to the Year of the Leviathan, but Mordecai promises to make the year of the Jabberwock a spectacular one indeed."

That answered one of Ren's lingering questions. Gideon's theory that Mordecai Davos had indeed left Rogue Destiny was correct.

Piqwic's thick sausage fingers picked up a crème puff and popped it in his mouth. He brushed at the crumbs on the front of his expensive red-velvet greatcoat trimmed in gold thread. He looked up as he finished clearing off bits of pastry, his face now a mask of cold steel.

"But with success comes change," he said, his voice low and serious. "Mordecai has decided that every territory is to fall under the jurisdiction of the *Black Rose*. This is how it will be from now on. No more freebooting. All jobs must be approved ahead of their execution."

The gang leaders at the table shifted about uneasily and murmured their disagreements amongst themselves. Ren knew these working-class gangs had neither the strength nor the will to resist Mordecai's *Society of the Black Rose* for long. Piqwic chuckled, incredibly pleased with himself.

The man sitting across from Piqwic stared at him, displeased with these new revelations. His tight, thin lips and gaunt features showed no emotion. He was bald except for the coarse facial hair protruding off his chin. The beard forked into two, each side braided with beads and carved pieces of wood. Ren knew him to be Ooturo Bacraan, the leader of the *Sons of Malachi*.

"Then why bother to pay tribute to Mordecai at all?" the man asked. "We supply you with muscle when you ask. We kill who you need dead, no questions asked. Doesn't that give us the right to earn a living in the way of our own choosing? The *Sons* do business with our homeworld. Will that be allowed to continue?"

Piqwic gave Ooturo a nod. "The *Sons'* loyalty has not gone unnoticed. Mordecai has decreed your annual tribute will be cut by one third, but from now on all decisions are to go through me. I speak for the Master until he returns. As for the smuggling operations from your homeworld, those can continue without interruption. According to his letters, it is only the ancient treaties among the gangs of Rogue Destiny that concern Mordecai."

"Are you saying Mordecai is breaking the blood treaties that have kept the peace between the gangs since before my father's father ruled the *Sons?*" Ooturo's voice was a barely contained hiss through clenched teeth. "Is that what I'm hearing?"

"That is *exactly* what I'm saying, Ooturo." Piqwic gave Ooturo a cold smile. "Mordecai was very adamant that all gang leaders sign a loyalty oath to the *Black Rose*, and immediately come under our direct protection." Piqwic pulled a piece of paper from his coat and unfolded it in front of him on the table. "Otherwise, they will have no protection from what is coming."

Ooturo pushed himself up out of his chair in a huff. Four of the five bodyguards standing around the table reached for their weapons. Only Odd Bod remained motionless. Ooturo raised his hands in front of him. "Just stepping out to the jakes, boys, nothing to worry yourselves about," he said gruffly, then looked to Piqwic until he nodded his consent. Ooturo disappeared out a hallway at the back of the room.

Ren watched Ooturo leave and saw it as his chance to ditch his current insect disguise. He dropped from the wall and flew toward the dark hallway after Ooturo.

He buzzed past the darkest corner of the wide room. It was in deep shadow, free from the glow of lamplight. An overwhelming wave of terror swept over Ren. It was not fear of being discovered by those in the room, but something deeper, more primal. His tiny heart fluttered in panic as his winged body shivered involuntarily.

He felt the stare of unnatural eyes on him. Something watched from the shadows. He changed his course and buzzed over the main table to get as far as he could from whatever lurked in the darkness. He landed on a tapestry hanging on the wall behind Piqwic and his bodyguards.

"There are big changes coming," Piqwic said. "Not only for us, but for all of Rogue Destiny. And once it is over, those who stood with the *Black Rose* will be on a permanent holiday. You just need to trust what I am telling you."

"And if any of us refuse to sign?" Hayeship Gribblin said. He was a gruff, older man with a flat nose that had been broken many times. The scars on his hands and face were a reminder of what it took to rise through the succession of leaders to rule the *Mad Dogs of Raparees*.

"I understand if you choose not to sign," Piqwic said with a cryptic smile. "Just because Mordecai is not physically here among us doesn't mean he is not in charge. And let me remind everyone sitting here tonight that we have the power to crush any who might decide to resist these changes. You will either abide by these new standards or be swept away under the tide of progress. I will not personally hold it against you, but there are others who might. Jester, if you would be so kind."

The room went cold. The rancid stench of decay and death blew across the still air. From the shadowy corner Ren had avoided moments before, a vaguely human-shaped figure emerged. A long tattered black cloak hid the body and face, except for the lower half of a human skull that protruded from under the hood. The creature's bony jaw was locked in a grotesque, frozen grin. Everything went silent as the wraith slowly glided across the room. Ren swore the dark hood paused for a moment to stare at the very spot where he clung to the side of the tapestry.

Piqwic's grin faded. "The Grimm Jester here is the liaison between myself and the Master. We have been in constant correspondence since his departure, receiving updates on his progress and instructions on how we should prepare for his return."

He reached inside the red greatcoat and pulled out a large manila envelope, bulging with papers. He handed it to the wraith. The Grimm Jester produced several letters tied with string from under its black cloak and traded them with the rotund financier. Piqwic's hand trembled as he took the letters.

Cassandra leaned back in her chair and sipped her beer. "Letters?" She scoffed. "Given the technology available to the *Black Rose*, Mordecai sends handwritten letters to his underlings? Isn't that rather archaic?"

"Mordecai is careful and secretive above all else," Piqwic replied. "He feels this method is the best way to ensure no one intercepts our communications. Who better than the Grimm Jester to keep our correspondence safe?"

Letters from Mordecai? Ren thought. They could lead to the criminal's whereabouts, or at least reveal what he was searching for. He needed to get to those letters.

"You don't scare us, York," a voice said. "Enough with your phantasms and empty threats." Dom Tarran Ran from the *Grand Excelsior Clan* sat up in his chair. He was a small compact man who wore a flat-topped black hat with no band. His long greasy hair flowed to his shoulders, and each ear sparkled with several dangling earrings. A sharp-cut black suit over a red shirt and glossy black tie with a red tie pin completed his look.

"Let's be real here," Dom Tarran Ran said. "Mordecai fears what the *Excelsior Clan* has become in recent years. He wants us to drop our guard so he can come at us when we least expect it. I won't sign, and my people bow to no one."

He pulled a chain from his coat pocket with a strange talisman hanging from it. It was a small, clear oblong globe wrapped in decorative wires. He held it up toward the hooded figure. The eerie blue liquid inside glowed with a blue light that grew brighter the longer he held it.

"I know what you are capable of, monster," Dom said. "And figured you'd play a part here tonight, so I brought my own protection."

The shrouded face of the Grimm Jester stared at the object in the gangster's hand. The creature seemed intimidated by the sight of it. "Where did you get that?" the wraith hissed, backing away slightly. Its voice was a whisper of harsh wind through hollow bones.

Odd Bod moved for the first time. He picked up an empty water glass and lofted it into the air toward Dom. It shattered on the stone floor next to the *Excelsior Clan's* leader. Dom Tarran Ran's head turned at the sound, and the Grimm Jester was on him.

The wraith covered the distance between them in a heartbeat and caught the wrist that held the orb in a bony grip. The sound of bones crunching filled the silence of the room. Dom cried out and dropped the glowing talisman. The *Grand Excelsior Clan* leader went for his shoulder holster, but the Grimm Jester grabbed him by the face with its other hand. Long, skeletal fingers wrapped around the gangster's head and lifted him into the air. Dom gave a muffled scream. The creature leaned in and hissed into his ear, "You have no idea what I am capable of."

The Grimm Jester held Dom Tarran Ran aloft as a wave of dark energy engulfed him. Anyone in the immediate vicinity jumped back from the sparks flying off the gangster. The air crackled and Dom's body twitched, then went limp in the monster's grip. Slowly, his skin shriveled until nothing remained, but a mummified leathery husk wrapped tightly around his skeleton. After the energy dissipated, the cloaked wraith tossed the lifeless corpse aside. A thin gray mist rose from the dead man's body as it fell to the floor.

Without a word, the Grimm Jester floated back to the shadows and disappeared. Cassandra stared wide eyed at the dark corner, and then down at the smoking remains of Dom Tarran Ran. A visible shiver ran through her. She cleared her throat. "Mordecai has long favored the *Nine Sisters*, so we will sign this agreement," she concluded. "The other Sisters may not be happy with the changes, but I will assuage their fears. For your fat sake, you better not be wrong about this, York."

"And that is why you're the leader of the *Nine Sisters*," Piqwic said. "Level headed and wise beyond your years. You know when to fight and when to cede power for the greater good. Let the Sisters know I have assured you this new agreement will in no way reduce the revenue they bring in. Your signature is merely a formality for the books."

Cassandra glanced at the black shadows in the far corner. "Is that thing gone?" she asked.

"No, he is awaiting further instructions," Piqwic replied. "The Jester is bound to our Master in some arcane way. I have no answers other than Mordecai Davos likes to collect unusual things. I will now open the table to questions."

Hayeship shifted in his chair. "There has been talk that Claymore Ives has been sighted in the City,"

Piqwic smiled. "We are aware of those rumors and have people looking into it."

Ren almost fell off the tapestry he was clinging to at the words. He needed to locate Claymore. His vision started to blur as he watched the conversation play out below him. The strain and exhaustion of holding his disguise made it difficult for him to remain in his tiny shape for much longer. He started to feel like he had been squeezed into a box too small for his body.

But the thought of getting those letters to Gideon intrigued him. They might fulfill his obligation to the Raconteurs, then he could begin searching for Claymore now that he knew his partner was in the City. His heartbeat pounded in his ears as his normally acute senses became blunted. He didn't see the newspaper until it was too late.

An enormous shadow engulfed Ren out of nowhere. The front page of the Daily Inquisitor smashed him against the wall. His world went sideways. It felt like a building had fallen on him. The impact should have crushed him to a pulp. Only the density of his one hundred and thirty-seven pounds of mass squished into a housefly the size of a man's thumb and held in place by sheer willpower saved him from instant death. But now his world was nothing but blackness and pain. Ren lost his grip and fell from the tapestry.

As he dropped, his tiny body changed, morphing bigger and bigger, until the naked, tattooed, human-sized form of Ren B'gatti fell on the middle of the table among the food and drink. He landed hard, glasses and platters clattered while every weapon in the room drew down on him.

Ren felt as if a train had hit him. His muscles were on fire, and they wouldn't respond to his desire to shift. He pushed himself up with great effort, but a massive hand grabbed him from the table. The grip engulfed the back of his neck and head. He found himself staring into the cold, dead eyes of Odd Bod.

"What do we have here?" Piqwic York cloyed, turning his attention to Ren. "A sneak-spy hiding among us."

Chapter 18
Under the Gun

Odd Bod stared at Ren, his lower lip curving in a cruel sneer. He gave a quiet chuckle, and then his expression returned to the emotionless mask he'd held moments before.

"I know you," the giant said. His voice was deep and menacing. "You're that doppelganger what turned down Mr. Mordecai's kind offer of employment way back when. But you haven't been around in a while, have you? Not since you let your partner go to prison for the *Angels of Avalon* debacle."

Odd Bod set his massive frame down onto a chair and pounded a mallet-sized fist on the table. The dishes rattled and cups overturned. "Ha! Mr. Mordecai was not happy when ya told him no. Then ya go and end up working for the Raconteurs. He was not happy about that either, no, sir." The chair creaked under his weight as he chuckled.

Even sitting, his huge frame loomed over everything around him. His head disappeared directly into a thick neck with small cauliflower ears and a broad nose. The gray-striped suit he wore strained under his sloping shoulders and massive arms. His soulless eyes never left Ren.

"So what brings you to us tonight, little trickster?" Piqwic asked. Ren did not answer.

Odd Bod relaxed his grip on Ren before whacked him on the back of the head with a flick of his other hand. "Mr. York asked you something, little doppelganger." Ren fell to the table, his head ringing from the blow.

Piqwic laughed. "Please, Bod, there's no need for violence. We can discuss this like gentlemen."

Odd Bod's eyes narrowed to slits as his grin turned sinister. "Speaking of gentlemen, it's a shame about the old gang, *The Gentlemen of Fortune,* isn't it?" he rumbled. "That's a terrible fate for anyone to suffer."

Ren's heart jumped. He rolled over on the table and pushed himself up slowly.

Odd Bod's deep voice continued. "You were the only one in that motley bunch that was worth a whit. But you knew that, didn't you? That's why you left them at the first chance you had to go work for Gideon Dumas and his intrepid troupe of Raconteurs, isn't it?"

Odd Bod chuckled and continued. "And where'd that get you? Couple years of running around playing hero, until your mentor Claymore Ives was put away for burning down a world. And they call me a criminal. I mean, I've killed a lot of people in my time, but never that many at once. I like to look into their eyes right before they realize what's about to happen to them."

Ren shook his head to clear the tiny star bursts that blurred his vision. One eye was swollen, and half closed. He tried to come up with something to say, anything that would buy him a few precious moments so he could figure a way out of this predicament.

The hulking giant shifted in his chair and leaned forward as the silence closed in on Ren. "You left your friends alone to deal with the mean streets of Rogue Destiny on their own, and now they're all dead. But that's the way of the world, isn't it? It's a dangerous place. You're still alive, so I guess it worked out to your advantage. But it's never a good thing to say no to Mordecai Davos, that's for sure. That will always come back around and bite you."

Odd Bod grinned, his uneven teeth shining in the dim light.

He sat back in his chair, his smirk disappeared, and his expression became indiscernible.

"I asked Mr. Mordecai if I could have you," Odd Bod mused. "But he told me no. Insisted you were too valuable to kill outright, that there was still hope you would see reason. But he didn't care what I did to your friends."

Ren's jaw tightened at the comment. He looked up at Odd Bod with his one good eye. The giant gave him a malicious grin.

"You're lucky I never got my hands on yah. We would have had a grand old time, you and me. But now it looks like I may get my chance after all." Odd Bod paused long enough to drain a glass of wine.

"Got them all too. Except that potbellied, seven-eyed freak that wears the vest and hat. He escaped me at every turn, didn't even know I was trying to kill him. Now that's what you call irony, my friend. Ah, good times! He even came around to one of our shops looking for work. By then I was on to other projects, so I didn't care. But now that you're back in town stirring things up, maybe I'll go look for him just for old times' sake. Finish up what I should have done back then."

"This night has indeed been full of surprises," Piqwic said. The rotund gang lord stared at Ren as he nibbled a piece of fruit with a curious gleam in his eye. He reached over with a pudgy hand and lifted the shape-shifter's chin for a closer look at his face. "Who sent you?" he asked softly. "Was it Claymore Ives? Where is he hiding?"

Blood ran down Ren's face. His right eye had swollen shut, but his vision began to clear in his left eye, and he saw a dozen faces staring back at him. He tried to hide his surprise at the question, but Piqwic smiled knowingly.

"You didn't know he was in Rogue Destiny, did you?" the rotund gangster said. "I see it in your eyes." Ren didn't respond.

Piqwic frowned. "Soho, he is not answering the question."

A burly bodyguard next to Odd Bod stepped forward and pulled a black rod from off his belt. He pressed the end of it into

Ren's chest. There was a spark and his body stiffened as a jolt of electricity went through him.

Piqwic leaned down with his elbow on the arm of his chair with one finger pressed against his temple. "I ask you one last time. Was it Claymore Ives who sent you?" Ren's mind raced, but in his current state, he could not come up with anything that would not end up getting him killed. "Soho, again," Piqwic said casually, biting into another tart.

The bodyguard hit Ren again with the shock rod. The trickster curled himself into a ball. He rolled off the table onto the tiled floor. The muscles in his limbs twitched as he tried to sit up. A massive hand grabbed him by the throat, pulled him from the floor, and slammed him back onto the table.

"The boss asked you a question!" Soho growled as he throttled Ren.

Unable to breathe or answer, Ren thrashed about, kicking things off the table as he fought to tear the hands from his throat. Soho eased up enough for him to suck in a lungful of air. The enforcer pulled his face close to his own. "Ready to answer the question?"

"All right. All right. No more!" Ren said. He coughed and choked, trying to get the words out. Blood dripped from his mouth and nose over Soho's hand. The bodyguard released his chokehold and wiped his hand on the tablecloth.

Ren kicked out with both feet, hitting Soho squarely in the face. He rolled backwards off the table and backed himself to the wall, rubbing his neck as he recovered from Soho's gentle grip. His breathing was labored. He leaned a shoulder against the wall to steady himself.

"Who are you spying for?" Piqwic repeated, his voice laced with annoyance.

Ren swayed drunkenly on his feet. He needed to buy himself more time. If he could cause enough confusion, he might be able to slip away in the chaos. A thought came to him, and he shouted it out. "They'll kill me if I talk! They have people in this room."

"Who will kill you?" Piqwic asked, his eyes darting to each of the gang leaders around the table.

Cassandra rose to her feet and made a sweeping gesture with her pistol. "There's a traitor among us? Tell us who it is?"

Ren glanced around for any means of escape, but too many weapons stood between him and freedom. He needed to bide his time a little longer until he regained some strength and could reach the door with his skin intact. A familiar itching under his skin told him his body was already mending from the beating. Just a couple more minutes and he could attempt to shape-shift again.

Ignoring the pounding in his head and the possibility of broken ribs, Ren pushed himself off the wall. If this was where it ended for him, he was taking as many as he could with him. The only person he could accuse of being a traitor was the one not in the room.

"It was Ooturo Bacraan," Ren said calmly, rubbing his neck. "He's been paying me to follow Piqwic for the last week. He's planning a coup against the *Society of the Black Rose.*" He paused for effect, letting the accusation settle in. "With Mordecai gone, Ooturo saw his chance for the *Sons of Malachi* to challenge the *Black Rose's* control of the City. With all their rivals in one place, the *Sons* are planning to make their move. They have hired assassins waiting for Ooturo's signal before they burst in here."

Everyone erupted into arguments about the possibility of a traitor amongst them. Ren smiled to himself, then noticed Odd Bod staring at him with dead eyes. The giant hadn't moved or said a word.

Ooturo Bacraan walked in from the hallway, his head down as he buckled his gun belt on. His head came up. "What'd I miss?"

The remaining gang leaders glanced at each other, and every gun moved from Ren to Ooturo. The leader of the *Red Dogs*, Hayeship Gribblin, spat on the ground. "I don't know what game you're playing here, Ooturo, but I'm not having it! The *Red Dogs* have always been the *Son's* closest ally."

"Calm down, everyone, and please put your weapons away," Piqwic interrupted, raising his hands for order. "This is only the desperate bluff of a desperate individual. Can't you see he's trying to sow discord among us? Soho, would you be so kind as to shut our little spy up before he causes any more mischief?"

The brute standing beside Odd Bod grabbed for Ren, but the trickster rolled away from him and attempted to shift. Under normal conditions, Ren could change his form in a heartbeat, but his body fought what his mind was telling it to do. Pain shot through his muscles and his head ached from the beating he'd just taken. He stumbled out of the reach of Soho. A heartbeat later, fueled by sheer adrenaline and will power, his body responded to his command. He took the shape of the raven, although it took him considerable focus to hold the shift.

A shadow loomed behind him, but Ren ignored it and took flight. If he could reach the hallway where Ooturo stood, he would have a chance to escape. A couple more seconds and he would be out of the room.

With lightning speed and an almost causal disinterest, Odd Bod reached out with a massive hand and batted the bird out of the air. Ren was thrown into the stone wall across the room. He landed hard and lost control of the raven's form. He slid down the wall in his true shape and collapsed at the feet of Cassandra of the Nine Sisters.

Ren looked down to see the huge handprint across his chest. It wasn't a bruise, but a splatter of his skin pigment. It would bruise later.

Cassandra hesitated, then holstered her gun. Hayeship followed, tucking his sidearm into its shoulder holster beneath his coat. The tension in the room eased and everyone sat back down.

Piqwic stared down at Ren crumpled on the floor. "Soho, please take our disruptive visitor to the Workshop and get him ready for a question-and-answer session. I want to find out exactly what he was doing here tonight. Montero, you go with him."

"Can we tenderize him a bit without you?" Soho asked.

"As long as he is still capable of answering questions when I arrive." Piqwic bit into a piece of spiced meat from the last platter of food left undisturbed on the table. He turned to the shadows where the wraith waited. "Jester, please escort them before you return to the Master. Watch him closely, for he will most assuredly try to escape."

The dark wraith drifted over from the shadows. Piqwic nodded but did not make eye contact. The room went cold as the creature glided to where Ren lay at the feet of the two burly bodyguards.

"And please warn the Master there are spies about and to watch himself," Piqwic added. "Assure him that everything is going according to his instructions, and we eagerly await his return."

The barely conscious trickster felt himself being lifted from the stone floor without ceremony. Piqwic's two bodyguards each grabbed an arm, and Ren was taken down the back hallway with his bare feet dragging behind him.

Soho shocked Ren in the side with the rod. "Don't go to sleep on us yet, little sneak-spy," he said with a laugh. "Your night is just getting started."

Ren's abdomen exploded in pain. He gritted his teeth so he wouldn't give them the satisfaction of crying out. Instead, he lifted his head and spat a bloody glob onto Soho's shoe.

"You're all out of tricks, little man," Soho said. "But you got spunk. I like that. I'm going to enjoy watching you bleed."

"There's always one more trick," Ren murmured, blood dripping from his mouth to the floor beneath him.

"Not for you, there's not," Soho said. He jabbed the shock rod into Ren's side again and held it there until Ren passed out.

Chapter 19
The Grimm Jester

The sound of a heavy door slamming shut reverberated through Ren's skull. It was followed by the jingling of keys turning a lock. The smell of the ocean filled the night air and revived his senses. He opened his eyes to the planks of worn wood and the booted feet of his captors. Ren hung limp in the arms of the two bodyguards on the outside of a massive door. Soho put the keys back in his pocket as Montero held Ren up by an arm. Behind him, the unmistakable presence of the Grimm Jester hung over them.

The precession moved silently along a narrow pathway underneath the public boardwalk next to the Pithy Fool. Ren heard water lapping under their feet, and the fragrance of the open harbor hung in the air. The last thing he remembered before blacking out was Piqwic ordering the two bodyguards to take him somewhere for questioning. He could not allow that to happen.

Ren sized up the two bodyguards dragging him along. Montero was a full head shorter than Soho and had said nothing the entire night. He was all business, doing what he was told without question. Soho, on the other hand, was all ego, quick to anger, and as impulsive as Ren. Neither man would ever be mistaken for suffering from too much intelligence. Ren could work with that.

He was still recovering from the night's misadventures and had no weapons to fight with or disguises to hide behind. He was naked and woefully out-muscled. The bodyguards thought they held the upper hand, but Ren had one thing no one could take away from him.

Utter desperation.

They walked ten yards before reaching a heavy gate. Stone steps lead up between two tall buildings. Soho unlocked it and pulled the iron gate open. Ren took a breath.

"Soho? Wait up," a deep voice behind them called out. It sounded like Odd Bod.

Both bodyguards turned back. The wooden walkway was empty except for the Grimm Jester floating silently in the air some distance behind them. The creature was another problem altogether for Ren, but if he could create enough of a distraction, he might find a way out of this mess.

"Bod?" Soho called, staring back into the darkness.

"Plans have changed," Odd Bod's voice echoed. "Piqwic wants the changeling brought back to the teahouse."

Soho released his grip on Ren's arm. "Watch him while I sort this out," he said to Montero as he headed back down the walkway, avoiding the Grimm Jester as much as the path allowed. Ren knelt on the boardwalk. Montero held his upper arm in a tight grip.

His heart pounded in his chest as Ren focused his thoughts. Fueled by his thoughts of the horrors awaiting him if he let himself fall into the tender mercies of Piqwic and Odd Bod. He acted on pure instinct, focusing every bit of his fear into anger, and allowing that anger to become strength, letting all of it boil up inside him until it erupted.

Ren pushed up with his feet, ramming his head into Montero's chin. Stars exploded in Ren's vision, but the adrenaline rush was enough to carry him through the pain. Montero stumbled back, letting go of Ren's arm.

Ren focused every ounce of willpower he could muster. He needed to get out of there, but his injured body fought against his command to transform. His temples pounded and his strength failed before he realized his body could not do what he needed to do. He remained in his natural form.

Montero chuckled and slammed a fist into Ren's stomach. He slumped to the walkway, fighting for air.

"You got nothing left, little man," Montero said. "At least accept your fate with a little dignity."

The smell of decay wafted through the air, and Ren looked up. He gave Montero a painful grin as a dark shape rose up behind him. The brawny enforcer turned to see the Grimm Jester looming over them.

"Looks like the Jester wants to take a shot," Montero said with a laugh before stepping aside.

The wraith stared down at Ren from the darkness of his hood. His jutting lower jawbone and yellowed teeth were all that was visible. A bony hand shot out and grabbed Montero by the back of the neck. The bodyguard's eyes went wide. There was a crunch of bone and the man's entire body went limp. The Jester tossed Montero's corpse aside with no effort. Beyond the wraith, Ren could see the lifeless body of Soho laying on the walkway, his neck contorted at an unnatural angle.

"Told you there was always one more trick," Ren muttered to the dead bodyguard. The Grimm Jester turned its attention toward him. The stench of death and rotting carrion washed over him. He felt his blood go cold and backed away until he hit the stone retaining wall. The cloaked monster remained where he was, silent, as if studying him.

The wraith bent down closer. Ren flinched as it came closer. He wanted to run, or at the least cry out. Instead, he sat frozen as the crooked finger moved through the air like the creature was feeling around for something it could not see.

"You are not Fae, Celestial, or Demigod," the Grimm Jester hissed softly, with a voice as dry as dust. "You are wholly unique. Where are you from, before you came to Rogue Destiny?" The bleached bones of his grinning jaw did not move, and the words seemed forced through the jagged teeth.

"I don't know," Ren said. "I don't remember anything before being pulled from the ocean by fishermen. Why?"

"There is a shadow you carry," the wraith said. "One that follows you everywhere. It is something I have not encountered before. I cannot discern or identify what it is, but it intrigues me."

Ren had always felt another presence hanging over him. There were small whisperings, murmurings in the dark recesses of his mind that he could never quite hear, let alone understand. Part of him had always been curious to find out what it might be, but another part of him wasn't sure if he wanted to know. The whispers only came to him when he was in Rogue Destiny, so he knew it was not the influence of any Muse. He had never mentioned it to anyone else, so how could the Grimm Jester know?

"So, are you going to kill me?" Ren asked. He was not sure why he would provoke such a creature, but the words came out without thought.

"Would you prefer I did?" the Jester hissed.

"No, I'm fine staying among the living," Ren replied. "Isn't Mordecai going to be upset you're going around killing his lackeys?"

"Mordecai Davos will never know," the wraith whispered. "I take who I wish and let live who I wish. And I have spared your life this night. So you are now in my debt."

Ren did not want to know the answer to his next question, but he asked it anyway. "What could you possibly want from me?"

"A favor," the wraith hissed. "To collect at a time of my choosing."

"What kind of favor?" Ren asked hesitantly.

"Whatever I need you to do." The wraith turned away. "When I call, you will make yourself available."

The Grim Jester was not flesh and bone. Ren did not do well against foes he couldn't shoot, stab, or punch. But the monster had direct contact with Mordecai Davos, and this opportunity would never come again. Ren swallowed his fear, as well as the urge to vomit.

Ren cleared his throat. "Wait," he almost begged. "Where can I find Mordecai Davos?"

The wraith turned back. "Why do you seek him?"

"He killed friends of mine," Ren said. "I want to talk to him about that."

A chuff of air that may have been a laugh escaped from the wraith's bony jaw. "That is not possible," the Grimm Jester answered. "He is very far from here."

"Then take me to him," Ren said.

"I travel in ways you cannot follow."

Ren shrugged. A small bit of courage returned to him from somewhere deep inside. "Then just tell me where he is," he said. "I'll find him myself."

"I cannot do that," the wraith asked.

"Then what is Mordecai searching for?"

"An arcane object of great power."

"To use against Rogue Destiny?" Ren asked.

"To take Rogue Destiny from those who now rule it."

"Where is this item?"

"If Mordecai knew that, he would no longer need to search for it," the Jester said with what sounded like a tired sigh. "I must return now. Remember your debt."

"How will you find me?" Ren said, again not really wanting to know the answer.

The Jester reached out a long, bony finger and touched him on the forehead. Ren could not move away, no matter how hard he tried. His muscles froze from the sheer panic that swept over his senses. Time itself seem to slow as the wraith grazed his skin.

"I have marked you," the Jester hissed. "As long as you are among the living, I can find you wherever you are."

Whatever unimaginable horror hid beneath that dark cloak was not alive. Ren knew that instinctively. He realized his entire body was trembling — not from the cool night air, but from something he was unfamiliar with. Fear. A primal dread rose deep in the pit of his stomach, and he clasped his hands together to stop them from shaking uncontrollably. Staring into the black abyss of that cowl left him empty and full of despair.

"Until we meet again, little trickster." The leering smile sent a shiver through Ren's bones. The raspy voice was barely a whisper, yet it came out harsh and unnerving. The wraith swept past Ren without another word. The shadowy figure floated up the steps and disappeared from sight.

Ren recoiled to avoid the flapping folds of the Jester's tattered cowl. Until that moment, he had feared nothing except boredom. Out of morbid fascination, Ren snuck up the stairs after the dark creature. The Grimm Jester drifted across the main boardwalk, disappearing into the shadows of the buildings on the other side. Ren hurried after him, but when he reached the same shadows, the wraith was gone.

Ren stood alone in the shadows, trying to process everything that had just happened. He would have followed the Grimm Jester to Mordecai if he could, but the wraith said it traveled in ways Ren could not. Overhead, the sky showed signs of daybreak.

Something warm ran down Ren's face. He touched his temple and saw blood on his fingertips. The cut could have come from Montero or Odd Bod or any of the punches he'd received in the past hour. He rubbed the blood between his fingers.

He sat down on the curb under a streetlight until his breathing returned to normal and contemplated what to do next. He'd taken a pounding tonight, yet had nothing to show for it. He lay back against the lamppost, trying to calm his nerves and clear his head.

Two choices lay in front of him. He could go back to Medesto's flat, but he hated the idea of returning empty-handed. Two of Mordecai's bodyguards lay dead in the hidden walkway across the street. Maybe not by his hand, but it meant the night wasn't a total loss. And Piqwic York sat in the *Pithy Fool Teahouse*, with a stack of letters given to him by the Grimm Jester. Letters written by Mordecai Davos that could lead the Raconteurs to the criminals they were chasing. They might be worth the bruises he'd already taken. He got up and headed back to the teahouse.

Ren went back down the steps to where the dead bodyguards lay. He dug the keys from Soho's jacket pocket and walked down the walkway to the rear entrance beneath the restaurant where the gangs' meetings took place. He hesitated when he reached the door. Those inside would be on their guard now, and Ren was in no shape for another fight.

He watched his shadow flicker on the door from the oil lamps above him. The voice in his head told him it was time to give up and go back to Medesto's apartment. He hated that voice and rarely listened to it, but now it seemed to make sense. He turned from the door, then stopped. Odd Bod had boasted about killing *The Gentlemen of Fortune* on Mordecai's orders. Now the Grand Enforcer said he might go back to searching for Mucluc and finish what he started, for no other reason than he could. That made it personal, and something Ren could not ignore.

Ren looked up at two ceramic oil lamps hanging from chains on either side of the door, and a plan formed in his head. He took one lamp down and blew out the flame. It was half full of oil. He checked the other, and it was almost completely full. He set them both down at his feet and unlocked the door with Soho's keys, leaving them in the lock. He picked up both lamps by their chains, one in each hand, and pushed open the door with a foot. It swung silently inward as he stepped into the dark hallway. The most notorious gang leaders in Rogue Destiny were still inside, drinking and plotting.

Creeping forward, Ren stopped just outside the circle of light coming from the inner sanctum where the criminals gathered. Ignoring the pain in his side, began to swing one lamp in a slow circle beside him and stepped out into the room.

Ooturo sat in his chair, lighting a cigar. He glanced over and saw Ren's silhouette standing in the hallway. His eyes went wide. Ren smiled and lobbed the oil lamp into the center of the room where it crashed onto the other lamps lined up along the tabletop.

The ceramic lantern shattered on impact, and the splattered oil caught fire. Everyone jumped back from the rising flames engulfing the wooden surface. The oil from the broken lamps spread across the surface of the banquet table and dripped down onto the floor.

Odd Bod moved away from the fire, brushing spots of burning oil from his suit. He looked around for the source of the disturbance. Ren met his eyes with a wry smile. He pointed at the giant and flung the second oil lamp at him. Faster than someone with such bulk should have been able to move, Odd Bod sidestepped the projectile. It struck the tapestry behind him, exploding into a fiery ball of broken ceramic pieces.

Burning oil splattered onto Piqwic and the bodyguards standing around him. Piqwic bellowed for someone to get him down from his wooden throne. He was helped to the floor by his men while the smoke and flames increased around them. Dense smoke filled the enclosed area quickly. People scrabbled for the exit.

Ren gave a satisfied grin before running back down the hallway. He heard shouts and the sounds of boots on the tile floor behind him as the room's occupants realized what had happened. The keys jingled as he slammed the heavy door and locked it behind him.

Bullets struck the inside of the thick door as panic erupted inside. Ren laughed to himself and ran the length of the secret path, his adrenaline racing. He reached the iron gate and listened for pursuers. There was no sound behind him. If anyone was going to avoid getting burned to death, their only escape was through the front of the teahouse. That's where he would find Piqwic.

Ren ran up the stone steps to the street above and around to the front entrance of the Pithy Fool. He waited under the eve of a shop at the corner of the boardwalk to admire his handiwork. The two-story building burned brightly, and the heat was intense in the night air. He felt a tinge of satisfaction.

Across at the Pithy Fool, crowds of people rushed out of the teahouse. Cassandra of the Nine Sisters was the first one he recognized, then Ooturo and the other gang leaders. The authorities would be there soon, and the criminal element knew not to be in the area when they arrived.

A moment later, a hulking man strode out of the front doors of the burning building. His massive frame was unmistakable in the glow of the flames consuming the structure. Once clear of the smoke, Odd Bod looked over the gathered crowd.

Mordecai's Grand Enforcer turned to watch the Pithy Fool burn. The flames reflected in his dead eyes. His face was empty of emotion. He straightened his tie, brushed off his suit, and skulked away from the devastation, leaving the others to fend for themselves. Ren watched the behemoth until he disappeared from sight up the boardwalk.

They would meet again, Ren thought. But after the trickster found Claymore. He would need his partner's help to take the behemoth down.

Piqwic emerged from the smoke, coughing and cursing. His bodyguard led him away from the crowd by his arm. His round face came up as sirens could be heard in the distance. He pulled his arm free and trundled away from the burning building in a panic, his other bodyguards at his heels. He glanced around to see if they were being followed before turning the opposite direction Odd Bod had taken.

Mucluc came around the rear of the building, carrying a bundle in his tentacled arms. He tilted back and forth like a windup toy as he approached. Ren ran over and the monster-from-under-the-bed held out the shoes and clothes Ren had left in the kitchen.

"Thank you, Mucluc," Ren said.

The monster's mouth broke into a big, goofy grin. "No problem. Dat what friends do."

Ren pulled on the shirt and stuck a foot in a leg of the trousers. Once dressed, he shifted to the guise of Axel Prospero.

"How long have you been working here?" Ren said.

Mucluc shrugged. "About a year now. It was after Sozo got himself drunk and killed. I have to take care of myself now."

"Well, it looks like you're out of a job now. Sorry about that."

"Dat okay. Never much like working here, but it all I can get dese days." Mucluc said. "Life tough for persons like me, even in Rogue Destiny. But we should stay in touch now you back in town." He dug into his apron pocket. He handed Ren a small card. It was bent and stained, but the shapeshifter could make out the writing.

"Dat my business card," Mucluc said with a wide grin. He untied his apron, pulled off his hairnet, and dropped them on the ground. "It help me find work. Look me up sometimes. The old gang gone, and I miss them. You and I are all that is left of those days now."

Ren nodded. At least Mucluc was learning how to look after himself. He started walking off, then turned back to the gentle, clueless beast.

Ren looked at the card before shoving it into his pocket. "Yeah, we should. This is where I can find you?"

"Yeh, dat my 'partment," Mucluc said. "I be there when I not looking for work. Come over some time and we have drinks. But you have to bring drinks."

Ren laughed. "Yeah, I'll bring the drinks. You know the Obtuse Turtle, over on the west shore? That's where I'm staying while I'm in town. Come by some time and I'll get you a job there. I know the owner."

Mucluc smiled big, saliva drooling down both sides of his lips. "I will do dat."

A thought came to Ren. Something he had forgotten in the chaos of the last couple of hours. The reason he had ventured out for Medesto's to begin with.

"You haven't seen Claymore, by chance, have you?"

"Who dat?"

"The guy who talked me into leaving the *Gentlemen* and joining the Raconteurs."

"Oh, da big guy wit da muscles?" Mucluc nodded. "Yeah, he came by asking about you."

"Claymore was here?!" Ren shouted.

"Yup," Mucluc replied. his eyes vacant of thought. "I told him he was supposed to be in jail, but he just laughed."

"When was this?"

"About eight or nine days ago. Told me he left message for you."

Ren waited for Mucluc to finish the sentence, but nothing else was said. "So, what was the message?"

Mucluc shrugged. His whole body quivering under the action. "Him not say. He said you would know."

Ren thought about the statement. Where would Claymore leave him a message, and how was Ren supposed to know where it was?

"And he didn't say anything else?"

Mucluc shook his head. "Him not say anyting more."

"It was good to see you again." Ren replied. He walked his bulbous friend along the boardwalk and watched Mucluc waddle down the street towards his home, his tentacled tail twitching behind him. His wide, webbed feet made a sticky sucking sound on the street as he walked. Mucluc eventually disappeared around a corner. Ren grinned and took off the other way.

Chapter 20
Reunions

Shortly after Ren had joined the Raconteurs, he and Claymore had made a pact. The two had agreed that if they ever needed to contact one another in secrecy, the message would be left in a place only known to the two of them. A spy had been uncovered inside the ranks of the Raconteurs, forcing Claymore and Gideon to enact new security protocols. Ren hadn't thought about the agreement because he and Claymore had never needed to use it.

Until now.

The message was to be left among the countless scribblings of graffiti on or near the ancient statue of Baltazar Gheddi that stood next to a street known for its rampant graffiti called Zealot's Alcove. The street lay in a desolate area in the oldest part of the city, not far from Beggar's Row. The area was empty given the lateness of the hour, but people kept lamps lit day and night out of respect for City's long-dead founder. This time of night, the cobblestone streets were empty.

A ten-foot-tall free-standing statue stood at the end of the alley. The centuries old sculpture was built in the earliest days of the City. As Rogue Destiny grew in population and expanded, the area around the statue fell into ruin. The original statue was replaced by an identical, fifty-foot-tall likeness erected near the government buildings in celebration of the formation of the Common Council of Eternal Vigilance and Public Sympathy.

Overtime, the smaller statue would be forgotten by the public. But the alley where it stood would become a location of veneration to Baltazar Gheddi. A place where local citizens came to write messages to lost loved ones or unrequited love, in hopes the dead founder of the city would somehow answer their petitions.

The stone sorcerer-king towered over Ren as he scoured the colorful graffiti and scribbled words that filled the walls and cobblestones under his feet. Finding no evidence of a message from Claymore, he turned his search to the statue.

He found nothing on the pedestal amid the flowers and trinkets left as tokens of affection for a man who had been dead for almost a thousand years. On tiptoes, Ren searched the upper reaches of the statue. There he spied a crudely drawn chalk picture of an oil lamp, high on the shoulder of the giant statue. It was not just any lamp, but a Persian lamp from an Arabian adventure. The kind of lamp that held djinns captive. The words scrawled in chalk under it read:

A well-prepared meal is a healing salve for the troubled soul.

His stomach growled as he suddenly realized how hungry he was, but Ren couldn't help but smile. He reached up and wiped the chalk markings away with his palm. He knew where Claymore was hiding.

He caught a ride on the back of a street trolley that carried him the majority of the way. He jumped down onto a street of shops and restaurants. The hour was getting late, and the crowds had thinned to nothing. Two blocks over, he came to a dilapidated, two-story structure built hundreds of years earlier.

The Djinni's Lamp was buzzing with activity. A handful of customers filled the inside of the tiny café and the front terrace under a stretched canopy was empty. Ren had been there once long ago, and little had changed.

Babak Ghasemi, his wife Asha and their seven children had

taken to life in Rogue Destiny well. When Ren first met him, he was a poor spice merchant, barely able to feed his children. Now he lived a quiet, content life with Asha and his children around him.

Ren watched one of the children slip in between tables with a tray of steaming food. The young girl was named Mahsa, if he remembered correctly. He marveled at how much she had grown. A small boy swept the flat stones on the walkway. He looked up at Ren and bowed.

"A table for one, sir," he said over the din of the noisy crowd.

"No, thank you," Ren replied. "I'd like to speak to Babak Ghasemi if I could. I'm an old friend."

The boy's eyes narrowed, and he shrugged. "Babak is not around this evening." Ren could tell the boy was lying, but he wasn't going to argue with him.

"Thank you," Ren replied politely. He scanned the inside of the café before returning to the sidewalk, looking up at the dark, second-story windows. He waited for the boy to go back to his duties, then headed around to the side of the structure.

In an alley behind the café, a high stone wall stretched the length of the building. Ren leapt up, caught the top of it, and pulled himself over. He dropped silently into a private botanical garden hedged by high bushes. People were talking in low voices, but he couldn't see them through the thick foliage. He crept forward through the catacombs of fragrant flowers and exotic plants to a burbling fountain at the center of a courtyard and listened. Through the leaves, Ren could see three people sitting at a table in the shadows of a canvas awning.

Babak Ghasemi wore a white turban and ankle length blue robes. He smoked from a hookah pipe sitting on the table. His wife, Asha, sat next to him sipping tea, dressed in a swathe of multicolored robes. A large dog slept at their feet.

The other man was tall, with muscular arms and wide shoulders. A cowboy hat and dark glasses hid his eyes. A thick growth of stubble concealed his face. His hair was longer than the last time

Ren had seen him, but he knew his old partner on sight. Beyond the small table, the doors to the arched entryway that led into the restaurant were closed, with the shades drawn.

"Are you okay?" Babak asked.

"It's just another headache," Claymore replied.

"They seem to be getting more frequent," Asha urged. "Baba, go get him some Kaaboko tea. It's good for the head."

"Thank you, but no," Claymore said. "I'll be fine in a moment."

"These are more than just average headaches." Babak shook his head. "Does this ailment have a name?"

"Nothing I want to talk about, but I can't thank you enough for your kindness." Claymore dug through his shirt pocket and removed the stopper from the small blue vial. He gulped the contents and leaned back, closing his eyes.

"Oh, you poor dear," Asha sighed. She took his hand in hers. "Is there anything we can do to help?"

"You've risked enough hiding me here," Claymore squeezed her hand gently. "This is something I have to deal with alone."

A warm breeze blew through the garden behind Ren. The flowers and their leaves waving gently around him. The dog's head came up. Asha looked over at the spot where Ren hid.

"I do not think we are alone," Asha whispered.

Claymore's hand dropped to the pistol lying on the table. Babak produced a curved knife from inside the sleeve of his robe. Ren stepped out into the open, then realized he was still Axel Prospero. He raised his hands in an unthreatening gesture. The dog stood up and growled.

"*Time fell asleep...*," Ren said. His frame quivered before the face of Axel Prospero shifted back to his natural form. The over-sized shirt hung loose on his lean shoulders.

Claymore rose from his chair. "*In the afternoon sunshine,*" he replied. A smile appeared on his tired face. "I was starting to doubt if you'd ever find me." He holstered his pistol. "How are you?"

"Just got back into town," Ren told him with a wry grin. The phrase was a password the two shared to prevent Ren from getting himself shot when he was hiding behind an unfamiliar face.

"I knew you'd come back," Claymore quipped. He took off his dark glasses and shook Ren's hand. "No one stays away from Rogue Destiny for long. You remember Babak and his wife, Asha?"

"I do," Ren replied, nodding to them both.

"Ah, of course, it's you." Asha gave him a relieved smile. "Please sit with us, Mr. B'gatti. Would you like some tea? Or something to eat. The honey biscuits are fresh."

Ren took the empty chair between her and Claymore. "Thank you, I'm famished."

Although Ren could hold the form and shape of someone roughly his own mass indefinitely, it left him feeling hollow inside. He dug into the honey biscuits with gusto, then turned to the hummus and pita bread. Across from him, Babak slid the curved knife into a leather sheath strapped to his forearm with a grin.

"So what are you doing out tonight?" Claymore asked in return.

"Looking for you," Ren replied. "Medesto insisted you had left the City. I had a feeling you'd still be here, even though everyone in Rogue Destiny is hunting for you."

The reason Ren had returned to Rogue Destiny suddenly seemed trivial. Claymore's world was crashing down around him, but his partner still wanted to see justice done with no concern of what it might cost him. Ren couldn't abandon his partner now. The Raconteurs would have to find a way to stop Mordecai without his help.

Babak let go a laugh. "Oh, Claymore, I forgot to show you something. I found this on a public board in the plaza this morning." He unfolded a piece of paper from his pocket, spreading it out on the table. It was a bounty notice with Claymore's face on it.

Claymore picked up the crinkled paper. "Public enemy number one. Impressive. And a bounty of a hundred thousand gold sovereigns. Can't say I like the picture, though."

Asha took hold of Babak's calloused hand. "It's getting close to closing time, dearest," she said. "We should probably go help the children clean up and let these two talk in private."

"Of course, my love," Babak replied.

Claymore stood up with them. "Now that I have some help, I need to be leaving, too," he replied. "There are things I need to take care of while there's still time." He grabbed Babak in a strong embrace. "Thank you, my friend, for all your hospitality. It will never be forgotten."

"Goodbye to you, Claymore," Babak responded with a deep concern in his eyes. "It was the least we can do to repay you for all you've done for us over the years. May your road be forever smooth."

Asha kissed Claymore on the cheek. "Take care, my dear friend,' she said, tears welling in her eyes. "Remember to always hold on to hope. There is an answer out there for you."

She took Ren's hand. "Take care of our friend. He is very dear to me and my family, as are you. But he is deeply troubled these days, and he's not doing well."

"I'll watch out for him, Asha," Ren replied. "I won't let him out of my sight."

She kissed Ren on the cheek. "Then good luck to both of you," she said with a gentle smile.

Babak shook Ren's hands and the elderly couple disappeared inside the café. The moment the door closed, Claymore turned to Ren.

"I think I know who killed Minstrel Cotty," Claymore replied. His eyes were cold and empty, his gaze distant. "It's a Common Council member. Serralto Cardus."

Ren almost choked on the bite of honey biscuit. "I saw him not an hour ago."

Claymore's expression came back into focus, like a fog was lifted. "Tell me everything," he said.

"I was at the *Pithy Fool* spying on a meeting of the *Black Rose*. All the leaders of the City's gangs were there, along with members of the Common Council. Then a fire broke out."

"A fire, huh?" Claymore said.

"It was an old building," Ren replied. "That kind of thing happens sometimes."

His partner chuckled. It was a carefree laugh, and for a moment, Claymore was his old self again. "I've always suspected someone from the Common Council was behind Cotty's assassination," he said. "After the breakout from Lazaranth, I figured the guilty party would disappear from public view, afraid I'd come after him. According to my sources in the registrar's office at the Hall of Records, only one council member has not been seen."

"Who's that?"

"Serralto Cardus," Claymore said. "Now that I have a firm lead, I can go after him. You want to go with me and check out this butcher shop? Or do you need to get back?"

"I'm with you," Ren said. "The Raconteurs can wait. This is more important."

A satisfied smile touched Claymore's lips. He didn't say anything, but his appreciation of Ren's loyalty was evident.

"Good. I wasn't sure when I could move on Serralto, but now that you're here, it changes everything."

Claymore put his dark glasses on and donned his cowboy hat. "Hide yourself. We need to leave." Ren shifted back to Axel Prospero and followed his partner through the café.

They cut through the kitchen. The aroma of wonderfully prepared exotic foods cooking over open fire stoves and fresh breads baking in stone ovens caused Ren to pause and take in the smells. Claymore grabbed him by the arm and dragged him through the kitchen, but not before Ren secured a small loaf of bread from a cooling rack.

Ren climbed the steps of a narrow staircase behind Claymore up to a small room in the attic of the restaurant. There was a bed, a washbasin, and a dresser among the cluttered mess. Claymore grabbed a duffle bag from the floor and began to load it with boxes of ammunition, stun grenades and small canisters of what the

Raconteurs called *conflict negotiators*, both non-lethal and other-wise, and finally, two holstered pistols.

He took a sawed-off rifle down from a closet shelf. It was holstered in a leather sheath with shoulder-straps. He loaded the weapon before sliding it back into its holster and stuffing it into the duffle bag.

"This is going to get bloody," Claymore said, opening a dresser drawer. He strapped a gun belt around his waist and loaded the revolver. "I'm bringing Serralto back, regardless of who stands in the way. You sure you still want in on this?"

Ren smiled. "I wouldn't miss it."

Claymore took a small wooden box from the dresser and slid the top open. Inside were a dozen small shiny silver balls of varying sizes packed safely in a bed of foam. He picked out three silver orbs and dropped them into a jacket pocket before closing the box and tossing it in the duffle bag.

"I've spent days shadowing one of Serralto's underlings, Ignatz Mountebank. He works as a legal-scribe in the halls of the Common Council. I've been staking out his apartment, hoping he'll lead me to his boss, but so far, no luck. Now that you're here, I can use your talents to flush him out."

"And the other thing?"

"What other thing?"

"The headaches," Ren said. "I heard you tell Babak and Asha you've been hearing words in your sleep. When I came to bust you out of Lazaranth Prison last year, you wouldn't leave. You said your moral compass had been compromised, and you needed to stay there to protect yourself."

"I'm doing better these days," Claymore said. "I have it under control." Ren wanted to believe him, but the hollow look in Claymore's eyes told him his partner was not doing better.

"Why didn't you go to the Raconteurs for help?"

"What makes you think I haven't?" Claymore said. "Natascha developed an elixir that has helped slow the progression of the symptoms. Gideon had them smuggled into Lazaranth since the trial, but it's only a temporary fix."

"Then we need to get more of them," Ren said.

"There's no time," Claymore replied. "We have to move on Serralto Cardus before he disappears for good. I can't involve the Raconteurs. If the Common Council suspected they were harboring a fugitive, it would be catastrophic for them."

"So, how do we flush him out if he's in hiding?"

"With this." Claymore handed him a telegram envelope from the nightstand.

Ren unfolded the paper inside the envelope. The message was on official Common Council letterhead from the office of Serralto Cardus and read:

Come at Once. Situation crucial. SC

Ren handed the paper back and Claymore slipped it back into the envelope. "Let's just hope it's enough to panic Ignatz into leading us to Serralto."

A half-hour later, Claymore waited in the shadows across the street as Ren strolled up to a quaint brick apartment building. He found the name *Ignatz Mountebank* on the residents' list and pressed the buzzer for apartment 21. After a few seconds, a tired voice answered.

"Hello?"

"Yes, is this Mr. Ignatz Mountebank?"

"Yes, want can I do for you?"

"I am a messenger from Bellegarde Telegraph Unlimited, and I have been tasked with delivering an urgent message to you."

"Just drop it through the mail slot. I'll look at it in the morning. It's really late and I'll be in the office in a few hours."

"I'm sorry, sir, but the sender paid extra to have it hand delivered, so you'll have to sign for it."

"Who is it from?"

"Serralto Cardus," Ren replied. There was silence on the other end of the intercom.

"One moment," Ignatz Mountebank said. "I'll be right down."

Chapter 21
A City of Assassins

A half hour later, Ren found himself looking out the back window of a horse-drawn Hansom Cab along a row of mercantile shops and businesses. Down the dark street, he watched another taxi pull up to a small shop called *The Chopping Block*.

Ignatz Mountebank got out and walked to the front door. He knocked as the cab pulled away from the curb. A light on the porch came on. The door opened a crack, and a face appeared. A moment later, Ignatz disappeared inside, and the porch light went out.

Claymore tapped his foot restlessly. "We need to hurry so we don't lose him on the other side," he said. "You go around back and through the rear of the shop. I'll wait for you to get in position before I go in through the front. Don't kill anyone unless they leave you choice. We're here to find the rabbit-hole, not kill people."

"Are you sure you don't want the Raconteurs involved with this?" Ren asked. He had watched for signs of loss in Claymore's mental acuity on their way over here. So far, nothing seemed out of the ordinary. "We don't know who or what we'll find on the other side of the rabbit-hole. Having backup might be nice."

Claymore's gray eyes hardened. "I don't know who I can trust these days," he rumbled. The tone of his words did not sit well with

Ren. "You're the only one who has stood by me this whole time. I want to trust the Raconteurs, but something's telling me not to. Besides, we may need to break a few rules on this one."

"Alright, I'll see you over there." Ren stepped back into the shadows. Focusing his mind, he felt the waves of pigment moving across his arms and torso, bleeding out over his skin until his color matched the shadows around him.

Avoiding the halo glow of the streetlights, he kept to the shadows and drifted across the street to the back of the butcher shop. He peeked in a side window. Three men sat at a table playing cards. Each was armed with pistols and had bladed weapons lay close at hand.

Ren hurried around to the back. Claymore's lack of patience was evident. His partner desperately wanted to reach Serralto Cardus before the faux telegraph aroused his suspicions. Climbing over the wooden fence, he dropped silently into the shadows on the other side. The yard lay cluttered with discarded boxes and scrap metal from machines and shipping containers.

A single sentry stood in the light of the back door. He carried a short rifle on a strap over his shoulder and gazed out into the darkness. Ren froze, tensing his muscles for an attack. The man pulled a cigar butt out of his pocket and lit it with a match. He took a puff, looking at the burning end to see if it had lit properly. Satisfied, he took a casual drag, blew out a large plume of smoke and turned his back to where the trickster hid.

Ren reached for a discarded meat hook lying in a box next to him, but decided to honor Claymore's edict, *Don't kill anyone, unless they give you no other choice,* and picked up a metal bar from the ground instead.

He crept up behind the man as he walked across the yard. Ren's foot kicked a pile of loose scrap metal hidden in the grass. Ren whacked the guard upside the head as he turned. The man crumpled to the ground. Ren took the rifle and emptied the bullets on the ground. He tossed the metal bar aside and pulled off the man's boots. He wanted to get inside before Claymore burst in.

Shouting erupted from inside the butcher shop, followed by a gunshot. Ren ran for the back door. Three more shots rang out in rapid succession. Claymore turned as the door flew open, his smoking pistol leveled at Ren.

"Claymore, it's me!" Ren said. He lifted his empty hands. His partner's gaze was empty and distant, like he was looking through Ren. The bodies of the three card players lay dead on the floor.

"You were supposed to give me time to get in through the back," Ren said.

"I had no choice," Claymore replied slowly, staring at his smoking gun. He pointed it at one of the dead men. "They pulled their guns on me. I had a split second to decide."

Ren glanced at the bodies at their feet. Only one man had his gun drawn. The pistols of the other two remained in their holsters. At any other time, Ren would have been glad he had three fewer bad guys to worry about. But now, with Claymore's mental state in question, it seemed to matter more. His partner's value for life seemed to have shifted during his time in Lazaranth Prison.

"But we're still the good guys here, aren't we?"

"Of course, but we have a job to do," Claymore replied. "I've waited long enough to make this right. I told you there'd be blood, and tonight we're taking no prisoners."

Clarity returned to Claymore's eyes as if he suddenly remembered Ren was there. He scratched the back of his head furiously, then pushed over one of the dead men with his boot.

"This one's Gronic Diabolus," he said. "These men work for the *Society of the Black Rose*."

Ren heard the creak of a rusty hinge. At the back of the room, a door slowly swung open. A shadowy figure appeared, a pistol in hand.

"Behind you!" Ren yelled.

Claymore spun on his heel and fired twice. Both shots hit the gunman in the chest. He fell forward onto the floor. A dark pool of blood formed on the floor under him. Claymore ignored the dead man and pulled the door open to reveal a staircase leading to a darkened cellar.

"This way!" he yelled. "The rabbit-hole should be down here. We can't lose Ignatz." Ren followed him into the darkness. Claymore stomped down the wooden staircase to the bottom. An iridescent lightbulb hung from the center of the room. It doused the basement in a dim glow. The air was musty, the walls constructed out of cut stone. Four ancient support columns held up the floor above them.

Claymore made his way across the floor to a cellar door with a brass ring handle. Recent repairs on the wooden door were evident in the ancient, musty surroundings of the basement. A faint glow of emerald light seeped through the cracks of the boards. Next to the door, a statue of a serpent posed to strike sat on a concrete stand connected to the floor. Its jeweled eyes reflected off the lightbulb.

"Go check the pockets of the guy at the top of the stairs," Claymore ordered. "He should have a peculiar-looking coin on him."

Ren dashed back up the steps to check the dead man for loose change. Inside a jacket pocket, he found a single coin of silver and black. It had a symbol Ren had never seen before on the silver side and the head of a serpent was on the other. It appeared to be more of a souvenir token than an actual coin. He returned to the basement and tossed it to his partner.

Claymore studied the coin, then held it up. "This is a sigil of Adezhda, the city of assassins," he said. "That's where Serralto Cardus hired Cotty Minstrel's killer." He placed it into the open mouth of the statue. The serpent's ruby eyes lit up and the audible sound of a lock opening filled the room. The edges of the cellar door glowed. Claymore grabbed the brass ring, and with a grunt, pulled up the slanted cellar door to reveal a tunnel. The emerald glow of the rabbit-hole filled the room.

"I always knew there was a rabbit-hole to Adezhda somewhere in Rogue Destiny, but I could never find it." His partner disappeared down the tunnel.

Ren stepped through the glowing doorway after him. He felt the shifting of realities and emerged from the rabbit-hole next to Claymore. They stood under the shade of a massive tree that sat atop a hill overlooking a rugged coastline. The leaves of the tree quivered slightly, even though Ren felt no breeze. The red evening sun sat low on the horizon above a dark blue ocean.

The tangled roots of the tree surrounded the circular rabbit-hole and sank deep into the earth beneath Ren's feet. The roots created the ley-lines that defied time and space, and every Wayward Tree created a unique doorway that stretched across the Mythic Cosmos to some distant world.

Ren walked down the smooth stone steps to a well-worn dirt trail that descended the hillside. In the distance, over the treetops, an island city sat off the coastline. Its bright, neon lights reflecting off the waters. A range of high, rugged mountains ran along the coast, separating the island from the mainland.

"Where are we?" Ren asked.

"In a sword and sorcery fantasy called *The Hallowed Empire*," Claymore said. "Swords, dragons, that sort of thing. I've been here once, long ago, but I came through a different rabbit-hole."

Claymore reached the bottom stair and pointed to the brightly lit island city. "That's Adezhda. The world's Story lies far to the east on the other side of that mountain range. The city was built beyond the Narrative of the world. It's a place of killers and mercenaries, where the powerful meet away from the eyes of Rogue Destiny. Business is conducted there, deals made, and contracts signed. That's where we'll find Serralto."

Ren stomped after Claymore down the winding path through the thick trees for half a mile before it ended at a dirt road. A windowed telephone booth stood beside the roadway.

The sound of a car shifting gears broke the silence. A billowing cloud of dust rose among the trees. The rear lights of a vehicle could be seen in the distance, headed in the direction of the neon city.

"Looks like they called for a ride," he said. "You want me to go after them?"

"Yeah, I'll follow you on foot." Claymore dropped his duffle bag to the ground and dug through its contents. He handed Ren a round compass the size of his palm. "This is a companion compass." He held up a second one, identical to the one he gave Ren. "One will always lead you to the other. Just stay with the car and I'll follow you. Wait for me, and don't do anything before I get there." His faced winced as if he had trouble finishing the thought and pressed a finger to his temple.

"You okay?" Ren asked.

"Just another headache. It'll pass in a moment."

"These are more than headaches," Ren said. "You're still hearing words echoing in your head, aren't you?"

"How do you know about that?" Claymore snapped.

"You don't remember?" Ren said. "You told me that when I came to break you out of Lazaranth Prison. When you said you were out of the game and told me to leave Rogue Destiny. And tonight, you didn't want to talk to Babak and Asha about headaches and words echoing in your head. It's the same thing you were suffering from in Lazaranth, isn't it?"

"None of that important right now," Claymore growled. "We need to find Serralto. He's all that matters to me." He scratched the back of his head until Ren thought it would start bleeding.

Ren wanted to push the conversation further, but he decided this wasn't the time. There would be other opportunities to argue with Claymore about what he was going through. He kicked off his shoes and began to unbutton his shirt.

Claymore waited for him to finish undressing. "Don't approach Serralto until I get there."

"I won't," he replied. Once he was done undressing, he gathered up his clothes and handed the bundle to Claymore. A small object fell to the ground.

Claymore picked it up and looked at it. "My old badge," he said with a smile.

"I found that in a crate at Medesto's flat."

"If all goes well tonight," Claymore replied. "I might even be worthy of wearing this again." He slipped the badge into his coat pocket.

Ren backed away and focused his will. "I'll see you over there," he said. Before dropping the compass to the ground.

The swirling strands of dark pigment snaking across his torso and arms bled out over his lean, muscled body as he morphed into a raven. With the compass clutched in a clawed foot, Ren took to the air, up over the trees, following the dust trail left in the car's wake.

Chapter 22
A Lingering Mystery

Moments later, he was high above a black limousine, feeling relaxed for the first time since his return to Rogue Destiny. To be back with his old partner, heading toward an unknown peril, was the only place he ever truly felt alive. The thrill of the hunt welled up inside him.

Ren glided on the coastal winds toward a small flock of seabirds. With a thought, his dark feathers rippled to the same long, colorful plumage as those flying around him. His beak grew in length and curved at its end. Blending in with the environment was the first rule of shape-shifting.

The automobile turned off the narrow, rutted dirt road onto a paved roadway that wound along the ocean's edge toward the island city. To the west, under a setting sun, lay the city of Adezhda. To the east, high cliffs rose along the coastline.

The flock of birds Ren flew with rose high enough to allow him a glimpse beyond the rocky clefts that separated Adezhda from where the Story's Narrative played out.

He knew the world's Story would not reach this side of the mountains or Adezhda would never have been built where it was. Secondary characters from the Story may venture over the high cliffs, but no one of any importance would leave the safety of their Story.

Ren pulled his attention back to the task at hand. Below him, the limousine turned off the main road to a wide bridge that led into the bright neon city. He broke away from the other birds and flew down across the water to a lamppost at the far end of the stone bridge.

He moved the companion compass from a claw to his beak as he waited for the limousine to make its way through the thick traffic. After the car passed under him, he flew up a couple of blocks up to wait for it again. Ren repeated this several more times through the congested downtown streets. Finally, the vehicle swung into the entryway of a nightclub with a gaudy neon sign that read *The Gallows Club*.

At the front of the nightclub, a set of gallows stood silhouetted against the brilliant lighting outside the building. Three bodies hung from the wooden crossbar, dangling over the open trapdoors of the scaffold. The structure stood in plain view for all to see as they entered to club.

The limousine pulled around a fountain of dancing water before rolling to a stop at the front entrance. Ren landed on top of a dragon statue on the grassy lawn. He glanced back at the hanging bodies. They looked real enough, but he couldn't tell for sure. He wondered what other surprises this place had waiting for them.

Serralto's underling, Ignatz Mountebank, climbed out of the car. He walked up the steps through the doors of the nightclub before Ren lost sight of him in the pressing crowd. He decided to fly to the side of the building and wait for Claymore there. The distance from the rabbit-hole wasn't more than a couple of miles, which meant his partner would not be far behind him.

He found a small grove of palm trees overlooking a veranda of partygoers. From his perch, he watched the nightclub patrons cluster and mingle on the circular veranda. Their voices were little more than a dull drone to him. The smell of exotic flowers filled the air.

Two men wandered out of the nightclub into the shadows of a side patio. Ren recognized both immediately. The first was portly and wore an elegant red greatcoat. The other walked with purpose to the edge of the terrace. His sharp, razor-thin features and dark suit of ash gray blended into the surrounding shadows. They moved through the crowd to a secluded spot. Ren dropped the compass to the grass and flew to the eve above the two men.

Piqwic York took a pipe out from his coat and stuffed the bowl with tobacco. He struck a match on the stone wall. Beside him stood Dmitri the Confessor, Mordecai's grand inquisitor. Together with Odd Bod, the three formed Mordecai's inner most circle, much like Medesto, Natascha and Ren were Claymore's.

Dmitri glowered into the darkness. "Why would you bring Ooturo, Cassandra and the council members here?" he asked. "Have they defied us and need to be dealt with?"

"No, no, quite the opposite," Piqwic replied between long puffs. "Our meeting was interrupted by the Raconteurs' changeling. Needless to say, chaos ensued, and the Pithy Fool was burned to the ground. I wanted to wine and dine them tonight to remind them that the *Society of the Black Rose* is still in charge of things. They know Mordecai has gone missing. Their cooperation is important if our plans are to succeed."

"So Ren B'gatti is back in town?"

"It would appear so," Piqwic said with a sigh. "Our spies inside the Raconteurs have said nothing, so they must not yet be aware he has returned."

"And Claymore Ives?"

"Only passing rumors that he has been seen in the City. No firm confirmation yet. If he is there, it is strange that he has made no attempt to contact the Raconteurs. Our spy has told us as much."

Piqwic took a drag on his pipe, blowing a cloud of smoke into the warm air. "Were you able to make Candree tell you who else was involved in the theft of the Terrill shipment?" he asked.

"No, he died on my table before I could get the names of his accomplices."

"That's unfortunate, Dmitri," Piqwic replied. "Mordecai will be disappointed when he hears."

"It was not my fault," Dmitri countered. His voice rising in defensive anger. "Candree came to me already beaten and battered beyond recognition. I would have waited for him to heal a bit before I cut into him, but you insisted I extract the identities' his co-conspirators as quickly as possible before any of them could flee the City."

"I understand," Piqwic replied. He paused, looking out into the dark trees.

"Any word from Mordecai?" Dmitri asked in a tone that indicated he knew the answer.

Piqwic blew out several smoke rings. "Still nothing. It's beginning to worry me. I fear something is terribly wrong."

Dmitri agreed. "It is strange. But he has disappeared before. He is a man of solitude, and besides, we know the Grimm Jester is with him, so he will be well protected."

"He has never been gone this long before. Not without letting anyone know where he was. It's out of character and doesn't feel right. My instincts are never wrong. The letters sent through the Jester are vague, and doesn't sound like Mordecai wrote them. I don't like it. Bod shares my concerns. And then there's the Lazaranth breakout."

"Do you think the two are connected?"

"The timing fits," Piqwic replied. "But if Mordecai is somehow involved, why didn't he warn us it was going to happen?"

"Who can know the mind of Mordecai Davos?" Dmitri replied. "I just don't like the idea of him being out there alone. I know the Jester watches over him, but still.

Piqwic shrugged. "I suppose we will just have to wait until this all plays out."

Above them, Ren listened intensely to every word. What did they mean *Mordecai Davos was missing?* He looked up to see

Claymore striding across the lawn. Piqwic and Dmitri remained engaged in their conversation, but all they had to do was look over and they'd see his partner.

In a desperate move, Ren dropped down on them. He flapped his wings in the faces of Piqwic and Dmitri, pulling at their hair and driving them away from the edge of the patio. The men cursed and swatted at the air. Piqwic covered his head with his arms as he ran for the doors. Dmitri followed at his heels. Ren pecked at them until the doors were pulled shut behind them. He returned to the corner of the roof. Claymore reached the spot where the companion compass lay in the grass. His partner picked it up and glanced around with a grim smile on his face.

Ren cawed loudly from atop the roof, bobbing his head up and down. He spread his wings and glided around the building, away from the crowds. He landed in the grass and waited for Claymore. His partner appeared moments later. Digging through his duffle bag for Ren's clothes, he tossed them on the grass next to him. Ren shifted back into Axel Prospero.

"Piqwic York and Dmitri the Confessor are here," Ren told him as he dressed.

"Then this is where we'll find Serralto," Claymore replied. "He's been trying to work his way into the ranks of the *Black Rose* for years. Watch yourself once we're inside. We don't know who in the crowd might be on the *Black Rose's* payroll."

"Got it," Ren replied, strapping on a gun belt from the duffle bag. "So, how do you want to play this?"

"We go straight in, grab Serralto Cardus and get out as quicky as possible."

"Is storming the dragon's den the best strategy?" Ren asked. "Shouldn't I go in and look around first? I can locate Serralto and get an idea of what we're up against. Then we figure out the best way to grab him. Or better yet, we could wait here for him to come out?"

"I've waited too long for this already," Claymore growled. His hands clenched into fists, his knuckling cracking. "Going in is the easy part. It's getting back out with Serralto. That'll be tricky."

"I have to ask, those bodies hanging from the gallows out in the public?"

"Spies, most likely," Claymore said. "Adezhda may be a refuge for despots and hired killers, but it has its rules. It's supposed to be a sanctuary where business can be conducted in peace. The city's inhabitants guard their privacy and any who interfere in someone else's affairs are dealt with harshly."

"So we're just going to walk up to Serralto and arrest him."

"That's the plan," Claymore replied. "We play the cards we've been dealt. We'll split up once we're inside, but stay close. When they recognize me, things will go south quickly. And remember, we're not in Rogue Destiny anymore. The magic here is real, so I'm counting you to watch my back."

"Without a doubt," Ren said. His partner's carelessness bothered him. He couldn't put his finger on it, but something was not right with Claymore's plan. Claymore was never one to rush into a fight without meticulously planning every possible contingency before executing any action. Especially if innocents were sure to get caught up in the middle of it. His impatience seemed wrong.

Ren pushed his concerns aside. They were about to arrest the individual responsible for Minstrel Cotty's murder and Claymore's imprisonment. That was all that mattered.

Claymore noticed Ren's hesitancy. "Why do you think I keep you around?" he quipped. "If not to watch my back."

"I thought it was because someone needed to rein in my tendency for wanton destruction where every I go."

Claymore let go a laugh. "That too. And remember, no shape-shifting until we have Serralto in custody. That'll be our ace-in-the-hole in getting out of there alive." He mounted the crowded steps leading into the casino. All Ren could do was follow.

Chapter 23
The Gallows Club

The nightclub was crowded. Live music drifted from a raised platform on the left side of the expansive room. Throngs of people milled about, some dancing, others engaged in raucous conversations filled with laughter. The interior décor was a mix of gaudy yellow, silver, and gold. Large decorative shields lined the walls from one end of the room to the other. Dimly lit chandeliers hung from the beams of the domed roof, casting a golden glow over everything.

Behind the eyes of Axel Prospero, Ren scanned the sea of nightclub patrons. He let his concern for Claymore's shifting moral indifference go for now, to focus on finding Serralto Cardus. They entered the main floor of the club as the infectious beat of the music rolling off the stage. It reminded him a bit of the Pithy Fool Teahouse where he had been hours before. Only the patrons there were working-class commoners trying to survive. The Gallows Club was different.

The nightclub catered to a higher level of clientele. Lots of money was being thrown about by people in expensive jewelry and opulent clothing. He also knew the place was full of elite killers hiding among the wealthy power brokers.

Claymore shouldered his way through the crush of intermingling humans and non-humans alike, his gaze searching the crowd. His eyes fell on a private table in the far corner of the room. He strode across the deep red carpet toward it. Ren circled around, keeping his partner in sight as Claymore headed for the large corner booth, where a dozen individuals sat.

Piqwic York caught Ren's attention first. The rotund gangster laughed the loudest and pounded the table in response to someone's joke while stuffing his mouth with shellfish. Around him sat Dmitri the Confessor, Cassandra of the Nine Sisters, Ooturo Bacraan and Hayeship Gribblin from the meeting Ren had broken up earlier in the evening. Two large bodyguards sat with their chairs angled out to the open room.

A hulking reptilian creature from some unknown science-fiction story eyed Ren as he passed its table. Glossy, black eyes stared at the revolver at Ren's side. The tight leather vest strained against the rough, scaly skin as the brute hunched over a card table. An assortment of bladed weapons filled a wide belt.

Ren glanced down at his holstered revolver. A toothy grin appeared on the creature's long snout before turning back to the card game. It was then he noticed that no one around him carried a firearm. That meant something, he just didn't know what. He took an empty stool at a long bar, dropping the duffle bag at his feet.

Ren watched Claymore approach the members of the Black Rose and lesser gang leaders sitting around the laughing and drinking at the wide table. Only Odd Bod was absent.

Claymore's intense gaze told Ren the man occupying a chair on the outside edge of the table had to be Serralto Cardus. Ignatz Mountebank stood with his head bowed in front of the man in yellow and blue robes. The young man nodded dutifully as he was berated in hushed tones. The others at the table glanced over from time to time, but none made any comments.

Sitting next to Serralto, a darkly dressed woman drank from a crystal fluke. She was the first to notice Claymore approaching them. Her eyes narrowed as he came closer. She set her glass down and dropped both hands out of sight under the table.

Serralto noticed her staring out at the floor and looked over to see Claymore walking up. The member of the Common Council jumped to his feet and grabbed the underling by his robes, before slapping him across the face, knocking him to the floor. Piqwic and the others in the booth stopped laughing and the table went silent.

"You fool!" Serralto spat. "You were followed!" Ignatz climbed up from the floor, rubbing his reddened cheek.

The two burly bodyguards pushed themselves out of their chairs to meet Claymore as he reached the table. His partner stood toe to toe with them. The hired thugs both stood as tall as Claymore's six-plus-feet of condensed muscle. Their hulking frames and swaggering bravado contrasted his relaxed stance. Each met Claymore's steely gaze with their own.

Claymore stepped back and drew his pistol in one quick motion. He stared between the two men at the man he and Ren had pursued there.

"Serralto Cardus," Claymore declared loudly for all to hear. "You are under arrest for the murder of Minstrel Cotty and the destruction of the novel, *The Angels of Avalon*, by order of the Raconteurs and the Common Council of Rogue Destiny. The rest of you remain where you are, and you won't get shot."

Ren watched the lack of reaction of those at the tables. No one seemed the least bit intimidated by the revolver pointed at them. Serralto sat back down, expressing nothing but disinterest. The two bodyguards stepped back from Claymore as if something were about to happen.

Ren slid from his barstool. His hand dropped to his own revolver. The gun handle tingled under his touch. He glanced around at the walls of the casino. The shields mounted along the wall above Claymore gave off a soft, reddish glow.

The room was protected by magical wards. Ren could feel the enchantment swirl through his fingers when he gripped the handle of his gun. That's why no one else carried a firearm. He let go of his pistol. If Claymore pulled the trigger, chances were the gun would not fire or worse. Serralto's smug smile reenforced Ren's fear.

"And you think you're going to just walk me out of here unchallenged?" Serralto asked indifferently.

"That's the plan." Claymore said, his gun leveled at the stomach of the bodyguard standing in his way.

"Then you might as well shoot me where I sit," Serralto replied. He took a bite of the fish on his plate. "Because I'm not leaving with you."

The tension at the table was palatable. Piqwic stared at Serralto, his face a mask of any discernable emotion before he turned to Claymore. He took a sip from his crystal goblet.

"Claymore Ives, what a surprise to see you," Piqwic said with a smile. "You look well."

"As do you, York," Claymore replied. "Serralto, we need to go."

There was hesitation in Claymore's words. He didn't have the sensitivity to magic that Ren did, but his partner had to sense something was not right. Whether it was the apathy on the faces of people at the table or Serralto's sanctimonious grin, Ren couldn't tell for sure. Claymore waited a moment longer before he holstered his revolver.

"So be it," Claymore said. He returned Serralto's smile. "It looks like we'll have to do this the old-fashioned way."

Claymore struck the first bodyguard in the throat, then grabbed the front of his shirt and bounced his face off the thick table. Blood spurted from a broken nose, and the man staggered back. The second bodyguard slashed at Claymore's face with a short, curved knife. The Raconteur caught the man's wrist in a vise-like grip and twisted the arm back until there was a cracking of bone and the bodyguard dropped the blade with a cry of pain. He followed that up with a solid punch to the man's sternum, before throwing him across the table.

Before anyone else could react, Claymore rolled three small silver balls across the table top. The largest of the orbs exploded in a brilliant flash of light, blinding everyone in the immediate area. The remaining two balls crackled and hissed before bursting into billowing clouds of thick gray smoke that engulfed the corner of the room. Claymore kicked the table into the wall with his boot, pinning those behind it in their seats.

Every head in the immediate vicinity turned toward the commotion. People jumped from their chairs and backed away from the smoke. The music stopped. Someone shouted *fire!* and a wave of chaos swept across the nightclub floor. Ren waited for any of the *Black Rose's* other henchmen hiding in the crowd to reveal themselves.

Down the bar from him, a man with dark, slicked-back hair and slightly pointed ears separated from the others along the row of benches. He threw back his black leather coat open to reveal the curved hilts of two long knives as he stalked the floor toward the corner table. He drew both blades in unison, approaching Claymore from behind. He crouched as he moved in closer for the kill.

Ren snatched a decanter of wine off the tray of a bewildered waiter and threw it. The heavy crystal container struck the man carrying the knives in the back of the head. He fell forward from the blow but turned his fall into a controlled roll, somersaulting back to his feet. He spun around to face his attacker.

The hulking reptile that had been eyeing the crowd earlier gave a deep growl and pushed himself out of his chair, his tiny black eyes settling on Ren.

Ren lifted a hand in a mock salutation. "The Raconteurs send their regards!"

The assassin hurled both knives at Ren. The twin blades sliced the air with whirling precision. Ren snatched the metal tray from the waiter's hands before pushing him out of the way. Ren deflected the first knife away from him, then the other. The flying blades continued through the air, defying the laws of physics. They swept out in a wide circle across the room in such a way that could only be magic.

Ren held the tray in front of him like a shield, searching the smoke for Claymore. He found his partner punching Serralto in the face as both were engulfed in the widening cloud of smoke.

Claymore never once looking over his shoulder, knowing full well his partner was protecting his back.

A moment later, Claymore emerged from the smoke with the unconscious Serralto flung over a shoulder. Ren watched his partner run to the far side of the room until he was lost in the chaos of the panicked crowds. The trickster returned his focus to the two killers in front of him.

"Gallo," the long-haired assassin sneered. "He's yours." He stepped out of the way as the hulking reptilian lumbered at Ren. Not knowing what else to do, Ren flung the tray. He was determined to give Claymore the time he needed to get away. The silver disk careened off the creature's misshapen head but didn't slow him down. The charging reptile quickly closed the gap between them. An increasingly loud hum caught Ren's ear.

Ren risked a quick glance over his shoulder. The assassin's twin blades whirled toward him. He evaded the first one with a quick sidestep, but the second blade sliced him along his left side. The impact knocked him to the floor. Blood seeped onto the carpet from a deep cut along his ribs. The flying knives boomeranged back to the gauntleted hands of the man who had thrown them.

Ren climbed to his feet. He grabbed a chair and swung it at the hulking beast lumbering at him. Gallo caught it mid-swing and wrenched it from Ren's hands. Clawed fingers caught Ren by the throat and lifted him off the floor.

The reptilian creature's grip tightened, cutting off his airway. Ren struggled to break the chokehold before he passed out from lack of air. He punched the lizard's chest. Gallo only smiled back.

Ren pounded frantically on the thick scaley arms, choking the life out of him, before a thought struck him. He reached blindly for one of the blades stuffed into Gallo's belt. His fingers touched the handle of a knife. He pulled it out and with both hands stabbed it upward into the soft underside of the reptile's snout with all his strength. He shoved until the hilt could go no further.

Gallo stumbled back, spurting blood and grabbing for the blade embedded under his snout. Ren dropped to the carpet, coughing and rubbing his neck. Behind him, the sound of whirling knives reached his ears. This time, he was ready for them.

Ren backed away from the Gallo to see if the knives followed. As he expected, the flying blades altered their trajectory toward him. He braced himself, letting the blades close in on him. Gallo yanked the blade free in a shower of pea-green blood. The reptile creature roared in pain. His beady black eyes searched for Ren. The hum of the deadly blades grew louder.

The second before the knives reached him, Ren darted to the side. His injured side screamed in protest. The distinct thud of double knives finding their mark told him his scheme had worked. Both blades lay buried to the hilt in the reptilian's chest. Gallo remained upright for a moment, staring down at the knives. He glanced up at Ren before collapsing onto the floor.

Ren got to his feet. Blood oozed through the fingers pressed to his side, as he grabbed the duffle bag. He saw Claymore waiting for him at the kitchen doors. The room was in chaos as Ren wound his way through the dispersing to his partner.

"Ready?" Claymore shouted as Ren reached him.

"Yeah, let's get out of here," Ren replied.

Chapter 24
A Fatal Escape

"You're bleeding," Claymore said.

"Yeah, I caught a knife in the scuffle back there," Ren replied. He peeked at the injury through his shirt. The bleeding had slowed, and the deep cut was already starting to heal.

The hum of spinning knives split the air. Ren looked up to see the blades pass over them. They boomeranged back to the assassin's hands as he walks toward them.

"He's messing with us," Claymore said. He stepped in front of Ren and dropped Serralto unceremoniously to the floor. "I know this guy. Keep an eye on our friend while I deal with him."

Claymore drew his gun and walked toward the assassin. "Stop where you are, Jopaquay!" he ordered. "It doesn't need to be like this. Don't make me kill you."

Jopaquay continued forward. "It's been a while, Ives."

"Yes, it has," Claymore replied. "How long have you been working for *The Black Rose*?"

"Going on three years now," Jopaquay replied as he continued walking forward. "Got to take work where you can find it."

"I hear you," Claymore rumbled. "Should've taken the job I offered. You might have made a good Raconteur."

Jopaquay shook his head at the remark. "Your world is too

black and white for me. I prefer swimming in the deep end of moral ambiguity."

Claymore cocked the hammer of his revolver back. The decorative shields along the walls glowed red.

"Claymore?" Ren said.

"I know," his partner replied.

"And if you're wrong?"

"Then take Serralto and run!"

Jopaquay spread his arms out, daring Claymore to shoot him. His twenty-inch long knives held loosely in each hand. Claymore glanced down at his gun, before pausing for several heartbeats.

Jopaquay smirked at him. "Do your worse, Ives."

"Remember, Joppa," Claymore rumbled. "This was your choice."

Claymore lifted the revolver and pointed it. But instead of firing, he flipped the gun around, caught it by the barrel, and threw it knifelike at the assassin in one fluid motion. Jopaquay's stride was unchanged as the projectile flew end over end toward him. His expression filled with contempt.

An instant before the gun reached him, Jopaquay brought his knives up and deftly blocked it with crossed blades. Metal struck metal. Sparks flew, and the revolver discharged on impact. The bullet struck the floor at the assassin's feet. The warded shields above him flared with an ethereal surge of fiery magic.

The remaining bullets in the revolver exploded in the assassin's face. Jopaquay screamed. He stumbled back, his bloodied face burned and peppered with scraps of metal shrapnel. He fell to the floor, writhing in agony.

Claymore threw Serralto's limp body back onto his shoulder. Ren followed him through the swinging doors. They entered the back kitchen and food prepping area. Claymore pushed his way through the panicked waitstaff and aproned cooks toward an exit on the far side.

"How'd you know that would work?" Ren said as they wove their way through the chaos of the kitchen workers.

"I didn't," Claymore replied. "I assumed the magical wards would cause the gun to either misfire or explode. Jopaquay wanted the satisfaction of seeing the gun blow up in my face too badly. Never underestimate someone's hubris. It's the easiest way to force them into a mistake."

"What do we do now?"

"We run!" Claymore replied.

"Run where?"

"They'll be watching every exit. We need to find a way out that won't get us killed."

Claymore opened a door that led to a narrow corridor used by the staff to restock the kitchen. Stacks of supplies stood along both walls. They hurried down the carpeted hallway.

"They'll have everyone looking for us now," Claymore said.

Ren found a door that led to stairs leading down. "We can find a way out through the lower levels!"

"No, we need to go up," Claymore replied. "Do you think you can fly all three of us out of here?"

"I don't know. The cut's not fully healed. I may need more time to recover."

"That's fine," Claymore replied. "When I was walking in, I noticed a wing of the third floor extended out over the bay. If we get up there, we can jump to the water before they realize where we went! We'll swim for the trees and make for the rabbit-hole. It's our best shot."

"You want me to stay behind and run interference?" Ren offered. "It'll give you time to get Serralto out?"

"No, you've done enough already," Claymore said. "Stay close to me."

Three security personal rounded the corner at the far end of the hall. Each carried a wooden staff the height of their body with a crescent-shaped headpiece on the top.

"Stop where you are!" the woman in front shouted. She held the staff in one hand and thumped it on the floor. A blue glow appeared inside the crescent before a small sphere of blazing light shot out. It whizzed past Ren, exploding in a silent cloud of smoke on the wall behind him. Several more struck the walls around them. The blasts left no scorch marks on the paint. Ren guessed the entire building of the nightclub must be ensconced with protective magical wards.

"They're not trying to hit us," Claymore said. "They won't risk hitting Serralto. Those are just warning shots to get us to surrender. There are smoke bombs in the duffle bag marked with blue tape! The red tape is the grenades. Be careful of which ones you grab!"

Ren unzipped the bag, digging through it until he found a cylindrical can with a strip of blue tape on it. He pulled the pin and tossed it into the middle of the hall.

Claymore took off up the stairwell. The deadweight of Serralto did not slow him one step. Fireballs flashed exploded in the stairwell all around them. When he reached the third floor, he threw open the door and Ren followed him out onto a carpeted hallway lined with sconce lighting along the walls.

A dense, unnatural fog rolled down the hallway toward them, covering the ceiling in what appeared to be dark rain clouds. The air was suddenly thick and humid. A drizzle of precipitation fell on Ren's face. Small bursts of thunder rumbled and boomed along the ceiling.

"What new level of hell is this?" Claymore growled.

"Is that rain?" Ren asked. He lifted his palm, letting the drops of water land on it.

"I think so. Be on your guard."

Soft laughter came from somewhere down the mist filled hallway.

"Did you think you were going to get away so easily?" an unseen voice said. It sounded female. "I knew you wouldn't try to sneak away in the chaos of the crowds. Too obvious. This seemed more logical. It was an educated guess, but it paid off."

Claymore threw Ren a glance. Without a word, he knew what his partner expected of him. Their years together had honed a level of trust between them. Once the grenade exploded,

Ren was to go in and take down whoever was behind the supernatural rain and fog. If she didn't fight him, she'd live. If she fought back, then things would end differently. He found himself nostalgic for how things once were between him and Claymore.

Ren peered into the thick fog. Visibility dropped to only a few feet in front of him. He took a grenade from the duffle bag, pulled the pin, and tossed it in the direction of the voice.

The still air of the hallway stirred. A gust of wind came up from nowhere and blew against their faces, followed by the sound of a metal object bouncing back toward them. The grenade canister bounced out of the fog toward them.

"Watch out!" Claymore threw his weight against the closest door. It burst open, and he was through. Ren ran after him. The grenade exploded in the hallway. The blast knocked Ren into his partner and they both fell to the carpeted floor.

"Check the balcony!" Claymore yelled. "See if we can jump to the water!" He left Serralto where he fell and slammed the door closed, pressing his shoulder against it.

Ren rushed to the railing of the balcony and leaned out. Below him, the lazy waters of the bay lapped at the white sands. "We're over the water," he yelled. "But I can't tell how deep it goes."

"We'll have to risk it!" Claymore replied. The pressure on the other side of the door caused it to buckle.

The door blew inward under the force of swirling winds. Claymore was thrown back. scrambled to his feet and dragged Serralto with him to the balcony. The heavy fog billowed into the room. Black clouds crept in across the ceiling, bringing with it a pelting rain.

The voice spoke again, full of calm confidence. "You have kidnapped someone who is under my protection, and I'm here to take him back."

A swirling wind swept into the room. It dissolved into a shadowy figure dressed in dark clothes and a cloak. Ren recognized her as the woman sitting at the table next to Serralto. But there was something else about her. He had seen that phantasmal whirlwind before. Then he remembered where.

"You were in Minstrel Cotty's study!" Ren yelled. "You assassinated him!"

The woman said nothing. A sly smile appeared at the corner of her mouth. "If you are not familiar with me and my work," she said. "My name is Audette Shoal. Trust me when I say I'm a professional, so none of this is personal. I'm just doing what I've been paid to do."

"Serralto told you when our meeting with Cotty would take place," Claymore growled. "So you could be there to pin his murder on us. Ren, you ready?"

"Now?" Ren asked.

"Do it!" Claymore answered.

Ren pressed against the wound in his side. Some pain was present, but he could tell his body was on the mend. Which meant he had limited choices of what to change into. It had to be something roughly his own size and mass. But still fast enough to reach the weather witch before she could react. The image of a sleek black panther came to his mind. He unbuckled his gun belt and tore open the front of his shirt, so he would not get tangled.

Audette Shoal lifted her hands toward the ceiling. The thunderheads crackled and the rain within the room increased. Static electricity filled the air around her. Ren felt his hair stand on end. His body quivered as he began to change shape. The sorceress brought her hands down like a maestro conducting the crescendo of a symphony.

Thunder exploded above her. Tendrils of electricity from the clouds struck them both. Excruciating pain shot through Ren's entire body as the electricity coursed through him. His back arched as his muscles and joints locked. He couldn't move. The paralyzing pain stopped a moment later, and he crashed to the floor in his natural shape.

The sorceress's face filled with unrestrained joy. "Controlling the primal elements of nature is a wondrous thing to behold," she said. "Don't you think so?"

A flurry of winds picked up around her. It blew her hood back. Wild black hair streaked in white flew about her head. She pulled what looked like silver needles from her pocket and held them out in front of her. She blew on them and a dozen thin silver-needled darts, each tied with a tiny red ribbon, flew from her outstretched palm.

Ren dropped to the floor as several darts whizzed over him. Claymore crouched and shielded himself with Serralto's body as he backed up to the balcony railing. A handful of silver needles struck the unconscious man in the back.

Ren pushed himself up. His legs wobbled under him. His body tingled all over, his extremities numb from the lightning strike. Claymore leaned against the railing.

"Claymore, we have to leave!" Ren yelled. He grabbed the railing to jump, then looked back to find his partner down on one knee. A single silver dart stuck in the back of his calf.

"Don't worry about me," Claymore said his words slurring. "You know what you have to do!" He dropped Serralto to the floor. Whatever poison or drug was on the dart, it was already doing its job. Claymore shoved Ren to the railing as he succumbed to the foul toxin and collapsed to the balcony floor.

"I'm not leaving you..." Ren replied.

"Just find me," Claymore murmured before he was gone.

The assassin whirled both hands in front of her. The rain subsided and Ren could feel the room's air pressure change, even from out on the balcony. Everything fell silent, as if the air had been sucked out of the room like the receding tide. Ren stepped to the railing but stopped. He knew he should run, but he couldn't leave his partner behind. He whipped around and drew his pistol, hoping the balcony was beyond the reach of the magical wards, and wouldn't blow off his hand when he fired the pistol.

A torrent of powerful winds slammed into Ren, strong enough to lift him off his feet. His pistol fired. The bullet struck the floor.

He slammed into the balcony railing. It knocked the wind out of him. He flipped over the polished wood, somersaulting head over feet above the water.

He struggled to draw in the air, flailing helplessly over the moonlit bay. He couldn't tell how far the harsh winds carried him, but the balcony was nothing but a distant portal of light when he hit the water. The last thing he saw before hitting the water was the sorceress, Audette Shoal, standing over Claymore.

He slammed into the dark waves, and everything went black.

Chapter 25
Dragon's Delight

Ren floated in inky blackness. He couldn't tell if he was unconscious or awake, dead or alive. It was not a good time to be dead. All he could remember was Claymore was in deep trouble and needed him.

He tried to move but found he couldn't. his limbs were limp and useless. If this was death, he didn't like it. Was he going to float in this nothingness forever?

A bright light appeared in the distance. The pale glow reminded him of a ley-line or rabbit-hole, yet somehow different. He floated toward it, like a boat caught in a river's current. The doorway grew closer. His speed picked up until the light completely engulfed him. His body tingled with the same sensation that came from the shifting realities that occurred while moving from world to world.

"Wake up!" A voice echoed in the back of Ren's head. It was strangely alien to him, yet familiar.

"They are drawing near!' the voice said. "You must run before they find us!"

The dream ended.

Ren lifted his face from the wet sand. He was lying alone on a dark beach. The water lapped at his boots. He had no idea how he got there, or any recollection of how much time had passed since the battle with the sorceress. The last thing he recalled was the murky waters of the bay as he sank into its black depths. He remembered dreaming of a coastal village destroyed in a raging storm. But that was only a dream, wasn't it?

He didn't remember swimming to the beach. He rolled over on his back, every muscle aching. Across the bay, the Gallows Club sat, its garish lights reflecting off the water, taunting him. He didn't like the idea of running from a fight. His first impulse was to go back for Claymore, but he knew his partner would not be there.

What was that voice inside his head? Was it the shadow that the Grimm Jester said followed him wherever he went? Was it the presence he sometime felt in the silent moments? Gideon insisted no one had ever figured out Ren's origin. Where he came from or how he fell out the sky into the ocean. Ren knew there was a connection between the two. But he also knew he didn't have time to worry about that. Claymore needed help.

The thought crossed his mind to contact the Raconteurs, but he dismissed the idea. He doubted they maintained a field house in Adezhda. And if they did, how would he find it? And even if he found it, Claymore could be dead before they got to him.

Claymore always kept Ren close to his side. The trickster was recklessly dangerous on his own. Ren didn't mind letting his partner be the moral compass for the both of them. But now Claymore was in the hands of the *Black Rose* and their Grand Inquisitor, Dmitri the Confessor.

That meant the rules of right and wrong no longer applied. He was on his own, unshackled to do whatever it took to save his partner, and there would be no mercy for those who stood in his way.

In the trees beyond the beach, voices reached him. The sound of people arguing and stomping through the underbrush. Ren pulled off his wet shirt and tossed it aside before kicking off his boots. His pistol was missing, so he unbuckled his gun belt and dropped it to the sand. The commotion in the trees grew closer.

He took the companion compass from his pocket and held it up. The large needle spun and wobbled, before it stopped to point across the waters to Adezhda.

He checked the injury he had taken from Jopaquay. The knife cut was nothing but a thin red line running along his side that seemed to have fully healed. Cuts and bruises, however deep, healed quickly. Broken bones took a longer. It was internal injuries that took the longest to heal. The scar from Jopaquay's would disappear completely in a few days.

He looked down at his bare feet, focusing his thoughts on one image, and shifted. Dark course fur grew over his naked torso and arms. Black feathered wings sprouted from his shoulders. He flexed his wings to their full span. His mass remained the same as in his natural form, but he lost several inches in height. Satisfied, he ambled forward on short, crooked legs and took to the air in the form of a flying monkey.

A warm wind blew in his face as Ren soared across the dark bay. Below him, the lights of Adezhda rippled on the black waters. He passed over dozens of pleasure yachts and leisure crafts that lay anchored for the night. The directional compass took him across the bay. Reaching the far shore, he continued up into the low lying-hills to the high-priced villas and estates overlooking the ocean.

Circling the hillside for several minutes narrowed his search to one particular villa at the western edge of the island. High stone walls surrounded the grounds of the estate. Claymore was down there. Ren was convinced of that.

He circled around again to survey the grounds and get an idea of what he may be up against. A small flat-roofed building stood outside the walls next to the front gates. He counted six armed guards waiting along a private road leading up to the villa. Beyond the walls stood an opulent multi-storied villa with a small tower built on one side.

The outside of the estate was lit by torchlight, while the glow of electric lights emanated from the villa's windows. The walls around the property were unusually high, making the villa resemble a fortified castle in contrast to its surrounding affluent neighbors. He glided high above the tropical trees that lined the long driveway to avoid being seen by those on the ground.

The moment he cleared the shadows of the trees, he spied a sentry silhouetted against the night sky. He leaned on the railing of a narrow walkway that encircled the tower. A thin trail of smoke from his cigarette floated in the air away from him.

Ren glided down to the front lawn. He remained in the shape of the flying monkey and crouched in the shadows. When no alarm sounded, he crept along the wall.

In the soft moonlight, Ren could make out charred areas of blackened ash where something had scorched the stones. The stench of brimstone filled his nostrils and burned his eyes.

His bare foot plopped in something soft and squishy, concealed in the darkness. He gagged at the smell and pulled his monkey foot out. The stench of animal scat wafted through the air. He glanced around for a beast capable of leaving such a deposit. Despite wiping his foot off in the grass, the horrible odor lingered.

Ren caught movement from the corner of his eye. A serpentine shape, at least thirty feet long, came around the building's corner. Another smaller one followed. The creatures lumbered into the torchlight of the villa. They were long, serpentine dragons propelling themselves across the expansive lawn on six stubby legs. The torchlight from the villa shimmered off their iridescent scales.

Both were wingless, with broad, tapered snouts. Two rows of foot-long spikes ran down the top of their scaley backs to the tip of their coiled tails. Twin horns grew in a gentle curve off the back of their wedge-shaped heads.

The larger of the two growled. A low guttural sound, somewhere between a yowl and a mewl, before spewing a ball of fire into the night sky. The smaller one snorted smoke out its nostrils and shot a fireball into the wall twenty feet from where Ren crouched. It exploded, illuminating everything in an eerie red glow for a few moments. Ren threw himself onto the grass. The smell of burnt brimstone filled the air.

Both dragons lifted their snouts and sniffed the air. Ren did not wait to see what scent they had picked up. Staying low, he ran along the shadows, spread his wings and lifted off the grass. He flew across the lawn up to a support beam under the tower's walkway.

Whether by scent or sight, the dragons slithered to the base of the tower. The larger one clawed its way up the side of the building until it stood on its hind legs, a dozen feet short from where Ren hid. He folded his wings in tighter, making himself as small as possible. He didn't dare move or shift.

Footsteps echoed off the wood deck above him. Ren could see a sentry approach through the slits in the boards of the walkway. He stopped right over the spot where Ren hid and leaned over the railing to see what the commotion below was all about. He leapt back with a yelp when he saw the serpentine dragon staring up from below. Ren looked out from the shadows of his hiding spot to find two large copper eyes reflected off the moonlight.

"Ludres, is everything okay?" a voice asked over the crackle of a radio.

"Yeah, I thought I saw movement on the lawn, but it was nothing," Ludres said. He ventured another peek over the railing. "The ladies are restless tonight. Toska's staring up at me right now. Kodota's coughing up fireballs into the wall again."

Ren couldn't tell if the Toska's eyes were focused on him or on the sentry standing on the walkway. Its enormous jaws hung open, exposing rows of gleaming dagger-length teeth and a long, flicking tongue. A fireball from this close of a range would be the end of him.

Without warning, Toska belched a glob of molten brimstone into the air. Ludres jumped back as the fireball flew past him. It exploded high above the tower.

The dragon tore into the stucco wall, trying to climb higher. Frustrated, she roared and spewed a second glowing ball of red and orange into the sky.

Kodota climbed up next to her larger companion, growling and snapping its jaws. Toska responded with a roar and clawed at the smaller one's head. The scaly beasts crashed to the ground, wrapped around each other.

"Why would anyone try to domesticate a Coiled Dragon?" Ludres laughed into his radio. He leaned over the edge of the railing, but with more caution this time. Below him, the dragons continued rolling around, locked in each other's jaws, biting and clawing the other with renewed vigor.

The radio in his hand crackled. "They're supposed to be trainable and make good guardians," the voice on the other side replied. "It's not for us to ask why. We are only cogs in a greater machine. Hang on, we have a car approaching. I have to go. Keep an eye out." The radio went dead.

Two headlights appeared down the road. The vehicle slowed to a stop at the gate. A crack of light appeared under the bottom slit of the front gates. Ren could see the guards move around with their guns held on the vehicle.

A few moments later, a somber pipe melody started playing from somewhere. Both dragons stopped fighting and became still as statues. Their long necks started weaving back and forth with the music, as if they were in a trance. Kodota moved first, slithering out of sight around the corner of the villa. A moment later, Toska disappeared after it. Ren breathed a silent sigh of relief and inched out of his hiding place.

The sentry's radio crackled above him. "The dragons are back in their cage. It's okay to open the front gates."

"Roger that," came a third voice from the front gates.

The high entrance to the villa swung inward, and a vehicle drove through. It was the same automobile Ren had followed into Adezhda earlier. The limousine circled the fountain and stopped in front of the villa. A servant rushed out to open the backdoor of the vehicle. A massive figure climbed out.

Odd Bod rose to his full height, dwarfing the servant in front of him. He adjusted his suit coat and disappeared through the front entrance. Ren found himself smiling at the appearance of the gang-ster. It was fitting Bod should show up. Now that all the players were present, the party could begin.

Chapter 26
Cloak and Dagger

Ren clung to the wooden beams under the tower walkway, waiting for things to quiet down. Eventually, the front gates closed, and the footsteps above him grew faint in the distance as the sentry returned to his rounds. He felt it was safe enough to venture out from the shadows.

He inched along the ledge under the walkway, his apish fingers finding handholds. His squat legs and tail dangled under him. He reached the corner of the watchtower and dropped into the open air, spreading out his wings as he fell.

Keeping to the shadows as best he could, Ren flew around the side of the tower, following the wide swathe of grass that encircled the building. The back of the villa looked out over a cliff at the incoming surf of a calm sea. The moon sat high in the dark sky and cast an ethereal glow over the walled-off terrace below him. A strong flap of his wings carried him up to the carved stone railing of a balcony on the second floor. Beneath him, enormous muddy tracks torn up the grass. They led to a closed iron gate built into the side of under the villa.

He climbed over the railing and crept to the French doors. Inside, a young servant girl busied herself drawing down the enormous bed that dominated the room. The grating sound of a gate opening caught his ear. He glanced over the railing to see the dragon's tail disappear underneath the villa.

Ren backed up into the shadows and shifted back into real form. No sense in scaring the servant with his flying monkey guise. He took the companion compass from his pocket and slid it across the deck in front of the glass doors. It bounced a couple of times before coming to rest within easy view from the inside.

The noise caught the servant's attention. She came up to the windows and peered out, shading her eyes from the indoor glare. The young woman looked down at the compass. She looked behind her before unlatching the glass door and opening it enough to reach the compass.

As she picked it up, Ren jumped from the shadows and grabbed her by the wrist. He put a finger to his lips for silence. Still holding her arm, he took the compass and forced the young servant back into the room. He pointed to a chair next to a small table of refreshments. The servant sat down without resistance.

Ren leaned in close to her. "They brought a man in earlier," he whispered. "Where did they take him?"

"There is a red door in a hallway beyond the kitchen," the woman muttered. "They take people down there that never come back out. The house staff is not allowed near it."

"Thank you," Ren replied. "Now give me your shirt, pants and shoes."

After the servant undressed down to her undergarments, Ren took her to the bathroom and bound her hands and feet with the cords from the bedroom drapes. He tied a napkin around her head to gag her mouth and lifted her into the tub. He drew the shower curtain closed and quickly dressed in the servant's clothing. As he reentered the bedroom, the door opened.

Ren shifted into the form of the young servant. He began fiddling with the tableware and food trays laid out on the table in the center of the room. The door swung open and a weary-looking Piqwic York entered.

Piqwic closed the door and removed his heavy red coat, tossing it over the back of a chair. The rich red material was singed with dozens of tiny burns from his fiery encounter earlier that evening at the Pithy Fool. He stepped to his dresser and removed the many rings from his fingers. He noticed Ren standing there for the first time.

"That is all," he grumbled, pulling on a robe. "You may go."

"Yes sir," Ren answered, mimicking the servant voice and cadence. He bowed and headed to the door.

"Wait!" Piqwic ordered, his voice flat and irritated.

Ren froze, his hand on the doorknob. He didn't want to have to kill Piqwic. Or maybe he did, but he would let Piqwic's next few words decide the man's remaining lifespan. He turned around.

"Sir?"

"Take the tray with you," Piqwic said, not bothering to look up.

Although somewhat disappointed, Ren dutifully grabbed the empty silver tray from the table. He bowed, casting his eyes to the floor. "Of course," he replied. "My apologies."

He stopped at the door. This was one of those indecisive moments where Claymore always had the answer. His servant's disguise would get him around undetected easy enough, but would it get him past the red door? Or should he take a more all-inclusive disguise? One with some authority behind it. Piqwic York's face could get him anywhere in the house, more so than any servant. Ren turned around.

"Is there something else?" Piqwic looked up with an agitated huff. He bit down on the pipe hanging from the corner of his mouth.

"Yes, just one more thing," Ren said with a bow. He stepped in and hit the financier in the throat with the edge of the round tray. Piqwic choked back a cry. He staggered backward, grabbing his neck, trying to call out for help but couldn't. Ren followed the blow with a swift kick in the chest, sending him flying back into the baseboard of the bed. The rotund gangster rolled on the floor. Ren locked the bedroom door.

"How dare you!" he choked out. "I'll have you skinned alive for this."

Ren shook his head and shifted back to his real form. "I don't think so."

"You?!" the fat criminal gurgled. "How?!" The words caught in his throat. There was panic in his voice. He started to tremble. Ren saw Piqwic's realization of the dire predicament he found himself in. Ren enjoyed seeing a little fear in someone he was about to interrogate.

"How do I get down to Claymore?" he asked, allowing the fury building up inside him to rise to the surface.

The gang lord tried to regain his composure. He did not have his bodyguards around him now, so his bravado was gone, replaced by wide-eyed fear. He cleared his voice.

"You are making a great mistake, changeling," the gang lord declared. His voice was deeper now, more in control, but the tone still lacked any genuine conviction. "I am a chief lieutenant of Mordecai Davos. To assault me is to assault the *Society of Black Rose*, and to attack Mordecai is to bring death upon yourself."

"Shut up!" Ren snapped. "It's been a long night, and you're giving me a headache. There's only you and me now, so I'm asking the questions. "Where is the Red Door?"

"At the bottom of the staircase, take a right," Piqwic said. "You'll come to another shorter hall. You'll see the Red Door down that hallway. That leads to the lower levels. Claymore is down there, but you better hurry. He will not last long under the tender mercies of Dmitri the Confessor."

"Good enough," Ren said quietly, trying to maintain the tone of intimidation despite the impatience raging inside him. "Now where are the letters the ghoul gave you at the Pithy Fool?"

Piqwic pointed to his red greatcoat thrown over the chair. Ren dug through the pockets. He felt the chain of a necklace and pulled out the talisman that Dom Tarran Ran used to keep the Grimm Jester at bay.

Ren studied the strange wire-entwined orb for a moment

before putting the necklace around his neck. He had no idea what its powers were, but he couldn't shake the feeling that he and the Grimm Jester would meet again, and the necklace might help make a difference in that regard.

He continued to look through the coat until he found the stack of envelopes in an inside pocket. He counted seven thick letters tied into a bundle and stuffed them into the back waistband of his pants. He held the necklace up.

"What is the Grimm Jester?"

"Some foul devil or fiend, or possibly even one of the Deaths themselves," Piqwic said. "No one knows. Mordecai bought the creature from a visiting necromancer many years ago."

"So Mordecai controls the monster?" Ren snarled.

"Yes, the monster obeys his every command." The fat financier rubbed his face with both hands. "No one dares challenge Mordecai while the Jester is at his side. Even Odd Bod avoids him."

Ren gave him a smile as he stood up. Piqwic was cruel and vicious, and Ren took great pleasure in watching him squirm. With Mordecai away, Piqwic's death would deal a heavy blow to the *Society of the Black Rose*. The resulting vacuum in leadership could lead to infighting, which would tear the criminal organization apart from the inside. Ren adjusted his grip on the tray.

"Take off the shirt and pants," Ren ordered. He didn't know why, but he couldn't bring himself to kill Piqwic even as he whimpered at his feet. Sparing his life and letting a heartless killer walk away unpunished did not sit well with him, either. He took a deep breath and searched the dresser for something to restrain Piqwic instead.

"You'll never get your partner out of here alive," Piqwic said softly as Ren dressed. The fear gone from his voice now that he realized he was not about to die. A smirk appeared on his round face. "I just came from there. He'll be in no shape to travel for some time."

Ren pressed his knee down on Piqwic's chest and grabbed the linen neckerchief wrapped around his thick neck. He twisted it until the fat man's eyes bulged and his face turned bright red. Piqwic tried to break the hold on his throat with his tied hands but could not. Ren released all his frustrations of the night into choking the life out of Piqwic York. He leaned in to the gangster's gasping face.

"Don't be so sure about that." Ren tightened his grip. "I'm very resourceful."

Piqwic thrashed under him as Ren twisted the neckcloth tighter. Finally, Piqwic's eyes fluttered, and he stopped struggling. Ren released his grip. Piqwic slumped down to the floor, his head bouncing off the tiles.

Ren watched the gangster's chest rise and fall as he finished dressing. He found leather belts in a drawer and bound Piqwic's hands and feet. He took a good look at Piqwic's face before he shifted into a near-perfect mirror image. He took the rings off the dresser and slipped them onto his newly acquired thick fingers. His charade was now complete. He pushed a cloth into Piqwic's mouth and tied the neckerchief tight around his head.

Closing the door behind him, he glanced up and down the empty hallway before closing the door. A brindle-colored house cat padded up the stairs as he descended. He knelt to scratch under its neck.

"You better make yourself scarce, buddy. The fireworks are about to begin," he warned the feline. The cat sniffed his foot. It hissed at him before darting up the stairs. Ren shrugged and continued downstairs.

The stairs ended at along a posh hallway, decorated with expensive accessories from across the cosmos. Lit sconces lined the wall, along with paintings and décor Ren knew were stolen from distant worlds across the Mythic Cosmos. He headed down the hallway toward the kitchen per Piqwic's directions. Voices could be heard coming a room ahead of him.

Ren picked up his pace, hoping to slip past the open doorway unnoticed. A glance out of the corner of his eye showed a dozen members of the *Black Rose* and gang leaders from the Pithy Fool sitting around talking and drinking with the other two Common Council members.

Ren exhaled in relief once he cleared the door, then a deep, booming voice spoke. "Piqwic? Please join us if you would." It was a command, not a request. Ren turned around and peeked his head into the room. Everyone had stopped talking and stared at him.

Odd Bod sat alone on a wide couch. He extended a giant hand toward an empty plush chair across from him. "Sit," he rumbled. "We need your input on a delicate situation."

Chapter 27
Small Mercies

Ren stuffed his hands into the pockets of his robe as he had seen Piqwic do and entered the lounge. Two tall, statuesque figures stood on either side of the doorway. Both were decidedly non-human, covered from head to foot in what appeared to be a single concealing hood and cloak. One was completely white, the other entirely black.

Each wore a porcelain mask the same color as the counterpart's robes and gripped a tall polearm. Ren assumed they were more than just bodyguards. He took the empty seat offered to him by Odd Bod and glanced about the room to get an idea at what he was up against.

At the other two access points into the lounge, two burly body-guards in leather vests stood, each armed with blades and pistols. The assassin, Audette Shoals, sat in a chair protectively close to a man stretched out on a divan near the unlit fireplace. A white cloth draped over the man's eyes, concealing his face, but Ren could tell it was Serralto Cardus.

Cassandra of the Nine Sisters gave Ren a self-satisfied smile. She reclined in her armchair, sipping from a wineglass. Next to her, Ooturo Bacraan smoked a carved pipe. The aromatic smoke floated to the ceiling and hung there. Hayeship Gribblin and three unknown individuals sat together at a table. Ren could only assume they were other high-ranking members of The Society of the Black Rose.

"I thought you were retiring for the night, York?" Cassandra asked. "You said the changeling's attack at the teahouse was too much for you?"

"I feel better," Ren replied in Piqwic's voice. "And I have a few more questions for our guest downstairs."

"You better hurry then," Odd Bod said. "I was just down there, and Ives was barely conscious."

Ren nodded at the comment. He needed to get out of here as quickly as he could. "What was it you needed from me, Bod?" he asked in an even tone.

"Since all the candidates who have made a bid for our open position are here," Odd Bod replied, "we have decided to take a vote on who it will be offered to. Fatima Magda and Garrow Halajan, would you join us at the center of the room?"

The two council members looked at each other and set their drinks down. Each took a place in front of Odd Bod. The giant leaned forward, putting his elbows on his knees. The couch he sat on sank even further under the distress of his immense weight.

"Serralto Cardus, if you could step over here, please."

Serralto removed the cloth from his face and sat up. He dabbed his forehead and neck before leaving the cloth on the arm of the couch. His eyelids drooped as he stood, swaying a bit on his feet. Audette caught his arm and walked him to where the other council members stood.

Ren smiled to himself, knowing he was still recovering from the effects of the tainted darts that had struck him earlier that evening. It took only a single dart to take down Claymore, but Serralto had a been hit by a half-dozen or more when his partner used him as a shield. It was surprising to Ren that the man was able to stand at all.

"The five members of the *Black Rose* present here today," Odd Bod said solemnly, "will each cast a vote for their choice of who will gain admittance into the society. If the vote ends in a tie, a second vote will be taken with only the remaining two candidates."

"Tanith Zella?"

A woman with short white hair who carried an air of magic around her stood up. She dressed in a kaleidoscope of layered clothing and threw back her blue cape dramatically. Her dark eyes seem to pierce each of the candidates as she studied them one by one.

"My vote will go to Garrow Halajan," she replied with a nod before sitting back down. Serralto seemed physical injured by her words. His feet shifted under his robes, but he remained where he stood. The other two next to him remained stoically silent.

"Caino Stratos?"

A brawny bald man sitting at the table looked up from his glass. He was impeccably dressed in an expensive outer jacket of red and gold and a freshly pressed blue linen shirt. He carried a short blade and gun at his belt. Ren could see in the man's eyes the dormant volcano of violence that lay beneath the fine clothes.

"Fatima Curzon," Caino growled. "She's the only one fit to run with the *Black Rose*."

Odd Bod nodded slowly. "Piqwic York?"

Ren found himself at a momentary loss for words. In the back of his mind, he had been debating if he should deny Serralto his chance of attaining more power, just out of spite. Or should he vote yes? Let Serralto feel the sting of having something he desired so much, be ripped away at the last second as Ren and Claymore dragged him back to Rogue Destiny.

"Piqwic?" Odd Bod asked. "Your decision."

"I vote for *Fatima Magda*," Ren said calmly. He decided it would be easier to get to Serralto if he were separated from the *Black Rose* rather than under their protection as a new member. That left two votes.

"That is two votes for Magda and one for Garrow," Odd Bod rumbled. "There are two votes left to cast. Elios Abass?"

A tall, not quite human looking, individual stood up. His eyes were pitch black, with golden slits for pupils. Elios was taller than Claymore, only leaner and more majestic in stature compared to Claymore's sheer physical presence. He wore high black boots and gray pants with a long sleeved scarlet shirt and vest under his outer black suede coat. He hooked his thumbs into his coat pockets and cleared his throat.

"My vote will also go to Garrow Halajan," he said. "The power he has consolidated within the Common Council benefits the *Black Rose's* interests far more than what either of the other candidates have to offer." Elios took his chair.

Odd Bod stood up. The couch creaked in relief as he rose. "That leaves the final vote to me," he said. His expression changed to an emotionless wall of stone. "Congratulations to both Fatima and Garrow for making it this far. Before I cast the deciding vote, we have one order of business to take care of."

"Serralto Cardus, you have successfully failed your initiation into the *Society of the Black Rose* and therefore will not be joining our ranks."

Serralto blinked in disbelief. "But I had Audette kill Minstrel Cotty as you requested," he said. "And I was able to lay the blame at the feet of the Raconteurs. I have done all I could to show my loyalty to Mordecai and the *Black Rose*. I would never act against your interests."

"Yes, you did as we asked," Odd Bod replied. "But none of that makes up for the total lack of discretion you showed tonight at the *Gallows Club*. Your underling led our enemies straight to us. This kind of negligence endangers everything we work towards and shows a personal weakness we cannot allow to taint our organization."

"Wait, a moment!" Serralto protested. Panic gripped him. Sweat broke out on his forehead. He frantically searched the room for any possible escape before turning back to Odd Bod. "We can discuss this! My position on the Common Council has provided invaluable information to the *Black Rose* for these last months. I demand to speak to Mordecai himself! I am owed at least that much!"

"That is not possible," Odd Bod said. "You have proven yourself a security risk we cannot afford. There is a long line of council members waiting to take your place. We have nothing left to discuss."

"Piqwic?" Bod said. "You've been quiet. Care to weigh in on this?"

Ren chose his words carefully. He couldn't allow Serralto to die, but if it came down to it, Claymore's life was more important. He kept his hands in robe to appear relaxed and stood up. He had done this a hundred times before, behind a hundred different faces, and knew it was all in the delivery.

"You acted foolishly, Serralto," he said. "That cannot be argued. But does a mistake committed by an underling warrant such a penalty? It has done nothing to make me doubt your loyalty. If we were all held to our shortcomings, none of us here would be fit to be part of the *Black Rose*. But in the end, you have brought our greatest enemy to our gates. I'm sorry, but a failure of that magnitude cannot be tolerated."

Ren repeated what the others before him had said, but decided at the last moment, he would throw Serralto to the wolves. He would no doubt be held somewhere until his fate was decided. It would be easier for Ren to grab him from a locked cell than a room full of gangsters. After Ren located Claymore, of course.

"Then our decision is final," Caino Stratos said. He stood up. "Onyz, Zabl, please dispose of Serralto in the dragon pit." The two statuesque figures at the main door to the room stepped forward.

Odd Bod shook his head. "Wait," he rumbled. "The presence of the acolytes upset the dragons. Lux, would you be kind enough to escort our guest down to the pits."

"There are votes coming up on the Council floor that I had to be present for!" Serralto explained. "My assistant needed to know where he could reach me! Please!"

One of the hulking bodyguards at the back of the room walked toward him. "C'mon, Cardus," Lux said. "No need to embarrass yourself any further."

Serralto shifted uneasily on his feet. "Audette!" he cried. "I'd appreciate some assistance here."

Audette Shoal stood up. Ren could tell she was taking in the demographics of the room and calculating her odds. She hesitated for a heartbeat before stepping in between the bodyguard and Serralto, taking a defensive position in front of her employer. Her hand ready to draw the blade at her side.

"I cannot allow you to do that," Audette said politely.

The hooded acolytes stepped toward the assassin and her employer. The tension in the room rose. Ren ran scenarios in his head of how to handle the situation. He might even find a temporary ally in Audette Shoal, at least long enough to get Serralto out of the room alive.

Odd Bod raised his hand. The two tall figures closing in on Serralto stopped. Bod chuckled. "It seems we have come to some sort of impasse."

"Yes, it does," Audette replied, her tone soft and confident. Ren felt the air in the room begin to stir.

Odd Bod chuckled. An empty, cruel gesture that was meant to ease the tension, but changed nothing.

"Then may I suggest a solution," Bod said, "before the bloodletting begins?"

"Such as?" Audette asked.

"How much does he pay you?" Bod asked her.

"Excuse me?" the woman replied. The wind picked up. It caught her hair, blowing it around.

"How much does Serralto Cardus pay you to work for him?" Odd Bod repeated.

"A thousand gold sovereigns a month. Why?"

"Audette, don't!" Serralto shouted. "We have a contract! You've sworn your loyalty to me."

The sorceress-assassin raised her hand to silence Serralto. "He's right. I never break a contract. Not good for my reputation."

"Then how about this," Odd Bod said. "The *Black Rose* will buy out your contract from Serralto. Will that ease your conscious?"

Audette lifted a curious eyebrow. "I'm listening."

"We will pay double the amount of your current contract if you come work for us. Will that be enough to assuage your conscious?"

"Triple."

"Done!" Odd Bod replied. "We've lost good people tonight, and you have proved your value by bringing us Claymore Ives. Will fifty thousand be enough to buy you out of your contract?"

The growing wind in the room ceased. Audette Shoal studied Serralto for a moment, her green eyes void of any emotion. "I think that's more than generous."

"Audette, please!" Serralto yelled. "You can't do this to me!"

"Sorry, it's only business," she said. "Even killers need to plan for a rainy day."

Odd Bod gave her a satisfied laugh. "Excellent," he rumbled. "Elio, please write Mr. Cardus a check for fifty- thousand sovereigns. We want to keep this legal and above board, after all."

Elio rose from his chair. He took out a narrow black binder from inside his vest. Clicking a pen, he opened it and began writing. When he finished, he tore the perforated check from the binder, folded the paper in half and slipped it into the chest pocket of Serralto's shirt.

"Your contract has been officially bought out by *The Otherworldly Import/Export Company*," Elio said with a cheeky smile. He patted Serralto on the back. "He's all yours, Lux."

Lux grabbed Serralto by an upper arm. "Let's go," he said.

Audette stepped back as Serralto was escorted to the door. He glanced over at her as the bodyguard ushered him past her. She shrugged and looked at Odd Bod.

"Yes?" Bod asked.

"I have to ask," she said. "Who were you going to vote for?"

Bod gave her a toothy smile. "Fatima, of course," he said. "Her off-world connections have proven invaluable to our business interests." He seemed impressed by the assassin's interest in the decisions made there tonight.

Audette turned to Fatima. "Congratulations are in order," she said with a sincere bow.

Odd Bod chuckled. "Now that you're in our employ," he rumbled, "please help escort Serralto down to the pits. When you're done there, come back here and we'll figure out who you'll be assigned to protect."

Audette agreed with a nod and fell in behind the bodyguard holding her ex-employer by the arm.

Ren gave a painful yawn and rubbed his eyes with the back of a hand. "Then I'm off to bed, everyone, this time for good. Right after I talk to Ives, of course, and raid the kitchen one last time tonight."

He gave a quick laugh at his joke and waddled out of the room toward what he hoped was the right direction. No one in the lounge gave him a second look. Things had been working in his favor so far, but now he had two lives to save and not just one.

Chapter 28
Dmitri the Confessor

Ren ambled out of the lounge imitating Piqwic's distinct gait. Audette walked behind the two thugs holding Serralto between them through the ornately decorated dining room to the kitchen area, passed what looked to be servant quarters, before turning down to a short hallway. A lone servant mopped the floors as they passed him to an adjoining hall. At the end of the short hallway, there was a red door.

Lux opened the wooden door, revealing a stairway. There was no lock or guard posted at the door, as if the *Black Rose* dared anyone who should be there to venture where they should not be. The bodyguard grabbed Serralto by the arm and lead him down to the lower levels of the villa. Audette followed behind Serralto. Ren waited until the other bodyguard descended into the darkness before following after him. A string of lights hung from the ceiling illuminated the passageway. The bottom of the steps led a tunnel chiseled out of living stone.

Ren grabbed the doorhandle. He paused until the others were out of sight. Again, he was uncertain what to do, stop Serralto from being fed to the dragons or rescue Claymore. An anguished moan from behind the door made his choice for him. Dmitri the Confessor lifted his head as the door swung open.

"Oh, hello, Piqwic," he said. "I didn't expect to see you again tonight. What brings you back down?" Dmitri held a stained cloth in his gloved hands and was administering something into one of the cuts that covered Claymore's naked torso.

"I had a few more questions for our guest," Ren replied. "How is he doing, Dmitri?" Ren asked flatly, hiding his building rage behind a wall of indifference. He buried his hands in the pockets of the robe, unable to take his eyes from the unconscious figure hanging in chains on the opposite wall of the room.

"Resting, quietly," Dmitri muttered. "He is unusually resistant to answering my questions. The usual ministrations are not working as quickly as they should, but he'll come around in the end. They always do."

Dmitri dressed in the shabby overalls of a laborer covered with dark stains that could only be dried blood. It was hard to tell in the low light. Splattered blood covered one side of Dmitri's gaunt face and neck. He hadn't bothered to clean it off. His surprisingly animated expression told Ren this was a man who enjoyed his work.

The rubber boots Dmitri wore squeaked as he stepped away from Claymore to a wheeled cart, filled with shelves of phials, decanters, and bottles of varying sizes. In the clear bottles, Ren could see liquids of different hues that bubbled and roiled under their own power.

Ren walked up to his partner. The blood dripping from dozens of cuts on Claymore's face and torso formed a dark pool of blood on the stone floor at Ren's feet. Each tiny slice was a precise incision that covered every bit of exposed skin, even his ears. Intermixed with the sliced skin were small circular burns that looked like they may have been caused by magic. Ren felt a lethal fury rise in him.

A discoloring brown substance had been rubbed into many of the wounds. It gave off a rancid stench. A bubbling ooze seeped out of them. Claymore twitched and winced in pain.

"I just applied a solvent that sensitizes the individual nerve endings, giving even the tiniest cut the equivalent of unbelievable agony. It magnifies the victim's pain a hundredfold and is quite effective in breaking through someone's hesitancy to answer my questions."

Ren stared at Claymore, his back to Dmitri. "Again, apologies for the late visit," Ren said pleasantly. "I've been so busy lately that I've lost all sense of time, like I've *fallen asleep in the afternoon sunshine.*"

Claymore lifted his head to meet Ren's eyes. His face was covered in cuts and his hair was matted with dried blood. He stared at Ren through half-open eyes. Fresh streams of blood trickled down his cheeks like tears. A weak smile appeared on his lips.

"Took you long enough," he mumbled, his voice raspy and barely audible.

Guilt tightened in the pit of his stomach as Ren examined the chains holding his partner. He should have gotten here sooner. Claymore would have.

His partner's body hung limp, suspended above the floor by shackles on his ankles and wrists. The thick chains stretched to a pulley system in the ceiling, then down to a wheel attached to the wall on his right. Ren ran a hand down the lever that operated the electrical hoist that raised and lowered the prisoners.

"Torture is an interesting business, don't you think?" Ren said. "So many ways to hurt a person." He turned to find Dmitri staring at him. The Confessor's eyes lingered longer than necessary.

Dmitri averted his gaze to the tray of razor sharp surgical knives he was cleaning. He picked up a thin, nasty looking blade and began wiping the blood from its gleaming surface.

After a moment of uncomfortable silence, Dmitri spoke, his accent thicker than before, his tone more serious. "As you know, Piqwic, I am a student of the human condition. And the most important thing I've learned about humans is their desperate need for routine."

Ren braced himself for an attack. Dmitri finished his cleaning and laid the ivory handled blade down on the tray with the other scalpels and instruments of pain. Next to the tray was a gnarled foot-long stick. It resembled any broken twig lying on the ground. Dmitri's boney fingers picked up the thin twisted stick.

"For example," he said, tapping the stick on the palm of his hand. "We might honor a loved one who has died by carrying a precious keepsake or piece of jewelry on our person."

"That's interesting," Ren replied, wondering what Dmitri meant.

"Routine is so important in understanding and dealing with grief. Like the grief you feel for your dead wife and how you wear that blue sapphire ring in honor of her. The one you're currently wearing on a different finger."

Dmitri lifted the stick toward Ren and shouted, *"Ala-Hestra!"* A bright flash of magical energy shot from its tip. Ren kicked the wheeled cart into Dmitri and ducked under the blast. The shot exploded off the wall behind him.

The cart knocked Dmitri back before it tipped on its side, glass jars and clear decanters shattering on the floor. Different substances mixed together, causing a crackling and rapid popping noise. A blue flame ignited on the floor creating tendrils of noxious smoke and discolored bubbles.

Dmitri scrabbled to his feet, choking on the toxic air. Ren ran and dove on top of him, punching him in the face repeatedly until the man lay bloodied and broken under his fist. He would have continued, if not for the violent coughing behind him. Letting go of the lifeless Dmitri, he climbed off him and ran to Claymore.

Ren pulled the lever on the hoist and the chains holding Claymore lowered him to the floor. He examined the shackles attached to his wrists. They were padlocked shut.

"I need the keys!" he shouted in between his own violent coughs.

"In the workbench," Claymore answered, trying to free himself from the tangle of chains wrapped around him.

Ren pulled open the top drawer. He fumbled with a set of keys, trying to locate the right one. He finally did and quickly removed the restraints. Claymore threw an arm over his shoulder and together they headed for the door. Claymore stopped.

"My bag!" Claymore groaned. "Grab the duffle bag!"

"I'll get it!" Ren lead Claymore out into the hallway, barefoot and bleeding, and helped him to the floor. He took a deep breath before returning to the dark fumes of the torture chamber. His eyes burned. The alchemical clouds mixed together into a thick multi-colored mist before separating again in a strange dance of chemical reactions.

He stumbled to the workbench and grabbed the duffle bag, throwing the strap over a shoulder. Dmitri the Confessor lay face down on the floor, his clothing seared by the corrosive liquid dripping from the blackened ceiling. The droplets burned smoldering divots in the stone tiles.

Ren realized he would need every trick he could come up with if he was going to get Claymore and Serralto out of the villa alive. Next to the worktable was a large cabinet. He opened the doors to find an assortment of items he guessed were left by the room's previous guests. Then a thought struck him.

He looked around for the wand Dmitri had tried to kill him with. He spotted it lying next to the wall, picked it up and stuck it in the deep pants pocket. He rushed through of the clouds of toxic chemicals into the tunnel next to Claymore. With his hands on his knees, he took several deep breaths in between coughs to clear his lungs.

Claymore sat down against the wall of the passage, fading in and out of consciousness. Ren helped him to his feet.

"Where are we?" his partner asked, looking up and down the dimly lit tunnel. His muscular chest heaving with exhaustion. Blood dripped from a hundred different cuts over his body and face. Ren listened for any sound of pursuit before answering.

"We're under a villa in the hills of Adezhda," Ren replied.

"Where's Serralto?"

"They took him that way to the dragon pits."

"They have dragons?"

"Yeah," Ren replied. "More like red-wyrms or ruby drakes, really. Wingless, but they belch fireballs and guard the grounds around the villa."

"Doesn't matter," Claymore growled. He spat a glob of blood onto the floor. "We need to go get Serralto."

"Forget him! I need to get you out of here!"

"No!," Claymore insisted. "If he dies, all of this will have been for nothing!"

"But you're in bad shape. You can barely stand."

Ren supported Claymore's weight as he got to his feet. They passed several wooden doors with barred windows. Behind the doors, Ren could see wine cellars and random storage. They had not gone far before Claymore fell to the floor.

"My skin's on fire," he groaned. He propped himself against the wall. "It hurts to move."

Ren set the duffle bag down, unzipped it, and dug through the contents. Claymore had his sawed-off rifle and the two six-shot revolvers inside. He grabbed one of the pistols, made sure it was loaded, and kicked the duffle bag over to Claymore.

"Your guns are in there," Ren told him. "Wait here. I'll be right back with Serralto."

Claymore leaned back against the wall and closed his eyes. Ren didn't want to leave his partner there, but he had little choice. He continued down the tunnel, peeling off Piqwic's oversized robe and shifted back to himself. He cinched the voluminous pants around his narrow waist with the belt. The familiar sound of pipes filled the air.

He crept down the corridor. The stench of brimstone grew more powerful the further he ventured. He looked back to see Claymore slumped over and motionless next to the duffle bag.

The passageway opened out into a huge cavern. On one side, a wooden door lead into a room in the solid rock under the villa. The dragon pit was a circular, barred enclosure, stretching fifty feet across and a hundred feet from end to end. The domed peak reached up thirty-feet, creating an underground arena. The metal bars of the cage were thick and interwoven, too small for an adult-sized individual to crawl through, but he wasn't worried about that. He never had trouble getting out of a cage.

At the center of the dirt floor, Serralto and Ignatz lay bound hand and foot.

Two figures stood at the door of the cage with their backs to him. The shorter one had dark graying hair woven into long braids. She wore layered, colorful robes and held a set of wooden pipes. Beside her, Audette stood waiting for the henchman, Lux, to reach them.

Serralto and Ignatz lay on the ground at the center of the dusty arena. Lux closed the cage door behind him and latched it. He opened the panel of a control box and pulled down a lever.

There was a slight hum from the bars of the cage. A red luminous essence crawled up the sides of the cage, joining together at the domed peak. A magical ward similar to the one at the Gallows Club glowed brightly for a moment then faded. The entire enclosure was shielded by a magical barrier to prevent the great beasts from reaching beyond the confines of their cage.

Lux pushed a button in the control box and the outer gates rose. The dragon-handler lifted the pipes to her lips and played the same sorrowful melody that had drawn the dragons away earlier. It was the same tune Ren had heard outside earlier.

The henchman turned away from the cage to see Ren walking out of the tunnel. Lux reached for the gun under his coat, but Ren put him down with two shots to the chest. The gunshots echoed through the enclosed space. Lux fell back to the stone floor. Ren pointed the pistol at Audette. The assassin raised her hands, glancing around for any avenue of escape.

"You," Ren said, motioning his gun at the woman next to Audette. "What's your name?"

"Dejha Min," the woman said.

"Play your pipes," Ren ordered, "and call the dragons off."

"I cannot. Once they've been called, they have been trained to come back to their cage."

"Then turn off the shield and close the gate to the pits."

Dejha complied. She pushed the large switch up until it clicked. The vibrant glow of rippling magic running through the bars of the cage faded as the ward was deactivated. She pressed the button below the one Lux had hit and slowly, the outer gate lowered.

"Now set the pipes on the floor."

Dejha removed the wooden pipes from around her neck and set them carefully on the stone floor.

"Good," Ren said, kicking the wooden instrument away.

"Both of you, inside the cage," Ren said, "One wrong move, and I will not hesitate to shoot." He knelt and pulled Lux's thin saber from its scabbard.

"Fair enough," Audette replied. She unlatched the cage door. Ren followed Dejha down the stone steps to the dirt floor of the arena.

Along the wall on one side of the steps, a long metal food trough sat. It was half-filled with the bones of what looked like rancid animal carcasses. Ren wondered if it was only animal remains. On the other side, a large round tank filled with putrid water stood next to enormous piles of muddy straw used for bedding. Somewhere in the darkness beyond the closed gate, the roar of a dragon echoed.

Chapter 29
Duel in the Dragon Pits

Beyond the outer gates to the pit, the larger dragon, Toska appeared. Kodota ambled up alongside a moment later. They both sniffed the air, trying to sense who dared invade their nest. Ren held his pistol on Audette Shoal as she lead Dejha to where Serralto and Ignatz lay bound, hand and foot, on the ground near the center of the arena.

"Step back," Ren said to both women. "And keep your hands where I can see them." Audette complied, backing away. Ren lifted his sword and sliced the ropes tying Serralto's wrists and his legs.

"Help him up," Ren said. He lifted the pistol at her.

Audette grabbed Serralto's arm and helped him up. She moved behind him, shielding herself with his body. A small, slim object flew from her hand. Ren had already faced her once that night and was familiar with her methods. This time, he was ready. He dodged to the side as a dart with a red-ribbon tied to it whisked past his ear.

Ren knocked Serralto into Audette with a kick to the stomach. They both stumbled back. Ignatz fell to the ground. A gust of dust and wind spiraled up around the assassin. A moment later, she was gone. Ren fired twice at the empty air but hit nothing.

"Will somebody please untie me?!" Ignatz yelled, struggling

against his bonds. Ren sliced the ropes binding his polished boots and pulled him to his feet.

"Hold your hands out," Ren said. Ignatz lifted his bound wrists. He winced as Ren cut the ropes tying his wrists in one swift motion. The young man rubbed the burn lines on his wrists.

"Get Serralto out of here!" Ren ordered. He stood next to Serralto and Ignatz, watching for the assassin.

Ignatz grabbed his employer's arm, ushering him toward the cage door. Serralto was out of breath almost immediately from the physical exertion. Dejha Min kept pace behind them, despite her shorter stature.

Ren scanned the pit for the assassin. A deafening silence filled the air. He backed up slowly and followed after the others to the cage door. As Serralto reached the steps, his foot tangled in his flowing robes. He tripped and fell into the dirt. Ignatz stopped to help him up. Ren waited behind them, searching the empty arena for any sign of the invisible assassin. He saw nothing.

Dejha continued up the steps. She was through the cage door before Serralto was back on his feet. Ren heard the gate to the cage clang shut.

Across the arena, Ren saw the faintest swirls of dust rise off the ground from unseen footsteps. Fighting an unseen assassin seemed foolhardy, but keeping Serralto Cardus alive was imperative. He fired at the spot where he estimated Audette Shoal stood.

In response, two darts flew at him from nowhere. He side-stepped and fired at the dust wafting off the ground. The footsteps changed direction, and he fired again.

"Show yourself!" Ren yelled.

A whirlwind of dust flew up and Audette appeared twenty-feet away. "We meet again, changeling," she said with a grin. "Your partner could've used your help earlier. But you sat there gawking while I took him down. Care for another try?"

"I'll try to do better this time," Ren replied. His eyes watched her gloved hands to make sure they remained empty.

She yanked back her cloak. Ren raised his pistol as Audette

pulled the hilt of a sword from the leather belt underneath. There was no blade attached to the foot long handle.

"Then I propose we settle this in a civilized way," she said. With a flick of the wrist, a segmented blade slid out of the sword hilt. "No magic. No changeling tricks. Just a duel of blades until one of us is dead. Or are you afraid to face me in fair combat?" She swung the weapon in a figure-eight pattern in front of her.

"I won't need to shape-shift to kill you," Ren replied. He tossed the empty pistol to the dirt and lifted his sword. He didn't care how the sorceress chose to die, he just needed to end this quickly so he could get back to Claymore. The assassin's offer of a *civilized duel* was nothing more than empty words. She would cheat at the first opportunity. But then, so would he. Only one of them would leave the dragon pit alive.

He had to be relentless in his attack so she couldn't draw on her magic and protect Serralto at the same time. He gripped his sword with both hands as he and the assassin circled each other.

Ren leapt first, attacking with a double slash to test her for weaknesses. Audette blocked both strikes with ease. She countered with a deft stab at his throat that he barely parried in time.

The assassin's skill with a blade was exceptional. Her sword blurred through the air as Ren fought to keep her at bay. She moved with lightning speed, in a sword fighting style he was unfamiliar with and just unpredictable enough to make her extremely lethal. He could not afford a single misstep. There would be no second chances.

The trickster considered himself an expert with a blade, but she matched him step to step. The ability to mimic actions and movements came naturally, and as with most things he did, he learned the art of sword fighting quickly. Within the first moments of the fight, Ren started to imitate her unique sword work. Audette noticed this shift in his style immediately.

"You've trained in the Bocchi- Zaavadri style," Audette quipped. "I can tell."

"I've picked up some things here and there," Ren replied.

Above them, the metal bars of the cage glowed a crimson hue as the magical barrier came on again. Audette stepped out of the reach of Ren's blade and raised her hand to cease fighting.

Dejha Min stood at the control box, staring down at them with a wicked grin on her face. She pressed a button on the panel, and the outer gates of the cage rose.

Both dragons gave low, restless growls as the gate rose. They hesitated entering until their luminous, yellow eyes settled on Ren and those with him. Toska lumbered down into the pit, with Kodota at her heels. Once the beasts were inside, the outer gate lowered.

"I may have trusted my new employer a bit prematurely," the assassin mused.

"If we work together, we can get out of this," Ren said.

The assassin looked at him. "That is kind of you, changeling," she replied, with genuine sympathy. "And a tempting offer. You seem competent enough, but the road I walk, I must walk alone."

The ground trembled as the coiled dragons rushed across the pit, their serpentine bodies slithering along on multiple stubby legs. Audette held her sword on Ren, but kept an eye on the approaching beasts.

Serralto backed away as they drew closer. Panic seized him and he broke into an awkward, gangly run. Ignatz followed at his heels. Kodota's head came up as they ran along the edge of the cage. It broke away from its companion to pursue them and launched a fireball at the fleeing figures. The dragon's aim proved imperfect. The blazing orb struck the enchanted bars above the men, erupting in a shower of flaming brimstone.

With a roar that shook the arena, Toska charged in Ren's direction. Audette took a combative stance with her sword.

"Still up for this?" Ren said. He brought his sword up.

"Of course," Audette replied. "Don't go soft on me now. But what we need is some privacy."

She circled her open palm in front of her. The air became thick and humid, obscuring everything around Ren. The same unnatural fog he had seen in hallways of the Gallows Club rose on all sides until visibility dropped to zero. Overhead, the thunder rumbled through the dark clouds that clung to the rock ceiling above the cage. Rain began to fall, picking up in intensity by the second.

"No magic, huh?" Ren quipped.

"Maybe just a little," she replied with a smile. With another twirl of her hand, a pocket of air formed around them, clear of all fog and rain. Ren shook the rain from his hair.

The assassin leapt at him, her sword a blur in the air. Ren blocked it and countered with a sideways slash that Audette parried with ease. They continued exchanging strike after strike, neither gaining ground on the other. The sound of the dragons skulking through the wind and rain grew louder.

Their eyes locked as swords clashed back and forth. An unseen battle of egos played out to see who would be the first to back down.

The floor of the pit vibrated as the great beasts approached. A second later, Toska's head emerged from the mist. Ren leapt out of the stampeding monster's path as the gaping jaws snapped only empty air. The assassin disappeared on the far side of the beast's enormous body.

Ren raced along the length of its long body toward the tail. He grabbed one of the spikes sticking out of its armored skin and pulled himself up onto its back. Footing was difficult on the slick scales. Ren crouched in between the two rows of protruding spikes running down the spine of the beast. He searched for the assassin, but she was nowhere to be seen. The dragon turned its serpentine body in a tight circle, searching for its lost prey. Ren's added weight seemed unnoticed by the beast.

Audette jumped on the tail and climbed toward him. Ren braced his feet on the spikes for stability as the assassin came at him. He teetered on the scaly back of the dragon, slashing, blocking, and trying not to slide off. Thunder boomed overhead.

The assassin gave Ren a broad smile before bringing her sword into play with a vicious downward strike that blocked easily. Lightning flashed from the assassin's blade. A powerful jolt of electricity shot through the metal into his arms. It continued through his upper body and into his legs.

The sword slipped from his numbed fingers. His feet slipped out from under him on the slippery scales. He tumbled down the scaley back, careening off the boney spikes like a billiard ball until he ran out of the dragon and crashed into the dirt.

Ren shook his head to clear it. "You want magic, I'll give you magic," he muttered to himself as he dug into the pocket of the pantaloons for Dmitri's wand. It wasn't there. He scanned the ground quickly for the gnarled piece of wood until his eyes fell on his sword. He snatched it up as Audette landed in the dust near him.

Ren pressed his attack on the assassin. Audette lunged at him. He blocked the strike and countered. They continued back and forth as the dragon could be heard skulking through the fog.

Toska came out of the dense mist, drawn to them by the sound of their clashing swords. It struck out at the assassin. Audette deftly dodged the snapping mouth. She ducked beneath the neck and ran to the far side of the beast.

Ren waited for the croaking rattle in the dragon's throat. He had to keep the assassin distracted long enough for the flaming sphere of death to be spewed in their direction. He knew when that would happen. She did not.

Toska gave a guttural retching sound deep in its throat and belched out a sizzling ball of brimstone. The accuracy was better than its smaller companion. The fireball struck the ground between them and exploded. Ren rolled beyond the blast radius in time. The assassin twisted away a moment too late. She pulled her cloak up to protect herself from the brunt of the explosion. The fabric burst into flames.

Audette discarded her burning cloak and turned toward the dragon. She dropped the sword into the mud and weaved her hands through the air. A fire blazed in her eyes. Winds picked up around her. The temperatures dropped precipitously, and the pounding rain changed into a storm of snow and sleet. Ren raised his arm to protect his face against the pelting winds.

The raging winds grew in intensity, assaulting the dragon from all sides. Toska roared in frustration and backed away. It fired another fiery ball of brimstone into the air. Ren heard it explode somewhere near the outer gates.

The frigid cold slowed the beast's movement. It became sluggish, stumbling backwards, searching for any way to get away. The sorceress held her ground against the massive lizard, striking it with bursts of icy winds again and again. The confused beast backed away, roaring wildly and shooting fireballs. A barrier of strong winds flowed over and around Audette, deflecting the fireballs to one side or the other.

Ren ducked under a hissing orb of brimstone as it whistled past him. He took the opportunity to reconsider their duel. Without a sword, he had to reestablish the rules of the game. But first, he needed to make sure Serralto was safe.

With a focused thought, he felt the dark swirling tendrils of pigment spread over his naked torso and down his arms and legs. The skin tone over his face and body changed to a hazy mosaic of colors to match the shifting fog around him until he was almost invisible to the naked eye. He turned away from the assassin and dragon, disappearing into the thick cover of fog.

Somewhere ahead of him, a high-pitched scream broke out. He untied the cord holding Piqwic's pantaloons around his thin waist and took to the air in the form of a raven. He followed the cries, trying to get his bearings. The air grew warmer, and visibility improved the further he flew from the assassin. He glided down until he could make out the swirling movements of the smaller dragon under the mist. The beast's head came up. A pair of black boots stuck out from the tip of its toothy maw.

The desperate screams were cut short by the crunch of bones and the wet chomping of flesh. Kodota swallowed and the leather boots disappeared down the beast's throat. If it was Serralto or Ignatz, Ren couldn't be sure. He saw neither of them, so he figured the dragon may have eaten them both. If that was the case, his desperate attempt to save Serralto Cardus from the *Black Rose* had failed. All he could do now was find Claymore and get him out of there. His wings tilted to the side and circled around the cage. First, he had an assassin to kill.

Below him, Audette Shoal had encased Toska's head and upper body in place against the side of the cage. Only the end of the snout stuck out of the solid ice. The majority of its long body remained free. It thrashed about, struggling to free itself.

Ren flew past the scene through the frigid winds and snow, dropping softly to the ground, morphing into a sleek saber-toothed cat. His thick fur blocked out the cold of the arctic winds. It was his turn to hunt.

He didn't know the extent of Audette Shoal's weather witchy powers and could only hope that she had neared the limits of those powers. He stepped on something that crinkled under the snow and ice. He pulled his paw off the pantaloons he had abandoned earlier. It gave him an idea where in the dragon pit he stood.

His eyesight was exceptional under normal conditions, but the driving winds and stinging ice cut his visibility to nothing. He stalked forward and almost walked into the assassin before seeing the blurred figure in front of him. Her sword came around in one fluid motion, but not before Ren slashed her across the side with a huge claw. Audette leapt backwards, grabbing at her injured side.

Ren pressed his advantage, knowing he may not get another chance to take the assassin down. He covered the distance between them in a heartbeat. But Audette recovered from her injury and threw out a hand. Ice crystals formed around Ren and his momentum ceased in midair. From the shoulders down, his body was encased in thick ice. He couldn't move any of his limbs to gain leverage against what held him fast.

Ren struggled to get free. He choked down his panic as the assassin climbed to her feet and approached him. Then he gathered his thoughts and focused. His body morphed inside the ice. Every muscle in his body tensed, pressing against his icy prison.

His body mass expanded. His arms and shoulders pressed against the icy prison that entombed him. He pushed out with all his strength. The ice cracked under the pressure, then it shattered. He pushed the crumbling ice fragments away and stepped out onto the dirt as a massive minotaur.

"You disappoint me, changeling," the assassin said. "You agreed to no shape-shifting." She lifted her sword and charged. As she brought the blade down, Ren blocked it with one of his twisted horns. A second blade came out of nowhere and stabbed him in the shoulder, cutting through muscle and sinew.

"And you agreed to no magic," Ren growled. "I guess that makes us both liars." He grabbed the foot-long blade embedded in his shoulder by its handle and pulled it free. Audette raised her sword. The frost bitten winds swirled around her.

"This is your last chance to impress me before I kill you," she said.

On the ground behind the assassin, Ren spotted the wooden wand. Audette's demeanor showed nothing but a grim determination to kill him. To reach it, Ren needed to distract her. He released the hold on the minotaur's form and slid back to his natural form, bent down and picked up the sword.

Ren clucked his tongue in the way he had heard the coiled dragons communicate with each other. Somewhere in the dense fog behind Audette came a mewling response from one of the behemoths. It caught the assassin by surprise, and she looked toward the unseen beast with her sword raised. Her face revealed the slightest trace of concern.

Ren rushed forward and stabbed the knife into the frozen ice where the wand lay. He pried the twisted wooden rod out of the ice as Audette came at him. He dodged a downward strike that would have split his head open if it had hit. She struck him across the face with the hilt of her sword. His vision blurred, and he fell back. She pinned him down with one hand and brought her sword up to gut him.

"I expected more from you, changeling," she scowled. "Aren't you supposed to be some kind of hero?"

"Still working on that," Ren replied. He pressed the wand against her side and shouted, "*Ala- Hestra!*"

The wand responded to the command. A blaze of magical light burst from the end of the stick. Audette Shoal flipped head over heels into the air. The sword flew from her hand, and she landed hard on the ground a short distance from him.

Ren grabbed the fallen sword. Audette struggled to her feet, drawing a dagger from under her cloak. Tendrils of electricity formed from the fingertips of her empty hand. Thunder boomed overhead. They came together as the chilling winds around them grew stronger. Sleet and ice stung his face.

Ren feinted a thrust to the assassin's head. Her dagger came up to block his sword. He twisted the blade away and slashed downward. Audette reacted a split-second too slowly. The razor-sharp blade sliced through the wrist of the hand controlling the growing strands of lightning.

Audette screamed. She stared with wide eyes at the bloody stump. Her dagger sliced him across the side. Ren gritted his teeth to prevent himself from crying out. His reflexes responded instinctively, without thought. He brought the sword down and drove the blade into her mid-section.

The assassin sank to her knees. Her dagger dropped to the ground. She grabbed the hilt of the sword with her remaining hand, trying in vain to pull it free. Ren stood over her, breathing hard. She looked up at him before collapsing to the dirt, the tip of the blade sticking out of her back.

"Sorry," Ren said. "It's just business."

As his anger cooled, he felt a deep sense of remorse. He realized he didn't want to kill her, but she was far too dangerous to leave alive. Even with only the one hand, she would have come after him seeking revenge.

If any other outcome had been possible, he would have taken it. But as it was, he did what he had to, just as she did. It was who she was, just as he was who he was. Still, he could not shake the feeling that in another world, in another time, they might have been allies.

Audette Shoal said she preferred to walk alone. That she needed no one else. Now she was dead. There was a lesson in there somewhere, but he was too tired to think about it further.

The fog began to thin around him now that the one who had summoned it was gone. He realized he was standing just outside the entrance to the dragon pit. Odd Bod stood on the other side of the bars with a henchman on either side.

Two shadowy forms emerged from the mouth of the tunnel, dragging an unconscious body with them. The bare-chested, bare-footed Claymore Ives hung unresponsive between the two men. The bleeding from his wounds seemed to have stopped. The henchmen dropped him at the foot of the stone wall behind Bod.

Ren pointed the wand at Bod, yelling, *"Ala Hestra!"* A bolt of energy erupted from the wand and struck the glowing bars in an explosion of blinding light. The blast was swallowed by the protective barrier in rippling wisps of magic.

"Give it up, B'gatti!" Bod said, his voice rumbling like the thunder of an approaching storm. "We have your partner. You've got nowhere to go. Drop the stick or we'll put a bullet in your partner's head."

Ren looked at the magical wand in his hand before tossing it aside.

Chapter 30
Heroic Masquerade

Odd Bod stared through the bars of the cage at Ren. He held Claymore's duffle bag in his hand.

"Clever trick, B'gatti," he said, setting the duffle bag down at his feet. "We found York tied up in his room. You're good, I'll give you that. Standing there right there in front of me, and I never suspected a thing. I'd be embarrassed if I felt such things, but I was an idiot for not seeing it. No wonder Mordecai wants to recruit you."

Bod motioned the lackey at the control panel, who nodded and pushed the lever up. The magical field that covered the cage sparked and faded. The man handed Odd Bod a pair of metal binders. He tossed them through the cage bars to Ren's feet. The lackey slammed the lever back down and the magical barrier came on again.

"Put those on, then get down on your knees.," Bod said. "They're shock bands and will prevent you from shape-shifting. And no games this time, little trickster, or your partner dies."

Ren glanced over at Claymore. His partner slumped against the stone wall, eyes closed, and his head hanging to one side. He looked to be in bad shape. The bleeding had stopped, but his muscular, naked torso remained speckled with dozens of small incisions administered by Dmitri the Confessor's scalpel. One of Bod's henchmen put a revolver against Claymore's head.

"Last chance, Bugatti," Odd Bod rumbled.

All eyes were on Ren as he bent down and picked up the metal binders lying at his feet. The restraints were nothing more than a short metal rod with locking handcuffs at each end. There was a tingle in his fingertips from the magical aura the metal gave off. He looked back at Claymore.

His partner opened his eyes. He gave Ren a winked. A small blue vial rolled from his hand across the floor. The henchman standing over him looked down at the sound.

Claymore grabbed the gun pressed to his temple and twisted it out of the lackey's grip. He slammed the man's face into the stone floor and fired in rapid succession his body. The three remaining henchmen went down before they could react. He leveled the revolver at Odd Bod and climbed to his feet.

The giant held his hands up in compliance. He stepped between Claymore and the control box, unintimidated by the pistol pointed at him.

"Impressive, Ives," he rumbled. "Twenty minutes ago, I saw you hanging in chains, half dead. What's that about?"

"Just getting my second wind," Claymore replied.

Bod glanced at the blue vial on the floor, before crushing it under his heel. "Found yourself a little pick me up, did ya? Not that it's going to make any difference by the time we're done here."

"Turn off the magical barrier around the cage," Claymore ordered. He cocked the gun.

"I'm not going to do that," Bod said. A deep chuckle, edged with menace, erupted from his lips. "And don't think the two bullets left in your pistol will prevent me from tearing your head from your shoulders?"

"Go for it," Claymore replied with a wry grin.

"I've been waiting for this moment for years," Bod said. His massive hands flexing at his side.

"I bet you have."

Bod rushed forward, his arms up to protect his face. Claymore dropped his aim and fired twice, once into each of Bod's kneecaps. Blood splattered with both bullet wounds but did nothing to slow the behemoth. Bod swung a massive fist, but Claymore ducked under it. The blow struck the wall, cracking the stone. Bits of broken rock exploded from the force of the punch.

Ren tried to reach through the bars to unlatch the cage door. The unseen barrier crackled and sparked as he disrupted it. The protective magical energy knocked him back into the dirt. He got up, rubbing his numb hand, and watched helplessly as the battle outside the cage played out in front of him. Claymore may not have been in his best form, but he had been on the verge of death minutes before. Now he was holding his own against the most dangerous individual in Rogue Destiny.

Even with bullet holes in both knees, Odd Bod was surprisingly quick on his feet. Claymore reached the gray metal box. Before he could throw the switch, Bod lowered a shoulder and slammed him into the stone wall. The giant landed a punch in his side, followed by another across the face that sent Claymore flying across the smooth floor of the cavern.

Ren remained trapped inside the cage, unable to help his partner in any way. He caught movement in the corner of his eye. Serralto Cardus peeked out from under the food trough to his left. The Common Council member was bruised and covered in dirt, but alive. Ren breathed a sigh of relief, even though he had no doubt Serralto had sacrificed his assistant to save himself. The fog began to disperse. Soon it would be clear enough the dragons would notice them.

Claymore scrabbled to his feet. He glanced around for anything he could use as a weapon as Bod hobbled toward him. He stepped in the direction of his duffle bag, but Bod cut him off. Claymore leapt into the air and came down on giant's knee with the full weight of his body.

The leg buckled with a loud crack and Bod caught himself on the cage bars. He screamed as the shield's magical energy surged through him. With a great effort, he pulled his hands free and fell to the floor on bloody knees. Claymore rushed back to the control box and pulled the lever down. The glow of the protective shield faded. He retrieved a pistol from his duffle bag and stood over Bod.

"Had enough?" Claymore growled.

"Yeah," Bod muttered. He grabbed the cage bars to pull himself up. Claymore took a step back, keeping the pistol leveled at the giant. With frightening speed bordering on inhuman, Bod struck out, knocking the gun from Claymore's hand. The pistol went off and struck the ceiling. Bod caught Claymore by the throat, lifting him from the ground as if he weighed nothing.

"I told you I'd rip off your head," he spat in Claymore's face.

Claymore fought against the massive hands wrapped around his neck. He punched Bod in the chest and pounded on his arms, but it had no effect against the giant. He was over a foot shorter than Bod, but his long arms could still reach the big man's face. He pressed his thumbs into Bod's eyes until he roared in pain, forcing him back against the bars.

An idea came to Ren. He ran back to where the dead assassin lay and carefully searched the body. He found what he was looking for inside a hidden sheath on the side of her glove. He gathered several in one hand and ran back.

The giant's grip on Claymore's neck tightening. Claymore seemed close to passing out. The veins in his forehead popped. His face grew purple from lack of oxygen. He struggled against the death grip on his throat.

Ren leapt up onto the bars. He reached through and jammed the handful of darts into Bod's thick forearm. He looked down to the slim projectiles protruding from his sleeve. His eyes drifted up to Ren. A flicker of fear appeared on the giant's face when he realized what had happened. Ren smiled.

Bod's grip on Claymore's throat slackened. His partner pulled himself free and dropped to the floor, choking and coughing as he fought to take in air. Dark bruises covered his neck.

Odd Bod lunged at the trickster through the bars. Ren dropped to the dirt floor, out of his reach. He watched the giant brace himself against the cage as the effects of the drugs took hold. His massive body swayed before he stumbled, grabbing the bars to support his weight. Claymore backed away as Odd Bod, the Grand Enforcer of *The Society of the Black Rose,* crashed to the floor.

The roar of the dragons echoed across the cavern. Through the thinning fog, Ren could see Toska breaking the melting walls of ice built to contain her. Both dragons bounded toward the cage door. He ran past Serralto up the stairs and unlatched the cage door. Serralto followed him out. Ren latched the door shut as Kodota slammed into the bars. The force shook the cage and bent the cage door from its moorings.

Ren jerked the lever down to turn on the magical barrier. The shield did not come on. Kodota clawed its way up the bars. The top hinge of the cage door snapped under the weight as the beast pushed its snout through the opening. The bars bent inward even further under the monster's weight.

Claymore struggled to his feet. He seemed relieved to see Serralto wasn't dead amidst all the chaos. He picked up his duffle bag and escorted Serralto to the mouth of the tunnel.

"We're not going to get out of here by going back through the house," Claymore shouted. "There has to be another way out."

Ren hurried past the unconscious lump of rumpled suit that was Odd Bod to the wooden door. He opened it to a ten-by-ten room that appeared to be the sleeping quarters for the dragon-handler. The short, plump woman stood at a desk talking to someone on a phone. Claymore walked up behind her, took the receiver out of her hand and set it on its cradle. He motioned for her to sit down on the bed. Outside, the dragons roared and thrashed against the bars of the cage. A fireball exploded against the wall of the cavern, lighting up the arena outside the curtained window.

Ren peeked through the curtains of the room's only window. Without the magical barrier protecting it, the cage would not withstand the rage of the dragons for long. The metal cage door buckled under the hideous strength of the reptile, bending inward as the beast fought to get through.

"You can explain to me later how you were able to take on Mordecai's Grand Enforcer like that. Because when I left you a half hour ago, you were unable to stand on your own."

"I kept one last elixir back for emergencies such as this," Claymore replied. "I can feel it already starting to wear off."

"We need to figure something out quickly," Ren said. He glanced over the room. Beside the small bed, there was an armoire for clothes and a writing desk with a small lamp next to a phone.

"You can't let me die down here," Serralto cried. Claymore grabbed him by the shoulder and forced him to sit on the bed. He turned to the dragon-handler.

"What's your name?" Claymore asked.

"Dejha Min."

"Can you control the beasts with your pipes?" Claymore asked. He set the duffle bag on the desk.

"No, it's more like the pipes guide them with the music," she replied. "It calls them into the pits, and they come because they know it's feeding time."

Claymore put on a wrinkled shirt from the bag, then pulled out his sawed-off rifle. He laid it on the desk and strapped its leather sheath onto his back. he looked at Ren. "Any ideas?"

Ren stared at the phone, trying to think of how to get them out of there. A piece of paper next to the phone listed a number of extensions to various parts of the villa. One was labeled *front gate*. He picked the receiver up and hit the corresponding button. A moment later, a voice came on the other end.

"Hello?"

"Bring a car around!" Ren said, mimicking the deep, rolling cadence of Odd Bod.

"Right away, sir!" came the answer over the phone. Ren set the receiver down. The walls of the small room shook as another fireball struck somewhere in the cavern outside. Fiery debris splashed against the window glass.

Ren went to the curtained window. "If I lead the dragons up the tunnel, you take Serralto out through the dragon pit around to the front. I'll meet you at the car."

"Are you sure you want to do this?" Claymore flipped the sawed-off rifle over his shoulder, sliding it into its sheath on his back.

"Not really," Ren answered. "But I don't see any other way out of this."

Chapter 31
Thrill of the Hunt

Ren slowly opened the door a crack and peeked out.

"I'll see you at the car," he whispered to Claymore, closing the door behind him. He crept along the wall toward the mouth of the tunnel.

Kodota fought to get through the twisted cage door. Her head came up and sniffed the air before two copper-colored eyes locked on Ren. It roared and forced its way through the narrow opening. The frame of the cage door groaned before giving way, and the dragon's long body slithered free.

With a roar, Toska followed its smaller companion through the broken cage door, but found the opening more difficult to navigate. Sparks flew as the beast clawed at the floor, leaving deep gouges in the stone. With a great effort, she squeezed into the cavern. Her scales scraped against the twisted metal until both dragons were free of their captivity.

Ren dashed down the dimly lit tunnel, calling the dragons to follow him with a low, mewling growl. Behind him, the clicking of sharp claws scraping the hard stone told him they were following. He glanced back to see their distorted shadows move across the walls of the tunnel.

Chemical fumes filled the tunnel in front of him long before he reached Dmitri's workroom. The sickly sweet stench burned his eyes and left a fetid taste on his tongue. He covered his mouth with both hands and forced himself through the billowed plumbs.

He emerged from the smoke, coughing and wiping his burning eyes. Coming down the hall toward him, Caino Stratos strode, flanked by a dozen security personnel. That must have been who Dejha Min talked to on the phone. Ren could see the two mysterious acolytes standing at the back of the group, polearms in hand.

Before he could retreat back into the smoke, Caino drew a pistol from his shoulder holster. Ren raised his hands. Behind him, the thundering slapping of giant clawed feet on the stone floor grew louder.

"What are you doing down here?" Caino growled. "And why are you naked? Where's Odd Bod?"

"Back there," Ren said, throwing a thumb behind him. The sound of the approaching dragons intensified. Caino peered past Ren into the dense smoke.

"What's that noise?" Caino asked.

An ear-piercing roar shook the tunnel as the snout of the first dragon appeared out of the smoke. An unmistakable guttural noise built up in her throat. Behind Kodota, her larger companion raced up the passageway, wanting to take part in the coming carnage of gangster meeting dragon.

Ren knew better than to be in close proximity of the dragon's fireball when it exploded. He shifted to a raven and flew down the low-ceilinged passageway as fast as he could to get beyond the ensuing chaos. Behind him, the dragon spewed a crackling orb of brimstone into the middle of Caino and his gangsters.

Ahead of him, the black and white acolytes stood with their pole arms ready. Neither looked up as the black bird approached. Instead, they seemed mesmerized by the flames and mayhem taking place down the corridor. Then, without warning, both vanished from sight. Neither had moved, they simply disappeared from where they stood, not unlike wizards Ren had encountered in the past.

The concussive force of the exploding fireball pushed Ren's tiny body further down the narrow tunnel. Flaming debris splattered the walls. Gunshots rang out, followed by the crunching of bone under the force of dragon teeth.

The screams lasted a moment longer before they were drowned out by more gunfire. Ren flew around a slight bend in the tunnel and found himself at the red door. He shifted mid-air to his natural shape and dropped down lightly in front of the door.

Turning around, he called to the dragons with a howl that echoed down the dark tunnel. It was answered a few heartbeats later. He left the door open behind him and ran down the short corridor to the main hallway. It was empty.

He stood there with no idea where the front doors to the villa were located. Down the hall, a dark, shrouded figure appeared out of nowhere. Ren ducked into the kitchen, startling the staff as he raced by them into a large dining room. He slid under the oversized banquet table and shifted into his best recollection of the house cat he had encountered briefly outside Piqwic's room.

The roar of a dragon echoed through the hallways. The kitchen staff scattered in all directions. Ren moved on the far side of a table leg as a dragon stomped down the hallway he had just exited.

He considered following one of the staff members, hoping they would show him an alternate way out of the villa. Before he could finish the thought, the white robed acolyte entered the dining room, gripping the seven-foot long glaive. Strips of colorful streamers tied to the pole arm fluttered as the mysterious creature glided into the room.

The long, knuckled fingers were like the talons of a bird. It was the only part of its body he could see and, for a moment, wondered what the creature looked like without its robes and mask. The graceful figure moved across the floor along the table, so silently

Ren wondered if the footsteps even made contact with the marble floor.

The hair on the back of his neck rose, not out of fear, but from a sudden surge of magical energy that filled the room. He froze, waiting to see if the cowled figure had detected him. The white figure reached the table where Ren hid.

A black mask appeared below the edge of the table. Almond-shaped eyes stared at Ren. The creature reached out a clawed hand for him, as if it sensed something was not quite right with the cat. Ren pushed himself away from the hand and hissed. He slashed at the air with a paw, careful not to make contact.

The mask was also oddly reminiscent of a bird. Pure black almond-shaped eyes stared out from behind it. The bridge of the nose descended too low to be human and gave the impression of a beak. Ren decided he had no desire to see what was behind the mask and hissed a second time. He arched his back, making his hair stand on end, hoping to convince the acolyte he was indeed just an ordinary house cat.

Ren had already wasted too much time getting out of there. He hoped his diversion would give Claymore the opportunity to escape with Serralto while the villa's security dealt with the drag-ons. If his partner was smart, he'd get away from the estate, knowing Ren would rendezvous with him back at the rabbit-hole.

His ruse appeared to work. The acolyte stood up and turned to leave when a brindle-colored house cat padded in through the arched doorway. At the sight of the shrouded figure, the real cat jumped back with a hiss before bolting from sight.

The figure stepped back. The butt of the pole arm lifted off the floor. Ren knew what was about to happen. He jumped out from under the table as the glaive came down with a thunderous crash. The thick, ornate marble tabletop shattered under the blow, but Ren was already out of the room.

He retraced his steps from the dining room to the stairs leading up to the upper levels. Down the hallway from him, he heard the heavy footfall of a six-legged dragon. He released his hold on the feline's shape and took the steps two at a time. He was almost to the top when a figure wrapped in black robes appeared at the top of the staircase. Ren turned to go back down, but the way was blocked by the white acolyte. For a quick second, he contemplated shifting into something big and nasty and fighting his way out, but he had seen the damage the glaives were capable of and decided it was best to run.

In desperation, he cupped his hands around his mouth and gave a blaring dragon roar. A long, mournful wail with hopes it would bring at least one of the dragons to him. The call was answered from somewhere down the halls of the villa. A moment later, the pounding footfall of the massive dragon shook the walls of the villa.

Toska waddled into sight. Her massive serpentine body filled the hallway. The white acolyte backed away as the dragon roared and rushed forward. She caught the white robed figure in her jaws. A shrill, ear-piercing cry broke the air as the dragon crunched down. The lower half of the body dropped to the floor in a spray of dark, blue-tinted blood.

Ren leapt from the steps onto the back of the coiled dragon. He dropped to the floor and sprinted down the hallway on the opposite side of the stairs.

The corridor led to a richly decorated front room. Outside the giant arched windows, he saw the water fountain and driveway leading to the front gates of the villa. He searched for something to break the glass, grabbing a red velvet cushioned chair and hurled it at the nearest window. The chair bounced off the thick glass and crashed to the floor. Ren cursed under his breath. Of course, the first-floor windows would be reenforced against any dragon mischief. Despite his rising anxiety, he had enough clarity of thought to realize from the position of the fountain where the front doors should be located.

He raced back across the hall through a small library and came out into another corridor. At the end of the hall stood two tall doors leading out of the villa. They were secured with a large crossbeam and security bar that ran from floor to ceiling, as well as a number of deadbolt locks.

Fueled by the adrenaline flowing through him, Ren lifted the heavy crossbar from its resting place and threw it aside. He unlatched the thick reenforced bar and slid it from its moorings, then began unlocking the deadbolts. He sensed movement behind him.

An excruciating pain exploded down his shoulder. It burned like a hot iron had been laid across his skin. He spun around to see the black shrouded acolyte lift its bloody glaive from the floor. The deep laceration burned with an excruciating fire. His legs weakened and gave out under him. He fell against the wall, sliding down to the floor, leaving a wide streak of crimson on the stucco surface.

The white masked figure lifted the glaive to strike, its sharp blade glowed an eerie, blue-tinted light. It came down at him. Ren caught the pole arm with both hands but felt his strength falter. The glimmering blade pressed closer to the trickster's face.

A muffled explosion shook the doors and front entrance way. The acolyte hesitated. Ren tried to push the blade away, but the unnatural strength of the robed creature was too great. He dropped to his knees.

The front doors burst open from a powerful kick. Claymore stepped into view. He fired his sawed-off rifle, hitting the hooded figure in the chest. He racked in another round and fired a second time, then a third. Each blast knocked the creature in black further back in a tangle of flaying robes. A fourth shot struck the wall as the shrouded from disappeared from sight.

Claymore grabbed Ren's hand. "You were late," he quipped.

"Sorry." Ren winced in pain as he was pulled to his feet. "There were dragons."

His partner laughed. "Let's get out of here."

Ren stumbled out the doors toward the car, each painful step a reminder of his injured shoulder. When they reached the limousine, he saw the back seats were empty. "Where's Serralto?"

"Unconscious in the trunk!" Claymore yelled as he ran around to the driver's side. "Climb in!"

Ren slid into the passenger seat and Claymore hit the gas. The limousine lurched forward, its wheels spinning on the cobble stoned driveway. The smell of burnt rubber filled the air. He turned the wheel hard to one side to navigate the tight curve around the fountain. Once clear of the water structure, he straightened out and sped toward the front gate.

Ren looked back to see Toska emerge from the front doors of the villa. she spotted the car and shot a flaming fireball at them. The blazing orb struck the rear passenger door, knocking the vehicle sideways. The impact shattered the back windows.

The dragon climbed through the decorative fountain, splashing through the waters in pursuit. She almost reached them before Claymore brought the car under control and floored the accelerator, staying ahead of the angry dragon. Another fireball flew over the vehicle, disappearing through the open gate into a grove of tropical trees across the driveway. The resulting explosion caused the brush and trees to burst into flames.

The guards at the outer wall fired at the approaching dragon. Claymore slammed the gas pedal to the floor. The limousine kicked up dirt and rocks as it roared through the closing gates. They were past the guards before anyone saw who was driving. A couple of uninspired gunshots struck the back of the vehicle before they were out of range.

Ren leaned forward, his elbows on his knees, and closed his eyes. The gash across his shoulder throbbed with a searing pain that burned him to his core. He wondered how quickly the cut would heal and if he'd finally be left with a scar.

Claymore let go a laugh, a wild look in his eyes. His face was bruised and battered from his encounter with Odd Bod, but his white teeth flashed in the fleeting light.

"I told you we didn't need backup," he quipped.

Chapter 32
The Sins of the Executioner

The wheels of the limousine crunched the rocks of the stony beach. Claymore parked under a high cliff overlooking the sea. A small waterfall fell from the heights into a lagoon that opened onto the open sea. He looked over at Ren.

"Well, that was fun?" he said. "How're you doing?"

Ren opened his eyes and sat up in his seat. His entire body ached. His shoulder ached with an unrelenting agony.

"Put some pants on," Claymore quipped, his voice tinged with humor even after all the horrors he had endured during the last hours. "There should be a pair in the duffle bag."

"Where are we?" Ren asked as he pulled on a pair of blue jean too big for his slight frame. He fastened a belt tight around his waist.

"This is another rabbit-hole that'll get us back to Rogue Destiny," Claymore said. "It'll take us by way of a couple of intersecting ley-lines." Claymore opened his door and climbed out. Ren followed much slower from the passenger side to the back of the vehicle.

Claymore pounded a fist on the trunk. "Wake up, Serralto!" he said with a smirk.

He unlocked the car's trunk with a key and lifted the hood.

Serralto lay on his side, facing away from them. Claymore grabbed his shoulder and shook him.

"C'mon, let's go," Claymore said. "We're at the end of the road!" Serralto stirred at the touch and rolled over. Claymore helped him sit up.

Serralto climbed out, supporting himself with a hand on the trunk. The other hand was concealed beneath the sleeve of his robes. His legs were shaky, but once he had both feet on the ground, he stood on his own. His hand slid out of the sleeve.

Ren saw the wand too late.

"Ala-Hestra!" Serralto shouted. A blast of blue and green flame hit Claymore and knocked him back in an explosion of lights. He landed on his back a dozen feet away and lay still. Serralto turned the wand on Ren and repeated the command.

It had been a long night and in his injured state, Ren was slow to act. The blast knocked him back to the edge of the surf. His skin tingled under the magical current coursing over him.

Claymore groaned and rolled over. Ren lay where he landed, barely able to move, his entire body numb and unresponsive. Water lapped at his feet.

"You cost me everything!" Serralto bellowed. "Because of you, I can never return to the life I had." He lifted the wand at Claymore again. "All I have left is revenge! Ala-Hestra!"

The end of the wand glowed, and a burst of flaming energy exploded against Claymore's chest. He was lifted from the ground and landed hard on the sandy beach. The magical essence of the blast writhed over his body. He slowly rolled over to his knees, pounding his fist into the sand. Bracing himself with both hands, he glared up at Serralto.

Ren watched the anguish and pain on Claymore's face melt away. He rose defiantly to his feet, his eyes cold and empty. His expression changed. As if the light behind his eyes had been extinguished. He began to mumble incoherent words.

Serralto held the wand on him. "Stay where you are," he said quietly. "Both of you put your hands on your head."

Ren's muscles wouldn't respond to his command to shift. He raised his aching arms and clasped them together behind his head. The wound across his shoulder throbbed.

Claymore shifted his feet, barely able to contain his building rage. He glanced at the ground, then over at his partner. Ren knew the look. He'd seen it a hundred times before. Whether from the wand or the waning effects of the elixir, Claymore's hand trembled slightly. Ren doubted he could draw his gun fast enough to shoot Serralto before the wand struck him again.

"Claymore, don't," Ren said.

His partner wavered a moment longer before obeying the command. He sighed, his shoulders slumping in defeat. With a slow, painful effort, he raised his hands and placed them on the back of his head.

"Because of you," Serralto said. "I will never enjoy a peaceful night's sleep again! The *Black Rose* will be hunting me for the rest of my days."

"Then put down the wand and surrender," Claymore said. "Lazaranth Prison will be the safest place for you."

"Lazaranth won't protect me. No place will be safe," Serralto replied, not taking his eyes from Claymore. "But I still have allies who will hide me. And from the shadows, I will not rest until the Raconteurs are destroyed. You will suffer as I have and watch helplessly as your life's work is wiped from existence. Now, remove the gun belt, slowly, with your left hand."

Claymore hesitated. He was in obvious distress. He took a deep breath and lowered his left hand to the buckle of his gun belt and began fumbling with the clasp. His right hand remained on his head. His cold steely eyes never left the man pointing the wand at him. He struggled to get the buckle unclasped. With a final tug, it came loose.

He let the gun belt slide off his hip. Serralto's eyes followed as it fell. Faster than Ren could follow, Claymore drew the pistol with his right hand and fired. The bullet struck Serralto in the hand holding the wand. He stumbled back. The wand fell to the ground.

Serralto scrambled for the fallen wand, but Claymore reached it first. The heel of his foot pressed down on it and snapped the thin rod in half. He leveled his gun at Serralto's face and pulled the hammer back.

"You took everything from me," Claymore rumbled. "Why come after the Raconteurs?"

"You were a convenience," Serralto said. "You showed up unannounced on the day Audette was to kill Minstrel Cotty. I figured pinning the murder on the leader of the Raconteurs would ensure I was accepted into *The Black Rose.*

"But why Cotty? He was an ally to the *Black Rose.*"

"True," Serralto replied. "The demand for enchanted off-world relics in Rogue Destiny has never been greater, and the money one could make selling them to the right people is beyond imagining. But Cotty got greedy. He started encroaching on the *Black Rose's* smuggling operations. I was liaison to Minstrel Cotty for the Common Council, so Mordecai Davos ordered me to oversee his elimination. In return, I was to be inducted into their ranks."

Claymore nodded, as if he already suspected as much. "So Mordecai didn't care about the artifacts that would be lost upon Cotty's death?"

Serralto took a slow, deliberate breath and cradled his wounded hand. Blood dripped to the ground. "Only one. Rumors have been circulating that *The Book of Days* had been found. Mordecai had reason to believe Cotty had it. He cared nothing for any other relics but was afraid this particular book would be lost forever. Audette questioned Cotty, but he said he didn't have it anymore. That it had been stolen recently by someone he would not name."

Claymore shook his head as if he was trying to gather his thoughts. "And what about the millions that died that day?" Serralto gave no answer.

"What's so special about this *Book of Days*?" Ren asked. His interested was piqued. Was this what Mordecai Davos was burning down dusty archives to find?

"It's an ancient book, written by Baltazar Gheddi himself, regarding the founding of Rogue Destiny and its dark secrets. Including how the sorcerer-king was able to bring his magick to a world with no magick."

"Is that why Mordecai wants it?" Ren asked.

"Possibly," Serralto replied. "What better way to take the City, then to be the only one who controls the magick?"

"Mordecai is no sorcerer?" Ren said. "And he would never abdicate power to someone else."

"So this is all about power and wealth," Claymore said slowly. His gun hand trembled, as if he was waging some great battle within himself. He lifted the revolver.

"Everything is about power and wealth," Serralto replied. "Only fools believe differently."

"Claymore, don't!" Ren yelled. "You're not thinking straight! We need him alive! He can prove we are innocent of Cotty's murder! Then you can return to the Raconteurs!"

"No," Claymore growled. "He'll never see the inside of a jail-cell. He has too many powerful friends." The barrel of the revolver quivered in his grip.

"You should listen to your partner, Ives," Serralto said. He gave them a wicked grin. "You can't kill me. You need me! I'm your only hope of ever returning to your precious Raconteurs. After what happened in Adezhda, the *Black Rose* will be coming for them. And there will be nothing you can do to stop that. You need to be there to protect them."

Claymore fired. Once. Twice. Three times. Serralto took all three shots in the chest and collapsed to the sandy beach. It happened too fast for Ren to react. He couldn't stop it. He could only watch his partner gun down an unarmed man.

Ren stood silent, unable to process what he had witnessed. Claymore had never killed anyone in cold-blood. It stood against everything his partner believed. Claymore was the culmination of everything that defined what a true hero represented. Selfless.

Altruistic. Honest. Courageous. Compassionate. Nothing had ever caused him to stray from that path. Until tonight.

He stared at Claymore. "What did you do?"

"What I had to," Claymore growled. "What needed to be done!"

"You just killed our only hope of setting things right."

"He took everything from me!" Claymore yelled. "My friends, my reputation, my dignity! He would never receive the justice he deserved in Rogue Destiny. Now the millions of lives lost inside *The Angels of Avalon* have been avenged."

"You used to tell me shooting an unarmed man was *murder*."

"Now I'm telling you its *justice!*"

Claymore sat down on a nearby rock. He dropped the revolver to the sand and scratched the back of his head furiously. For a moment, the fire returned to his eyes. He was himself once more.

"I don't know why I did that," he said. His breath came in short bursts. "In that moment, it seemed the right thing to do. I wanted him dead more than I wanted to prove our innocence. Part of me knew it was wrong, but I couldn't stop myself. I couldn't see past my desire for revenge for what he did to me."

It was at that moment Ren realized how far Claymore had fallen. The trickster had suspected things were bad for his partner before now, but killing Serralto in cold-blood proved his worst fears were true.

"It'll be okay," Ren said.

"I don't it will," Claymore replied. "I thought killing him would calm the madness eating away at my soul, but I was wrong. It's only made our situation worse. Now the only guy who could have proven our innocence is dead. I'm sorry."

"In Lazaranth Prison, you told me something had broken inside you. What's happened to you?"

"They call it the *Paradigm Madness*," Claymore said. "It's the mind's inability to cope with the sudden realization that we are, at our core, nothing more than a character from a books. Some cannot deal with this truth. They begin to lose their grip on the reality around them."

"But why you and not me?"

"I was there when the *Logos Persona* died," Claymore said. "Caught in the shifting realities, when the mystical bond between Minstrel Cotty and his Story was torn asunder and the destructive death spiral that burned the *Angels of Avalon* to ash was unleashed."

"But Audette Shoal was in the room with you?"

"I don't know how all this works," Claymore replied. "It's one of the greatest mystery in the cosmos. What causes it in some people, but not others, has never been fully understood. I suffered a traumatic head injury. She hadn't. That could explain it. I just don't know."

"When has this happened before?"

"Only once that I've witnessed," Claymore said. "One of our first recruits, Shala Barrick. She was young, with a lot of potential, and had only recently moved to Rogue Destiny. We missed the early signs of the madness. She was able to hide it from us until three agents died due to her lapse in judgement."

"What happened after that?"

"We couldn't have her continue as a Raconteur, and it seemed cruel to let her be locked away for something so out of her control."

"What did you do?"

"We took Shala home," Claymore replied. "By then, it was too late. She had been completely consumed by the Paradigm Madness by then, to the point she forgot everyone and everything she ever knew. We left two agents to watch over her until the end. Then one day she disappeared. She left a note claiming to be on some personal vendetta. No one ever saw her again."

His partner's voice was distant, like he was having trouble digging up the details from so long ago. Or was he thinking the same fate awaited him?

"We'll find a way to fix this," Ren said.

"There is no cure," Claymore snapped. "Something inside me

broke. I felt it when I woke up in Minstrel Cotty's study and you were standing over me. The headaches are more frequent now. The injuries I suffered tonight, the torture, my tussle with Odd Bod, and the blasts from the wand have only made it easier for the madness to take me."

"But you just took an elixir not that long ago," Ren replied. "Shouldn't that give you some relief for a while?"

"The elixirs slow the process, but it's always been a temporary fix. Each one is less effective than the last, like the madness is building a resistance to it. Now it feels like I'm falling down a dark hole. It's getting so dark I can barely see."

Claymore pushed himself to his feet and exhaled. "We should get moving," he said. "There's only a handful rabbit-holes along this coastline, so it's only a matter of time before they come here looking for us."

Ren looked back at Serralto's body. "What should we do with him? We can't just leave him there on the ground."

"We don't have time for a proper burial," Claymore said. "Here, give me a hand." He lifted the front half of the corpse under both arms. Ren picked up the boots, and they carried Serralto to the trunk of the limousine.

Claymore laid Serralto's limp body inside the trunk and Ren dropped his legs in after. The booted feet landed on something solid under the blanket. There was the jingle of coins. Claymore pushed the feet aside and lifted the blanket. He pulled out the backpack underneath it.

"Whatever it is, it's heavy." He unzipped the pack and laughed.

"A nice bonus for a night's work," he said. He showed Ren it was filled with golden coins of all shapes and sizes. The trickster recognized several Rogue Destiny Gold Sovereigns among the mix. Claymore zipped it closed. He threw the heavy pack over his shoulder and closed the trunk.

They completed their grisly task by pushing the limousine down the beach into the water. Once the vehicle disappeared under the surface of the quiet lagoon, Claymore pointed to a massive tree that stood at the top of a distant cliff.

"Our rabbit-hole's up there in the cliff beneath that Wayward Tree," he said.

They gathered their belongings. Claymore strapped on his gun belt. Ren grabbed the duffle bag, and they took a narrow path concealed by the dune grass at the base of the rock face.

Ren found himself excited for them to get back to the Raconteurs. It would put his world back in place. He found himself missing the chaotic metropolis of his adopted home.

Chapter 33
And So It Goes

A warm breeze blew in from the ocean as they followed a stony path up the incline. A giant windswept tree waited at the top of a high escarpment overlooking the moonlit sea. The massive trunk hung precariously over the edge of the cliff. Its twisted roots clung to the rocks and held the massive tree in place. The mountainside continued up, disappearing into the misty heights above them. Ren glanced back at the lights of Adezhda shining off the waters down the coast.

"How's your shoulder?" Claymore asked as they climbed.

"It's fine," Ren replied, even though he was not fine. The cut down his shoulder blade burned with an intense fire, but complaining about it wouldn't change anything, so he lied. "How long do we have before the *Black Rose* shows up?"

"Fantasy worlds, like the one we're in, accumulate ley-lines at the edges of its Story," Claymore replied. "The coastline's dotted with rabbit-holes and Adezhda was built here for that reason. It makes it easy for the city's clientele to come and go in secret. Many lead back to Rogue Destiny. Mordecai's people will search those first. Where we're headed is less traveled but will take us to a labyrinth of ley-lines like Bones Martyr Isle. We'll be home long before they can reach us."

"And then we can work on figuring a way to help you," Ren replied. Claymore said nothing. He became quiet and spoke no more as he hiked up the steep trail.

The rabbit-hole lay hidden far below the roots of the trees in a narrow crevice among the rocks. The glow of the ley-line peeked out at them. Claymore slipped through first. Ren followed him into a misty cave. Ten feet in, Claymore pushed a thick stone door open. The doorway came out at the dark end of an alley. Once they were through, Claymore shoved the stone door back into place. There were no cracks or evidence the door existed after it closed, with no way to open the door from the outside.

"To get back through, you have to contact the owner of the building and pay him for passage," Claymore said, as if he knew Ren's thoughts.

He led them along the waters of a bustling seaside port. Despite the late hour, the crews of sailing ships loaded and unloaded goods with mechanized cranes. They hired a private boat across the moonlit bay to the mercantile district. From the surroundings, the architecture reminded Ren of the European worlds he had traveled, but the climate was too humid to be Europe. He thought about it a moment longer and decided he was too exhausted to care.

"This is West Haven," Claymore said. "A port city at the edge of the novel, *The Darkest Mirror*. It's a romantic, mystery-driven Regency world. The story takes place during the Napoleonic Wars, and the tropical climate is well suited for dinosaurs to live alongside humans. I traveled through here a couple of times, but that was years ago."

The small boat docked, and Claymore strode down the narrow dock to a long avenue lit by streetlamps. His boots clicked off the cobblestone streets. They wound through the narrow lanes of the coastal town for a while longer before exiting down a dirt road.

Claymore wiped his brow. "Nothing here for us other than the maze of ley-lines in those hills. They lead to dozens of different locations throughout the cosmos. One of which will take us home."

A cart rumbled down the road toward them, drawn by a massive, hunched-back beast. Ren knew a dinosaur when he saw one. The two-legged animal waddled past them, pulling the creaking wagon full of goods toward West Haven. Claymore lifted his hand in greeting. The driver nodded back.

Ren watched the overladen wagon as the man went about his day. People just living their lives, unconcerned about the greater problems of the cosmos. He wondered what that was like.

A mile down the road, they reached a weathered stone marker, partially obscured by the tall grass. It was the first *guide-stone* Ren had seen, either here or in Adezhda.

To the causal onlooker, the symbol carved into the face of the stone meant nothing. But to anyone with knowledge of what lay beyond their world, the stylized compass over a crescent moon was the sigil of Rogue Destiny, City of a Thousand Moons.

The three-foot tall stones were embedded along trails and road-ways to show travelers they were near the entrance of a rabbit-hole that would lead them toward the fabled city.

Claymore followed a path off the main road at the guide-stone. They continued down a dirt path through a jungle of tropical trees. Slanted beams of filtered sunlight through the dense foliage over-head. The humid air stuck to Ren. He didn't sweat, but Claymore had beads of moisture dripping down his face.

They traveled for a short way before coming to the ruins of a crumbling structure built into the side of a rocky hill. The ancient ruins were overgrown with thick vines and green moss, but the path under Ren's feet was well-used. Claymore lead the way to the opening of the crumbling structure and a wide, dark passageway.

The walls of the ley-lines glowed, revealing dozens of corridors on either side of the tunnel. The intersecting rabbit-holes were a well-traveled epicenter used by those who wandered the Mythic Cosmos. The two Raconteurs walked another hundred yards before taking a side passage that led them into the depths of the earth.

They continued in silence under the greenish light of the ley-lines. Claymore strode down several adjoining passageways without warning, his long stride forcing Ren to almost run to keep up. It only took a couple of turns before Ren found himself hopelessly lost.

Ren heard voices. A light appeared ahead. The three travelers stepped aside to allow a donkey-drawn cart to roll by. The two occupants waved politely to them.

They took the circular tunnel the cart had emerged from. Traffic picked up in all directions from the various tunnels that fed into a main passage. Many individuals and groups passed them, some pleasant looking, others not so much. Ren kept an eye out for trouble.

His partner appeared more restless the further they continued down the tunnel. Soon they came to a large iron gate. They waited in line. Two sentries stood at the open gate processing travelers into the City of Rogue Destiny. Both wore the red and black colors of the city officials.

Claymore stepped out into the light, pulling the brim of his hat down to hide his face. He shifted his feet, repositioning the backpack on his shoulder in annoyance. He muttered words Ren could not make out. After what seemed forever, they reached the front of the line.

"Reason for your visit?" the officials asked, staring down at a clipboard and pen.

"Commerce," Ren said.

The city official eyed Claymore intently as he passed by her.

"What happened to your face?" she said to Claymore.

"He had a run in with some bandits yesterday," Ren said quickly. He gave a strained laugh.

The other guard stepped up. "What's the other guy look like?"

"You can probably guess," Claymore said. He tapped the handle of his revolver. The guards both laughed.

"That'll teach them, won't it? Enjoy your stay. Move on through, please."

They walked up a narrow corridor into a wide plaza of shops

and restaurants that waited to entice the weary traveler with food and overnight accommodations.

Ren looked over at Claymore as they fought their way through the crowds of people. "You finally ready to go home?"

Claymore's expression was unreadable. He didn't respond to the question, but continued to force his way through the crowded plaza until they reached the fountain at the center of the square. He sat down on the stone rim of the fountain's cascading waters and rubbed his face with his hands.

"I'm not going back with you?" Claymore said in a low voice. He gazed out over the plaza, his thoughts unknowable. His words left Ren thunderstruck.

"What do you mean?!" he said. "Gideon's going to want to see you. The Raconteurs can help us. I killed a lot of people to get to you tonight. And I'd do it again if I had to. Now you're just leaving?"

"You think I want it to be this way?" Claymore said. "I started the Raconteurs to preserve life, and I dedicated myself to that single purpose. It was something I intended to do until the day I died. Now it's been taken from me."

"None of us wanted this, most of all me!" Ren yelled. "I hoped after tonight things would return to how they used to be."

"So did I." Claymore shook his head. "But that's not the cards we were dealt. Now, I will only be remembered as the man responsible for the deaths of millions of people. I can't even walk the city streets freely. I'll have to hide who I am for the rest of my days." He turned away, but Ren grabbed his arm.

"Gideon and Natascha can help us figure this out. We'll figure this out. Just come back with me." Claymore clenched his jaw and pulled his arm from Ren's grasp.

"Don't touch me," he growled. "If the authorities find out I came back, it'll endanger the Raconteurs' very existence. They have spies everywhere, even within our own ranks. Then people just like Serralto Cardus will have the excuse they need to disband the Raconteurs."

"Then we'll hide you somewhere," Ren argued. "Until we figure this out."

Claymore stepped away from him, his head down. "Until now, I've always known my purpose in life, the reason I exist. Now I'm not so sure who I am or what I stand for. It's getting worse with every sunrise, and that terrifies me."

Ren set the duffle bag down and stepped in front of him. "I can't let you do this," he said. He pressed his hand against Claymore's chest. Usually, when they argued, their roles were reversed. It was Ren who needed to be reined in and forced to listen to reason. Claymore looked down at the hand on his chest.

"You need to back away," Claymore quietly said. His eyes went cold. His face lost all expression.

Ren didn't remove his hand. "No, we're going to talk about this."

Claymore paused for a moment, muttering words under his breath that Ren couldn't understand. His partner fell to his knees, grabbing his head with both hands. "No!" he yelled. "Not here! The words, they won't stop!"

"What can I do?" Ren asked, desperate to do something, anything, to help.

"Stay back!" Claymore shouted. He shoved Ren away from him. "Just give me a minute. I'll be fine." He pressed his palms against his temples, his face contorted in agony. Words began to escape his lips unbidden, like he was reciting something from memory:

Rip Rogers stumbled out of the tavern onto the streets of a warm Marrakech night. In his hand, he held a jug half full of the bitter wine the region offered. From the shadows behind him, the assassin slid out of the alley, silent as a panther. If not for a glint from the uplifted blade off a streetlamp, Rip would have died there.

He caught the wrist holding the knife with a massive hand and smashed the clay jug into the man's face. It shattered against the would-be killer's nose, giving Rip time to pin him against the wall by the throat with his free hand. Rip drew his two-foot long knife from his belt and drove it into the man's belly.

Claymore gritted his teeth and dropped his head. "Not now," he mumbled to himself. "Not while there is breath left in me to fight against it."

Beads of sweat broke out on his forehead as he strained to control himself. "I am Claymore Ives," he said slowly. "A Raconteur. Protector of Rogue Destiny. We fight, we endure, we continue on. I cannot forget that. I am a good man. That will never change."

Ren took a step back, watching his friend battle the madness eating away at his soul, horrified and furious. There was nothing he could do to help. The sound of Claymore's voice petered out, but his lips kept moving. He stared intensely at the ground, mouthing silent words for a dozen more heartbeats.

Gradually, Claymore brought himself under control. He looked up at Ren, his eyes bloodshot and the veins on his forehead evident. His face was pale, exhaustion weighing down on him. Ren laid a hand on his shoulder, because he knew no other way to comfort his friend.

"I'm sorry this is happening to you," he said.

Claymore's head whipped around. His eyes flared in anger. His hand closed into a fist.

"I said *Don't touch me!*" Claymore caught his partner with a right hook that Ren felt should have taken his head off. He flew off his feet into waters of the fountain. The impact of the blow shook him to the core. Claymore stepped toward him. His hand fell to the pistol at his side. His breath was heavy, his hair wet with sweat.

Then Claymore hesitated before dropping his hand from his gun. The expression of mindless fury on his face faded. The rise and fall of his brawny chest slowed and the light in his eyes returned. He held out an empty hand and pulled his partner from the fountain. Ren saw a little old lady with a pushcart full of cut flowers staring at them.

"Hello," Ren said. He gave her a wide smile. The last thing

they needed was to draw attention to themselves. "Everything's fine. My friend here has had a little too much to drink. I was just sobering him up before we head home." He bumped his partner softly on the chest with a fist. Claymore smiled and smacked him on the back. Ren grimaced as pain shot through his shoulder, but made no sound.

The elderly woman studied Claymore up and down for a few more moments, then snorted her disgust and continued on her way. Once she was gone, he turned back to Ren.

"I told you," he said. "I'm a threat to everyone around me. My behavior is erratic, and it's only getting worse. It comes on without warning and the next time I lose control, it might be a friend I shoot. I could never live with myself if I did that. That's why I have to leave. My time with the Raconteurs is over."

"Then I'm coming with you," Ren said. It only made sense. Claymore would need someone to help him navigate the dark days ahead.

His partner sighed and shook his head. "No, I need you to do something else for me. I'm leaving the Raconteurs in your hands. Watch over them. They are my legacy. My greatest work and their mission must continue. Can you promise me that?"

"Where are you going to go?"

"Don't know yet," Claymore replied. "Maybe find some place that needs a hero. Do some good before the end. Either way, I won't be coming back here. The others don't need to see me like this."

"Are you sure you want to be alone?"

Claymore took a deep breath and adjusted the backpack. The coins inside jingled. "You should get back to the Raconteurs. Medesto and Natascha are going to need your help. Do whatever it takes to stop Mordecai from finding the *Book of Days*. Kill him if have you to."

"And you're okay with that?"

"You once told me, right and wrong are whatever you decide it is," Claymore said. "This all goes back to Mordecai. If he's dead, the *Book of Days* will remain lost. He cannot be allowed to use it against the City."

Claymore wasn't incorrect about that. If Mordecai was gone, all the suffering he caused would stop. But the statement didn't sit right coming from Claymore.

"There's a storm coming," Claymore said. "And you need to make sure the Raconteurs are ready when it hits."

"Mordecai's no wizard," Ren muttered, almost to himself. "Why would he want to bring magic back if he won't be in control of it?"

"That's the question you need to answer," Claymore replied. "I don't know what Mordecai has planned. He must have figured out some way to control it because he'd never give that kind of power to someone else."

"Then stay and fight with us."

"I told you I can't do that," Claymore growled. "I feel hollowed out, like my soul is dying. I have no purpose anymore. No real sense of right or wrong. I feel only empty nihilism."

"Don't say that," Ren said. He watched the light die in his partner's eyes and knew not to push the situation further.

Claymore scratched his head vigorously. "We don't talk about death because we all hope to avoid it, even though it catches up to us all, eventually. And after everything that's happened tonight, I'm just glad to be alive."

"Will I see you again?"

"Who knows?" Claymore said. "Probably not. I feel the elixir already wearing off, so I don't have a lot of time."

He unknotted the string tied around the top of the pack and held it open. The morning light glinted off the gold coins inside. "Half of this is yours," he said. "Take however much you want."

Ren chose a single coin. "For cab fare," he said. He never had much need for money. No matter how easier it seemed to make life, it always felt like an encumbrance to him.

"Hold on, I have a couple of things for you," Claymore said. He dug through the duffle bag at his feet and pulled out a stack of letters tied with string he had taken from Piqwic, along with the talisman necklace. "You left these on the table back at Babak's diner. Give them to Gideon. They may help him piece together whatever Mordecai's ultimate strategy is. I found the necklace on the floor of the dragon pit next to Piqwic's pants. Thought it might belong to you."

Ren slid the letters into the waistband of his pants and put the necklace around his neck. Claymore stared down at him. A shadow of sadness passed over his face.

"And this." Claymore dug in his pocket and set his Raconteur badge into Ren's hand. The trickster reluctantly accepted it and slid the badge into his pocket. He glanced over to see the lady with the flower-cart across the plaza talking to two city officials. She pointed in their direction.

"We need to go," Ren said. "Our fight has drawn unwanted attention."

Claymore stuck out his hand. "Goodbye, Ren B'gatti," he said. "You've always been a good partner and a better friend. Maybe we'll see each other again one day. Take care of my Raconteurs."

Ren shook his partner's hand one last time and watched as Claymore strode off across the crowded plaza. A moment later, he disappeared from sight.

If his partner had any emotion at their departure, Ren could not see it. The trickster choked down his grief and rage, holding back tears he would never reveal to anyone. He never showed weakness in front of his partner and wasn't about to start now. But he was still convinced there was a cure for Claymore's condition.

A new dawn broke across the cloudless skies overhead, fueled by the waking of the hundreds of worlds that filled the Great Void above Rogue Destiny. Another day in the City of a Thousand Moons would soon begin. Despite everything that had transpired since he had reunited with Claymore, life would go on as it always did. Ren disappeared into the bustling crowd himself.

Ren needed to get back to Medesto's flat before the gnome woke up, if only to avoid a lecture about responsibility or his duty to the Raconteurs and how they all had his best intentions at heart. Things he was too tired to listen to again. A dozen blocks later, he found a Hansom Cab. The driver was asleep inside, but Ren did not hesitate to wake him, flashing the gold coin Claymore had given him.

Ren collapsed onto the cushioned seats of the first Hansom Cab he could find. He clenched his teeth against the impact. His injured shoulder burned with a vengeful rage. The bruising and cuts he had suffered would be gone soon enough, but the slash across his shoulder from the magically infused glaive was more stubborn.

He fingered the talisman hanging around his neck. It had kept the Grimm Jester at bay, so perhaps it might be his greatest weapon against the wraith. He pulled the Raconteur badge out of his pocket. It was the last thing that Claymore would give him before leaving Rogue Destiny forever. And with it, Ren was now burdened with protecting the protectors of the fabled City. The Raconteurs were now his responsibility, for better or worse.

The cab let him out at the public house. He gave the single gold coin he had in his pocket and shuffled wearily up the last couple of streets to Medesto's apartment building. He smiled in relief and limped up the steep front steps. He couldn't remember the last time he'd felt so sore. The effort up each step took what little strength was left. Ren couldn't wait to fall into bed and get a few hours of sleep. He grabbed the handle and pulled. The door was locked.

Ren pulled on the door again, as if it would somehow open this time. Throwing his hands up in frustration, he stepped back, looking up ten floors to where a soft feather bed awaited him. He tried to shift again, but as he began to morph, his body refused to heed his command, and he remained himself. Too exhausted to try again, Ren sat on the top step. Yawning, he laid down on the stoop, curled up in the warm morning light, and was asleep in no time.

. . .

If you feel so inclined, and while the story is still fresh in your head, consider leaving an Amazon review. Nothing helps an independent author more than a quick review to help entice new readers to give their work a chance. Link to review

To learn more about the Rogue Destiny Universe go to paultallmanauthor.com

Ley Lines and Rabbit Holes
Book Two of the
Rogue Destiny Saga

Chapter 34
Somewhere in the Pages of
Cossacks: A Winter's Tale

Natascha Devi fought back a painful yawn. She looked out the front windshield of *Nevermore*. Hunting the trickster had taken weeks with little rest, and she was reeling from the exhaustion. The few stolen hours of sleep were all she had got while Gustav flew *Nevermore* to the origin of the distress call. It was not enough, but it would have to do for now.

Even though she and Medesto had located Ren B'gatti, there was no guarantee he would make the difference in ending the escaped prisoners' rampage. Ren had always been a flight risk, especially in his early days with the Raconteurs. Claymore Ives was the only one able to control the trickster's impulsive nature, but Claymore was not a part of their world anymore. She missed him even more than she realized.

Gustav 7 sat at the controls of the slipstream, directing them through the floating worlds toward a small, bluish-green ball in the distance. He clicked through several maps on the wide dashboard screen with one of his utility arms.

"Mapping has come back from the Wayfinder," he replied. "The distress signal from *Fool's Errand* is coming from that world directly ahead."

Natascha yawned and sat up in her seat. "What do we know about this place?"

"It's a novel called *Cossacks: A Winter's Tale,* an alternate Earth history regarding. She's a relatively new world, only recently formed a couple of years ago, so we have no established safe houses. Montagu and Keating may have been the first ones from Rogue Destiny to step foot inside."

Natascha's co-pilot continued. "The Book's description says it takes place in the Russian steppes during Earth's First World War. Invaders from the planet Mars seek to enslave humanity. The Story centers on a small outlaw band of fiery Cossacks led by the world's *Logos Personae, Mykhaylo Rodchenko.* He and his army of horsemen are the last line of defense against an over-whelming, superior alien technology. It looks like there may be some supernatural elements as well, but nothing magical that I can see."

"Sounds interesting," Natascha said. "Too bad we're here for work and won't have time to look around. Once we're through the Word Canopy, try to patch through to *Fool's Errand.* Hopefully, we'll get a response."

"Roger that," Gustav said. The automatron hit a button with a metal appendage and pulled down a small lever on the console with another. A tiny flash of light shot from the front grille of the slipstream. The small ball of energy hit the giant globe. Tendrils of electrical charge spread over its outer surface and an opening appeared. *Nevermore* shot through the keyhole.

The turbulence outside the ship died down as they descended into a new world. The distress signal indicated they needed to head west through a thick blanket of clouds. Natascha picked up the radio receiver.

"*Fool's Errand,* do you copy?" she said. "This is *Nevermore.* We are in-world. Do you copy?"

Static crackled over the line, and then a voice answered. "*Nevermore,* this is *Midnight Run.* Good to hear a friendly voice. We picked up the same distress call and have a location on *Fool's*

Errand, but no word from Montagu or Keating. Sending you our coordinates now."

The WayFinder screen flashed to life and a series of numbers and symbols scrolled across the bottom of the screen. Natascha scanned them and replied, "We have a fix on you. Be there in twenty."

"Watch your step, *Nevermore.* We've got possible hostiles north and east of our location. They appear to be part of the greater storyline and not interested in us, but they could still be dangerous."

"Roger that *Midnight Run,* out," Gustav replied. They descended from a dead gray sky to a world blanketed in white. Large snowflakes swept across the windshield. Gustave adjusted course and brought the slipstream in low over the tree line.

They followed the glyph on the screen until the tail of *Midnight Run* came into view. The seventy-foot-long slipstream Runabout looked like a giant insect crouching in the snow. *Nevermore's* route thrusters slowed their descent through the snowy sky and brought them around to land. Natascha scanned the white landscape below as Gustav searched for a place to set down. He chose an open area hemmed in by trees twenty yards from the other ship and landed *Nevermore* in the deep snow.

Natascha opened the suitcase that held the vestments of her alter ego, Doctor Enigma. She stepped out of the confined space of the cockpit and threw the long coat around her, sliding her arms into the sleeves. She donned her gas mask and pulled up her hood. Two Tesla Peacemakers sat on the charging stations under the dashboard. She shoved them into the holsters strapped to each leg.

Gustav opened the skylight above them, letting snow drift into the cabin. The pilot's seat glowed blue from his anti-gravitational burner. He retracted his utility arms and flew up into the frigid winter day. The roof slid closed after him. With a push of a button, the side hatch opened and Natascha followed Gustav out into the cold. Snow and wind swirled around her as she sank to her knees in the snow piled up around the ramp. She pulled the keybox from her pocket to lock down *Nevermore.* The ramp rose and clicked shut.

Natascha could feel the icy chill even through her insulated clothing. The readings in her mask registered the wind chill at 24 degrees below zero. She adjusted the thermal heater in her coat to stave off the bitter cold. She pushed through the snow around the deeper drifts toward *Midnight Run.*

As she approached, the hatch on the side of the slipstream opened and Gossamer 99 slid his eight-foot metal frame free from the confines of the cabin. The ship tilted as his weight shifted toward the door. He planted a large metal foot deep in the snow-bank and stepped out. The slipstream rocked back into place when he cleared the opening and stood in the silent falling snowflakes.

"Hello, Gossamer," Natascha said. The cyborg mech turned to her.

"Oh, hello, Doctor Enigma." His words were deep and rumbling, a fusion of human intonations and mechanical syntheti-zation. "We still have had no contact from Keating or Montagu. Nasty business."

Natascha leaned into the open hatch. "So what do we have, Danique?" Natascha asked.

"The Story's Narrative is playing out about five hundred kilo-meters to our east," Danique replied. "So we're pretty far from the *Logos Personae.* The ships should be safe here."

Danique, Gossamer 99's older sister, sat in the pilot's seat and removed the headset from her dreadlocks. She put on a leather bomber jacket, a thick wool cap, and wrapped a scarf around her neck. After buckling a holstered Peacemaker on, Danique dropped out of the ship to the snow.

"You still have a bead on Montagu and Keating's signal, Gossamer?" Natascha asked.

"*Fool's Errand* is about 1500 meters west of here," Gossamer 99 said. "Over that rise and through those trees, very close to the edge of the Story."

"They must have found Mordecai," Natascha said. "That has to be why they're here."

Danique shrugged. "Don't know, but if we do run into the outlaws, Father will be relieved you're with us."

Sebastian Poe was protective of his children. His youngest daughter, B'Tori was 14 and worked with him in his shop, always within sight. Danique and Gossamer 99 were older, 19 and 17, and insisted on working in the field with the other Raconteurs. Sebastian had agreed to that only if the two teenagers took every precaution. They had to stay in constant contact with the WayFinder and were never to engage the enemy without experienced backup.

Even then, they were given only menial tasks, like transporting dignitaries or picking up machine parts for their father. Both agreed to those terms, because the alternative would have been to die a slow death, cooped up in their father's shop, dismantling and rebuilding slipstreams all day long. But every so often, they found themselves in an emergency situation, such as searching for missing Raconteurs in cold winter worlds full of alien invaders. Natascha could see the excitement on the young girl's face.

Gossamer 99 led the way, forging a pathway through the snow-drifts for the others to follow. Harsh winds swept down from the surrounding hills and forests as they trudged through the cold. Danique complained immediately.

"I'm freezing, brother. Can't you go any faster?" She wrapped the wool scarf tighter around her neck.

Gossamer shook his metallic head and looked back at her. "The snow's deep. I'm doing the best I can." His metallic-tinged voice was full of sarcasm. "It's winter in a Russian novel about winter. It doesn't get any colder than this."

"Shut up," Danique shot back with a smirk. "Just because you're not bothered by the cold doesn't mean I'm going to stop griping about it." She shivered and patted her gloved hands together. Large snowflakes continued to fall. "Since you have internal thermal heaters to keep your innards warm, you could at least fake a little sympathy for your sister's plight and offer me a ride."

"I am sorry you are cold, and I am not, my sister," Gossamer replied. "You have my sympathy. Is that better?"

Natascha smiled behind her mask. She wasn't about to mention the heating elements in the lining of her long coat kept her quite comfortable in the sub-zero climate.

Gossamer 99 knelt in the snow and Danique climbed up onto his shoulders. She sat on the smooth flat area behind his massive head and wrapped a hand around the leather handholds for stability. Her younger brother continued pushing his way through the deep snowdrifts toward the direction of the signal. Natascha followed in the wide track left by the cyborg. Gustav floated behind her.

"Are you getting any closer to locating Ren?" Danique asked.

"Medesto and I found him in a grimdark fantasy novel. He's on his way back to Rogue Destiny as we speak."

After a short hike, they came to a break in the trees. Natascha could tell from the frozen rocks crunching underfoot that there was a road buried somewhere beneath the snow that had not seen daylight for many months. The signal from their missing compatriots' transponder was getting stronger. They crested a forested hill, and in the distance, an ancient monastery of stone and mortar came into view.

The structure was two stories high, set on a wide span of open ground. Next to it, covered in snow, sat *Fool's Errand*. The area around the single stone structure was flat and empty of trees. A thin stream of smoke rose from the chimney.

"That's where their signal is coming from," Gossamer rumbled.

He stayed in the shadow of the trees. Danique dropped from her brother's shoulder to the snow. She pulled out her binoculars and surveyed the front of the monastery. "No movement from what I can see. What's the play?" Her voice was just above a whisper, but it still echoed in the still air.

"Danique goes with me," Natascha said. "We have to assume

Montagu and Keating are in trouble, or we would have heard from them by now. We neutralize any sentries we come upon — don't kill them unless you have no other choice. Then we deal with anyone inside."

There was a sound in the woods behind them. Natascha grabbed Danique by the arm and pulled her down as the whine of a large hydraulic machine broke the crisp, cold air. Natascha saw movement in the trees to their left. She crouched in the snow next to Danique. Gustav hovered just off the ground behind her. Gossamer stepped behind a thick tree trunk. Overhead, a massive saucer mounted atop a tripod of long spindly legs moved through the trees in fluid, elongated steps. The Martian invader's machine came within fifty yards before lumbering past them.

Gustav nudged Natascha from behind. "I am intercepting a radio transmission. Thirty yards to the east, there are three humanoid-sized hostiles moving this way. Lots of metal on the outside, but they appear to be organic underneath. They are communicating with each other, but I am unable to translate their alien dialect."

Natascha motioned for Danique to stay down, then raised three fingers and pointed east. Danique nodded and crouched lower until she was hidden in the snow. Natascha peered over the snowdrift.

Forty feet away stood three alien figures. They were seven feet tall with large, bulging heads encased in clear glass helmets. Their faces were small and squat, with prominent foreheads and exposed brains.

The trio of alien foot soldiers seemed to be having an argument amongst themselves. The tallest one's brain pulsated in rhythm with the wild gesturing of his mechanical arms. Natascha drew her Peacemaker and waited. After a back-and-forth conversation went on for several minutes before the three armed soldiers continued on their way. She waited until they were out of sight before she signaled the others to come out.

"Gossamer and Gustav," she said. "Stay here and monitor the

area. Let us know if they come back. Danique and I will investigate the building and see if we can find Keating and Montagu."

The two metallic Raconteurs remained in the woods as Natascha and Danique crept through the snowy field toward *Fool's Errand*. They reached the slipstream and crouched down by its rear engines. "I still don't see anyone," she said. "You?"

Danique surveyed the snowy fields beyond the ship. "Nothing," she said. "No, wait. Thirty-five yards out, near the tree line. There's a lone figure heading toward us. Looks like another alien foot soldier."

Natascha pointed toward the monastery. Danique followed her lead and they moved to one side of the stone structure as the alien approached from the field. It appeared to be armed with a heavy gun that hung from a strap over one shoulder. It stopped at the front of *Fool's Errand*. There was a hum, and a flat grid of light emanated from the soldier's chest and scanned the metal shell of the ship. The alien walked to the rear engines, continuing to scan the underbelly, and began talking in an unknown language to unseen comrades.

Danique drew her Peacemaker. Natascha gestured for her to stay where she was, but the command was ignored. The younger Raconteur made her way from the corner of the building to *Fool's Errand* and hid behind the front claw of the landing gear. The alien ended its transmission and went back to scanning the right engine. Then it stopped, suddenly aware of another presence, and turned on Danique. Natascha stepped into the open.

"Over here!" she shouted.

The foot soldier brought his weapon up on Danique, but hesitated at the sound of Natascha's voice. Both Raconteurs hit the bulbous-headed alien from different sides with their Peacemakers. The foot soldier lit up as the blue-red electrical charges from both weapons shook its body. The whine of gears fought the electricity coursing over it. The creature gave a high-pitched squeal that sounded like pain and fell forward into a drift of powdery snow.

Natascha went over to the alien and picked up its fallen

weapon. It was a ray gun, short and hefty, with a series of coils encased in thick glass. The barrel tapered to a large porcelain insulator wrapped around a silver electrode rod that protruded off the end, not dissimilar in makeup to her own Peacemaker, but no doubt more powerful. She lifted the alien's weapon with a grunt, but it was too heavy for her to use effectively, so she dropped it into the snow.

The side ramp on the slipstream stood open. Snowy footprints led up to that spot, then back to the building. Danique climbed the ramp to investigate the inside of the ship. She appeared moments later, shaking her head. "It's empty, and the keybox is gone," she said. Natascha nodded and pointed to the monastery.

They followed several sets of footprints in the deep snow to the front entrance of the building, still unchallenged by any guards. Danique put her nose to the window and shaded her eyes from the reflection. "There are only embers burning in the hearth," she said.

Natascha tried the doorknob of the large wooden door. It turned in her hand, and the door swung in with a push. The foyer area was small and narrow, leading into an open sanctuary lined with statues of saints and angels. At the back of the room, a set of wide steps led up to a second story. A baptism fountain burbled in the far corner. The room was empty.

Both entered silently and looked over the wide room. Natascha searched the areas adjacent to the foyer but found no evidence of anyone having been there. She walked down a short hallway to the backroom Danique was inspecting. It was the only place that had any hint of warmth. The smell of ash and smoke came from a fireplace on the far wall.

Danique took off her gloves, added kindling to the glowing embers, and stirred the coals with a poker. A small flame licked up over the wood. She rubbed her hands together. "Looks like we missed the party," she said.

"Yes, it does," Natascha answered. "But there's no doubt Mordecai was here." Something caught her attention. On the back of a chair facing the hearth was a long silk scarf. Natascha picked it up. There was an intricate flower design surrounded by swirling Chinese dragons. She recognized it right away. A birthday gift from a shy seven-year-old girl to her mother. Was it left behind by accident? Or as a warning?

"One problem at a time," she muttered.

Amazon link – Leave a Review Here
Amazon link – Buy Book Two

GLOSSARY OF MAJOR PLAYERS

The Good Guys

Ren B'gatti – Shape-shifting trickster of dubious morals
and mysterious past.
Claymore Ives – Founder of the Raconteurs and Ren's partner.
Natascha Devi – aka – Doctor Enigma – Senior field agent for
the Raconteurs.
Medesto Bodenhammer – Senior field agent for the
Raconteurs.
Tempest Vondersteen – Security Officer for the Raconteurs.
Oversees general operations.
Charlie Lovejoy – Tech specialist for the Raconteurs.
Gideon Dumas – Director of the Raconteurs.

The Bad Guys

Mordecai Davos – The shadowy overlord of Rogue Destiny's
criminal underworld who has kept his true identity hidden,
even from his innermost circle.
The Society of the Black Rose – A secret society controlled by

Mordecai Davos whose influence extends throughout the Mythic Cosmos.

The Grimm Jester – Mysterious wraith under the control of Mordecai Davos.

Piqwic York – The overseer of Mordecai's vast fortunes. He uses his financial expertise to increase the Black Rose's wealth and help them maintain their dominance over Mordecai's criminal underworld empire.

Odd Bod – Mordecai's Grand Enforcer.

Audette Shoales – Hired killer from the Adezhda, the City of Assassins.

Serralto Cardus – Member of Rogue Destiny's Common Council of Eternal Vigilance and Public Sympathy.

GLOSSARY OF PLACES AND TERMINOLOGIES

Rogue Destiny – The infamous city that stands at the crossroads of the Mythic Cosmo.

The Mythic Cosmos - a universe filled with the mythos of every fable, myth, legend and fairy-tale.

The Raconteurs – A self-appointed band of world-hopping troubleshooters who protect the Mythic Cosmos from the corruptive influence of Rogue Destiny's criminal element.

Ley-lines – The mystical pathways that grow from the roots of the Wayward Trees and connect all the written worlds of the Mythic Cosmos.

Rabbit-hole – A doorway between worlds created by the ley lines.

The Word Canopy – The mystical veil of words that surrounds every world.

The Narrative – The continual progression of a world's Story that must remain uninterrupted and free of outside corruption. If that narrative flow is broken, the consequences will be catastrophic.

The Logos Personae – The main character of a world's Story. The individual who is intertwined with the Narrative and the linchpin to the world's survival.

The Crucible Event – A catastrophic event that leaves consumes a world until it is burned to ash. Occurs at the death the Story's main character, the *Logos Personae*, or when the flow of the Narrative is altered beyond what can be repaired or restored.

The City of a Thousand Moons

Throughout the Mythic Cosmos there are an untold number of worlds. Every fable, myth, legend, and fairy-tale exists within this reality, where its inhabitants live out their existence, unaware of any part they may play in a larger Theater.
The continuity of these worlds are defended by the vigilance and sacrifice of a band of independent agents, known as the Raconteurs.
These heroes travel the far reaches of the Mythic Cosmos, dedicating themselves to the protection of these worlds from the corruptive influence of Rogue Destiny's criminal element.
At the center of this mythos lies a place outside the natural laws that bind the rest of cosmos together. It's a world unique unto itself, where the outcast creations of the written word find sanctuary. Where rogues and heroes, exiles and pariahs, live together in an uneasy alliance.
They are the flotsam and jetsam of Literature. Forgotten characters, discarded bit players and wayward denizens of countless stories that have nowhere else to go. They are all drawn to one point in the universe.
To a city called Rogue Destiny.

About the Author

Paul Tallman lives in the wet and wonderful Pacific Northwest with his long suffering wife, Tina.

After having worked for far too many years in the insurance industry, he finally broke away from the security of a steady paycheck to pursue writing.

A geek by birthright, he has spent his life in the social awkwardness of his calling, ever since reading *The Lord of the Rings* for the first time in middle school.

Paul can be found holed up away from the society, working on his next book.

He still mourns the cancellation of the TV show *Firefly*.

To find out more about the Rogue Destiny universe visit: paultallmanauthor.com

Also by Paul Tallman

A Rogue Destiny

Rogue Destiny: Beginnings

Ley Lines and Rabbit Holes